No Good Deed

Jack N. Lawson

No Good Deed

"Kyle, goddamnit, you know better than I that you were *at war*. Those kids had a grenade, and you had barely escaped from that landing zone—and one of your crew was dead. And besides, you tried to scare them off. You didn't just open fire."

"Yeah, but I could've fired high to scare 'em off, couldn't I?"

"But you were scared, Kyle. Who wouldn't have been in your situation?"

"I just acted."

"No, damn it; you *re*-acted!" I countered. "You told me yourself that Duke and Ches were shouting at you to shoot them."

"Well...I shoulda fired *high*."

"Then they might have killed *you*—unintentionally, I grant it—but they might have killed you."

Kyle's head fell back on the chair. "They *did*."

What They Are Saying About No Good Deed

No Good Deed by Jack N. Lawson is a coming-of-age story wrapped in a mystery. Jon and Kyle were inseparable school chums in the late 60's, each confident and self-assured. But they were soon pulled apart, Jon becoming a college peace activist and Kyle flying missions in Vietnam. How each ended up where he did is revealed in the first chapter; how they ended up that way is the mystery. There are moments of unforgettable descriptive clarity and uncommon insight into the hearts of two decent people, moments when war experiences, personal betrayals, ecclesiastical hypocrisy, and spiritual turmoil forced course changes and identity changes. Riding these rapids with them, we watch helplessly as one drowns in guilt but we watch joyfully as the other finds wisdom and vocational clarity. An unforgettable read!

—Rev. Professor Richard Prust

Jack Lawson's novel creates an extraordinary and gripping picture of the life of a Vietnam veteran. The central figure, Kyle Weston, is a US Army helicopter pilot who is badly wounded in Vietnam. The novel focuses on his life and tragic death, as told by his closest friend Jonathan Braddock, a Presbyterian minister.

The story is told in a series of fascinating events covering Kyle's life from his schooldays as a lively, popular young man in touch with the latest trends, to his military career during which, it gradually becomes clear, he suffered an extremely depressing experience. The novel moves on to Kyle's post-war career, at first working in the world of entertainment and then, by a startling development, becoming a Presbyterian minister like his friend Jonathan.

Underlying the story is the relationship of these two young Americans through the turbulent world of the 1960s, focusing on the impact of events like the deaths of John F. Kennedy and Martin Luther King Jr. Their story is played out in the American South, against a religious background of the Southern Baptist Church and the demands of the Presbyterian ministry, with which both Kyle and Jonathan struggle to come to terms.

Opening with Kyle's tragic death, the novel poses vital questions about the significance of life and death. Jack Lawson's deep understanding of American life in the second half of the twentieth century gives the book true depth. Underlying and unresolved historical issues such as the War between the States, are contrasted with the USA of the 1960s, the nature of the Vietnam conflict and the choice made by some young men to avoid the draft.

One of the best elements of the novel is its continuously exciting development. The story grips the reader by its extraordinary sequence of events, right up to the final happenings which dominate the second part of the novel. In creating a character of such interest and complexity as Kyle proves to be, Jack Lawson has written a remarkable novel and has opened up for the reader an amazing range of thoughts and questions.

—Dr. Michael Honeybone, Norwich, England
Retired Academic and Historian

No Good Deed

Jack N. Lawson

Literary Fiction

RESOURCE *Publications* · Eugene, Oregon

Resource Publications
A division of Wipf and Stock Publishers
199 W 8th Ave, Suite 3
Eugene, OR 97401

No Good Deed
By Lawson, Jack N.
Copyright © 2020 by Lawson, Jack N. All rights reserved.
Softcover ISBN-13: 979-8-3852-6926-6
Hardcover ISBN-13: 979-8-3852-6927-3
eBook ISBN-13: 979-8-3852-6928-0
Publication date 11/4/2025
Previously published by Wings ePress, 2020

This edition is a scanned facsimile of the original edition published in 2020.

Dedication

This book is dedicated to all the young men of America's Vietnam generation, whose lives were lost or forever marked by those years.

One

I've just buried my best friend, Kyle. I say "buried," but it was more than that. You see, I had not only thrown the first shovel full of dirt onto Kyle's coffin, I had also led the service *and* acted as a pallbearer. These were all Kyle's wishes—bastard. He was my best friend, and with him I buried much of my life as well. It will be the last service I ever intend to lead as a minister. It's not that I'm retirement age—nothing of the sort—it's simply the end. Dust to dust. And it's not simply because Kyle is dead, either. I should have seen the end coming—in fact, I probably had—but it took Kyle's death to crystallize that latent knowledge into clear, translucent understanding. Part of me wanted to make that end known by making a dramatic statement—you know, like taking off my collar and tossing it into the grave. And although it had crossed my mind to do so, while we were lowering Kyle into the earth that was to be his home, I had enough presence of mind to recognize that, at best it would have been misunderstood and, at worst, it would have seemed cheap theatrics by those who knew I was well and truly pissed off. So, no Gary Cooper for me, throwing his tin star in the dust. Life always looks so much nobler in celluloid.

Only a handful of people at the service had known Kyle for many years; the majority had known him for about eighteen months. Nearly all had loved him—at least to some degree. The fact was that most people couldn't help liking Kyle—and most, given the chance, came to love him. One could say he was truly blessed that way. But it didn't stop him from killing himself. Bastard.

Kyle was blessed—and I'm sure, at some level, he knew it; but he also had a secret. At one time, there were three of us who knew it: Kyle, Dave McChesney—his buddy from Vietnam—and me. Burdensome secrets are like the old three-legged milking stool my grandpa used to have: three legs will bear a man's weight; two will wobble like hell and eventually topple over; and one, well...one can't stand at all. Kyle fell over.

So, as I was saying, the congregation knew Kyle and they knew I was pissed off, because I had told them so. Those who had known Kyle the longest managed to handle my anger with him. Whether they understood it or not was a different matter. They knew that I was Kyle's oldest and best friend, so perhaps they thought that the preacher was emotionally unhinged at the untimely and macabre demise of his friend. The righteous indignation of those shocked at my ire stemmed from the simple fact that Kyle had been *their* minister. Very few of their small number—and it was only a handful who attended their minister's funeral—had any inkling that it might well be within the bounds of Christian propriety to be angry with a friend who not only takes his life, but leaves another with that life's detritus. Well, as their now former minister often said, in his unguarded moments: "Fuck 'em, if they can't take joke."

I had managed to shake off most of the mourners—particularly those who had wanted to berate me, the hypocritical jerks—so I could make my way to Kyle's mother and sister. I had noticed they had been waiting patiently for me in the shade of a pin oak, avoiding the late

June sunshine, which must have seemed like a searchlight aimed at their grief and loss. Between handshakes, condolences, and harsh looks at me, I had noticed the mourners self-consciously make their way toward Kyle's mother Ellen and her daughter, Kyle's younger sister, Marie. None stayed to chat with them for very long. In fact, they could barely make eye contact with either Ellen or Marie. This, I had discovered over the years, was typical at the funeral of a suicide. It's hard enough for parents to see any child die before them; suicide simply magnifies the pain and bewilderment. Mourners almost seem to have a look of guilt about them, such that they dare not look too long into the eyes of the surviving family. In Kyle's case there were some in the crowd who indeed bore culpability. They might not have put the rope around his neck, but their actions had certainly woven its strands and then tied it into a neat hangman's noose.

The last of those who had helped lay Kyle in his grave, Shirley Huntley, realized that she was not going to have the satisfaction of hearing me repent for my words in the funeral service. As I looked at her impassively, Shirley placed one hand on her hip, shook her head at me and blew a puff of air that signaled her exasperation with such a rogue minister as I. My eyes had already drifted back toward Ellen and Marie. Ellen gave a weak smile, dropped her head onto one shoulder and shrugged. I wiped the sweat from my brow and strode over to the two women.

"They giving you a rough time?" Ellen looked in the direction of Shirley Huntley as she joined a small clutch of people standing by the parked cars. I leaned down to kiss her cheeks. Although they were dry, I could taste the salt from earlier grief. I stepped back from Ellen but lightly held her upper arms.

"No less than I expected. And not as bad as it could have been. The woman you saw is Shirley Huntley, Kyle's nemesis. I'll tell you about her in due course."

Ellen nodded in silent acknowledgement, and I turned to Marie.

"Hey, Kid." My lips made a semblance of a smile. We embraced. I had called her 'Kid' for as long as I could remember.

"Hey, 'Nother Brother," she spoke softly into my shoulder. This had been Marie's nickname for me ever since Kyle and I had started to pal around in elementary school. Kyle, her only sibling, was five years older than Marie. Naturally, as I hung around their house a lot, I became 'another brother' for Kyle's little sister. I released the embrace and kissed Marie gently on the forehead.

"Your husband not with you?" I cast my eyes around the cemetery.

"No. Michael never really warmed to Kyle, as you know, so he's staying home with the kids. Although they're seventeen and fifteen now, I somehow didn't think it was a good idea for all of them to come…given…well…the circumstances. Besides, I got time off work, so Mama and I could go through all of Kyle's things, take care of the legal paperwork…well, you know."

"Y'all want to sit down? There's a bench under that magnolia over there."

The two women looked at one another and Marie answered for them both: "Let's."

They each took an arm and we wordlessly trod to the bench. As the bench was covered in pollen, I took out my handkerchief and gave it a quick dust. "Ladies," I motioned to the seat with a flourish and bowed from the waist.

"'Nother Brother," Marie's voiced cracked, but still she managed to smile. "Don't ever change."

"As though he would—or could," offered Ellen. We sat together, mother and daughter still on either side of me.

"You're the only brother I've got now," sobbed Marie. That did it. I had held my own loss and grief in check because I had had to officiate my dearest friend's funeral. My anger at Kyle had helped me through the service and through all of the inane remarks from those who opined that my feelings should have had no place in the service. Marie's tears released my own. And then, as she had done all those years ago whenever Kyle, Marie, or I got hurt playing in their back yard, Ellen's arms enveloped and comforted us.

"Dear Jon, I'm so glad you were able to say what you did in the service. It helped a lot of us to acknowledge what we were feeling but just didn't want or know how to say." Ellen's fingers, knotted from arthritis, stroked my sweat-matted hair. I found both her touch and her Tidewater accent soothing, with its characteristic pronunciation of vowels, wherein 'ou' was pronounced a long 'o.' "What's the phrase people use today? 'White elephant' or something?"

"'Elephant in the room,' Mama," laughed Marie between her sobs.

"That's right, dear. Well, the fact that Kyle took his own life has hurt all of us." And then more quietly, "And the way he did it. It must have been terrible for you, Jon, to…to find him…*like that.*"

I simply nodded. We hadn't had much time to talk before the funeral. Marie and Ellen had to drive for several hours from coastal Virginia to reach this part of North Carolina. Their family had moved to nearby Lawrenceville when Kyle and I were young and then returned to their Tidewater home after Ed Weston, Kyle's father, had died. What time we did have up to this point had been taken up with the police, county coroner and then the service preparations. With those things behind us, we could now address Ellen's "white elephant."

Ellen continued, "I'm only glad Kyle's father didn't live to see this day. Ed and Kyle…well, they never really understood each other…but Ed did love Kyle."

"How…" Marie's voice faltered. "How did it all happen?"

As though on cue, we all adjusted ourselves on the bench. I used my now pollen-coated handkerchief to dab my eyes and blow my nose, and then rested my head against the cool bark of the magnolia behind us and began.

"Kyle had been depressed again and nervous. The worst I had seen in a long time, since 'Nam. The bad dreams were making it almost impossible for him to get a good night's sleep. I urged him to think about hiking another stretch of the Appalachian Trail with me. He always liked the high country and the woods…fewer people and all that. So we were looking ahead a couple of months—maybe late August—when church life would be quiet and lots of folk would be on vacation. 'Just hang in there, Kyle,' I kept telling him. 'There's light at the end of the tunnel'…God, that sounds so weak now…and just plain stupid! A lot of good it did. Shit!" I cursed myself.

Ellen gave me a pretend smack. "Wash your mo'th, Jonathan Braddock! What would your mother say?"

"Yeah, and me a minister—I know," I replied.

"She'd probably say 'Let him finish telling us what happened,'" cut in Marie.

"Well, after we had finished with the worst of the church pre-school mess that Kyle had inherited, and once the trial was over, things went kinda quiet from Kyle's end. I hoped no news was good news and that our planned getaway would help him cope for the short run. We exchanged a couple of e-mails on the idea, and the last one sounded rather upbeat...so, I naturally thought he was through the worst...until... well...I got his note...and the key in an envelope left on the front door mat."

"The church key, right?" asked Marie.

"Yeah," I sighed. "That's the one. He left that and the note and roared off in that old camper van of his."

"Have you still got the note?" enquired Ellen.

Her question gave me pause and I sat up, looking across the cemetery at the mountains beyond. "I think the police still have it...I suppose we could get it back now—that is, if you want it."

Ellen shook her lovely white hair. "I don't know what I want. Well, I *do*, but I just can't have it."

"Go on, Jon," interjected Marie. "I think Mama and I both want to know what Kyle said in what was probably his last communication."

Why did I pause before I told them? Was it to protect his mother and sister? Perhaps it was to suggest that I had to dredge those words, the last my best friend ever shared with me, from the mental sludge at the bottom of my memory. They were, however, branded into my mind's hard drive verbatim.

"Well," I began, "Kyle said something like this: 'Hey, Jon, can't explain now, but I have a favor to ask. I got a meeting tomorrow morning at the church with the elders and our "friendly" officers from the Presbytery—you can probably guess who—at nine o'clock sharp. I've fixed it so they can't get in any door except the main one to the sanctuary, and you, old buddy, have the only key. Sorry if you had other plans, but I need this favor. Please don't let them in before nine—got it?—and then stick around for the meeting. I will need a witness. I owe you one.' That's it." I looked slowly from Ellen to Marie.

"W-what did you think he meant?" queried Marie.

"Certainly not what I got," I said, a little too harshly. "I'm sorry. That's not aimed at you. I…I thought there was going to be some kind of showdown with the elders and officers from the Presbytery. As the court case was over, I thought Kyle simply wanted to draw a line under the past and all that had happened. Since I had been barred from his original meeting with the General Presbyter and the chairman of the Ministry Committee, I just thought he wanted me there as a friendly witness this time. I…I don't know. I thought it was going to be something like that and that Kyle would probably tender his resignation at the same time."

"Kyle was planning to leave Carson Presbyterian Church?" asked Ellen. I simply nodded.

"Well, Jon, did he have plans to go somewhere el—" Ellen never finished 'else;' she realized the futility of the question…and Kyle certainly was *somewhere else*.

"Did you try to speak with Kyle before the meeting?" Marie asked.

"Yeah, I tried—but he was unreachable. Nobody knows for sure, but he probably spent the night in his van and went straight to the church from there. Please understand, there was nothing I could have done. I had no idea…" my voice broke, and I tried to stifle a sob.

Both women spoke at the same time: "No, of course not. We understand."

I gulped, fought back the tears, and continued. "I got to the church just before nine. Most of the elders were there and the two officers from the Presbytery. We exchanged a few words. They expressed their puzzlement at being locked out. I shrugged and said I was just there to let them in, as I had been asked. So I produced the key and opened the door. It was a bright morning, not unlike today, so it took a few seconds for everyone's eyes to adjust to the faint light inside the narthex. I was closing the door when I heard one of the women—Bea Franklin—scream. She was pointing into the sanctuary. The rest of us pushed through the double doors and...well...we saw Kyle...hanging from one of the beams..." My voice trailed away. I turned to look at Ellen and then slowly turned to Marie. "I think I need to know when you've heard enough," I said.

"We'll tell you," was Ellen's firm reply. She breathed deeply through her nostrils and jutted out her fine chin, looking out toward the silhouette of the Blue Ridge. Marie reached over and squeezed my hand. She simply nodded.

"Okay. Well, we all went in. It was like entering a bad dream. The church seemed ever so still. Apart from Kyle, the first thing I noticed was the stepladder lying on its side. I was pretty sure Kyle had kicked it over. I...he...I don't think he wanted to give himself a second chance." I leaned forward, put my elbows on my knees, and rested my face between the palms of my hands. I kneaded my forehead as I continued. "Once the shock was over, it seemed like everyone spoke at once. Some of them wanted to put up the ladder and get Kyle down, but I stopped them. Kyle was dead. His lips and fingertips clearly showed cyanosis; there was nothing we could do. And, like it or not, it was a 'crime scene' until the police and coroner said otherwise. Kyle had on his old Air Cavalry T-shirt that he only ever wore as a kind of sick joke. I'm sure you've seen it; it had 'Death from Above' emblazoned on the front. I guess it was his way of having a last laugh. I don't know."

I sat up again and looked first at Ellen. Her lips were pursed as her deep blue eyes stared straight ahead. Shifting on the bench, I gave an enquiring look to Marie. Her moist eyes met mine and she simply said, "Let's hear it all." Now it was my turn to nod.

I rolled my neck and shoulders, breathed deeply, and set about finishing this final chapter in Kyle's life. "There were letters addressed to all present, neatly arranged on the front pew. The church and presbytery folk just looked at them as though they might be booby-trapped. I picked mine up and headed for Kyle's office to phone for the police and an ambulance. I had just closed the door behind me when I heard the scuffle of hurried steps behind me and the door swung open. It was Milton Peebles, the General Presbyter of the presbytery in which Kyle and I work.

"'Whut're you doin', Jon?' he asked me in his nasally twang.

"Calling the police,' I told him.

"'Well, hold yer horses, son. We all got to talk this thang through,' he said."

"Talk *what* through?" asked Marie.

"Exactly," I said. "It sounded too much like what Peebles had told Kyle when he first reported all of that mess just over a year ago. He hadn't wanted the police involved then, either. The shitheel." Ellen snorted a short laugh at this last remark. No chastisement this time—mock or otherwise.

"What did you do about Peebles?" asked Marie.

"I told him to get the hell out of Kyle's office and..." I took a deep breath, "And I told him in no uncertain terms that it was his kind of talking that put Kyle up on the church rafter. That porcine, dickless wonder stood frozen in the doorway for a few seconds, so I put the phone back in its cradle and took a step toward him—ha! I thought he was going to wet himself." I laughed for the first time today. And in my mind's eye I could see Kyle's face, bursting with laughter. It wasn't a vision or anything; it's just the way Kyle was, especially when he and I were together, ever since we first met. Our mothers used to joke that they could never lose us as they would always find us by our laughter.

I hadn't realized that I had been sitting in silence until Ellen's hand took hold of mine. "You okay, hon?"

"Yeah—yeah! Sorry. Where was I?"

"Milton Peebles was abo't to pee in his pants," chirped Marie.

"Yeah." I laughed again.

"It's good to hear you laugh, 'Nother Brother, particularly today." Marie rested her head on my shoulder, clutching my upper arm with both hands.

"Well, honestly, that's about it. I reckon you know what happened next, as you have had to deal with the authorities, just like I have."

"There is one other thing," Ellen's voice was almost a whisper. "What was in his letter to you, the one he left on the pew?"

"Ah, yes," I replied. "I wasn't sure about bringing it, but I did think you might want to see it. I've got it with me." I reached into the breast pocket of my suit jacket and produced the folded sheet of paper. I started to hand it to Ellen, who only looked at it. I then proffered it to Marie, who had let go of my arm and was sitting up.

Ellen spoke first. "Kyle wrote it to you, Jon. Why don't you just read it to us?"

"All right, then." For some reason I straightened up, as though I were about to read the Sunday lesson. When my arms had reached their full length, I remembered that I hadn't put on my spectacles. "Blast," I mumbled at myself, while Marie sniggered. Why did I always put them in a different pocket? "It's typical Kyle," I offered as a prelude, "short and sweet."

Hey Buddy,

I told you I owe you one. Now you see just how big the debt is. What can I say that hasn't already been said? You know that peace of Christ that I always wanted—that passes all understanding? Well, it surely has passed mine! I hope our Roman Catholic brethren are wrong and that this isn't THE unforgiveable sin, 'cause I'd like to talk a lot of this over with Mr. Jesus. Shit, I've taken the lives of others. What's mine by comparison? Anyway, I'm taking my nightmares to my last sleep with me.

Well, Brother, it's down to the final business: the van's unlocked and my house key is under the front seat. My will's up to date and is on the kitchen table. Everything else you need to know is there. Look after Mom and Marie for me. You always were like one of the family. I haven't written to them, so your words will have to suffice for mine. Thanks for everything you did or tried to do. It did help, or maybe I would have done this sooner…I don't know. I'll finish this before I start rambling.

I love you,
Kyle

As I finished reading, I wondered: Was I now the one-legged stool, left to bear up Kyle's burdensome secret? Or was it truly laid to rest? I slumped back on the bench and again rested my head against the magnolia. This time, two heads made their way to my shoulders, and we all dissolved into tears.

~ * ~

Ellen, Marie, and I had spent the better part of an hour on the cemetery bench talking, hugging, and crying. When our backsides were sufficiently numb and our throats parched, we decided to get some lunch, so I drove all of us to a little café I knew not far from the Blue Ridge Parkway in Virginia. It was run by a first-generation American, born of Cuban refugee parents, Jorge and his wife Elizabeth, who was a part-time lawyer in this sleepy but somewhat counter-cultural mountain community. It had the funky, punny name of 'Jorgie & Beth's.' Jorge ran the kitchen and produced his own style of Cuban-American cuisine, with whimsical names such as "Fidel Fries," "Che's Burger," and "Bay of Figs" fruit salad. It was furnished with old, wooden, high-backed booths which provided privacy, if desired. Beth kept one booth for her general legal business with the locals, when not looking after their two young children. There was no other place vaguely like Jorgie & Beth's, but it worked. People drove from as far away as Galax, Mt. Airy, and Martinsville for its unique atmosphere. Kyle and I used to meet there to discuss our pastoral triumphs and tragedies. It had a country store feel about it without being tacky. Each booth had controls for the juke box, which was loaded with country and western music, mainly from the 1950s and '60s, and was played just loud enough to obscure spoken confidences. It was exactly what Kyle's womenfolk and I needed. As we entered, Hank Thompson was singing his bewilderment at how God had made "honky tonk angels." He wasn't the only one questioning life's puzzles in this day of puzzlement.

"Kyle never told us much abo't that business between him and the presbytery—you know, all the crap that had been happening at Carson Presbyterian," Marie mused aloud as the fork in her hand toyed with the country ham salad on her plate. "I always thought Kyle and I were close—maybe not close enough to share everything, but at least the really important stuff. I don't know...if he were here right now, I wouldn't know whether to hug him or slap him. Probably both." Marie looked up at me and smiled weakly. "But he did talk with you, right? He never had anyone else like you, 'Nother Brother."

"Yeah, he did talk to me. He told me about the problems at Carson from the beginning. I suppose it's one reason I feel so damn bad about it all. I had helped in the process of getting Kyle into the pastorate at Carson Memorial. And y'all don't have to say it," I quickly added. "I know it's not *my* fault. But I guess we all will be thinking of things we wish we had or hadn't done. In any case, Kyle kept me in the picture from his first misgivings about what was taking place just after his arrival right through to the court case and convictions."

Ellen had been relatively silent in our drive to the restaurant and had not said very much since our arrival. Now she quietly spoke up.

"Jon," asked her weary voice, "what do you think pushed Kyle to..." and here she paused, "...to...do...*what he did*? Was it the court case or all of the investigations or..." Ellen's voice drifted away, perhaps in recognition that this line of questioning would never yield a satisfactory answer.

And what was I supposed to say? Should I tell my best friend's mother that, in fact, Kyle had been a 'dead man walking' since 1972, since the events that happened in a small clearing near Pleiku in Vietnam, now more than thirty-five years ago? Should I tell his sister that the really amazing fact is that her brother didn't kill himself earlier? This is the hell of suicide: all those who loved the deceased will spend at least some portion of their surviving years trying to unravel the Gordian knot which binds the *why?* of self-immolation, and whose solution ultimately lies in the grave with the deceased.

And does the grave release one from things held in confidence? Even if the secret which had held Kyle in its thrall for more than three decades—and the burden of which I had helped carry throughout that time—even if the death of him who had needed my trust and confidence now released me from the promise of confidentiality, would sharing that information help—in any significant way—a grieving mother and sister? How was I to balance their need to have some knowledge of what triggered Kyle's death with revealing what, for Kyle, was the blackest deed he had ever done? And how does one explain how a basically peace-loving guy ends up as a helicopter pilot flying combat missions on 'Hueys'—the Bell HU-1 Iroquois—workhorse helicopter of U.S forces in that misbegotten police action in Southeast Asia. For answers to all of those questions, I have to go further back than Carson Memorial Presbyterian Church and even Kyle's tour of duty in Vietnam.

Two

And the soul of Jonathan was bound to the soul of David.
                                                  —1 Samuel 18:1b

Kyle Weston and I had met during our final year of elementary school in 1962. As both of us later became ordained ministers in the Presbyterian Church—a good, Calvinist tradition—I suppose I could say that it had been predestination. But it was just as likely due to the fact that we were both new boys at the school and in the same sixth grade class. The rest of the children had either grown up together and/or had known each other since their first day of school. Thus, it was only natural that Kyle and I—unknown quantities in a small-town school— should have thrown our lots in together. What began in solitude that day on the playground formed a bond that was to last a lifetime.

Both of our families had moved to Lawrenceville, North Carolina, during the summer of 1962. Lawrenceville was a small town which occupied a lovely, forested section of the rolling upland Piedmont in the north central part of the state, where it met with the eastern slopes of the Blue Ridge—not far from the Virginia state line. What precipitated my family's move was the fact that my father, Phil Braddock, had made the momentous decision to leave his career as a Marine aviator. But the actual decision to move to Lawrenceville belonged to my mother. Although my father was a lieutenant colonel and squadron commander, mother outranked him when it came to decisions about the family home. As the younger of two children—my older brother, Ron, was nearly four years my senior—the only home I had known up until that move was the one our mother had made for us in New Bern, North Carolina, just twenty miles up the road from the Marine Corps Air Station at Cherry Point, where my father was based. Mother always made sure we had a civilian home, and those twenty miles served as a moat between the raw barbarity—as she saw it—of USMC pilots and the civility she craved for all of us.

Although Dad had left the Marine Corps in mid-1962, he had not left the real love of his life: flying. In fact, if the F-4 Phantom were a woman, my father—like so many Marine pilots of that day—would have been guilty of adultery. And if the Phantom were his concubine, then Cherry Point was his love nest. These facts, though never openly discussed between my parents, were certainly understood by my mother. Thus, she jealously guarded what place and authority she commanded with regard to her children and home.

Nevertheless, Dad had made his decision, helped by the fact that an old Marine flying buddy, Craig Benson, had encouraged him to catch the growing wave of civilian aviation, along with the money and lifestyle it afforded. Benson had left the Marines shortly after the Second World War and become a founding partner of a fledgling airline based in Winston-Salem called Pilot Aviation. The name wasn't a tautology; rather, "Pilot" came from a nearby rocky granite outcrop at the top of a lone "mountain" standing southeast of the Blue Ridge. Its distinct silhouette, visible from all compass points, made it a natural point of navigation; thus, the name—Pilot. In true, World War II fashion, this emblem was emblazoned on the nose of all the company's aircraft: ex-military C-47s, now known as DC-3s, and newer Martin 404s. And now, soon to be added to their fleet was the new three-engine jet, the Boeing 727. After all, Craig had reasoned with my father, his age was going to militate against his doing any future operational flying, and soon—except to keep up his hours and ratings—his only cockpit would be the squadron desk. Why not swap this inglorious inevitability for another twenty years of actual flying—and on good pay? Besides, with jets beginning to make their way into air travel, my father would be a natural senior pilot to the young wannabes sitting at the controls of the ageing DC-3s.

~ * ~

Philip Braddock had joined the USMC just after graduating with an engineering degree from North Carolina State University in 1941. However, with a university degree and excellent physical health, Dad set his sights high—sky high—and applied for pilot's training as soon as practicable. Having grown up on a farm near Pilot Mountain in Surry County during the darkest days of the depression, and having helped his large family to eke out a living from the unforgiving red clay—only to lose the farm when bills couldn't be paid—hugging the earth (whatever the color) as an infantryman, and slogging through mud weren't for him. Once airborne, "Blackie"—as he became known to his fellow pilots, due to his thick jet-black hair and permanent five o'clock shadow—served in two different fighter squadrons from late 1942 through 1943, later commanding the second squadron. A flak burst earned him a trip back to the US where, after convalescence, he was given a generous liberty and spent time back with his parents, who had become tenant farmers in Forsyth County and were living in a small house amidst tobacco fields. Once his furlough ended, Blackie was stationed at the Marine Corps Air Station at Cherry Point, North Carolina, helping to oversee combat instruction for replacement pilots. Over the next two decades—between deployments—Cherry Point became his life's center of gravity.

He had met my mother, Rachel Lawrence, at a dance in Raleigh, where she was a student at Meredith. Their marriage took place not long after my father began his basic training. The fact that he *first* joined the Marine Corps and *then* married my mother set a pattern that will be familiar to military brats the world over. His priorities were clear. Proud as she was, my mother wore her status as cuckolded wife to Dad's mistress—flying with the Marines—with a pride which suggested indifference.

My family had come to Lawrenceville for two reasons. First, my mother, Rachel, had grown up in Lawrenceville; it had long family associations as her surname suggests, as it had been named for her great-grandfather, a Methodist circuit-rider and educator. We still had aunts, uncles, and cousins from my mother's side of the family spread around that area. Second, my father's new base would be some twenty miles to the south of Lawrenceville—once more giving mother her required degrees of separation between our home and her rival: flying.

Kyle Weston's family had moved from Portsmouth, Virginia, to fit and troubleshoot new electrical systems in textile mills within the triangle of rolling country between Winston-Salem and Mount Airy, North Carolina, and Martinsville, Virginia. It was a lucrative opportunity in those golden years following the war. And so it was that the Westons came to pick Lawrenceville as the logical place to settle down, as it fell in the middle of the triangle.

Ed and Ellen Weston were from Suffolk, Virginia. Their lovely, soft Tidewater accents had been passed to both of their children. It was one of the first things I remembered about Kyle—the long O's he pronounced in words like "out" and "house." He often played on it just to make me laugh.

Kyle and I met just a day or two after the start of school in September of '62. During the recess after lunch, we were the only two kids not engaged in some frenzied activity with the other children. We were outsiders. Kyle and I stood about ten yards apart, casting sidelong glances at one another, each pretending to be focused on something other than the fact that neither of us had been asked to join in ball games and the like. A basketball came rolling Kyle's way, and he picked it up and threw it with easy grace to its owner, who barely acknowledged the favor before returning to the game. Kyle noticed me looking his way. He nodded and said, "Hey."

I returned the greeting, moved a few paces closer to him and said, "Can't wait 'til school's out."

"O't?" he replied. "It's only just started!"

"No, I mean today—in a few hours."

"Oh, I got you." Kyle laughed. We moved easily toward one another. "So why do you want it to be o't?" he queried.

"Oh, I don't know," I shrugged, "Guess it's because I don't know anyone here. It feels weird to come back to school this year and not know anyone. What about you?"

"Yeah, it feels the same. We just moved here from Portsmo'th—in Virginia. Where do y'all come from?"

"New Bern—down near the coast. Dad was stationed at Cherry Point, at the Marine Air Station. But he's out of the Marines now."

"What's he doing now? Is he retired?"

"Nah, he's got a job with Pilot Aviation down in Winston-Salem. He's helping them move into jet airliners."

"That's cool," Kyle said thoughtfully, then added, "So why don't y'all live down there?"

"My mom's from here. She grew up in Lawrenceville, and we have lots of relatives around here."

Kyle nodded. "My old man used to work for the Navy—well, his company did, around Norfolk. He's in electronics, but now his company's got him working with Farrington Mills, all around this area." Kyle watched the pick-up basketball game while drawing lazy circles in the dust with the toe of his shoe. "What's your name?"

"Jon—Jonathan—but everybody calls me Jon. What about you?"

"I'm Kyle, but, for some reason, everybody calls me Kyle." He grinned. It was a cheeky grin that I came to know well over the coming years. It seemed to come from nowhere, and before you knew it, his face was alight and his eyes sparkling. It was as natural as the sneakers he wore—at least through those carefree years. But that was before he went to Vietnam and long before he encountered Carson Memorial Presbyterian Church. We were not quite twelve years old then.

"Where do you live?" I asked.

"'Bo't half a mile up this road—not far," he pointed languidly without looking. "I can walk it. You?"

"Less than that, but the other way. It's closer just to cut across the fields—over yonder," I indicated. "Fields" was the shorthand name for several large public baseball diamonds and football fields that were also used by the town's schools. "I can ride my bike there in about two minutes. You got a bike?"

"Sure. I thought just about everybody had a bike—except our parents!" He grinned again. "You like baseball?"

"Sure. A lot more than football. Why?"

"Can you get your glove—and a ball, if you have one—and meet me ab'ot four? That is, if your parents say it's okay."

~ * ~

And that's how it began for me and Kyle—innocuously, the way I suppose most childhood friendships begin. We met up that afternoon, played catch for an hour or more, threw each other our best fast and curveballs, grounders and pop-flies until our arms ached. Over the course of the afternoon, we discovered the things that were of importance to us as children: siblings, the parental regimes under which we lived, the subjects we liked or disliked in school, what church each attended—his family was Episcopalian (which I had *heard* of, but couldn't spell) and mine was Presbyterian (which hardly anyone could spell and even fewer could describe). The common ground was that neither of us was Southern Baptist, so we were united in the simple fact that we were both of Christian minorities. Another uniting bond was the fact that we had the same favorite baseball team: the Boston Red Sox. The fact that the Red Sox had their Triple-A farm team in nearby Winston-Salem was an incentive—we also discovered that afternoon— that both our sets of parents had used to encourage us to accept the move from the known worlds of our hometowns, friends, and schools to Lawrenceville.

All Kyle and I knew at the end of that September afternoon in 1962 was that we each had a *friend*—a lifeline—and we wouldn't be left alone to founder in a sea of strangers. Neither of us could have begun to understand just what cords were being entwined in those days, nor how time, distance—and even war—would be unable to sever them. And although each of us slowly gained a widening circle of friends and acquaintances in Lawrenceville, we each—unconsciously—came to treat the other as an irreplaceable mainstay.

~ * ~

Whenever I am tempted to look back on those days as idyllic, I remind myself that we were barely six weeks into the autumn term when the Cuban Missile Crisis loomed large over all of our lives. As our state had major bases for the Marines, Army, and Air Force, many people, young and old alike, talked about the likelihood that North Carolina would certainly be targeted if war should break out. As for us schoolchildren, our anxieties were not helped when we started having to engage in air raid drills, in which we had to form orderly lines and march outside to practice lying face down on the ground. With the benefit of maturity and hindsight, such drills take on the character of a sick and cruel charade. Perhaps our charred, irradiated little bodies would have been easier to find, lying in neat rows, for anyone who just happened to survive a nuclear attack. No doubt it was the government's way of keeping us busy—a sort of 'whistling in the dark' exercise to make us feel that, in the face of a nuclear attack, we weren't totally helpless, which, of course, we were. Looking back, part of me thinks it odd that, during recess, we children should have been discussing the odds of our surviving the school year, but we did. But then such may well have been the nature of children's discourse during Sennacherib's siege of Hezekiah's Jerusalem in 701 BCE, which we had read about in Sunday School, when he held the city in his grasp "like a caged bird" or that of the children of Leningrad during its nine-hundred-day siege in the early 1940s. Kyle and I listened with rapt attention to the grave words of our fathers during those dark days. As they had been to war, our fathers had wisdom we did not hope to possess. We were still too young to quibble with the fact that neither man had ever experienced a *nuclear* attack.

It was in the worrying days before Kennedy, through the United Nations, negotiated the removal of the Soviet missiles from Cuba, that I heard my older brother utter one of the few pietistic statements of his life. What was even more amazing for me, at age eleven, was that his words were said to comfort me. Normally, his chosen method of addressing me was to employ some derogatory put-down—part of the job description for older siblings. But on this one particular occasion, such was not the case. We had watched the *Huntley-Brinkley Report* and were both headed upstairs to do our homework. For once, while watching the news, my father hadn't added his own running commentary or argued with points of view. The Russkies had their missiles aimed right down our throats and we, on the East Coast, were within ninety minutes of destruction. I took the stairs slowly and thoughtfully as I tried to digest the news and contemplate the fact that my life, short as it was, might soon be over. Ron, no doubt shaken by the news as well, came alongside me. I felt his hand on my shoulder. His act of kindness had the odd effect of both providing comfort and adding to my insecurities, for my brother was rarely wont to show me any kindness. The USA must really have been in danger!

"How ya doin' little brother?" Ron asked.

"I don't know. It's scary...I mean—do you think we'll really have atomic bombs dropped on us? Do you think the Russians will launch those missiles?"

Ron thought for a few seconds as we mounted the landing. Then he turned to me and said, in all earnestness, "Jon, the Russians are *atheists*. How could God let atheists beat *us*, huh? I mean, God has to be on our side, right?"

I looked up at Ron and said, "Yeah. I hadn't thought of that. You must be right." Such fillips did a world of good to my juvenile mind, which had just about experienced a total shutdown when trying to imagine non-existence. Perhaps the hand of Yahweh would once more show itself strong in power, just as in the days of Hezekiah? In any case, such comforting thoughts released my worried brain to the compassionate hands of sleep, that balm of hurt minds.

Happily, we didn't have to wait long for our reprieve from a possible Soviet attack. Kennedy, through tough talk as well as public and secret negotiations, got Khrushchev to back down. My parents were elated, and since they were happy, I was, too. My father, a staunch Republican, surprisingly couldn't say enough good about JFK. And my mother, normally a Democrat, but suspicious of Kennedy's Roman

Catholicism, also felt the papist president had proven himself in her Protestant eyes.

Thus, apart from the threat of total nuclear annihilation, the school year passed much as other years had done with the exception that Kyle and I were coming to the end of our time in elementary education and would be bound for junior high school in the following autumn. We had both turned twelve years old in the first half of 1963. Despite liking the mature sound of twelve, we nevertheless resented having to pay adult prices at the movie theatre. For matters of such gravity, we hung onto our kid status. I barely earned two dollars for mowing our lawn. Why should I have to sacrifice twenty-five percent of that hard-earned money just to see a movie, not to mention buy popcorn and a soft drink? We hadn't even entered that halfway house between childhood and maturity known as "the teens."

~ * ~

"Damn fool teenagers..." Kyle's father, Ed, was declaiming aloud as we coasted our bikes into the Westons' driveway one late spring day. He was squinting with disapproval, through smoke from the cigarette that seemed to permanently adorn his lips, at the trees in the front yard of the house opposite. The house was owned by the baseball coach of the Lawrenceville high school team which had just won the conference title. In celebration, some "damn fool teenagers" had "rolled" the pines, oaks, and magnolia trees with toilet paper. But like so many of the things children of WW2 veterans got up to, from Kyle's dad they only earned the deprecating utterance "damn fool teenagers." Over time, Ed's epithet became something of a joke between Kyle and me. Whenever one of us did something silly or stupid, the other was quick to say, "Damn fool teenager." The fact that we weren't yet teenagers didn't matter. The phrase stuck in our vocabulary, and we used it right up until the last time we saw each other.

Ed Weston's firm opinion that all young people in their teens were "damn fools" occasionally led Kyle and me to muse aloud whether we too would automatically metamorphose into something unrecognizable from the selves we had known. Would we both—at age thirteen—mysteriously and magically become malevolent ogres, in the same way that Kafka's Gregor Samsa awoke as a cockroach? Kyle and I simply saw teenagers as 'older kids,' but not so for Ed Weston. It appeared to Kyle and me that his father thought all the youth in America were in a conspiracy—against him. What was it Ed Weston saw that we couldn't? Was it simple genetic determinism that we, too, should become damn fool teenagers? The closest we could come to solving this riddle was that it must actually be something that happens in the adult brain which turns perfectly comprehensible youngsters into damn fool teenagers.

With the arrival of June, our elementary school days ended and summer lay before us with the promise of sun, baseball, bikes, and swimming—the daily toil of white, middle class kids of the baby boom generation. The house my parents had bought in Lawrenceville had about three acres of land with it. At the lower end of the property were some woods. A large creek—Stuart's Creek (named for Jeb Stuart, who had been born just across the Virginia line, in the adjacent county)—ran through the middle of our property, and there was even a small pond at the bottom of a spillway where the creek left our land. An old, wooden bridge connected the land on either side of the creek. When nothing else took our fancy, Kyle and I spent time building a raft which we propelled by poles made from saplings we had cut in the nearby woods. The pond was only about four feet deep at most, and the stream was certainly no Mississippi; but this didn't stop our boyhood imaginations from turning it into our own versions of Huck Finn and Tom Sawyer. Across the creek from our house stood an old, semi-dilapidated horse stable, in which my family used the ground floor as a storage area for the lawnmower and gardening tools. However, there was a small hayloft above, and some evenings, Kyle and I would put our sleeping bags in the loft and sleep there, looking out at the stars through the opening in the gable end. In many ways, this was as close as our lives ever came to being idyllic.

~ * ~

That summer of 1963 also provided enough leisure time to introduce Kyle and me to the borderland of damn-fool-teenager-land. We were tempted over the invisible boundary by my older brother,

Ron, who was then sixteen. Through some friends of friends, Ron had managed to lay his hands on a selection of fireworks—and not just any fireworks (which, in any case, were illegal in North Carolina)—but four M-80s as well. For the uninitiated, M-80s had been designed for training use by the military to simulate mortar and light artillery explosions and contained up to three grams of explosives, not to mention fuses which could burn under water. For Ron, it was a way to relieve his younger brother and friend of their weekly allowance and money earned through doing chores. Neither Kyle nor I had ever seen an M-80, but we had heard their reports from the playing fields at Halloween, when teenagers gathered for their special forms of mischief. Further, having been raised on a diet of war films, such as *The Sands of Iwo Jima* and *The Guns of Navarone,* as well as television programs like *Combat!*, Kyle and I were keen to enact our own missions and lay some demo charges—but where or when? Our mission was to lie in an unexpected quarter.

~ * ~

Every summer since I had started school, my mother had liked our family to spend a week at the John Knox Conference Center. The Knox Center, as it was more commonly known, was a church retreat and conference center in the mountains of western North Carolina and named after that stalwart of Scots Presbyterianism. The Knox Center even suited my "Flyin' Leatherneck" father. Although Dad considered himself a Christian, he let it be known that he didn't get along too well with *all* of Mr. Jesus' teachings. For instance, when it came to such instructions as "turning the other cheek," Dad simply opined, "Giving in to bullies only encourages them. Just look at Hitler."

At such points of intransigence, mother would simply reply with, "Yes, dear." However, Dad also reckoned that any man who could stand up to the Romans and the punishment they dealt out would have made a fine Marine. That was the highest accolade Dad could have given anybody, even the Son of God.

Normally, our entire family went to the Knox Center, but this particular summer, Ron had been invited to spend part of the summer back down in New Bern with a friend from his former school. Mom and Dad agreed, as they thought it was high time Ron had some independence. Seeing that this left a space in our normal complement, I decided to ask my parents to let Kyle accompany us for the week. I carefully prepared my mental list of good reasons, such as how it would help to have someone my own age to pal around with. I decided to wait until after supper, when Dad would be well fed and enjoying his evening beer over the daily paper. As I helped clear the dishes away, I began my pitch. "Um...Mom and Dad...um...you know how Ron isn't going to Knox with us this summer? Well, I was thinking—"

"That you'd like to invite Kyle, right?" interjected my father. "I don't see why not. What about you, honey?"

Mother, who was washing dishes in the sink, answered over her shoulder, "Long as you two mind yourselves and do as you're told."

I was so unprepared for an affirmative answer that the arguments I had amassed in support of Kyle's going with us crumbled beneath me. My face must have had the look of a drunk stopping to rest against an open door. Dad cocked an eyebrow over the newspaper at me. He was enjoying himself. Even without seeing the rest of his face, I knew he was grinning.

Our week at the Knox Center encompassed the Fourth of July weekend. So after assuring the Westons we would both be on our best behavior—with the normal amount of "yes, ma'ams" and "yes, sirs"— we two co-conspirators made our way to Kyle's room.

"You got 'em?" asked Kyle excitedly.

"Yep," I said, magisterially drawing two M-80s from my jeans pockets and holding them gingerly in cupped hands.

"Wow!" admired Kyle.

"Ron says if we get caught or do anything stupid with them, we didn't get them from him. Got it?"

Kyle nodded, "Right."

~ * ~

As is common in the land of youth, the anticipation of our trip to the mountains made the waiting seem interminable. Whenever Kyle and I met up to play ball or ride bikes, our conversations kept turning to the M-80s and what wonderful mischief we would make with them. We were too young to realize that we were treading the same eastward path from youth's Eden as had virtually every adult, who later had cause to look back wistfully at vanished innocence. Kyle and I were, for the first time in our lives, deliberately planning to do something wrong—and illegal.

As it has a way of doing, the time for our mountain adventure did arrive. We sat through our Bible classes with some degree of attentiveness, but we were itching to execute our explosive plan. Kyle and I had brought two of our four M-80s to the Knox Center; we saved the others for devilment back in Lawrenceville. As July Fourth was our only evening free from adult supervision, we decided to set off both M-80s at one time. To our disappointment, we soon discovered that there were absolutely no fireworks displays planned for the Fourth. Instead, there were cookouts during the afternoon, followed by a patriotic concert and sing-song at 7:00 p.m. in the main auditorium. Our fireworks—apart from those of any other reprobates—would be the only "planned" pyrotechnics of the evening, thus making them all the more manifest. However, in our insouciance, this fact made our lone illicit endeavor all the more appealing. It would be noticed.

On the evening of July Fourth, knowing that neither Kyle nor I would be able to sit through the evening musical program, my parents tentatively announced that we would be given our freedom after supper. With this emancipation came the usual stern warnings about what unspeakable fate awaited us if we misbehaved, transgressed, brought the family into disrepute, etc. We accepted the conditions with youthful naïveté, bordering on arrogance. We knew we were too clever to be caught or even accused. It was all Kyle and I could do to keep from squirming in our seats as we grinned at each other over glasses of milk.

Immediately after supper, we retired to our bedroom to check over our equipment. While keeping one ear cocked toward the door in the event of parental invasion, we spread out our demolition supplies: two M-80s, Scotch tape (to fasten them together and secure them to our target), one cigarette (taken from Kyle's father) for a delayed fuse, matches, and my Swiss Army knife.

The conference center was situated in a bowl-shaped valley, at the center of which was a modest lake fed by mountain streams. It had been created by damming the main stream. Our plan was simple: we would take one of the rowboats, launch it from the stream-fed side of the lake, row out to the diving platform, deposit our charges, and then use the water's current, plus our adrenalin-spiked energy, to row like mad toward the dam, where we would jump from the boat, climb the bank and then walk nonchalantly back toward the cabin my family had rented for the week. We reasoned we should be nearly home before the cigarette fuse burned down.

One thing we hadn't counted on was the simple fact that early evenings during mid-summer weren't completely dark. Therefore, our movements across the lake would be visible. Having chosen our boat, Kyle and I waited by the lakeside as long as we could for some measure of darkness to envelop us. But as the concert ended at 9:00 p.m., and my watch read 8:30, it was now or never. And what fun it would be, we chuckled, if we got back to the cabin at the same time as my parents, and then heard the explosions. Kyle and I clambered into a rowboat and sat side by side, each taking an oar. The boat eased away from the shore as we made our way to the diving platform. Laughing and giggling with nervous excitement, we forgot to drag our oars to slow the boat and smacked into the platform with a sound that, to our guilty ears, was like a gunshot. I involuntarily looked toward the auditorium, which stood on a knoll some thirty feet above the lakeside and where my parents were enjoying the concert. Certainly, we would be found out. I almost expected to hear my father's strong baritone voice calling out to me. To our surprise and relief, nobody—not even the Almighty—called us to account for what we were doing. The auditorium remained bathed in the tranquil glow of the lights within. Kyle and I sat silently for a minute or so and peered around the lakeside. Unbelievably, there seemed to be no one about at all. Both of us breathed audible sighs of relief, looked at each other, and smiled at our luck and cleverness. I loosely tied the boat's mooring line to a rung on the platform's ladder, and we began preparing the M-80s for detonation.

I carefully taped them together while Kyle took out the badly crumpled cigarette. As he tried to push the two fuses into the cigarette's end, the tobacco simply sprinkled out. Soon there was barely a third of it left. Our escape time would be critically shortened. Kyle looked at me with frustration. The minutes were ticking by. "What're we gonna do?" he implored.

"Why don't we tape the cigarette to the fuses?" I offered.

"Yeah! That'll do it."

I felt a swell of pride at my obvious solution and duly pulled off about six inches of tape and handed it to Kyle, who methodically wound the tape around our delayed action fuse.

"There," Kyle said, as he held it up with satisfaction. "Now it's ready."

I checked my watch one last time. "It's a quarter to nine. We'd better make a move." My hands were shaking with an admixture of excitement and fear. "You light it." I handed the matches to Kyle.

He looked at me with brief hesitation and then said, "Okay. Here goes." I noticed—with some relief—that Kyle's hands also shook as he tried to strike the paper matches. He threw the first one into the water and took out a new one. The second match flared into life and Kyle touched it to the tape-encased cigarette. Then the unexpected came into play. While waiting for the tobacco to catch alight, the cellophane tape burst into flame, and the flame was racing toward the M-80s' fuses. I was momentarily stunned by the fast-burning torch in my hands. "Holy shit!" cried Kyle, "Drop it, Jon! Drop it!"

I followed Kyle's command—it no doubt saved my hands. The problem was that I had dropped the charges into the bottom of the boat and neither of us wanted to pick them up and toss them onto the diving platform. We stood staring, like deer caught in headlights—until we heard the sinister *sputter* as the fuses came to life. Now it was my turn to give orders. "Jump!" I shouted. Kyle and I both flung ourselves over the side of the boat and started flailing at the water in demented strokes, our bodies galvanized by the icy shock of the mountain water. A thunderous double explosion seemed to smack me in the back of my head, followed immediately by a powerful tremor through the water.

The echoes of the explosion seemed to accuse us from every mountainside. As the cacophony subsided, I called out to Kyle, "You okay?" gulping for air and swallowing mouthfuls of water at the same time.

"Uh-huh," was the breathless response from Kyle as we frantically plowed our way toward the water's edge.

~ * ~

Unbeknownst to me and my accomplice, my father, along with a half-dozen other war veterans, was on his feet and out the door of the auditorium within seconds of the blast. They had made their way down to the lakeside to survey the scene and ascertain whether all was well. "Sure as hell sounded like it came from the lake," offered one man, just as Kyle and I pulled ourselves out of the water.

"Over there!" Someone had pointed us out and the men came toward us at a trot. Kyle and I sat on the bank, shivering with cold and too much adrenaline. We looked at each other like condemned men. "You boys okay?" the same voice earnestly enquired from above, and then, "Y'all fishing with dynamite or something?" He laughed.

"Yeah," we responded to his first question in a bare whisper, afraid to look up. "But we weren't fishing," replied Kyle to the second question.

"Isn't that your boy, Phil?" another man asked my father, nodding toward me.

Dad pushed by the other men and fixed his gaze upon me. Laser-like, it could burn the truth out of me no matter what cover story or excuses I had tried over the years. "Yes," he answered curtly. "He's my son—and that other boy's his friend."

"Uh-oh," laughed one of the group. "Send in the Marines!"

"Come on up," said Dad, his voice flat, emotionless. This was always the scariest time when I had done wrong, because I knew the outward calm in the voice belied inner, pent up, raw anger. The Marines had indeed arrived.

Kyle and I slipped and sloshed our way up the bank of the lake, our waterlogged sneakers squishing with every step. Dad scanned the lake as we approached him. His keen eyes spotted the rowboat, settled up to the oarlocks in the water. Although my eyes weren't meeting his, I knew my father was looking at me. I was starting to shiver, as much from the soaking as from fear of what lay in store. I cast a furtive look at Kyle. It didn't occur to me at the time that the fear I saw in his eyes simply mirrored what he saw in my countenance; and that he, as children often do, had been waiting to take his cue from me. We stood dripping before my father. Without another word he reached out, took us each by the crowns of our heads, and turned us into an about-face beside him. His hands moved from our heads to the napes of our necks and firmly guided us toward our cabin. As we moved away from the lakeside, my father's hand suddenly released its grip on my neck. I had no sooner started to draw a breath of relief when I felt the sharp snap as his middle finger was released from behind his thumb. It made a dull thud against my skull and I flinched forward. I knew not to reach up and rub the spot. Out of the corner of my eye I saw the whites of Kyle's eyes as he looked in response to the flick of my father's finger. Dad's hand rested again on my neck—this time a bit more relaxed—and, without anyone calling the cadence, even Kyle fell in with Dad and me as we marched back to the house: Left...left...left, right, left. It felt as though we were condemned men making our way toward a firing squad. The only saving grace was the fact that, in our shame, we were just ahead of the crowds emerging from the evening concert.

After about three-hundred yards, my father spoke. "So, you boys going to tell me what happened and what that explosion was?"

My shoulders unconsciously moved backwards and my chin came up, as I answered: "Yes, sir." Kyle just nodded. He had never been in the custody of the USMC before.

"Son," my father stated, "I'm waiting, but don't try my patience." He tended to call me "Son" when he was at the extremes of his emotions. It usually signified one of two things: either he was very irate with me (the more usual signification) or it was one of his rare, tender moments, which should have comforted me, but tended to have the opposite effect, as they seemed so out of character.

"Well," I started, "well, it's like this. You see, Kyle and I had some firecrackers, and we wanted to set them off on the Fourth of

July—you know—today, and well, we kinda wanted to pretend we were blowing up a Jap installation on an island in the Pacific back in the war with demolition charges, and—" My father interrupted me.

"Whoa, son. Slow down. What do you mean 'firecrackers?' That explosion was more than some little ladyfingers. Inside the auditorium it sounded like a bomb going off. What the hell was it?" Dad's strong hands had released our necks. Both Kyle and I flexed our neck and shoulder muscles.

"Um...yeah, well they were...um, like M-80s."

"*M - 80s*?!" My father emphasized each component in the name of our pyrotechnic devices. "Where in the hell did you get M-80s? For cryin' out loud, did you realize what those things are capable of doing?"

"No...I don't know...uh...I guess we do *now*." I tried to bring a smile to my chilled lips.

"Jesus Christ." Dad was shaking his head. "I don't know whether to tan your hide or congratulate you for not blowing your hand off or blinding yourself—either of you." He looked at Kyle who looked blankly at Dad—probably wondering whether his parents had okayed it for my parents to exercise corporal punishment. Dad looked over his shoulder as small groups of concert-goers walked lazily back toward their mountain retreats. Dad guided us off the road and along a path which ran past the tennis courts. It afforded us some privacy.

"Okay, son. The M-80s. Where'd you get them?"

"Do I have to tell you? You won't like it," I began, as though that had ever stopped an interrogation by my father before.

Dad looked at me with exasperation. "Ron. Ron got 'em and he sold them to Kyle and me." Kyle nodded vigorously as at last it seemed something or someone else might take the heat off us.

"Your brother, Ron, sold you the M-80s?" I merely nodded assent. "Dad-blame it!" My father resorted to ersatz swear words when he was calming down. This was a good sign. "Your brother supplied you, a twelve year old, with TNT charges? If that doesn't beat all." Dad shook his head.

"*TNT?*" gulped Kyle. Dad stopped our march. He positioned himself in front of us and laid each firm hand on one of our shoulders. To a stranger's eyes, he could have been blessing us; and, in fact, his words and mood had become a sort of benediction.

"Yes, TNT." Dad took on a confidential air. "Boys, M-80s are used in military training to give Marines or soldiers the sound and feel of real combat—so they contain *real* explosive—enough to hurt, maim or even kill you." Dad sighed heavily and looked at us with real pity. Kids. "So, what did you do, sink the rowboat?"

"I guess we did," I replied, "but it wasn't on purpose!" I then related the events, with Kyle's occasional input, of how we came to sink the boat and had to swim to shore in our clothes. By the end of our tale, Dad not only smiled, he even laughed! Kyle and I sneaked a look at each other. We couldn't believe our luck. Dad returned to a grave tone momentarily and addressed the two of us. "You know you'll have to pay for any damage to the boat? It will have to come from your pockets."

"Yes, sir," we answered. Kyle and I were hugging ourselves as the cool mountain air accentuated the discomfort of our already chilled bodies. Dad then pointed us toward the cabin. "Let's go home and get you two dried and changed."

"Okay," we assented, with chattering teeth.

"And one more thing." We stopped and looked at Dad. "Do you boys have any more of those M-80s?" The laser-eyes were directed only at me.

"Yes, sir, two. That's all. But they're at home."

Dad studied my eyes and face until he was satisfied he had the truth. "All right then. When we get home, they're confiscated."

Truthfully, after the fright Kyle and I had put ourselves through, I had no intention of ever touching an M-80 again.

I learned later from Mother how Dad had squared things with her. Ironically, she said that Dad was almost proud of what Kyle and I had done: rigging the explosives, diving for safety when it went wrong, and then swimming for shore. Mom felt Dad was thinking he would make a Marine of me yet.

~ * ~

Ellen smiled at the memory of tales from Kyle's and my youth, as she slowly spread butter over one of Jorgie and Beth's corn muffins. "Y'all were lucky not to have blown your hands off."

"That's true," I nodded, "But there's an epilogue to this story you must have heard both Kyle and me tell more than once."

Marie shrugged. "Remind us."

"Well, y'all remember that our family property was divided by Stuart's Creek, right? In dry weather it was about four to five feet wide and eight to ten inches deep. *But*, whenever we had heavy downpours of rain, it became a raging torrent that could reach twelve to fifteen feet wide and at least five feet deep! All of the smaller creeks and branches from the surrounding hills fed into Stuart's Creek. This worried my mother to no end, but to make matters even worse, with the rising water came the escaping denizens of the creek bank—in particular: water rats.

"Although my mom was born a country girl, the rat was the one variety of rodents from the bucolic days of her youth she could not abide. And the idea of so many rapacious rodents living within close proximity of our house made mother so ill at ease that, whenever summer thunderstorms approached, she would stand at the kitchen window and fret aloud: 'Lord, I hope that creek doesn't rise with the rain.' She would study the clouds with furrowed brow and, no doubt, offer up silent prayers that the good Lord might send only the rain that was *needed*—and not so much that the rats would challenge the sanctity of her home. This is where my confiscated M-80s came in."

Both Ellen and Marie listened expectantly, their faces, having been so grief-stricken, were smoothed over by a story from happier times.

"About a month after our week at the Knox Center, Dad decided to put an end to the rats' tenancy on our section of Stuart's Creek. Kyle and I were down in the pond that afternoon, messing around on that raft we built—do you remember? We saw Mom come out of the house, looking very worried, wiping her hands nervously on her ever-present apron. Dad had his Marine Zippo in his hand, along with a roll of black, electrical tape and—" I looked again at my rapt audience of two and smiled as I paused.

"Dad reached into his pocket and pulled out the two M-80s. Well, Kyle and I looked at each other pie-eyed in bewilderment as we hadn't a clue what Dad was going to do. He didn't say a word as he looked around at the ground. Then he saw what he had been looking for: a nice round stone. Dad pulled off a length of electrical tape, cut it with his pocket knife, and secured both M-80s to the stone. When his explosive charge was ready, Dad looked at me and Kyle and said, 'You boys had better go wait with Mother.' He nodded toward Mom who stood on the bridge, about twenty yards away."

I halted mid-narration and looked from Ellen to Marie. "You know, it had never really hit me until then, that, as an airman, Dad hadn't actually *handled* explosives before. He had dropped bombs and fired rockets from underneath his aircraft, but unlike the Marines on the ground, he had never flung grenades or satchel charges into Japanese positions. For the first time in my young life, I felt that my father and I were 'level-pegging.' So, despite the words of warning Dad had given to Kyle and me about the power of the M-80, my father was learning— just as I had and just as badly!" I shook my head and took a big gulp of iced tea.

"Well, with a self-satisfied smile, Dad put the knife and tape in his pocket and flicked open the cover of his Zippo lighter. 'Honey Doll,' as he sometimes called my mother, 'your rat problem is about to be history.' Dad ran his thumb over the flint-wheel and touched the lighter's flame to the fuses...and the rest...well, that has been burned into my memory like a film in slow-motion. The M-80s' fuses hissed angrily. Dad quickly closed the Zippo and dropped it in his side pocket; he leaned over the creek bank and threw the explosives into the largest entrance of the rats' burrow—which was *beneath and between* his feet!

"Mother, Kyle and I waited one, maybe two seconds, and KERBLAM!" I threw my hands into the air in gesticulation. Other diners glanced over at our table. "Well, the ground shuddered as the M-80s went off with a ferocious blast. Dad never got a chance to get out of the crouch he was in as the bomb left his hand. He had thrown the M-80s far enough into the rats' tunnel that, when it went off, the ground actually convulsed beneath him. The upward thrust of the explosion lifted him up and over in a complete flip right into the middle of the creek!" Marie and Ellen were convulsing with laughter, and the joy of seeing them laugh made me want to prolong the moment.

Painting the picture with my hands, I resumed my story. "Mud, rocks, and water all came down on top of him. Dad sat there for a moment or two—stunned, but all right—with a quizzical 'What the *hell*?' expression on his face. It was like something out of a Road Runner and Wily Coyote cartoon! Mom, Kyle, and I were all silent for a moment, hardly believing what we had just witnessed, and then we all started laughing! We laughed so hard we couldn't stop! Our laughter soon brought him around, and ol' Dad was loath to find humor in his situation." Again mimicking my father's voice, I growled: "'Goddamnit! If you think it's so funny, maybe I'll throw you in here as well!'"

Tears were streaming from Ellen's and Marie's eyes, but these were the refreshing tears of laughter. "Well, Mom turned to Kyle and me, gave us a weak smile and said, 'Y'all had better go inside and get washed up for lunch.' Over her shoulder, Mom shouted toward Dad, 'I'll run a bath for you, dear.' She knew what Dad was like when his dander was up. So Kyle and I turned and headed for the house at a trot. Even after we'd closed the door, we could still hear Dad cussing up a storm!" I paused for a sip of tea. "Needless to say, that was one lunch that passed in near silence. Dad was unusually quiet. He seemed truly embarrassed and humiliated at having been defeated in his battle with the water rats. I had never seen him in such a state. It was a new experience. Kyle and I had to keep from looking at each other for fear we would break out laughing again, so we stared at our plates. After lunch, Mom whispered that we might want to get our bikes and go for a ride. We needed no encouragement. Once we got clear of the house, Kyle was the first to let his gut-bursting laughter out. 'Lord, that was fun-ny! Did you see the look on your dad's face?!'"

I was wiping my eyes from mirthful tears. "It was years before we could openly mention these misadventures in front of my father; and even then, we had to be careful. But for those of us who witnessed it, the story always got better with the re-telling." Ellen, Marie and I sat back and savored the joy of the moment, each of us lost in our private thoughts and memories.

As we sat in silence, my mind dredged up one more memory: After Dad's close calls with the M-80s Mother had tried to keep quiet about our diminutive, disgusting denizens. However, on one occasion, the household .22 make an appearance, when Ron tried to dispatch several adult rats. Having fired and missed, Dad decided he would show us how it was done Marine-style—cocking, taking aim and nailing a rat as it was swimming *over the spillway*. "Drilled it a new A-hole," Dad said with a smile as he handed the rifle back to Ron. My brother and I looked at one another with near disbelief. Could Dad have hit it *end-on* from over thirty feet away?

Ron and I went to verify the kill, fetching the inert body from the pond. Dad was right. One hole at each end. "Wow," we both uttered. But Dad had known it all along and didn't need to see the body which we brought back and laid by the creek bank. He simply smiled at us again. And it was the mental image of my father's smile that brought fully into conscious memory a photo of Dad that hung in his study, a twenty-three-year-old, leaning against the canopy of his Corsair, with twelve Japanese flags painted on the fuselage—and he had that same smile.

Three

Man must rise above the Earth—to the top of the atmosphere and beyond—for only thus will he fully understand the world in which he lives.

—Socrates

When we weren't waging war with vermin, Dad took Ron and me flying from time to time. He could never seem to get enough of flying, and the simple truth was he was a different man in the air. He was "Blackie." And Blackie took on a calm that was generally missing with his earthbound persona, Phil. Owners of small, private planes were happy to let Dad take their aircraft up, just for the cost of the fuel. They knew their aircraft were safe in his hands. Dad seemed to become one with whatever airplane we were flying in. He was sensitive to the engine's pitch and vibration, hands resting easily upon the controls. Dad could have been an expert equestrian the way he coaxed the aircraft to do what it was capable of doing. I enjoyed watching him from the co-pilot's seat as he smiled to himself and whistled ever so softly. He taught both my brother and me the basics of reading the instruments and gauges as well as how to keep the aircraft straight and level.

Depending upon the seating capacity of the airplane, Dad would let Ron and me bring along friends from time to time. Kyle was always the first to be asked. He loved flying. For my brother and me, flying was *fun*, but for Kyle, it was something *more*. And it was a fact that Kyle had a light, confident touch at the controls. Dad seemed to recognize this kinship in Kyle and, thus gave him more time in the co-pilot's seat than he gave me. I remember feeling more than a little jealous of the attention and tuition that Kyle received from Blackie. Was it that fathers and sons at certain levels just take one another for granted, or was it that Kyle was such a willing pupil? Perhaps a mixture. In any case, I learned to live with the jealousy because I loved them both, but in very different ways. With my father, the love was like that of the Hebrew people for God as reflected in the Old Testament: God was this wholly Other Being, who expected much of his people and made them aware of it in no uncertain terms, including punishment, whenever they strayed from his path. This God was not warm and cuddly, but was steady, firm and trustworthy. But as regards my love for Kyle, it was simple: he was my best friend. And having a best friend was just one of life's basics.

I never worried when in an airplane with Dad. It never occurred to me that, if anything had happened to him—heart attack or whatever—I would be left thousands of feet in the air with no ability to land the plane. But that was the kind of confidence my father instilled in those around him when he was flying. On the ground (as with the M-80s) or behind the wheel of a car—well, they were entirely different matters. Although Dad had managed to master the art of formation flying, he never learned the art of being in a line of cars, regardless of speed. His idea of driving was the same as flying his passenger plane: there should be *nothing* in front of him. Nice theory, but not very realistic on America's highways, and it was to cost us dearly a few years later.

As the years passed, the difference between my earthbound and airborne father increased. I began to see him as a sort of Jekyll and

Hyde character. The longer he was out of the Marine Air Corps, the more pronounced the difference became. Thus, I began to absent myself whenever he was around the house, especially I as moved into my teen years. Dad seemed to confer his restlessness onto me. Whenever he found me reading a book or sitting in the porch swing, he would launch in with his standard, "Why don't you *do* something?" When I was twelve, I had made the mistake of asking, "Like what?" whereupon I was marched around to a neighbor's house and given the job of cutting her grass for the princely sum of two dollars. Before long, eight or ten of our neighbors enlisted me as their lawn boy. Despite the vast difference in the size of their lawns, the figure of two dollars became the acceptable recompense, and I was too young and naïve to question it. The money I made did come in handy, and I hoped this bit of youthful entrepreneurial spirit might appease my father's work ethic. Not so. Therefore, I learned to become evasive and melt away whenever I heard my father's approach. The refrain "Why don't you *do* something?" became my life's reproach and instilled some indefinable sense of guilt and unworthiness. In my world view, I *was* doing something. I was reading—I loved to read—or worrying about school or thinking about girls—whatever.

Like so many new adolescents, I couldn't imagine that my father had ever been young like me. As far as I could tell, he had always been just as he was at that time, he had just looked different. It couldn't have begun to occur to me that Dad was staying busy to keep out of reach of his inner demons.

Whenever my Dad-evasion tactics around our house were exhausted, then Kyle's house was usually the next port of call. I was always welcome there. Kyle's mother, Ellen, thought I was such a "lovely boy" and Kyle's little sister, Marie, just thought of me as an adoptive, older brother. However, even the safe-haven of Kyle's house wasn't far enough away when Dad's restlessness deemed it necessary that Ron or I should be doing something constructive: pulling weeds, chopping wood, repairing a fence, etc. The next best escape was to arrange a couple of nights' camping in the nearby woods. Kyle and I had both joined the Scouts as soon as we were eleven. The troop was based at the church my family attended, so by our thirteenth year, we were well adept at looking after ourselves in the wilds. Summer or winter—it didn't matter to Kyle and me—when I had all of the lawns mowed or household chores done and knew that Dad had a few days off flying, we would prepare our backpacks, walk to the grocery for provisions, and then disappear into the woods. Sometimes at night, we would go for long walks in the woods. In summers, we would listen to the evening cacophony of night creatures and insects. In the winter, we enjoyed the deep stillness of the frosty air.

We especially liked walking the railroad line that ran a few miles behind my family's place. It was easier walking the ties with their regular spacing than making our way through trees and brush. Kyle and I would literally walk for miles, talking about everything that was important to us: the bands we liked, the girls we hoped liked us as much we did them, our incomprehensible parents, teachers we hated and what we hoped to do with our lives—once we had made it through what seemed to be interminable damn-fool-teenagerdom.

Sometimes, during our nighttime rambles and for reasons we could not express, Kyle and I would slip back to our homes and observe— from a safe distance—our families. There was a fascination in seeing our parents without us around the house. More often than not, they would be doing things separately: reading, washing dishes, mending something. Sometimes they would be together: talking, watching television, looking at a newspaper article. We would laugh and nudge each other if our parents showed any affection—a hug or a kiss—but there was also poignancy about such times, such that Kyle and I would muse aloud what our parents would have been like without us. Would their lives have carried on the same? As that line of enquiry also had the effect of negating our existence, it usually ended with a shudder and a "Whoa." How could anything be the same without us there to observe it?

~ * ~

Barely a year after the Cuban Missile Crisis and just when most Americans were breathing more easily, our world was upended once more. At the end of a school day, I, along with a few others, was helping tidy up our classroom after we had made decorations for the up-coming Thanksgiving celebration. Our teacher was momentarily out of the room and our small group was laughing and joking as we worked. Suddenly, a student from another class came rushing through the door. She stopped, her face pale and blank, and remained almost rigid for about a minute, before she blurted out, "Somebody has shot President Kennedy."

To say we were dumbstruck would be putting it mildly. I don't think I can ever remember another time when such a short message brought total silence from a boisterous group of young people. After a moment's silence, one or two students burst into tears. Then others started asking questions for which our messenger could have no answers: "Who did it?" "Why was he shot?" "Where did it happen?" And of course: "Is he dead?" The girl who came to tell us—and I can only remember her face, but not her name—shook her head at all of the questions we fired at her. Then she, too, fell into floods of tears and returned to her classroom. I was still glued to the spot where I heard the news. I realized that I was totally numb. Our president was shot, perhaps dead. Only a year ago he had been our savior from a Soviet maelstrom. Was our country once more in danger? Why had this happened?

"Why?" responded my father to the string of questions I posed regarding Kennedy's assassination. "You ask *why*?" He chomped his food angrily. The mood at our dinner table was subdued. "Have you heard of Castro or Cuba? Have you heard of Khrushchev and the Communists? Any one of these slimy bastards would have a hundred reasons to shoot our president—and you ask 'why?'"

"Phil, calm down," Mom interjected. "Jon's still young. It's only natural that he wants to know why our president was shot and killed. And for that matter, I want to know as well. I'm sure millions of other Americans do, too." Mother dabbed her eyes with a handkerchief she had been holding in her hand throughout supper. Ron ate his meal vacantly.

Life's questions were starting to pile up at a rate that boggled my twelve-year-old mind. Khrushchev wanting to nuke the US; now our president was shot dead. What next? It would only be a few short years before I would learn one key lesson to maintaining sanity: life is comprised of a series of questions, very few of which have satisfying answers.

~ * ~

When our lives weren't being shaken to the roots by national or world events, Kyle and I—along with our other male friends—were finding our days made tolerable with sports, music and girls. As for sport, Kyle and I continued in our love of baseball and played for the school team, Kyle on third base and me in outfield. As regards music, we were confirmed rock 'n' roll fans, the US being firmly under assault by the "British invasion" led by the Beatles, the Dave Clark Five, the Rolling Stones, and others. We sat around stereos in each other's houses, listening to the newest 45 RPMs and debating the merits of US groups like the Beach Boys versus the British groups. At the same time—when we knew our parents were out of earshot—we discussed the girls who were developing curves and which ones we fancied. No longer were they merely weird, long-haired versions of boys who wore dresses. Now they really were different and causing sensations within us; they attracted us. And the damnable thing was—they knew it. And so we stumbled and crashed our way through the turmoil which is adolescence, going through all of the same things that previous generations had gone through but feeling that we alone were the first to experience them, something that defines the very essence of being an adolescent.

Four

It's silly talking about how many years we will have to spend in the jungles of Vietnam when we could pave the whole country and put parking stripes on it and still be home for Christmas.

—Ronald Reagan, 1965

As 1965 rolled into 1966, American involvement in Vietnam steadily increased. Johnson had resumed bombing targets in North Vietnam—after his hopes were dashed that a cessation over Christmas of '65 might be an incentive for the Communists to negotiate a settlement. When Dad's former squadron was posted there, Dad chafed at the thought of their going off to war without him, even an undeclared war. He even, to my young mind, seemed to have a sense of guilt about not going to fight with them. I, of course, thought he was crazy, as I couldn't understand why anyone wanted to go to war in the first place, especially when it was so far away and there was no clear and present danger to our country.

America's police action in Southeast Asia became a common topic of conversation at our family dinner table as well as in my youth group at church. Because our youth group incorporated current events into our Bible studies, Kyle had deserted the small Episcopal church his family attended, as it only offered a Sunday evening Eucharist and no time to discuss Christian faith in the light of everyday life, which to our young eyes, was growing more complex with each passing year. For Dad, the problem of Vietnam was simple: Communist desire for world-domination. And America, the champion of democracy and freedom, had to stop it. However, at church I heard more nuanced analyses of Vietnam from a variety of sources—our minister for one. Rev. Gavin McLaurin was a kindly and thoughtful man. He was a scion of good Scots Presbyterian stock who had found a new life as farmers in the Sandhills of North Carolina during the early 19th century. Like my father and the fathers of most of my school friends, he had served his country during the Second World War. Gavin had finished college in the spring of 1942 and joined the Army Air Corps; he then served in the Eight Air Force flying B-24s out of East Anglia.

One Sunday evening, he came to speak with our group about a debate we had been having as to whether or not there could be a just war. He spoke to us from his experience of war. He began by saying that he would not tell us war stories—there was nothing glamorous or romantic about warfare, certainly not in our technological age. Neither would he indulge in the middle-aged man's preserve of reminiscing. Instead he wanted to tell us three things that stuck with him from World War II. The first was the tragic loss of so many promising young men. One day they were full of life and joshing around in the local pub frequented by so many from his squadron, and the next day they weren't there; those young lives had been snuffed out by flak or fighters.

The second thing Rev. McLaurin told us was that, following the Third Reich's defeat, he had helped fly former Allied prisoners of war from various places in Germany back to England. On one of these missions of mercy, he had been offered the chance to see firsthand what contribution to the war effort had been made by his bomber crew and hundreds of others like it. An enthusiastic army artillery spotter took him up in a Piper L-4 to view the ruins of Cologne. As it was late spring, the side windows were open. As they flew over farmland on the edge of Cologne, Gavin told us that, at a mere one hundred feet off the ground, he could smell the rotting flesh of dead farm animals below. As they flew above what was left of the city, he saw the once proud cathedral with its blackened towers pointing accusing fingers at them as they passed over. The city had its own smell of devastation: a combination of burnt wood and undiscovered corpses. Gavin said he leaned out of the window and vomited. The pilot looked at him, mystified, and asked: "Aren't airsick are ya, buddy?"

"He just couldn't get it," said Gavin. "It had been one thing to drop bombs from an altitude of four-to-five miles. It was entirely another matter to see at close range some of the devastation that I myself had wrought. That put an entirely different slant on war. When flying a mission, my main concern had been getting my bomber and crew home. Our immediate war was with the unseen flak and the ever-menacing fighters. But to see how many homes, parks, schools and hospitals had been blasted when our targets were supposed to have been factories or military installations, well, this turned my view of war into a personal, *human* matter."

From that point onward, Gavin said he believed, "However just the cause, war was something that should only be undertaken as the very last resort." Although he felt the Nazis had to be stopped, he wished that England and France had "clipped Hitler's wings" before he had led them all into a total war which engulfed the whole of Europe and much of the rest of the world.

Our minister's third and final reflection had to do with the aftermath of one particularly difficult mission. "We had just returned and taxied to our dispersal hardstand. We'd fought nearly all the way from our target in the Ruhr back to the Dutch coast. The gunners had expended nearly every round of ammo. Our B-24 had taken a lot of hits and one engine had been shot away, but we had all made it safely home. As I prepared to exit the cockpit, I noticed my co-pilot, Harvey Morris, a nice young guy from Des Moines, Idaho, tracing his finger around a spot on the canopy and staring at it, obviously lost in thought. When I touched Harvey's arm just to say, 'C'mon, Harv, let's get to debriefing,' he just looked at me silently. And then he pointed at a bullet hole in the metal frame of the canopy. That's what he had been looking at so intently. But I was eager to get out of the airplane, so I just nodded an acknowledgment, and said: 'C'mon, Harv, let's go.' But before I could turn to leave the flight deck, Harvey grabbed me by my right arm and then pointed toward a parallel hole in the other side of the cockpit—my side.

"I'll tell you this because I have never forgotten it: Harvey's face was drained of all color and almost looked like a wax mask. And then, with a voice which seemed to come from somewhere far away—or deep inside him—Harvey said these words to me." Gavin then repeated them to us slowly and deliberately. "'Don't you see, Gav? That bullet was *head height*—almost as though it was *meant* for one of us...or maybe both of us. I mean, it was only the smallest fraction of a second that stopped it from hitting you or me. If one of us had leaned forward—or if we had...' Harvey's voice halted at that point, and I never heard him speak again. Our group's Flight Surgeon sent Harvey to a nearby 'Flak Farm'—that's what we called centers for rest and recuperation—with the hope that some R & R, plus evaluation by a psychiatrist, might aid in his recovery. I guess it was about a week later that I went to see Harvey, but as far as I could tell, he never seemed to recognize me and neither did he utter a single word. Soon afterwards, I heard Harvey had been shipped back to the US. I never saw him again, but I did hear from some of my group comrades that Harvey had never recovered."

Gavin paused as he reached the end of his talk with us young people, who had only ever known the fruits of peace, and then, with moist eyes and a voice that slightly quivered, he said, "So you see, that bullet didn't have to hit Harvey for it to destroy his life. But it did that just the same. And he wasn't the only one. If you remember nothing else of what I've told you, remember this: war makes no distinction between the just and the unjust."

Rev. McLaurin's words struck a chord with me and Kyle, serving to strengthen our questioning of America's growing commitment to military action in Vietnam. As we walked home that evening, we discussed what we had heard. Kyle turned and asked me, "What do you think your old man would say about Rev. McLaurin's talk? I mean, they were both pilots in the same war—okay, I know your dad flew fighters in the Pacific—but still...has he ever told you anything like that?"

I shook my head. "Nah. Maybe it's the Marine thing, but it almost seems like he *liked* the war. I don't know. He's shown me his photo album and pointed out guys he knew who died out there, but he's never really said much of anything like we heard tonight. Next time he starts talking about America's duty to fight in Vietnam, I might bring it up and see what he says."

It wasn't a long wait. Not more than a few days after Rev. McLaurin's visit to our youth group, French President de Gaulle called for American forces to withdraw from Vietnam. It was the main topic of discussion on NBC's *Huntley-Brinkley Report* when I came in after a pick-up baseball game. Mom and Dad were in their normal places, Mother curled up the sofa and Dad in his recliner, except this evening he wasn't reclining. Instead he was sitting forward and carrying on a one-way argument with David Brinkley. "That big-nosed Frenchman didn't waste any time in getting his ass to England in 1940!" Dad grumbled. "I suppose we should just pack our men and weapons and abandon the South Vietnamese to the Communists and their Red Chinese masters?"

"Just try to calm down, dear," Mother chimed in. "They can't hear you, and we might as well listen to what Brinkley is saying."

Dad harrumphed away her suggestion. "The only way the French know to fight a war is to *retreat*."

Because I was fifteen and Dad was Dad, I interjected. "But I thought the French were our allies in World War Two."

"Only if you call *liberating them* being an 'ally,'" retorted Dad.

I was munching a sandwich which Mother had left for me on the table. "Yeah, but we learned in history that the French helped with the D-Day invasion—didn't they help take Sword or Gold Beach?"

Dad fired that look at me. I think he was trying to discern whether I was just jerking his chain or being serious. Any possible smirk that might have been on my face was camouflaged by a mouthful of sandwich.

Dad spoke slowly and with great emphasis. "The French army, such as it was, made it back to their *occupied* homeland on *American* ships and landing craft, *and* they were using *American* arms, ammunition and tanks." My father's eyes kept me fixed for a moment before turning back to the television news. I noticed my mother nervously smoothing out the nonexistent wrinkles on her dress, something she unconsciously did whenever Dad's temper or authority was being tested.

I perched on the end of the sofa while I finished my sandwich supper. As the news came to an end, I ventured a new tact. "Rev. McLaurin came to our youth group last Sunday night. He told us about his experiences in World War Two as a bomber pilot."

"And?" Dad asked without looking at me.

"And he feels that war should only be used as a last resort. Yet Vietnam is halfway around the world—and they haven't done anything to us—so why are we sending our men to fight there?"

"Are *you* a Communist?" retorted my father.

"Oh, Phil," Mom interjected, "you know very well that our Jon is *not* a Communist!"

"And just how do I know that?" asked Dad. "They have infiltrators nearly everywhere. Besides, let the boy speak for himself." Dad then focused his gaze on me.

"I am not a Communist, Dad, but I thought we were supposed to be Christians."

"What's that got to do with it?" asked Dad.

"Well, you're not the only man who's been to war." This was a bold statement from me and tantamount to rebellion. Was this what being a damn fool teenager was all about? My father studied me coolly. I continued, "What about Rev. McLaurin? He feels we should only go to war when we have no other choice; we shouldn't go looking for a war."

"Gavin McLaurin is welcome to his opinion. But Vietnam is *different*. Communists are looking to exploit every weak spot in the world. We have to fight them wherever they are."

"But it's still war, Dad. What about the Ten Commandments: 'Thou shalt not kill?' And what about Jesus? I've never read where he said we should go to war."

"Just leave the Bible out of it," snapped my father, "and just stick with reality!"

My mother's eyebrows rose so high at Dad's last remark that I thought they would join her hairdo. But before she could speak, I burst out, "So why the hell do we bother going to church, then, if it's nothing to do with reality?!" I had never before sworn at either parent.

Dad started to push himself up from his armchair, but Mother shouted, "Phil!" She started to speak to me as well, but with anger brimming inside me and eyes burning, I had fled to the kitchen to return my plate before storming up the stairs to my room. Discretion told me this skirmish was over.

Five

Nothing is as approved as mediocrity. The majority has established it and it fixes its fangs on whatever gets beyond it either way.

—Blaise Pascal

The autumn term of 1966 brought with it an air of change. I started high school after Labor Day and my brother, Ron, was bound for his freshman year at UNC a few weeks later. Although we weren't always the best of allies—how many siblings truly are?—it would still be the first time I was alone with my parents. There would no longer be two of us for Dad to call upon to do chores around the house and yard. That worried me. And there were changes for Kyle and me: we were both enrolled in the first stage of driver's education—the in-class module, wherein we learned the rules of the road and watched informative films such as *Signal 30*. The film took its title from highway patrol radio code for an accident with injuries and contained color footage of gory car crashes and mangled bodies of every description. I believe the intent of the film was to encourage safe driving. But by the time Kyle and I saw it, it had become a cult, teen classic. "Man, did you see the guy whose car ran off the road, and just as he was falling out of the car door, it was slammed shut by a tree trunk? Cut 'im right in half...whoa!" Did the film ever really help anyone become a better driver? (Do the Ten Commandments keep people from lying, killing, or stealing?) All I know is that our high school yearbook had the usual number of black-bordered photographs of students who would never graduate because they had ignored the warnings of *Signal 30*.

In any case, for Kyle and me—and thousands of other fifteen-year-olds like us—learning to drive was seen as a passport to freedom. In those halcyon days of gasoline for twenty-five cents a gallon, no one could even envisage anything like an Arab Oil Crisis, which lurked not a decade away. Driving meant we could date from the *front* seat, not sitting in the back with a parent as chauffeur/chaperone. Apart from becoming a teenager, learning to drive was the first discernible landmark that one was moving closer to being considered grown up and responsible. And for once, my father seemed keen to speed up the clock. He volunteered to teach me to drive the following Saturday. As Kyle's birthday was two months before mine, I swelled with pride, thinking that this might give me the jump on my friend. When my brother, Ron, heard what was on offer, he just shook his head at my gullibility and laughed, "You do realize, don't you, what this means?"

I shrugged and said, "Well, yeah...I guess...I mean, Dad says he'll teach me to drive, that's all."

"Jesus, Jon, wake up! He'll teach you to drive *his* car. Think you can handle that rusted-out heap's clutch and three-speed manual transmission on the column?" Ron shook his head in disbelief at his younger brother. My father kept a '54 Chevy Bel Air at the airport for when he got in too late for Mom to go get him. "Man, that Bel Air just about killed me three years ago, especially with Dad shouting instructions in my ear. It sits out in all kinds of weather at the airport, so it's even worse now. Come on, did you really think he'd let you learn to drive Mom's automatic?"

I nodded lamely. "Uh...yeah, I did." I had pictured it being something like flying in the cockpit with Dad, a scenario wherein my father was calm and methodical. However, with Ron's dire warning, the serene picture in my head immediately changed to that of our father angrily chomping on his cigar and running his hand nervously over his Marine buzz cut whenever we were stuck in traffic, while uttering a string of colorful Marine expletives. That night, I had a nightmare in which Dad handed over to me the controls of a light aircraft—but the moment I said, "I have it," the airplane morphed into the wingless '54 Bel Air which immediately plummeted toward the earth below. I woke up shouting, "It won't pull out!"

It was with a similar sense of impending doom that Saturday morning arrived. I had hoped I would wake up with a fever, tonsillitis, scurvy—anything to postpone *the driving lesson*. I wondered whether I should ask Dad about having Kyle come with us, but then I worried about how I might react if Dad really let me have it with one of his verbal barrages. More than once he had reduced me and Ron to tears. I even remembered eavesdropping from upstairs when Dad had taken a telephone call from his boss at Pilot Aviation, Craig Benson, asking him to apologize to a co-pilot whom Dad had so belittled for a bumpy landing that the man had burst into tears before they taxied to the terminal. No. Whatever fate awaited me, I had to walk that road alone. Of course, it hadn't helped that Ron was playing his favorite Kingston Trio song on the record player that morning—no doubt on purpose. I kept hearing their mournful voices singing about life as a lonesome valley that one had to traverse alone. It felt as though they were addressing me, and so, when the time came to take that long walk to the Chevy, it indeed seemed like I was walking toward my own lonesome valley and the shadow of death.

My father thought his pedagogical skills extended from flying to all other areas of his expertise. Such was not the case. Whether it was outlining the principles of a jet engine or mathematics, Dad thought anyone should be able to watch or listen to him go through something once and then repeat it with similar ease. This was one of his major blind spots, and it caused not a little friction between him and his family. Monkey see, monkey do might well apply to the limited repertoire of simian tree dwellers, but if it that simple philosophy were applied to all human skills and science, then every baseball player should have been able to smack as many home runs as Hank Aaron or any science teacher establish Nobel Prize winning theories like Albert Einstein. Somehow, Dad put all of his native abilities down to mere hard work and repetition—anybody could do it. Again, the one exception was flight instruction; but outside the cockpit, he forgot all of the myriad tacit aspects to learning any skill. That lesson was about to be driven—literally—into my memory.

Dad walked out to the car with me. When we got in, the closing of the heavy doors sounded like the slamming of my coffin lid. Dad put the car into reverse and let out the clutch, all the while giving me a running commentary. "You see, just a little clutch and the transmission engages." Similar instructions followed as we left our driveway and headed out to a deserted stretch of road. With my voice, I uttered a few uh-huhs or yeahs to reassure him that I was following him. But in my head, I was fervently praying for a flat tire, an engine blow-out, a sudden fever to strike me or Dad—"'cause it doesn't really matter, Lord; just make this driving lesson end in any way You see fit! Amen." But the Lord didn't intervene. My childlike faith in the interventionist God of the Old Testament suffered another blow that day. My prayers had failed to deliver up one fire, earthquake, or storm. And the car had stopped.

Dad looked over at me as he switched off the engine and said, "Over to you, Jon." He got out and walked around the car while I slid over on the well-worn bench seat, the friction of my jeans causing tiny pops of static electricity. As Dad hadn't tripped and broken his leg nor had the earth opened and swallowed him, there was nothing for me to do but initiate my own execution.

As my hand reached for the key in the ignition, I stalled. "Um, how would it be if I just practiced finding the gears before I actually try to drive?" Dad's heavy sigh needed no words, but I decided to take his lack of verbal response as assent. My left foot pushed in the heavy clutch and I stabbed around at finding the three forward gears and reverse. Dad drummed his fingers on the arm rest and looked at his watch. My execution had fallen behind schedule.

With no deliverance in sight, I depressed the clutch and turned the key in the ignition. The six cylinders sprang to life. Next came the scary bit: left foot on clutch, right foot on the accelerator, giving a bit of gas while I slipped the gear shift into first—but I had forgotten to release the parking brake. In so doing, I took my foot off the clutch, the car jerked forward and died. I might as well have released the trap door on the scaffold. Dad swore at me, "Damnation, son!" My ears and cheeks turned scarlet. I knew without looking in the mirror; I could feel them.

I apologized to my father, who made no response, and then tried again. This time, I remembered to release the parking brake first, but as the car started to roll backwards, I panicked and let out the clutch too fast. Amidst the cacophony of metallic clunking, the car died once more. In concert with the car's dying gasp came my father's dramatic sighing. He folded his arms across his chest and slowly shook his head in disbelief. He might as well have said, "I've only been doing this for *thirty years*; why can't you do it the *first* time?"

Now I was flushed *and* sweating—despite the autumnal temperature. From that point on I could do nothing right and only became more nervous and self-conscious. After one more instance of "Galloping Chevy," Dad blew up. "Goddamnit, son, that's enough! Put on the parking brake and get out!" Although I had entered the driver's seat my full height of five-feet-eleven-inches, I felt I practically needed a booster seat by the time I got out, so reduced was my stature—or so I felt—in my father's eyes. Although my eyes burned, I knew I couldn't cry in front of my father—not over something as "simple" as driving a car. We drove home in silence, for which I was thankful. I could keep my eyes fixed outside the car as I recovered from my belittlement. I don't know what my father felt, but I felt myself to be a complete disappointment as a son, not to mention a human being. And, hell, it was a just a car.

As soon as we were home, I went to grab my bike so I could ride over to Kyle's. Mother was in a corner of the garage where we kept the washing machine, and I heard her ask my father, "Well? How did it go?" Dad just shook his head and waved a hand in exasperation as he went into the kitchen. I took to the security of my two wheels and pedaled away my shame.

As I wheeled into the Westons' driveway, Marie was curled up in a lawn chair in a patch of autumn sunshine, reading a book. "Hey, 'Nother Brother." She smiled as she looked up from her book.

"Hey, Kid. Is Kyle here?" I tried not to look directly at her; fearful that my face might give away my failure.

"Yeah, I think so. Didn't think you'd be around today. Kyle said something abo't your having driving lessons." Marie shielded her eyes from the sun as she looked at me. "You don't look very happy, 'Nother Brother—is something wrong?"

"Sort of," I mumbled. Pride dictated that I not share my predicament with a ten-year-old girl. "Um, so where is Kyle?"

"Well, probably upstairs. See you later then, 'Nother Brother."

I never had to knock when I entered the Westons' house. I flew past Mrs. Weston in the kitchen, greeting her in passing. "Hey, Jon— what's the rush?"

"Oh nothing," I replied, taking the stairs two at a time.

Kyle was lying on his bed, flipping through a popular music magazine. "Hey, buddy," he said in a quizzical way. He tossed the magazine aside and swung his legs around so he was sitting up. Meanwhile I had pulled out his desk chair and flopped in it with a huge sigh of relief.

"Man, am I glad *that's* over."

"You talking abo't the driving lesson with your dad?" Kyle looked at his bedside clock and mused aloud, "Y'all must've left early to get back here at ten-fifteen." He looked me over for a few seconds, read the distress in my countenance, and then asked, "So, um, how did it go, um, driving with your old man?"

I gave Kyle a what-do-you-think look and simply shook my head.

"Oh. That bad, eh?"

"Yeah, *that bad*," I replied. "In fact, it sucked. He took me out in the Bel Air, for God's sake! I've never used a clutch before." I started to flush again as the experience re-surfaced.

"No synchromesh gears in that baby, eh?" ventured Kyle.

"No way! You should have heard the clanking! And when I did manage to get the thing in gear, it bucked like a bronco." I managed a weak smile. "The old man nearly smashed his nose on the dash board!" But then my father's haranguing came back to me and, once again, there was no humor in it. "I don't think 'patience' is in Dad's vocabulary and neither is 'understanding.' I mean, Jesus, he just doesn't remember what it's like to *learn* something—and for the first time."

"So...how long were you o't with your old man? How long did the torture last?"

"Maybe ten minutes—hell, maybe just five—I don't know. But it wasn't long. Dad just blew his cool, cussed at me, and that was that."

"That's tough. Guess you'll be waiting for the Driver's Ed in-car training then?"

"Yep. Next spring…the autumn class was full."

"Be here before you know it," grinned Kyle.

I picked up a paperback from Kyle's desk and threw it at him. "Jerk! Now you sound just like Mom!" Finally, I could laugh, even at myself. "Yeah, it was a fiasco. Can you imagine if Dad had broken his nose? Would've served him right!"

"Yeah. You can console yourself that at least your old man won't be volunteering to teach you to drive again—so forget it. And—hey!—I've got some news for you."

"Like what?" I picked up a baseball from Kyle's desk.

"You know Karen Thomas—who lives two doors down from me?"

I nodded distractedly as I rolled the baseball along my arm and tried to flip my hand to catch it. "Yeah?"

"Well, she's friends with Wendy Sullivan." The baseball fell to the floor as I began to flush. "Ha! I thought that would get your attention."

"Okay—so? You know I like her."

"Yeah, I know. And according to Karen, so does Wendy. But she wants you to ask her o't."

"Ask her *out*? And what am I supposed to do, let her ride double on my bike?"

"No. But you know what I mean; go somewhere—to the movies, a concert down in Winston-Salem—anywhere really."

"But Kyle, that means either getting one of my parents to drive us or my brother, Ron. I'd feel like a chump or something. Besides, Dad would see it as an imposition, so he'd tell Mom to do it. Mom would worry about me and give me last minute instructions; and Ron, he'd just enjoy making my life a misery. In any case, he leaves for college soon. So I guess meeting up with Wendy at school dances and ball games simply seems the thing to do until I can drive."

"Well, what if we all squeezed into my parents' Bonneville? You could double-date with Jean Edwards and me. Then you wouldn't have to worry abo't one of your family driving. And—hey—with four of us in the back seat, we won't have to sit a polite distance away from our dates. Think of that."

I did think of *that*. Sometimes it seemed as though I thought of little else. As I was particularly bad at math, in class I would easily find myself being lulled into a trance as the teacher droned on about the quadratic equation, while instead I studied girls' breasts, legs, and hair. Everything about them was fascinating. They even held their pencils differently than boys did. They tossed their hair in seductive ways when puzzling over a problem or would slowly wind their hair around a finger when deep in thought. There was so much to take in. Like many boys caught in the throes of adolescent hormonal high-gear, I quickly learned to bring my thoughts back to more mundane matters before the bell rang. Otherwise, a certain stiffening in the groin region made walking to the next class an embarrassing undertaking, and I didn't fancy limping along the corridors like a youthful Long John Silver with his peg leg.

There was just one problem with Kyle's offer of a double date. I first had to have a date. Wendy Sullivan and I had noticed each other at school since shortly after the start of the autumn term. It seemed that wherever I went in the school, I would run into Wendy with a group of her friends. She was alert to the fact that I couldn't take my eyes off her, but at that age, I was still too shy to approach her when she was surrounded by girlfriends. By the spring term, it was becoming stupidly obvious that we fancied each other, but it was also clear that I wasn't the only guy who had eyes for her. And why not? Wendy had it all: wavy brown hair that cascaded round her shoulders, alluring green eyes and a very shapely body…oh, and she had brains—she was a member of the student council (the sort of thing I avoided like the plague). But I am being honest as to what first attracted me to her: her looks. At that point, I had yet to have a conversation with her so as to judge whether or not we had anything in common. I only knew that watching her approach brought a pounding in my chest.

"There's just one thing about asking Wendy out, Kyle. Her family goes to Zion Baptist Church"—a church known for its fundamentalist theology and strict social mores.

"There is *that*," mused Kyle, "but then, what's the worst that could happen, huh? Maybe her parents would have you castrated—but that's all!"

"Gee, thanks, Kyle. That's made asking her out a *lot* easier."

"Think nothing of it," responded Kyle with a wave of his hand. He then took on a more serious approach. "Look, Jon, you say Wendy always smiles when she sees you, right? Gotta be something in that." He winked at me and said, "I'd say you're in with a chance." I began to take heart from Kyle's words and determined I should pluck up the courage to ask her out.

A few weeks after my conversation with Kyle, fate took a hand. I had been taking a short-cut to my German class by going down the "up" staircase when, as I turned on a landing, I ran smack into Wendy. My books and hers went flying from our hands and under the feet of a dozen or more students. Wendy's girlfriends just smiled at us slyly as they continued on their way. One or two looked knowingly at me and with coquettish smiles said, "He-ey, Jo-on." Perhaps they thought I had engineered the encounter. But swishing their hair and looking over their shoulders as they climbed the stairs, one fired a Parthian shot laden with innuendo. "Y'all don't be late for class, ya hear? Y'all don't want the teachers to come lookin' for you."

Wendy and I stood looking at each other and waited for the last of the students to pass by. It was clear I had to make the first move. "Uh—Wendy—hi! I'm—uh—sorry about crashing into you…I was…um…"

"Going the wrong way?" Wendy gazed up at me, for she only came to my chin, and released a smile that seemed to bathe me in light.

"Yeah. Um…guilty as charged." I couldn't think of what to say next, but to have the object of my desire standing barely a foot away and looking straight at me left me immobilized.

"Well, I guess we'd better pick up our books and papers before they're trampled on again." Wendy stooped to retrieve her lost items. Her words and movement released me from my suspended animation.

"Gosh! Uh—let me! After all, it was my fault."

"Yes, it was," she laughed. She stood back up and watched me collect our things. Whenever I found a shoe-print on a paper or book, I used my trouser leg as a duster. This brought even more laughter from Wendy. The sound of her laughter filled me with joy, so I pretended to spit on one of the books and clean it under my arm. At that, Wendy gave me a gentle shove and the outpouring of laughter echoed in the stairwell. I joined in.

When I had gathered everything, I presented them to Wendy with a slight bow. She curtsied in return, shook back her hair from her face, and then cocked one eye at me. "You're Jon, aren't you?"

"Yeah—gosh—sorry! I should have said." At that moment the manic ringing of the class bell pierced our ears.

"It's okay. I knew your name anyway." A coy smile crossed her face. "Where were you going in such a hurry when we collided?"

"Me? I was heading to German class. What about you?"

"Study hall—so no rush for me. But you're late."

"*Es macht nichts,*" I replied—trying to sound my cosmopolitan best.

"What was that?" The curiosity wrinkled Wendy's nose.

"It doesn't matter."

"Yes, it *does*!" Wendy playfully grabbed my arm. "What did you say to me in German?"

Now I was laughing. "That *is* what I said in German! 'It doesn't matter.'"

"*What* doesn't matter?" Wendy asked demurely. I was about to take the bait and engage in our own version of Abbott and Costello's

'Who's on first' routine when I saw the twinkle in her eyes. We both had a good laugh and then made our way leisurely to Wendy's study hall. By the time we got there, I had secured both her telephone number and the promise of a date in the near future—but first she had to speak with her father who, evidently, was not as great an impediment as her mother. She would bring up the subject with him after supper; thus, I could try calling her between 7:00 and 8:30.

After school, Kyle noticed that I seemed to have a spring in my step as we walked home, so I flashed Wendy's phone number in front of him. I was greeted with a rendition of Walter Brennan's TV character, Grandpappy Amos: "Well, gal' durn it, Jon—I knowed you had it in ya."

~ * ~

That evening, I spent a long time staring at the piece of paper on which I had scribbled Wendy's telephone number. Silently, I practiced what I would say to whichever parent answered if Wendy didn't get to the phone first. Whenever I had worked up the nerve to call her, either our phone would ring or Mother would need to make a call. By the time there was a lull in the telephone activity, the piece of paper with Wendy's number was damp from my hands' perspiration. With trepidation, I turned each number on the dial. After a few rings, I heard the click as the receiver was lifted from its cradle.

"Hello?" I felt an arctic wind rush through the telephone, burning my right ear.

"May I please speak with Wendy?"

I was met with the silence of the polar region. Then a voice cracked like ice breaking on a pond. "Who is this?"

"This is Jon—um, Jon Braddock."

"Wendy's never mentioned you."

"Well..." and now my ears were aflame, as much from embarrassment as frostbite. "Wendy does know me—from school—and she knows I was going to call her...tonight." My voice tightened from humiliation and anger.

And then I heard Wendy's voice in the background, "Mama? Is that Jon?"

I next heard the rubbing sound of a palm being placed over the mouthpiece; but I could still make out Mrs. Sullivan's words, "You need to finish washing the dishes and cleaning the kitchen." The palm twisted on the mouthpiece as though trying to erase the caller.

I then heard Wendy with a pleading tone say, "Mama, I finished in the kitchen *ten minutes ago!*"

Then came the baritone voice of what must have been Wendy's father, Earl. "Mah-tha, let the girl talk to her friend." This was followed by a clunk that must have been the phone being dropped onto a table. It was so loud that I instinctively jerked the phone away from my ear.

The next voice I heard was so subdued I couldn't recognize it as Wendy's. "Hey, Jon. Sorry about that." It was such a barely audible whisper that for a moment I feared it might be Martha Sullivan luring me into some kind of trap.

I was so flustered I was lost for words. All I could manage was, "Ahh…"

"Jon? Are you *there*?" It was definitely Wendy.

"Yeah, yeah, I'm here. I just wasn't expecting, um…"

"Mama?"

"Yeah, you got it! I wasn't expecting your mother. I mean…um…well, I mean I *knew* she *might* answer…but…well—I just…wasn't expecting…"

"I know." For a fifteen-year-old, Wendy's voice sounded suddenly old and tired. I could see why. In my head, I was trying to picture Wendy's mother and whether or not Wendy resembled her, but all Martha Sullivan's voice conjured up was a refrigerator.

"So…did you get to talk with your father about me?"

"Yeah, I did…but when I heard him talking—or *trying* to talk—with Mama, all she did was go very quiet like she does and then leave the room. Daddy said you could call me, but that we can't talk long…at least not *yet*. Mama takes time to get used to things. Well, things, *anything* I suppose—*different*—kind of upsets her."

"So would it be *too different* if I asked you out?"

"It might be…I don't know…" My spirits foundered as did the hope in Wendy's voice. "I'm sorry, Jon, I'll have to go in a minute. I have to walk over to the church and bring my little brother home. He's at the junior choir practice."

"You have a little brother?" My interest was genuine, but I also wanted to keep Wendy on the phone—to learn more about her, to listen to her voice. "How old is he? What's his name?"

"Tommy is twelve and is only in junior high. That's why you haven't seen him."

"Any other sisters or brothers?"

"No. Just Tommy and me." Then, in hushed tones, "Jon, I'm getting a look from Mother, so I have to run. Okay?"

"Yeah. Okay…but, hey—wanna meet in the cafeteria at lunch tomorrow?"

"Yes! And, Jon?"

"Yeah?"

"I'm really glad you called."

~ * ~

The wait until lunchtime the next day required every bit of patience that I did not have at age nearly-sixteen. But in the end, as is often the case, it was worth the wait. Next came the promised double date to the movies with Kyle and his girlfriend, Jean. The ignominy of dating with a parental chauffeur was made bearable by the fact that it wasn't my parents. As Kyle and I bought tickets, we discussed our strategy of sitting with our dates in the back row, the traditional preserve of courting couples. We made the obligatory stop for popcorn and drinks and then entered the darkened world of celluloid fantasy. "Wow! I can't see!" exclaimed Kyle. "Let's just duck in here." The back row was ours. Kyle led Jean in toward the middle of the row, followed by Wendy and me. We chatted, munched, laughed and slurped our way through the coming attractions.

The main feature was some innocuous film that appealed to Wendy's parents and was eminently forgettable. My attention that night was focused solely upon Wendy—the warmth of her shoulder next to mine, the smell of her perfume, the way her hand curled up inside mine, the dance of light from the movie screen on her eyes when she looked up at me. I was intoxicated by her presence. And my insides were in an uproar. Each section of my body felt like it was at a funfair of its own. My head was in the whirling teacups; my lungs were replaced by helium balloons; my lower abdomen was on the parachute drop; and over in the music tent, Buddy Rich was playing the drums on my heart. Surely such cacophony was audible to Wendy? While the film droned away in the background, my whole being was caught up in the desire to kiss Wendy. Because of our height difference, I had slumped in my seat so that our faces might be closer together.

In retrospect, I'm sure Wendy knew my intentions and was probably wondering why I didn't get on with it. But, of course, in the naïve heat of the moment, it felt as though I were in control and directing events toward the desired outcome. And what would girls know of desire?! Weren't they passively waiting the advance of young, hot-blooded suitors? My left hand held Wendy's right; our fingers were interlaced; our shoulders were snug against each other. But as our heads leaned in toward one another, I felt a hand tracing its way gently up my right thigh, which both startled and aroused me. Was Wendy putting the move on me? My eyes strained for light in the darkened cinema as I looked for Wendy's left hand, which I discovered was resting on the arm of her seat. I knew that no one had taken the seat immediately to my right, but still the mystery hand was on the move, patting its way toward my groin. In near panic, I jerked my head to the right in order to confront its owner, only to be greeted by the wizened visage of an elderly lady. "Jesus!" I gasped, as my whole body involuntarily recoiled.

The owner of the hand was equally shocked and let out a yelp as she bolted backwards and fell onto a man sitting in row ahead of us. He growled: "Hey?! What gives?" while pushing the old dear back into the empty seat beside me, where she plunked down unceremoniously, exclaiming, "Oh, Lordy me! Oh, Lordy me!"

Our area of the cinema erupted with competing voices—including those of Wendy, Kyle and Jean—saying: "What's going on?" "Are you okay?" "Keep the noise down!" "What's happened?" "Shhhh!"

In the aftermath, my accidental groper told me that she had gone out to the restroom, but when she returned, she couldn't remember where she had been sitting with her friend. Thus, she had been trying to feel her way in the dark, which is how she came to my aggrieved thigh. In the end, due to the turmoil, an usher came over and helped the bewildered lady back to her friend. "You probably made her night, Braddock!" quipped Kyle. I had to stifle my laughter so as not to attract the usher again. At the same time, I turned toward Wendy, whose face was only inches away and seemed to be waiting.

Lest another farce interrupt my plans, I pressed my lips against Wendy's. Although this was not my first kiss, it was the most delicious that I had experienced to this point. My only previous experience of kissing had been with June Hinkle—a girl on whom I had had a crush the previous summer. June was a cute, strawberry blonde who had a turned-up nose and wore braces on her teeth. One late afternoon we had spent an hour or so sitting on a grassy bank overlooking Stuart's Creek, experimenting on one another with kissing. I well remember the tingle of excitement as our lips first brushed against each other. However, when I tried to experiment with French kissing, my tongue found itself not in a lush tropical lagoon, but in a cavern full of stalactites and stalagmites composed of metal wires and rubber bands. After one sharp scratch, made bitter by the taste of metal, my tongue beat a hasty retreat. Still, with ardor undiminished, June and I confined our passion to the mangling of our lips on the crucible of her braces. Thus, with only this experience to go by, I was sensually overwhelmed by the incredible softness of Wendy's kiss. Without the obstruction of wires and rubber bands, our lips were able to explore and play without let or hindrance.

Kyle, Jean, Wendy, and I spent the remainder of the movie making out. The lights had come up and the audience was leaving when I felt a tap on my shoulder. "Y'all better come up soon for air." It was the usher. "We gotta clean up before the next picture."

I smiled sheepishly and said, "We're gone."

The usher smiled knowingly. "Y'all have a good evenin'."

Wendy and Jean immediately started fretting about their hair and dashed to the women's restroom to have a brush-up and re-apply the little make-up they wore, thus hiding the evidence of our back-row passion party. When we emerged from the theatre, we saw car lights flash us from across the street where Mr. Weston awaited us. As Kyle and I opened the rear doors for our dates, Mr. Weston, in a manner calculated to annoy, patted the huge bench seat in the front of the Bonneville and said, "There's plenty of room up here."

"Yeah. Right, Dad," growled Kyle, as the four of us piled into the back seat. The rear-view mirror revealed to me the grin that creased Mr. Weston's face as his taunt hit home. The internal lights shone like lighthouses in a sea mist through the blue haze left by the cigarettes Mr. Weston had smoked while waiting for us. "Good Lord, Dad!" gasped Kyle, "Ever hear of opening a window?"

"Ever hear of winter?" came Ed Weston's retort. "It's cold out there."

"Yeah, well, thanks," grumbled Kyle. "Maybe we can all end up on the same hospital ward when we get lung cancer."

Before the lights dimmed, the conspiratorial rear-view mirror showed me Ed's look of grim satisfaction in this round of verbal jousting with his teenage son.

Wendy's house was the first stop on our homeward journey. As I got out of the car to walk Wendy to the door, Mr. Weston blurted out, "Kiss her quick! This taxi has two more stops before I can get back to my warm house!" I found myself wondering whether he had always been an asshole and I hadn't noticed it until now or was this something that had come upon him with age in the same way that some people got arthritis? And he thought of us as 'damn fool teenagers'!

Six

A good landing is one from which you can walk away.

—Pilot lore

Each passing week brought Kyle and me nearer to the Promised Land of automotive autonomy. Soon, as with Joshua and the Israelites, it would lie a mere Jordan's breadth or, in our case, a driving test away.

Kyle was right. Spring did arrive before I knew it, and with it came the eagerly awaited in-car training. Because of his earlier birthday, Kyle finished his Driver's Education before I did and kindly passed along essential tips so that, by the time my turn came along, the disastrous experience with my father was all but forgotten. As the car in which we received instruction was an automatic, I passed without a problem—and then wondered what all the worry had been about. But, of course, whenever I drove on my Learner's Permit with my mother or father, it was always in Mom's Caprice and never in the '54 Bel Air. I wasn't a glutton for punishment.

Only a few weeks before I was to take my driving test at the local Highway Patrol headquarters, my parents announced that we were going to Mother's family reunion near Stuart, Virginia. As Ron was away at college and I wasn't deemed responsible enough to stay at home alone, I had to go. Although I enjoyed most of my cousins, these huge gatherings were, for me, too full of cheek-pinching ("My, isn't your boy adorable?") and hair-tousling ("Getting' a bit long, ain't it? Looks like one of them Beatles, don't he?") and all of the usual statements of the obvious, such as, "Haven't you *grown?*" I once answered one of my older relatives with, "No, I haven't grown; you've *shrunk,*" only to receive a sharp finger flick from Dad on the back of my head. Thus, all I could picture was a boring drive to a boring clan gathering.

In order to break the monotony, I asked my parents if I could drive at least part of the way. Dad immediately dashed my hopes by telling me that, as a new driver, I would be too cautious on the mountain roads. "I want to get there and back on the same day," he jibed.

Crestfallen, I took my place in the back seat and didn't even bother asking whether we might listen to my favorite radio station. I settled down for what promised to be a journey of *tedium tremendum*—but I had no way of knowing how wrong I was. I watched the spring colors from my slumped position in the back, occasionally responding with a grunt whenever my parents directed their attention to me. Soon we crossed over into Virginia on Route 8. Along the way, Dad had tried to use the car's cruise control, much to Mother's dismay. He fumed whenever he had to tap the brake because we had fallen in behind a slow-moving truck or tractor. But he positively raged when drivers in front of us refused to acknowledge that *he had his car on cruise control and could still handle the sharp bends, so why couldn't they?* Dad was constantly setting and re-setting the cruise control, and Mother was patently worried. She said to him, "Phil, honey, this isn't an airplane. You can't expect to keep a constant speed on these roads." Dad just glared at her.

However, things went from bad to worse when we turned off Route 8 and onto the windy roads that led to the country church where the reunion was taking place. Despite the fact that we were fully in the terrain of S-bends and hairpin curves, Dad was locked in a contest of wills with the cruise control. The cruise control had been switched on and off so many times, it started to release whenever Dad let up on the accelerator. That did it. Dad was determined he should be able to set it once and for all: a speed for all seasons. By this time, I was no longer my mopey adolescent self. I was sitting upright and watching the drama unfold in the front. Still, partly to calm myself and partly to send a message to the driver, I started singing "Thunder Road." I was barely into the second verse when I saw Blackie's coal dark eyes giving me that look in the rear-view mirror and quickly shut up.

"There!" my father exulted triumphantly when we were on a relatively straight stretch of road. He had been holding the control button down until it wouldn't switch off when the speed varied. Now he had it on what he felt was an appropriate speed: 50 miles-per-hour. He hummed a satisfied tune and winked at Mother. For the first time ever, I saw my father in the light of *Mad Magazine*'s Alfred E. Newman character: "What? Me worry?" However, Dad's joy at his victory of human will over inanimate machine was short-lived as we all discovered when we arrived at the next sharp bend. As he pressed on the brake, the car's engine kept revving at 50 MPH, so the wheels started to spin, resisting the brakes. We careened out of that curve into a downhill series of bends. The cruise control wouldn't release. The tires screamed as we banked around the first turn. And the tires weren't the only thing screaming.

I heard my mother shouting: "Phil! You've got to stop!" I quickly looked behind us and saw the blue-grey smoke from the burning rubber. We could smell the over-heated brakes. My heart was thumping rapidly—both from excitement and fear. The excitement was from watching my father as he tried to rectify his screw-up with the cruise control. The fear derived from the fact that my brain kept conjuring up catastrophic scenes from *Signal 30*. I could even hear the voiceover as we sped along the mountain roads: "This family was killed when the maniac father jammed his cruise control into the 'on' position and at a speed in excess of the safe limit for the road conditions. Just look at their mangled bodies…"

Meanwhile, Dad was fighting to keep the car on the road. As we flew out of the last bend, Dad put the transmission into neutral and pumped the brakes gently, both to slow us down and, most likely, to ensure they were still functioning! We coasted to a gentle 25 MPH, and I began to breathe more easily. However, we noticed that the engine was still racing at its previous speed. Undaunted by such inconveniences and determined to get us to a service station about a half-mile up the road, Dad dropped the gear shift back into drive. The torque from the transmission jerked our heads backwards like marionettes as the car resumed doing what Dad had told it to do: drive at 50.

Once more the car burned rubber as we tore into the next bends. Mother screamed again as we approached yet another sharp turn, so Dad popped the car back into neutral and successfully negotiated our way through that danger. We could see the service station which sat in the middle of a Y-junction about a quarter of a mile ahead. However, in order to get there, we had to go down into a dip and over a small bridge, then back uphill and over a railroad crossing before reaching the fork in the road where we hoped to stop and get assistance. Coasting down the hill was not a problem; but in order to reach the brow of the opposite rise, the car needed to be *in gear*. So, just as we began the ascent on the far side of the bridge, Dad put the car back into drive with the same result as before: crying tires, big smoke, scared passengers.

No one could have missed our arrival. We flew over the brow of the hill and were onto the railroad crossing in no time. We hit the small ramp leading over the rails with such force that the front wheels left the ground. Mother and I hung on for dear life. With no more than fifty yards to the gravel forecourt of the service station, Dad instinctively hit the brakes. This caused the car to swerve in a fish-tail manner, with the rear wheels spinning out of control as we hit the gravel. In my mind's eye, I can still see the two old boys who had been sitting in their ladder-back chairs, leaning against the front of the building and sipping colas. They probably hadn't moved so fast in years as they did when they saw our car spewing smoke, dust, and gravel—and headed straight for them! One fell to his knees as he tried to jump out of the way of impending disaster, his chair tumbling over behind him. The other took refuge behind the gasoline pumps. Although the Caprice had no drag chute like the Phantoms Dad used to fly, he managed the automotive equivalent by switching off the engine, slamming on the brakes and using the handbrake. We ground to a halt about five feet from the pumps.

It took a few moments for the dust to settle. The two old fellows gathered their wits and came around the gas pumps to the car. The garage mechanic, in greasy overalls, emerged from the bay where he had a car on the hydraulic lift. He wiped his hands on a rag and looked curiously at the Caprice and its bewildered passengers. Dad got out of the car first, followed by me. I looked at my mother in the front seat; her face was in her hands and her shoulders were shaking. The mechanic had a wad of chewing tobacco in his cheek and spat a stream of juice before speaking. "Y'all alright?" he asked laconically.

"We're okay," Dad responded but in a way that invited no other questions. He gave a sharp wave of his hand that seemed to say, "Dismissed." I had never before seen my father embarrassed in front of other men, but I could see without a doubt that he was truly embarrassed. The only other time I had witnessed my father in a state of chagrin was the episode with the M-80s. But then his only witnesses had been two kids and his wife. Now, in this instance, he could hardly start shouting and swearing at Mom and me—after all, *he* had been in the driver's seat. And he was in the presence of complete strangers; thus, Southern etiquette demanded calm. The station owner soon appeared and joined the others in forming a semi-circle around my father as he opened the hood. I was certain Dad kept his eyes on the hood and searched longer than necessary for the release latch so he didn't have to look these bucolic gentlemen in the eye. I watched my father's discomfort with morbid fascination and not a little *schadenfreude* because I could not believe my luck: Blackie, the Ace, had been shot down by his own bull-headed pride! And I was around to witness it. It felt as though I were looking at him with someone else's eyes. He was no longer just my father. Now I saw him as a man like any other of the millions of men on this planet. And, like many of them, he could be a complete jerk.

I could see, as I stood beside the left front fender, that Dad wanted to speak first and take control of the situation so that he did not have to answer questions which curiosity would surely draw forth from his spectators. He swiveled his jaw around and leaned his head right and left, almost like a boxer loosening up before a bout. Dad pulled his handkerchief from his pocket and wiped the back of his neck. Keeping his eyes firmly on the engine, Dad addressed his audience. "Had a little problem with the cruise control."

"Sounded like a *lotta* problem, the way you come flyin' an' screechin' in here," commented the mechanic.

The squadron commander in my father flinched at being addressed that way. "Ye-ah," he exhaled slowly, without looking at anyone. He was trying to keep his anger in check. The muscles in his jaw were clenching and releasing. "Must be something wrong with the vacuum line that controls it. Could I borrow some tools?" I turned and looked at my mother. She was dabbing her eyes with a tissue and checking her make-up in the mirror on the sun visor. It wasn't long before the vacuum line to the cruise control was disconnected and we were ready to take to the road. My father offered the garage owner a few bucks for the use of his tools, but he waved the money away. Dad nodded his thanks and resumed his rightful place at the wheel. The last few miles were driven in total silence.

It was a much-chastised Dad who attended the family reunion. I noticed how he made a point of telling and re-telling the story, trying to make a joke of it all, until he had the version I knew would become canon. Mother smiled weakly whenever she was in earshot of the conversation. As for me, I moved a cautious distance from Dad around the crowded church fellowship hall, watching and listening. And in those moments, I realized two things: that I was pissed off with the way he had nearly killed us all and that I could despise him.

~ * ~

The evening after my "Thunder Road" experience with my parents, I rang Wendy to tell her of the near disaster. Granted, the manner in which I told it had her in stitches with laughter. But when I had finished, I said to her, "You know, sometimes I really hate my old man." The laughter ended abruptly.

There was a silence at Wendy's end before she spoke. "You can't really hate him."

"Can't I? He nearly killed us all! And he didn't seem to care. I mean—he didn't even apologize. Can you believe that?"

"But still, Jon, he's your father. And it is one of the Ten Commandments."

"Ten Commandments!? Are you kidding me? 'Honor thy father'—even if he's behaving like a homicidal maniac? One commandment does not give Dad the right to take risks with Mom's life and mine. It doesn't make him right...or good...or even *caring*. The Bible says something about those things, too." Somehow, I knew—deep inside me, where there were no words but only the knowledge contained within feelings—that this conversation was as much about Wendy's mother as my father. But I dared not voice it. And there were no words.

"Well..." Wendy thought better about whatever she was going to say and changed tack. "Jon? Want to come with me to my church youth group meeting this Friday evening?"

Caught off guard by the abrupt change of tack and my own overpowering swell of intuition, I responded without thinking, "Sure. Yeah. Why not?" Anything to get out of the heavy atmosphere at our house for which I was as responsible as anyone. "Shall I meet you at your house?"

"Yes, please," Wendy answered with a sweetness that somehow drained me of the bile I had been venting.

Seven

The function of prayer is not to influence God, but rather to change the nature of the one who prays.

—Soren Kierkegaard

"Let's all pray for Jon!"

Given their spiritual marching orders, eleven fresh-faced teenagers—including Wendy—surrounded the chair on which I was sitting, and twenty-two hands were duly laid upon me. I wanted to run, but I never had a chance. I felt as helpless as the day Dad took us on the hell drive to the family reunion. Earnest prayers were offered to God on behalf of this near-patricidal and spiritually-benighted Presbyterian who had only ever been sprinkled with water and not fully-immersed, sea-changed, washed clean and spotless, world without end.

"A-men." The huddle dispersed and the group of teenaged intercessors broke into twos and threes, chatting excitedly from their spiritual high and casting less than furtive glances at me as though waiting to see me transformed.

Walter Binkley, the one who pronounced the amen which ended my ordeal by prayer, laid his hand, in a patronizing fashion, on my shoulder. "There's the root of your problem, Jon. You haven't been fully and truly baptized." Simple. I cast a how-could-you-do-this-to-me look at Wendy.

"Do you really think so, Walter?" I replied in false-earnest, something he didn't pick up. "Help me out here. What has my father's driving got to do with how I was or wasn't baptized? I really don't see the connection." I lifted my shoulders and arms in a Gallic shrug.

"Well, Jon—if I may use a pagan example—it's like the story of that Greek fellow—um—Actilles—that we studied last year in European culture and history. You know how his mama was supposed to immerse him when he was a child in that special river…um…the Steecks?" Replete with Southern, rural intonation, Styx came out like 'stee-ix.' I bit my lower lip to keep from laughing—what would Homer have said? "And remember that the water didn't touch that teeny, little bit of his heel where her hand covered it?"

"I think I recall," I replied, casting another look at Wendy, who, funnily enough, showed a twinkle of mirth in her eye.

"Well, baptism is like that—don't you see? You gotta go *all the way* to have the full protection of Christ's saving mercy. Jesus doesn't just want a *bit* of us; he wants *all* of us!" Walter beamed. I fumed.

"So, let me see if I understand this correctly," I began. "It's all about the amount of water in contact with body surface, right? The more water, the better, right? Because that means more grace, more mercy, and thus more protection, correct?" I stood looking at Walter, nodding my head in agreement with my pseudo-casuistry.

Somewhat flummoxed, Walter replied, "Uh…ye-ah…something like that…"

"Oh—and what about my Dad's bad driving?" Walter shook his head with the dazed look of the perplexed. "You know—y'all we're praying for me because I was angry with my Dad for nearly killing all of us because he got the cruise control stuck when driving on mountains roads." I cast a mock accusatory look at Wendy. "So will my getting baptized by full immersion make him a better driver or will I just not care anymore because I'll be saved, so if we crash and die, at least I know I'll go to heaven?"

"W-what?" stammered Walter, "I-I don't…"

After a moment's pause, during which I rubbed my chin thoughtfully, I adopted a look of serious concern and said ponderously, "Actually, Walter…I think I'll put off baptism by full immersion…that is, until I've gained more weight!"

"You…I…*what*?!"

"You've made it all so clear. If I can eat my way to—say—Sumo size, then just think how much more Christ's grace will abound! More body surface—more water. More water—more grace! You said it yourself." Gesticulating, I spread my hands to arm's length on either side. "Thanks, Walter!" I proffered my hand. Walter stared at my hand for a brief moment and then took it with some hesitation and uncertainty; but I received his hand in both of mine, in the sincere way I had seen so many politicians do. "And now," I looked at Wendy who had the countenance of a cat hiding a canary in its mouth, "I must walk Wendy home."

Wendy said her goodbyes to Walter and the others. They cheerily replied, "See you on Sunday!"

Once outside, I closed the mock-Gothic door of the church and leaned against it. As I rested my weight on the heavy dark-stained oak in world-weary fashion, I took a long, deep breath, let it out slowly, and said in clipped tones to Wendy, who was behind me, "If you ever expect me to come with you to another of these meetings, we shall have to re-negotiate the nature of our acquaintance." The silence behind me was pregnant with foreboding. I turned, poker-faced, and looked at Wendy. She had turned slightly pale and her eyes were searching mine—and then I burst out laughing.

"Jonathan Braddock!" She pretended to slap me, but joined in the laughter. Then, with much effort, she formed her face into a grimace and pointed an accusing finger at me. "You were *so naughty* in there! What you did to poor Walter…that was cruel…but so funny!" The laughter refused to be contained. "I was afraid I would crack up! How could you say all of that with a straight face?" Wendy put her hand over her mouth as more guffaws erupted. She took me by the arm and pulled me away from the church. "Let's go before anyone hears us!"

Wendy held onto my arm and then wrapped her other hand around it, laying her head against my shoulder while we walked in silence. We were both lightly dressed on this spring night; the warmth of her skin against mine caused an electric ripple to run under the surface of my skin, making the hairs on my arms stand up. An intermittent cool breeze off the lower range of the Blue Ridge fought a losing battle with the warm air rising from the Piedmont. This was early April, and winter had already been banished to the higher slopes, there to lie dormant until awakened in late autumn. But the occasional cool gust was welcome as it gave Wendy reason to draw in closer to me.

After a few minutes, Wendy lifted her head slightly and looked up at me. "You know, Walter is planning on being a Baptist preacher. He's going to Bible college after he finishes high school."

"He'll probably make a good Baptist preacher," I replied noncommittally.

"He won't if he has someone like you in his congregation!" I felt a thump on my ribs.

"Hey! What's that for?"

"You *know* what it's for! You had poor Walter going in circles."

"Whoa! Let's be honest—he got himself going in circles with his nonsense about 'full body contact' with the water."

I felt Wendy stiffen suddenly. "Baptism is nothing to joke about. Don't you want to be saved?"

"I wasn't joking about baptism. I—"

"Jonathan Braddock, you were so!"

"Okay—hang on a minute! Can we sit and discuss this?"

We were passing the small park across from the courthouse. Wendy let me guide her to a bench in front of the Confederate war memorial. We took our seats under the melancholic gaze of a Confederate soldier. The motto on his pedestal read, "*Dulce et decorum est pro patria mori.*" It may have been 'sweet and fitting to die for one's country'—but his 'country,' as it were, had only lasted four years and was now only a distant memory, along with all those who died for it. Then another thought occurred to me: would this be how Vietnam would be remembered in a hundred years' time? Perhaps I should have chosen another bench on which to carry on what was becoming an increasingly heated discussion on baptism and salvation?

"Look Wendy, I believe in baptism as well—you know I do. But you're an intelligent girl…you know there's nothing in the Gospels that tells us *how deep* Jesus went in the Jordan. Right?"

"We-e-ll…"

"You know I'm right—the Gospels just say Jesus was baptized by John. They don't say, 'He took a deep breath, held his nose, and John kept him under for ten seconds,' now do they?"

Wendy suppressed a giggle. "No, Jon, they don't."

"So why do Baptists have to make such a big deal out of something that nobody really knows? Wouldn't one of the Gospels tell us if it were so important? I mean, have you ever seen a painting of Jesus coming up out of the Jordan wearing an aqualung like Mike Nelson in *Sea Hunt?*"

"Don't you start again! Jesus in an aqualung! How do you come up with these ideas?" I received another playful jab. "Sometimes I think you're too clever."

"What do you mean?"

"Oh, the way your mind works; the way you can turn things around and look at them in different and funny ways."

"It's no sin *to think,* is it?"

"No…of course not…but…it's just…I don't know. I care about you…a *lot.*" Wendy's voice dropped to a whisper. "So I just want the person I love to be saved."

In the months that we had been dating, neither of us had mentioned the L word: love. I had wrestled with telling Wendy I loved her—but then part of me wondered whether it was just a teen romance, puppy love like in the songs, and that would only fade with time. It certainly *felt* more than that. But if it were, what would that mean? Marriage? A lifetime commitment? This was too much to contemplate at sixteen. One had to be careful with words like love. Shotgun weddings were not a myth in rural North Carolina. But here was that word being spoken to me and about me. And yet there seemed to be a rider on this love policy: the salvation clause. And so I found myself in the same instant both thrilled to the core and yet frustrated. It felt like the time when I was six and my brother told me to hold my nose and cover my mouth when I had to sneeze. I tried it—once. And I thought I'd blown my brains out through my ears! Love should be a word-event that sets a person free just like that sneeze was meant to *release* pressure, but the salvation clause had had the same effect on my expression of love as the implosion of my lungs and ears from that contained sneeze.

"Jon?"

"Yes?"

"Did you hear what I said?"

"I did—*really*. It's just that…I mean…oh, I don't know!"

"Don't know *what*? Whether you love me or not?"

"No, it's not that. I do know how I feel about you—and believe me, I've wanted to tell you. It's just that you…well…you've left me confused about *why* you love me. Is it for Jesus' sake—so that I can be saved—or is it that you love *me* because…well…because you love *me*? I mean, am I loveable because I'm a potential Baptist, or can you love me for who I am right now? Because, Wendy, I can honestly say I love you just as you are." I looked up at the Confederate soldier to see whether he might give me some clue as to how I was doing, but he seemed preoccupied with far gone battles.

Aware now of what existential/theological dust clouds she had raised, Wendy wrested control of the situation by nestling her head into my shoulder and kissing my neck—just below the ear. "I love you, Jon. Let's just leave it at that."

I needed no encouragement. My lips found hers and I blissfully lost myself in sensuality. I reveled in the taste of her lips and mouth; I inhaled the scent of her hair and skin. I even delighted in the texture of her blouse as my hand traced its way along her shoulder, back and arm—it had never dared venture into the foreground. Unconsciously, my fingertips were following the straps of Wendy's bra. Suddenly but gently Wendy pulled her lips away from mine. My fingers stopped at the invisible, undeclared border. Was I about to be reprimanded? Uncertain of Wendy's intention, I saw her eyes dart left and right, reconnoitering the park. She then looked deeply into my eyes and said, "Your hand doesn't have to stop," as she pulled my lips into hers.

If the warmth of Wendy's touch had sent electric currents running through my skin earlier that evening, those words of hers set off a depth charge in my loins. I was both thrilled and shocked that Wendy wanted to be touched in ways I thought only I had imagined. The idea that both she and I might entertain similar desires and fantasies had previously seemed incredible. My mind raced to picture what my hand caressed and which only lay beneath thin barriers of cotton and nylon.

And so in the space of one brief evening, we had both fashioned and clamped tight the dual jaws of our moral vise: the first being the biological imperative implicit in physical attractiveness and the second being the otherworldly calling of our Christian faith. Our desire to be moral beings was real, but equally real was our discovery that we were created as sexual beings and we enjoyed the thrill of each other's touch. We also discovered how easily we had slipped between those seemingly contradictory realities and entered the map-less, moral *terra incognita* of those who lived beyond the barred gates of Eden's paradise.

Eight

But far more numerous was the herd of such who think too little and talk too much.

—Dryden

For Kyle and me, our junior year shaped up to be a year in which the ideals being taught in our civics and American history classes were not matching up with the events unfolding around us. High school was supposed to be the place where we laid the foundation for our futures, but with all that was happening outside its walls, it seemed to many of us that it was becoming increasingly irrelevant. As unsettled as the autumn of 1967 had been, nothing could have prepared us for the fast-paced descent into the chaos of 1968. The first quarter of the year saw the Tet Offensive in Vietnam, wherein nearly 70,000 North Vietnamese regulars, with the support of the Vietcong in the south, overran or attacked dozens of cities in South Vietnam. Every night on television, we saw the scores of body bags being unloaded at various air bases back in the US. As with so many Americans, that brought the reality of the war in Vietnam, some 12,000 miles away, closer to our front doors. Among the dead were guys Kyle and I had known as high school seniors the previous year. Their average age was nineteen, so they couldn't even vote for or against the war to which they were sent to fight and die. Hot on the heels of Tet came a call for an additional 200,000 young men to be sent to that most curious of conflicts. Vietnam seemed insatiable in its appetite for blood.

But conflict wasn't restricted to Southeast Asia. It was also on American streets and campuses; it was around the family dinner table, in churches and synagogues, and on Capitol Hill, the two main causes being Vietnam, of course, and civil rights. But the latter had been brewing far longer than the former. The Civil Rights Act of 1964 had legally done away with segregation, but not racism. Thus, racial tension had continued to increase, both in rhetoric and in action, even in sleepy towns like Lawrenceville. Clearly, Jim Crow was not going to lie down in his grave without a fight, and our school was no exception.

The fact that Kyle and I had befriended one of the few black students who had made the choice to attend our formerly all-white school made us pariahs for the unabashed racists, who were not few in number. Wesley Crawford was the student's name. He was not only academically gifted—he had to be to survive in that environment—but also one hell of a first baseman. Happily, our coach was no racist and saw Wes, as he liked to be called, for the athlete he was. The fact that Wes replaced a duffer at first base did nothing to appease the racists on the team: the duffer was white. After Wes suffered a couple of uneven fights with groups of rednecks on the team, Kyle and I appointed ourselves as his unofficial and uninvited bodyguards. Wes was made of stronger stuff than most of our classmates. As one of only three black students in our school, he took whatever the white kids threw at him. Wes would never have asked Kyle's or my assistance; we simply gave it. If Wes was glad to have our help, he never indicated it. The fact that he accepted it was enough for Kyle and me. It was an unspoken pact. Whenever Wes's parents couldn't drive by the school to give him a ride home, Kyle and I walked with him or got one of our parents to give him a lift with us.

Once, when Dad was late picking me up from an after-school meeting, I had begun to walk home. Not far from the school grounds, three of the school's morons, led by an overweight, pasty-faced bully named Alton Wilkins, started following me, throwing racial epithets and the occasional stone at me. They, of course, wanted me to react so they could give me a collective beating as they had done to Wes. I burned with anger at their words and flinched whenever one of their rocks found its target, but I kept my nerve and walked on. Meanwhile, having not found me at school, my father came driving along the road and saw what was happening. When he pulled up alongside me, I was crimson, both with rage at what I had endured, as well as the embarrassment of being rescued by my father.

Dad seemed to sense my predicament and said nothing until we were nearly home. Then, using a tone I could imagine he had used with younger pilots in his Marine days, he said, "That looked like unfair odds back there." I simply nodded.

Dad slowed the car in order to turn into our drive and then stopped. I was staring at the dashboard, still feeling my inadequacy from the earlier run-in, but I could tell my father was looking at me. "Know what we used to do in the Pacific whenever we were outgunned against the Japs?"

I slowly turned to look at him. "No." I shrugged.

"We acted like we didn't know or didn't care that we were outgunned. We flew straight for the group leader. If we could flame him, the other Japs knew we meant business—or that we were just plain crazy! That would usually break up their formation." Dad reached over and gripped my shoulder. "Son"—was he going to comfort me or berate me?—"is this about your friendship with Wesley?" My eyes began to burn and once more I just nodded and bit my lower lip. "I haven't wanted to step in or try to advise you." Dad paused. "But I'm mighty proud of what you and your friend Kyle have been doing. I've even heard from Wes's father—he rang me and thanked me for what you have done for his son. It shows...well, it shows real Semper Fi." Dad gave my shoulder a squeeze. "But there's something else..." Dad waited for me to look at him before he resumed. "You can't let those boys buffalo you. If you want it to stop, *you* have to do something about it."

"But, *Dad.*" I lifted my hands to indicate how helpless I felt. "I can't take on *all three* of them."

Dad added more pressure to his grip on my shoulder. "Did you hear what I said about taking on the leader like we did with the Japanese?"

"Yeah, I did."

"Well, I guarantee you that only one of those boys is the leader. You drop him and the others will fold."

"But what if they *don't?*" I was beginning to feel queasy at the thought of being pounded into the ground.

Dad looked at me for a moment and then continued our drive around the house to the garage. "We'll finish this talk after supper."

By the time supper was an hour past, I was beginning to hope that Dad and I weren't going to carry on the conversation about how I was meant to get my ass kicked by three rednecks. But my hope was mistaken. Dad had simply wanted our supper to settle so he could take me out in the back yard and show me the basics of self-defense, which was Marine code for "how to drop the other guy before he gets you first." For the next ninety minutes I was taught jabs, punches, and even kicks. We were both sweating when we finished. Dad nodded approvingly at me and said, "Remember, don't let them get in the first punch. If they have you cornered, just go for the leader. He'll be the one with the biggest mouth. Just focus your anger and adrenalin on him. The rest will take care of itself. Got it?"

"Yes sir, I understand."

"Good. Go get yourself washed up." I noted that my father not only seemed pleased with himself, but that he was also pleased with me, his reluctant warrior.

~ * ~

If the two root problems which divided America were its undeclared war in Vietnam and its racism, those same two issues were united in one figure: Martin Luther King, Jr. Not only were a disproportionate number of young black Americans being sent to

Vietnam—an inequity which King decried—but they were being sent to fight and kill a people who were equally as downtrodden as black Americans. For King, the war was not only unjust, it was also inherently racist and only served to add another page in that sad chapter of American history. Love him or hate him, King was one preacher the American conscience couldn't ignore.

Mr. Haynes, my civics teacher, not only couldn't ignore King, he openly condemned him as well as the de-segregation of our schools. On one particular day, when the topic of discussion was the American constitution, he began extolling the values of the original Founding Fathers, saying that there had already been "too many amendments to the constitution and we should leave well enough alone."

Without following the classroom etiquette of raising my hand, I blurted out a question, "What about the Three-Fifths Compromise?"

"What about it, Braddock?" Haynes responded testily.

"Does it seem a good idea to you that black people should only count as three-fifths of a person? That's what they thought in 1787."

"Yeah," added Kyle, "and Indians didn't count at all."

"I'm glad to know y'all have been doing your reading, but I was talking about later amendments, if y'all don't mind."

"Oh, like the Thirteenth Amendment, which abolished slavery? Guess that was a bad one, huh?" My blood was up.

"Must've been a bad ideer or wouldn't be havin' so many pro'lems with colored people these days—especially that Martin Luther Coon," sniggered Alton Wilkins.

"The real *problem*, Alton, is redneck-shit-for-brains like you," snapped Kyle.

"Say whut?" Alton swung his chair around and seemed ready to square off with Kyle. But Kyle was fired up and the look he gave Alton made the latter reconsider.

"Yeah, well, at least I ain't a nigger-lover," he lamely replied as he turned his chair around.

"That's enough!" shouted Mr. Haynes, "Weston, I'm sending you to the principal's office for using foul language! Get your things and go."

"Me?" countered Kyle, "What about Alton and his 'nigger-lover' comment? Is that okay in your book?"

"I didn't hear Mr. Wilkins say anything." Haynes had a self-satisfied look on his face as he hastily scribbled a note for Kyle to take with him. He proffered the note to Kyle. "Now git!" The classroom was becoming restive and seemed equally divided in their support for Kyle and Alton. I wondered if our civics class would become the latest battleground over civil rights.

"Mr. Haynes, may I ask a question?" I waded into the troubled waters.

"Is it pertinent?" asked the now petulant Haynes.

"Yes, sir, I believe it is." Kyle cast me a furtive look as he slowly gathered his belongings.

"Make it quick." Haynes was clearly distracted by Kyle, who was in no hurry to leave.

"Earlier this term, you kept making the point that the US has been known as the world's melting pot. It seems like you only meant that as regards *white* people."

Now off his guard and riled at Kyle's behavior, Haynes fulminated at me, "Some things you just can't change and you don't mess with! A melting pot doesn't mean the mongrelization of the races!" I fell back in my seat, incredulous at what I had just heard.

Kyle stood. All eyes were on him as he looked around the room at the various posters and quotations by famous Americans proclaiming the nobility of the American system of government. Then he laughed out loud as he shook his head and turned to our teacher. "*Mongrelization of the races*?! You know something, Mr. Haynes?" Our teacher simply looked at him without responding. "Everything abo't you and this class is a crock of shit."

Half of the class began roaring with laughter in disbelief at what had just transpired. Mr. Haynes went a deep shade of purple and became apoplectic. He spluttered as he tried to speak. Kyle gave a cheery little wave and left for the principal's office. Too late for Kyle's hearing, but as a stab at trying to regain control both of himself and his classroom, Haynes veritably gurgled the words, "That'll earn 'im a full week's detention, just see if it doesn't." Somehow, I didn't think that was going to worry Kyle. What worried me, however, was how I was going to survive another day—not to mention *year*—in this school. It was all beginning to feel claustrophobic.

I was still preoccupied with the events in civics class as I turned to enter the locker room before going home. I hadn't expected a reception party. "Looks like this nigger-lover is all by hisself." Alton was standing in front of me, blocking my way. My books were suddenly flipped from under my arm by one of his two cronies, who had approached from behind and stood either side of me. "You dropped sumpthin', Braddock," sneered Alton.

Both instinct and common sense told me not to bend down to collect my books, especially when outnumbered three-to-one. But as my agitation from the injustice done to Kyle had yet to subside, it didn't take long for my temper to flare. All I could hear in my head, aside from the blood pulsating through my ears, was my father's voice, saying, "Don't let them buffalo you, son." Keeping my right arm in close to my body, I veritably growled as I jabbed my fist into Alton's soft gut just below the solar plexus. His flabby mouth formed a perfect 'O' as he fell back against the lockers. I immediately followed the jab by quickly swiping my right elbow across his face, breaking his nose in the process. Wordlessly, and with blood gushing down his chest, Alton melted like one of Salvador Dali's clocks into a puddle on the floor. The surrealism continued as I prepared to take on his buddies. With Alton down for the count, an outcome neither of them had expected, I heard footsteps on my left as one accomplice bolted straight out of the locker room door. The third boy, Larry Jones, was trapped between me and three walls of lockers. Alton had gone down so fast I hadn't begun to burn up the adrenalin, a surfeit of which was coursing through me. Because my glands had powered me up for a three-on-one fight, I was shaking from the potent cocktail of hormones and rage. I don't know what Larry saw in my face when I turned to confront him, but whatever it was, he didn't like it. He tried to hurtle past me but slipped in Alton's blood and fell flat on his face. I pounced on his back. I grabbed hold of his collar and pulled his face from the floor.

"Whassa matter, Jones? You wanted a fight, didn't you? Well come on—let's have it!" As I was virtually sitting on Larry's back, I could feel his convulsing as he started to cry. My heart was pounding and I was breathing heavily like when our coach made us run windsprints. I had never been so worked up in all my life.

"Don't hit me, Jon," whimpered Larry. "I-I'm sorry...it was Alton's idea...I-I shouldn't a'gone along with it. Please let me go. Please!"

All of a sudden, the rage was gone. In its place was another feeling: power. I had flattened one foe, sent another fleeing, and was perched atop the third one who was begging my mercy. A fellow student turned the corner to enter the locker room. When he saw Alton's bloody face and me sitting on top of Larry, he made a quick about-face. Lost in my adrenaline haze, it seemed as though I sat on Larry for half-an-hour, but it was probably no longer than forty or fifty seconds. Alton's voice brought me around: "Jon, let Larry go—okay? You win."

I had almost forgotten about Alton. "Yeah, okay," I replied absently. I pushed myself up and watched Larry scamper to his feet and disappear out the door without another word. Then—and to this day, I can't say why—I extended my hand to Alton and helped pull him off the floor. Was it the *noblesse oblige* of the victor or was it simple compassion? Maybe it's the case that we all find some occasion to act without thinking according to "the better angels of our nature."

With Alton on his feet, we both looked at his blood-stained shirt. He gingerly touched his nose. "Ow! Shit! Man, you got me good, Braddock." He looked at me sheepishly. "You gonna report this to the principal?"

I shook my head. "It never happened. But you might want to wash your face before you leave—and cover that mess with your jacket." I pointed toward his shirt.

Alton nodded, almost obediently. He started to leave but then turned and said to me, "My daddy'll prob'ly whup me for this."

"For *what*?" I asked. "Getting in a fight?"

"No, for losin'..." his hangdog voice trailed away.

"So tell him you won," I suggested, "or...or that you got slammed in a game of razzle-dazzle football. Either one of those ought to work."

Alton's face brightened, but he winced from pain when he smiled. "Hey, Braddock?"

"Yeah, Alton?"

"You ain't so bad."

I started to retort with "For a nigger-lover?" but let it go. "Yeah? Well, thanks. Go get yourself cleaned up, okay?"

"Okay...uh, thanks."

Alton hastily turned and left while I finished exchanging the books in my locker as I had originally intended to do some minutes before. I leaned against the cool metal of the lockers and mused over Alton's parting word: thanks. "He thanked me," I said out loud. "He *thanked* me." I had just broken the guy's nose and humiliated him, and he thanked me. I shook my head incredulously and chuckled under my breath. I can't say Alton and I parted as friends, but we were certainly less than enemies. And with that realization, something surged within me, as much a feeling as a thought: Why did we have to shed blood to get to that point, the point of recognizing our common humanity? I left the school knowing what I had to do.

Nine

Let war yield to peace, laurels to paeans.

—Cicero

Rev. McLaurin was in his study when I arrived at the church. His secretary wasn't in, and his door was half opened. The minister appeared to be deep in thought, poring over a commentary, so I lightly tapped the door. McLaurin looked up and smiled. "Well, hey, Jon. Come on in."

"I hope I'm not disturbing you?"

But McLaurin was already on his feet. "No, sirree!" He beamed as he came around his desk and motioned to one of his two easy chairs. "Sit down, sit down, Jon. And to what do I owe this unexpected pleasure?"

I sat in the chair and squirmed a bit nervously. "I...uh...I got in a bit of trouble today at school." I looked at McLaurin who considered my words as he studied me with his kindly eyes.

"Tell you what, Jon. Why don't we just close the door so folks know I'm busy?" He laid his hand gently upon my shoulder as he passed by me and, with this unexpected tenderness, I felt a lump rising in my throat.

McLaurin returned to his chair and smiled invitingly. "Now go ahead, Jon. Just what sort of school trouble was it?"

"I—uh...well, it wasn't exactly *school* trouble. I mean, it happened there...but it was more of a...well..." I looked up at McLaurin, "It was a fight."

"A fight, eh?" McLaurin nodded thoughtfully. "That doesn't strike me as your style, Jon. What started it?" Before I responded I noted that he had not said, "*Who* started it?" as my parents would have done.

"Three guys cornered me."

McLaurin's eyebrows rose at the number of opponents. "Mmh-hmm...mmh-hmm," he contemplated my words briefly while rubbing his chin. "Three of 'em, you say?"

"Yes, sir."

"Well, Jon," the minster smiled. "If you don't mind my saying, you don't look the worse for wear."

"No, sir, I clobbered the biggest guy and the other two kinda changed their minds." I went on to explain about how Kyle and I had befriended Wes and how this had led to trouble with the school racists. Then I related the fracas in Mr. Haynes' class, my father's advice, and finally the resultant fight and its aftermath.

Rev. McLaurin had settled back comfortably in his chair and listened to me, the fingertips of each hand lightly resting on one another. He looked at me deeply and knowingly, and then asked, "So why have you come to see me, Jon, as opposed to going home and telling your father how you kicked the butt of the boy who's been bullying you? Oughtn't he to be proud of you?"

"Hmm—" I snorted a short laugh. "I see what you mean. I guess...I guess he would be proud of me, but..." I paused for several moments. "But I'm not proud of myself." The minister just looked at me and waited for me to find the words. "When...when I punched Alton in the gut, at first it felt good. It's hard to explain, but there was this look of shock on his face and I felt like, well, 'So now *you know* what it feels like—what you've done to Wes, and probably others.' I mean...it all happened so fast I guess I thought it—but maybe I just felt it—'cause next I busted his nose. And...well, I've told you the rest except that...I don't know...I felt really *powerful*—do you know what I mean?"

"Sure enough, Jon, I do know what you mean." He smiled: "If you can believe that of a middle-aged man of the cloth like me." His eyes twinkled.

I stumbled on. "I mean, after I had dropped Alton and then found myself sitting on top of Larry—" even the minister joined me in smiling at that image, "I felt powerful, but at the same time, it was a feeling I didn't want. Does that make sense?"

"It makes perfectly good sense," responded McLaurin. "You know, Jon. People like me and your father—men in their late forties—well, we were young once. And we got into fights, no different than you. And then came that terrible, terrible war, a war with more destruction than I hope you can ever imagine or ever have to witness." He shook his head at his inner visions. "And even in the war...well, flying a bomber like I did or a fighter like your father...well, that's a pretty powerful feeling. And some men liked it. I don't know why or how, but they did."

"Yeah, I remember seeing a film with Steve McQueen called *The War Lover*. Did you ever run into guys like that when you were in the war?"

"Not exactly like that," McLaurin replied pensively, "but there were one or two who were full of bravado...or bullshit—if you'll excuse my language! I was never sure which."

I let out a guffaw at the preacher's swear word and then changed tack. "Do you think my father liked it—the war?" I asked.

"Oh, I wasn't meaning to suggest that, Jon." McLaurin waved his hand as though trying to erase his words.

"But really...I mean, you fought in the war, but you became a minister, right? But my dad...well, he stayed in the Marines. That seems to be the most important thing in his whole life. It's almost like peace was an interruption to his profession."

The minister sat and pondered my words for a full minute before he spoke. "Jon, son, I can't say I know your father *well*, but I know him well enough to say I don't believe your father *liked* war. He had—and has—a passion for the Marines. You know the saying, 'Once a Marine...'"

"Always a Marine," I finished the sentence for him and chuckled. "Yeah, believe me, I do know the saying."

"Well, I think your father and many men like him see military service as a way of preserving the peace and protecting the freedom we enjoy in this country. I don't know if that makes sense to you, especially with this Vietnam thing growing all the time. But when you've seen the world under threat from dictators like Hitler, Mussolini, and Tojo—well, you know what it means to have a democracy like ours. But here I am preaching at you—a real liability for a preacher!" He smiled in such a way that I felt warm inside. "Jon, it may be hard to do, but perhaps try to think of your father as a knight of old, who saw as his duty the protection of all he held dear—if that makes sense?"

"Yeah. I guess it does. But all I know is, seeing Alton's bloody face and having Larry on the ground crying...I just think this is the same kind power over other people that I'm against in Vietnam. And yet, here I go doing the same thing...Do we human beings ever learn anything? Will we just continue to fight one another and go to war?"

"Well, Jon, that's a very good and very tough question. It's one I've wrestled with for many years." He paused. "Will you let me try to answer it?" McLaurin rested his chin onto his right hand, the index finger curled and rubbing his nose and top lip pensively. We sat in comfortable silence for several minutes. It hit me that my father always had a quick answer to my questions, no matter how tough. I had never seen him ruminate over a question, and Dad's answers did not invite conversations. I was still mentally comparing my father and our minister when the latter spoke again.

"Jon, in the Second World War, I saw what the human race was—and still is—capable of doing. I saw how vile and base we can become. I remember how surprised I was after the war to see Germans going to church just like we did back home. And I suppose they prayed to God for protection and victory just as we did. It all seemed so absurd to me. Hitler's was one of the worst regimes this world has ever known. I asked myself, 'How could anybody support him and still pray to God?' And, Jon, that's when it came to me: humanity is not saved as nations or entire societies. It just happens one human soul at a time." McLaurin lifted his hand away from his chin and raised one finger. "That's all. Just one soul at a time. And so, when I got home from the war, I decided not to take up law, which is what I was going to do, and went to seminary instead. I vowed that I would do everything one person could do to help prevent the world going to war again and that I would live my life peaceably with all. I won't pretend it has been easy, but it has been worth it."

Now it was my turn to keep silence as I weighed McLaurin's words in my heart and mind. I had not only liked what my minster said to me, but what is more, I had liked the way he spoke to me. He hadn't patronized me as my father or older brother would have done. Nor had he tried to hurry me up or get rid of me. Rather, he had simply spoken to me, man to man. I felt somehow liberated.

"I'd like to devote my life to peace." My voice almost sounded foreign to me.

McLaurin had been accompanying me in active silence. When he spoke, his tone was grave but gentle. "That's a mighty big undertaking, Jon—a mighty big undertaking." He nodded from experience as he spoke those words. "But I'm here to tell you that I would like to support you, if you would like that."

I had no idea of the path on which I was embarking, so with youthful naïveté I said, "Yeah...I guess."

McLaurin could see my lack of understanding, so he spoke again. "Jon, here's what I mean. You've been in a fight today—you've drawn blood—and you're shaken up."

Thinking he was about to diminish my newfound commitment to a peaceable lifestyle, I started to speak. "Yeah, but—"

McLaurin lifted his hand to silence me and smiled. "Please hear me out first—okay?" I nodded. "I'm not saying yours isn't a heartfelt decision. I believe it is. But what I am saying is this: it won't be easy. Wiser people than I have often said that if one prays for patience, then prepare for it to be tested! Be prepared for life to throw a whole herd of annoying people in your way! This also applies for any other virtue that one might wish for oneself, especially with that most elusive state of being, peace. Just look at what Gandhi went through—and Rev. Martin Luther King right now. Gandhi was shot; and King...well, a lot of our fellow whites want to destroy him. Jon, wanting peace is one thing, but living peaceably in the face of aggression and violence is another.

"That rage you say you felt when you were confronted by those three lads? Well, it's in all of us. It's part of our human nature. Rev. King talks about non-violence because he knows human nature well enough to know what we're like when people attack us. We're probably the most violent creatures on the planet. We're anything but *pacific*. For that reason, a true pacifist is a rare thing indeed. But non-violence, that's another matter; that is something that *we can learn*. King and associates like James Lawson are making great strides to train people in non-violence. But make no mistake, it takes courage, strong faith, and prayerful support. So if you'll let me, I'd like to offer you that support. What do you say?"

"Yeah, I think I understand what you're saying...so what kind of support do you mean?"

"Just this," replied McLaurin. "We'll agree to meet once a week to talk about situations that...well, piss you off." I snorted with laughter at the minister's choice of words. "We'll talk about how you felt, how you dealt with the situation. If you weren't happy with your response, we'll work out a strategy for the next time. If in any week there's nothing much to report, we'll still meet, if only for five minutes. Just to check in with each other and pray for strength. How's that sound?"

"It sounds good. I think I'd like that."

"Fine!" beamed McLaurin. "I'd like that, too. With our son in graduate school up at U.Va. and our daughter married and living in South Carolina, it will be good for me to have a younger person's point of view. The world's changing fast, so you can help keep me in touch, eh?"

"Okay," I agreed with a smile and stood to leave.

Rev. McLaurin took my extended hand in both of his, shook it vigorously and warmly, and then said a prayer. He walked me to the door, but before I had taken two steps, he called to me, "Oh, Jon?"

I turned to face him. "Yes, sir?"

"What will you tell your father about the incident this afternoon?"

I scratched my head in Stan Laurel fashion and asked, "What incident?" He gave a hearty laugh and waved me off.

~ * ~

Kyle took the week's detention in his stride. Like me, his grades were always A's and B's, and—until the fracas in Mr. Haynes' class—Kyle had not been in trouble at school. He told me later the principal had been embarrassed at having to agree to the detention, but felt he couldn't undermine decisions made by his staff. He even offered to write a letter to Kyle's parents explaining the questionable judgment of Mr. Haynes, but Kyle shrugged it off and told the principal it was no big deal.

Meanwhile, a variety of stories floated around the school about the incident in the locker room. As part of my vow to myself and God, I had decided I wouldn't mention the run-in between me and Alton. Apart from Rev. McLaurin, only Kyle—and to a lesser degree, Wendy—knew the true account. Kyle had asked me about it straight out, so I told him. Wendy came to hear about the fight through the school grapevine, but when she queried me about it, I told her that I had made a promise of sorts to my minister not to talk about it. Unintentionally, this increased my stature with Wendy! Whenever other people brought it up in my presence, I would either shrug it off or, if someone had heard about it from the boy who had seen me sitting astride Larry Jones, I would gleefully make up absurd stories about standing on Larry's shoulders to climb on top of the lockers when I slipped, accidentally kicked Alton in the face, and fell on top of Larry. I knew implicitly that reveling in my triumph over Alton & Co. would lead me down a path that I did not want to tread. This was far from a desire to be holy, per se, but it was an earnest desire to be peaceful.

~ * ~

I shared with Wendy some of the things I had discussed with Rev. McLaurin as well as the fact that he and I had agreed to meet on a regular basis. Although my intentions for meeting with McLaurin were straightforward, I also hoped that these meetings with the good reverend might go some way to salving Wendy's wound from my refusal to attend further prayer meetings with the youth group at her church. Perhaps they would even add a touch of sanctity in the eyes of her mother, but that seemed beyond hope.

In the weeks following the locker room fracas, Rev. McLaurin and I discussed many things. However, the one area of my life that we definitely did not talk about was my ever-awakening sexuality. Because I was too young to reconcile Christian faith and my being created as a sexual being, I couldn't imagine my minister doing any better. To the contrary, having seen too many old black and white movies wherein the clergy always seemed to be Catholic priests, I could only picture the contradictory image of my Presbyterian minister warning me of mortal sins and telling me to repeat so many Hail Marys. This would never have happened, of course, but it is also the case that I so much enjoyed the kissing, touching, and passion that I didn't want to spoil this delicious secret by telling any responsible adult.

There was only one confessor I trusted and that was Kyle—not that we ever gave each other explicit accounts of our forays into sins of the flesh (we were brought up to be gentlemen!); but these explorations and discoveries were much too delightful not to be shared with someone. Meanwhile, along with Johnny Cash, I "walked the line"—in my case between body and spirit, albeit not without much mind-numbing inner debate as to why any God would create humanity as such a bundle of contradictory impulses.

~ * ~

The remainder of that spring semester was an even greater test of peace, patience, and love than could have been imagined, not only for myself, but for the rest of American society as well. In April, Martin Luther King, Jr., was assassinated in Memphis where he had gone to support a sanitary workers' strike. The voices of peace and reconciliation—black and white—were drowned out by the deluge of violence which swept across more than one hundred American cities. The US was becoming as dangerous as Vietnam. There was plenty of talk by white racists around town and in the school about how "King got what was coming to him" and "just let the niggers try to riot in Lawrenceville—we know how to deal with 'em." And I found myself torn between two poles: On the one hand, I wanted people to see reason and to deal with each other according to our common humanity. And on the other hand, I wanted to smash some of the faces of loud-mouthed bigots, who saw the violence in America's cities as the pretext for enacting our own final solution of the race problem.

I brought up my dilemma when I next met with Rev. McLaurin. "Apart from being in the war, did you ever want to flatten anyone?" He laughed out loud.

"Jon, I often tell my wife, 'A lot of people don't know how lucky they are to be alive!'"

"Really?" I queried, "You mean *you...*"

"Of course, Jon! Of course! So many people think we ministers are above having strong emotions, unsavory ones in particular. If they only knew!" He laughed again and shook his head. "I'll tell you something funny. When I was newly ordained just after the war, I was the minister of a little church outside of Atlanta. I was only there for three years, but it seemed like thirty! Now in small churches with only forty or fifty members, there is often one individual or family who rules the roost. And didn't we have one there?! Mmh-mmh! Buddy Elkins was his name. He was short, stocky, bandy-legged and, as you would expect, loud-mouthed. He chewed so much tobacco that he had taken to speaking out the side of his mouth whether or not he had a chew."

McLaurin got to his feet and started to imitate the way Elkins walked and talked. I guffawed, as I had never seen this side of our minister. "So there was this one Sunday, just after the service 'cause that's when he usually liked to hold forth, and I was talking to a lady who had just lost her husband in an automobile accident. Well, up walks Buddy. And although he can see perfectly well that I'm talking with this poor, bereaved lady, he takes me by the shoulder and turns me toward him in order that he can sound off about something or other. I don't have to tell you the widow was mightily offended, and I wasn't any too pleased. And mind you, I towered over him by at least six inches and had arms that were well-muscled from flying B-24s. In short, I could have snapped that little bastard in half!" I involuntarily hooted at the minister's choice of words. "But I guess he reckoned he was perfectly safe to throw his half-pint weight around as I was a minister. Jon, it was all I could do to refrain from knocking his block off." McLaurin smiled to himself as his mind replayed the scene.

"So…what happened?"

"Well, Buddy Elkins finished haranguing me about whatever it was he found so doggone important. But when I turned back to the widow, I found that I was actually shaking with anger and nearly busting a gut from wanting to cuss—and believe me, I still had all of the vocabulary from my Air Force days. So there I was, in such a state that the widow felt the need to comfort me! Anyway, when I finally regained my composure, I put on my best ministerial voice and said, 'Ma'am, if you weren't a lady and I were not a gentleman, I do believe I would swear upon the legitimacy of his birth!'" McLaurin gave a full-bodied laugh. "Can you believe I said that?" The minister removed his handkerchief from his pocket, wiped away the tears of laughter and resumed his seat opposite me. "Sounds like something Ashley Wilkes would have said in *Gone with the Wind*, doesn't it?"

"Yeah, I guess," I chuckled in reply. "But at least you didn't hit him."

"No, sir, I did not. But, Jon, he's just one of the people on that list who don't know how lucky they are to be alive. As we've discussed before, this is the discipline of non-violence. Not many of us are truly pacific, without an ounce of aggression. If you stamp on another man's toe, he's just as likely to do the same—if not more—to you. That's why, in Old Testament times, they set a limit on retribution: 'an eye for an eye.' Too often today people understand that to be a license for retribution; but its intention was to set a limit on reprisals. If someone struck another person and rendered him blind in one eye, that was the most retribution one could exact in return: like for like. Our biblical forebears were well aware what violence lurked within the human heart from the time Cain killed his brother, Abel. They were fully aware that violence breeds violence. This is what we're witnessing now in the wake of Dr. King's assassination. But if his legacy is to have any meaning, good people will have to resist that natural urge to strike out at aggressors. It requires both self-control and stamina 'cause it's a long haul, son. A theology professor of mine used to have this motto on his wall: '*Illegitimi non carborundum.*'" McLaurin's hand traced the words in the air.

I shook my head. "What's it mean?"

"It's mock Latin for 'Don't let the bastards grind you down!'" Once more I burst out laughing. But McLaurin took on a very serious tone as he leaned toward me. "And, Jon, with a bright young man like you, they will try. The real challenge for you in this life will be to retain your integrity in the tug-of-war between simply selling out to the powers of this world and being crushed beneath their wheel." Nothing that had been said to me up to that point in my life had struck me as deeply as McLaurin's words. And their import only became more profound with passing years.

Ten

Peace, peace—but there is no peace!

—Jeremiah 6:14b

I have never been happy with truisms such as: the difference between a pessimist and an optimist is that the pessimist sees the glass as half-empty, but the optimist sees it as half-full. I have always had to ask qualifying questions: Just *where is* this proverbial glass? Is it in a desert country or a temperate country? Did it catch rainwater or was it filled by a kitchen faucet? How long has the glass been standing there? How desperately does someone need the water? There are so many ancillary questions! Thus, context is always the determining factor.

The context of our lives in 1968 did teach me the validity of one truism, however. No matter how bad things are, they can always get worse. Some might call that pessimism, but I know it to be realism. This was poignantly brought home to me on the morning of June fifth, when we awoke to the news that Senator Robert Kennedy had been shot during the wee hours of the morning. He had just won the

Democratic primary election in California for the nomination for president when he was gunned down by Sirhan Sirhan, a young Palestinian immigrant. The next morning, we learned of the senator's death.

It didn't take long before I was on the phone to Rev. McLaurin to arrange a chat. The only difference was this time I asked if I could bring Kyle along with me. I had often told Kyle about my meetings with McLaurin and how helpful they had been for me in trying to make sense of this violent world. As Kyle attended the church youth group anyway, McLaurin, as I expected he would, said it was fine for Kyle to join me.

Like a lot of young men our age, we had placed great hopes in Bobby Kennedy. We felt he understood the youth of America and would also take seriously our concerns about the country's growing involvement in Vietnam, which millions felt not only to be illegal, but immoral as well. Both Kyle's father and mine were staunch Republicans and anti-Communists. Because they saw Democrats as soft on Communism, both overseas and at home, any discussions about politics or world events usually turned into verbal combat. Kyle and I thus found a safe haven in Rev. McLaurin as both spiritual guide and voice of reason. He was the only World War II veteran I knew who did not support the war in Vietnam as a simple knee-jerk reaction. He took pains never to spew out simplistic civic virtues such as, "Our generation went to war for America; now it's your turn." It never really occurred to us self-absorbed youngsters how lonely and isolated our minister must have felt. He was a Presbyterian in a sea of Southern Baptists, a war veteran who deplored war, a moderate Democrat in an area becoming increasingly right-wing Republican, and he was well-educated and thoughtful in a time and place wherein both of those qualities brought suspicion. These were the days of "America—love it or leave it."

~ * ~

"So what hope is there?" asked Kyle—in a voice that was more plea than question. "First they kill JFK, then King, and now Bobby.

Will right-wingers and racists simply gun down anyone who tries to make a difference to this country?"

"Kyle," answered McLaurin slowly and deliberately, "I have to admit that sometimes...well, sometimes it indeed looks that way. Every country that has valued its freedom has had to decide whether the bullet or the ballot box would have the ultimate say. I can't help the way you're feeling right now...because...well, because it's good and right that you should feel outraged. It means you have heart, and it means you care—both you and Jon. Nothing and no one can ever replace anyone who dies. We are all unique and our particular gifts die with us, but what we bring to this world, what we give, well, these things can and do live on. And they can influence others just like the two of you. But let's also not forget that there are others out there who are following in the footsteps of Dr. King, the Kennedys, and others who have died for social justice and peace: Ralph Abernathy, Andrew Young, William Sloan Coffin, and even though I'm Protestant, I don't mind mentioning the two Jesuit brothers Daniel and Philip Berrigan. Not everyone, for good or ill, gets the sort of publicity given to a Martin Luther King or a Kennedy, but that doesn't mean there aren't a lot of folk out there who want to make this world and this country a better place."

"Yeah, I guess that's true," Kyle murmured both softly and pensively. "And most of 'em are ministers." He smiled at McLaurin, who returned the smile and nodded.

"But Rev. McLaurin," I chimed in, "Kyle and I have just finished our junior year in high school and...and well, we just wonder *why* we're getting an education, what's it all for? What's the point? When you look at what is going on in the world, it feels like we should be *doing* something."

McLaurin ran his hand over his graying hair and then scratched his scalp as he pondered his reply. "Man!" he laughed, "Y'all are sure enough throwing hard balls at me today!" He breathed in deeply and exhaled as a sigh. "Jon, Kyle, y'all are probably going to think I'm an old fogey for saying this, but getting your education is *doing something*. Every one of the men we have mentioned has had a good education. If you want to be taken seriously by the powers that be, then that's one criterion you can't be without. Our country has always needed good leaders, and good leadership requires two things: knowledge and the ability to use it. Don't y'all short-change yourselves at this critical time in your lives."

Kyle and I were silent for a moment as we weighed McLaurin's words. I was the first to speak. "You're not an old fogey, Rev. McLaurin, or Kyle and I wouldn't be sitting here with you. And you know I've been meeting with you because...well, because you're one of the few adults I can relate to and who can relate to people our age." I nodded toward Kyle. "I mean, you talk *with* us, not *at* us or *down* to us."

"Amen to that," seconded Kyle. "To most adults, it seems guys our age are old enough to die in Vietnam but not old enough to vote or to have anything to say that's worth listening to."

"How do you keep going?" I asked McLaurin. "You always seem so...I don't know, *even* and easy-going. I mean, with all of the assassinations, riots, Vietnam, etc., how do you keep hope alive?"

McLaurin laughed genially. "Oh, Jon. If you only knew." He chuckled again and shook his head. "I guess I'm like the proverbial swan." The minister drew his hand slowly across the desk. "You know—who seems to glide effortlessly across the water, but underneath he's paddling like mad! Believe me, son, I do my paddling. But you've asked a good question and it deserves an answer." McLaurin shifted in his chair and rubbed his chin as he considered his response. "Jon and Kyle, one major difference between us is the fact that I'm a good thirty years older than y'all. But lest I be heard as patronizing or 'talking down the years' to you, let me first qualify that and say that age does not automatically confer wisdom. I'm afraid many people—too many— just get older, but they don't get smarter. I hope I am not one of them, but I'll leave you to judge."

Kyle and I both protested that we did not see McLaurin as an old buffoon.

He bowed slightly to us and thanked us; then he continued. "What age can do for a man is to give him some perspective on life. And this only comes through experience, like living through the Second World War. You know, in 1942, none of us could see that the war would have an end. And even after the fall of Nazi Germany in 1945, there were many in our government and the military who thought the war against Japan could go on for another year or two. I was half certain I would have to fly bombing missions over there. Of course," he paused, "that was *before* the atomic bombs were dropped." The minister closed his eyes as he resumed speaking. "The point is that *during* the war, it felt like it might go on forever, or at least until all my friends and I were dead. But it didn't. And neither did Korea. As bad as it was, it, too, had an end. With the passing of years, one discovers that even the worst of times has an end. But I hasten to add that this applies for those of us who *survive*." McLaurin opened his eyes and looked from me to Kyle while he gave us a moment to let his words soak in.

"Jon, you've asked about how I keep going, and I've given you a partial answer. You've told me that you would like to dedicate your life to peace. That's the reason we began meeting. So the other thing I would say is this: a man has *to live* his words and ideals. Even when— and *especially when*—life seems like 'a tale told by an idiot, full of sound and fury, signifying nothing,' even then the peaceable man has to live as though peace were possible, come hell or high water. Once the man of peace makes one exception and says, 'In this situation, war is the answer,' then he unravels all that he has done up until that point in time. The Bible speaks of 'beating swords into plowshares' but never the reverse, and I think that's for a reason. As Mr. Jesus put it, 'Those who live by the sword shall die by the sword.'"

"But," Kyle interrupted, "what if people with swords killed all of those witho't?"

At first, I wondered if Kyle might be joking in his smart-ass way, but one look at his face told me he was not. "Yeah," I added, "how can there be peace if all of the peaceful people are dead?"

"Now you fellas are starting to understand the cost of discipleship. But answer me this: What does resorting to violence do for the cause of peace? Being killed is always a distinct possibility. But no one can say he's truly a pacifist unless he's grappled with the risks and the cost."

No one said anything for at least a minute. Kyle and I were both lost in thought. It was Rev. McLaurin who broke the silence. "I hope y'all will excuse me, but I've got to get home for supper before coming back here for a meeting with the church elders tonight." Then he chuckled. "If there's anything that would make me forget my pacifist commitments, it's dealing with a bunch of cantankerous elders on an empty stomach!" Then he laughed aloud. "My darling wife ought to be awarded the Nobel Peace Prize for keeping me fed. It's done more for world peace than most treaties!"

Kyle and I shared the laugh with him as we stood and shook hands. We walked down the church steps into the balmy warmth of early summer. I caught a hint of honeysuckle as we ambled along to Kyle's house where I had been invited for supper. We kicked at stones on the sidewalk and joked with one another. Suddenly Kyle took a more serious tone. "Jon, are you really serious abo't this pacifist stuff?"

"Yeah, I guess I am," I replied, "Why?"

"I don't know. I mean...well, what if you got cornered again like that day with Alton? What would you do? I mean, would you just let 'em kick your ass?"

"I gotta admit, I don't like the sound of that," I averred. "I remember reading about how once, when Martin Luther King was attacked by a lady with a knife or something, he just kinda took a defensive posture. But he didn't try to fight or struggle with her."

"Yeah, I remember that, too," said Kyle. "But he got wounded, though, and came damn close to being killed."

"Yeah, there is that," I said somewhat curtly. "Where is this headed, Kyle? Do you think I'm off my rocker or something?" I found myself getting annoyed with Kyle, something that rarely happened, and whenever it did, it felt doubly bad because he was my best friend.

"No, I don't think you're off your rocker. I'm just thinking about what happens to most—or at least *a lot*—of the people who take a stand against war and violence."

"What? You mean like King and Bobby Kennedy?"

"Yeah, but not just them. I mean, why does Christianity have the cross as its main symbol? Answer: Look what happened to Jesus Christ—

and most of his disciples. And Gandhi. You gotta admit he was a pretty peace-loving guy. And I admire all of 'em, I do. It's just...oh, I don't know. Why the hell does this world seem to favor the violent? And why can't God do something like he did back in the Bible days, huh?"

"What, like wipe us all out with a flood? Like in Genesis?" I laughed despite myself.

"Asshole," grinned Kyle. "You know I don't mean that. But how come God supposedly took care of the Israelites like in the Exodus and then lets the European Jews get gassed by the Nazis? And why do the Communist regimes do whatever they please? I don't get it, that's all."

"Yeah, well, join the club," I said. I couldn't answer Kyle's questions and struggled enough with them myself. But happily, my thoughts were turning elsewhere because, as we rounded the corner to Kyle's street, a gorgeous young woman was leaving a house and walking out to a waiting car.

Kyle followed my gaze. "Forget it, Braddock—she's o't of your league."

"Man!" was all I could utter.

"Don't you know who that is?" queried Kyle. "Maryanna Creighton. Remember? She was a senior when we were sophomores. She was a runner-up in the Miss North Carolina contest this year. Anyway, she's at Meredith College now—when she's not gallivanting around getting her picture taken."

The car was just about to drive away when I noticed Maryanna had left a book on the roof of the car. Kyle must have thought I'd flipped out over her as I darted toward the car. "Braddock?! What are you doing, man?" But the car pulled away and the paperback fell onto the road. So I stooped and picked it up. By then, Kyle was alongside me again.

"I was going to try to tell her the book was on top of the car..." my words drifted away as I studied the book's cover.

"Yeah, and she was going to swoon into your gallant arms for rescuing her book. Right!" Kyle laughed.

"You ever hear of this?" I asked Kyle, who was also now studying the book.

"Ken Kesey? Nope," replied Kyle. *"One Flew over the Cuckoo's Nest,"* Kyle slowly read the title. The cover had a picture of a man in a strait jacket, laughing. "Is her name in it?" enquired Kyle.

"No. No name," I answered after looking inside the book.

"Then it's meant to be yours," said Kyle, airily.

Most of us only recognize our life's turning points long after we have passed them, and even then, only with the aid of 20-20 hindsight. I certainly had no clue what doors that paperback novel would open for me.

~ * ~

Kyle and I soon arrived at his house. We walked up the driveway and entered through the screen porch on the side of the house. "'Bo't time y'all got here," said Marie, who was setting the table.

"What did the good preacher have to say that kept y'all so long?" asked Mr. Weston, invisible behind his newspaper. Only the tips of his fingers on the newspaper and the smoke rising from his cigarette gave away his presence.

"Oh, the usual ministerial stuff. He told us to stay away from liquor and wild women—oh!—and not to smoke, because it causes lung cancer."

Ed Weston lowered his newspaper to give us his damn-fool-teenager look. "Wise ass. Y'all've probably been at Johnson's drug store looking at the girlie magazines on the top shelf."

"And how would *you* know about them, Dad?" fired back Kyle with his most innocent look.

Before Ed could reply, Mrs. Weston breezed into the room. "Now, you two can just stop it," she chimed in brightly as she carried a steaming casserole dish from the kitchen with, "After all, we have a guest tonight. And in any case, we ought to be glad the boys were with Rev. McLaurin instead of many other things they could get up to." She smiled brightly at me and then added, "Kyle, you and Jon go wash your hands before we eat."

"What's wrong with the Episcopal Church?" asked Ed, as Kyle and I headed to the bathroom. "Haven't *we* got a minister?"

"Now, dear," we heard Mrs. Weston using the tone of voice that seemed universal to Southern mothers when calming their men folk, "you know perfectly well that Rev. Hazleton is seventy, if a day…" We lost Mr. and Mrs. Weston's voices as we closed the door and washed our hands.

Kyle soaped his hands until they dripped with froth, then he squeezed them together sending a stream of soapy bubbles at my face. "Hey! You jerk," I growled and laughed at him.

"Temper, temper!" Kyle wagged a forefinger at me, with a mischievous sparkle in his eye. "Remember, you're a pacifist!"

"Your dad was right, wise ass!"

Kyle threw his head back in laughter. Then he stopped suddenly and looked at me in the mirror, where we stood side by side. "Jon, do you think this is how we'll wind up one day?" Kyle jerked his head toward the door, wordlessly indicating his parents. "I mean, I love my parents and everything, but…is this what life is all abo't? Is this why we're supposed to get an education and get a job—just so we can end up with…" and here Kyle mimicked his parents' voices, "'now, dear,' 'yes, dear,' 'damn fool teenagers,' and blah, blah, blah?" Kyle shook his head in puzzlement.

"Beats me," I said. "Sometimes it seems like it's either that or becoming the kickass Marine my father wants me to be."

Our musings were interrupted by Ed Weston's bellowing, "Would y'all kindly get your behinds to the table? Some of us want to eat!"

And then we heard Ellen's kind tones: "Now, dear…." Kyle and I just looked at one another and laughed.

~ * ~

I walked home that evening breathing in the perfumed night air and listening to the dusk chorus of cicadas, tree frogs, and other creatures for whom night was the beginning of their working day. As there was nothing I had to do, I took my time. I nodded to people who were using the cool of the day to mow their lawns or trim back the ever-encroaching honeysuckle. Dad was away on an overnighter, and Mother would be out at her Women of the Church meeting. As I turned down our winding driveway, I continued past the house and walked out onto the old oak bridge over Stuart's Creek. The ever-changing music of its water spilling over the rocks was a natural symphony of which I never tired. I stood in the middle looking down toward the pond. While lingering there, my mind's eye conjured up the images of Dad's episode with the M-80s. The associated scenes made me laugh out loud. But it was the buzz of bloodthirsty mosquitoes in my ears that brought me back from my reveries, so I headed up to the house.

The walk from Kyle's house made me thirsty, so I went to the kitchen to find that most catholic of Southern thirst-quenchers, iced tea. It stood on the main shelf of the refrigerator. For as long as I could remember, it was always to be found in a hand-painted glass jug that Mother had inherited from her mother. Its principle property was that it seemed to replenish itself miraculously overnight.

After pouring a tumbler full, I sat down. The chairs at our kitchen table had come from my father's parents. They were ladder-back, wooden chairs with seats made from woven strips of saplings. Sitting in them made one sit Marine-upright. Feeling a lump in my rear jeans pocket, I retrieved the Kesey novel I had found in the road and plunked it on the table. I upended the dregs of iced tea. The glass was covered with beads of condensation from the warm night air. I ran the glass across my forehead and enjoyed the cooling sensation. In doing so, my eyes fell upon the paperback novel I had tossed onto the kitchen table. The character depicted on the cover, even though trussed up in a strait jacket, seemed to be enjoying a joke his bindings couldn't contain. "What have you got to laugh about?" I asked him as I started to thumb through the pages. What I read enticed me to read more, so I refilled my glass and repaired to the screen porch which overlooked the creek and woods beyond.

~ * ~

For as long as I can remember I have had a love affair with reading. One of the most amazing discoveries I made as a child was that words printed on a page could paint pictures in my head and transport me far beyond my small, contained world. Books gave me the power to become or experience whatever their words described: mountaineer, deep-sea diver, Confederate cavalryman, ship's captain, or astronaut—all I needed were the words. I would rush to get my homework done so I could dive into whatever book I happened to be reading. Books became my friends, and they never let me down. Often, I read under my bed covers with the aid of a flashlight long after I was supposed to be asleep. This was my time and my world, uninterrupted and unfettered. My hungry mind devoured words the way my growing body demanded food—and lots of it.

So it was that night. Within a matter of minutes, I was pitched headlong into the story of Randall Patrick McMurphy, a sane man in an insane asylum which turns out to be saner than the world outside—and the staff who move freely between both worlds. I went to the refrigerator, poured myself another glass of iced tea, and returned to the screened porch and my book. By the time I was halfway through the novel, the characters of McMurphy, Chief Broom, Big Nurse, Billy Bibbit, and others had become firmly fixed in my mind, such that they became cairns, marking the boundaries between the different worlds that each of us must inhabit. Big Nurse evoked my parents and the stalking world of the superego; Chief was the part of me who observed the world uncomprehendingly; Billy Bibbit was the good, obedient and responsible me; but McMurphy!—well, he was the rebellious wild-child trapped inside this baptized, polite, and obedient Son of the South. It's not that I wanted to dismiss the mores with which I had been brought up; I simply wanted to experience *more*. This guy Kesey had, through the medium of imaginative literature, formulated insights that started my adolescent mind spinning, and what it spun were the makings of a rope which I could throw over the wall of my imprisoned innocence and shinny down to the world of experience, for which most of us are never really prepared.

The headlights from mother's car brought me back into the here and now. I was almost resentful at being distracted from my reading. My neck ached slightly from being bent over the book for two or three hours. As I rolled the kinks out of my neck joints, I noticed I had gathered quite an audience of moths and mosquitoes on the screen. Bats whizzed around the yard, waiting to pick off any bug that decided to forsake the light and fly away into the darkness, thus becoming a delicious meal for a fellow night creature.

I heard Mother come in the back door and up the stairs. "Jon? Jonathan? Are you okay, honey?"

"Yeah, Mom, I'm okay."

She opened the door and came out onto the porch with me. "What're you doing up this late, Jon? It's nearly eleven-thirty."

I flashed the paperback at her. "Reading a book. It's good. Guess I just got lost in it and forgot the time. But speaking of late, you're not usually back so late after one of your meetings. What's up?"

"Oh, it was that Thelma Clemments. She practically threw a hissy fit because some of us wanted to send this year's benevolence fund to the United Negro College Fund. She said…well, I won't repeat what *she* said." My mother started to flush as she recalled the remarks from her meeting. "Let's just say she thinks the Negro colleges are only training centers for social revolutionaries and communists." She sat beside me on the glider, a sort of suspended settee, which rocked back and forth on its sprung suspension.

"*That's you,* Mom—a revolutionary *and* a communist!" Mother shook her fist at me, but giggled at the thought. "So what did y'all decide?"

"Oh, I don't know! Jon, would you be a sweetie and run get me glass of tea? My throat is parched from all of the arguing."

"Sure." I got up and took my glass with me. I poured mother's glass first and then finished the pitcher in my glass. "This will be a test for the refrigerator genie," I thought, as I placed the empty pitcher back into the refrigerator.

Mother had kicked her shoes off and was gently rocking herself, pushing with her stocking feet. Her head was resting on the back cushion of the glider.

I handed my mother her glass. "Oh, thank you, darling." She patted the seat beside her for me to sit.

"I thought you said it was late." I was thinking about going up to my room and reading until I fell asleep.

Mother shrugged and smiled sweetly at me, melting my resistance in the way that only a mother's love can. "I did. But I don't work and you're out of school. Just for a few minutes. Your father's away flying and Ron's working in Chapel Hill this summer. I'd just like some company." She sipped her tea quietly for a moment and then surprised me by saying, "Sometimes I wish I drank liquor like your father." She turned her head toward me and smiled. "Does that shock or surprise you?"

I expelled my breath through my teeth and said, "Well, yeah! You've preached the evils of alcohol for as long as I can remember."

"I know. And it's not without reason."

"Your grandfather and Uncle Tyler, I remember." Was her desire for company just another excuse to lecture me? I started to squirm in my seat and was just about to say I wanted to go to bed when she surprised me once more.

"There was also your father."

"What do you mean?"

"His drinking. When he came back from the war. Oh, I know he drinks now, but it's nothing like it was then. It was different. He...he was different."

"I don't understand." As far as I could see, Dad was just Dad.

"Jon. The Marine you grew up with—Colonel Braddock— well...he wasn't always like that. I knew him when he was young and before he went to that horrid war. He went away 'Philip' or 'Phil,' but he returned as 'Blackie.' And he drank—*a lot*." Mother saw the anxious look on my face and placed her hand on my shoulder. "No. He never hit me, if you're thinking about the way Uncle Tyler treated Aunt Ruthie. But he disappeared into himself. I'd wake up at night and find he was not in bed. At first, I would go and look for him, but then I learned it was better to leave him. He just had to work through those things."

"What things?" I asked.

"Jon, has your daddy ever told you why he came back from the war?"

"Well, yeah. He got wounded by Japanese flak or something."

"That's true, but it's only part of it. Did he tell you that he was shot down?"

"Shot down?" This was news to me. "To hear Dad tell it, he and his buddies blew every Jap they ran into out of the sky! But now you say he was *shot down*?"

"Yes. And now I wish I hadn't started this. But, son, please don't tell your father I shared this with you, okay? I would have preferred you heard it from him."

I nodded and said, "Sure. I won't say anything." This was turning into one crazy night.

"All I know is this: Phil—your dad—and his squadron were attacking some Japanese transport ships somewhere around the Solomon Islands. They were flying low and attacking with bombs or rockets or something—but anyway, that's when your father's plane got hit and he was wounded. He said he tried to gain some altitude, hoping he would be able to get back to their base, but he couldn't control the rudder due to the wound in his left leg. And he also had a wound in his left arm. I'm sure you've seen the scars. Well, when flames started appearing from his engine, your father knew he had to bail out, and luckily, he was just high enough to jump. So he radioed to his—oh, what do you call him?" Mother waved her hand in the air—as she was wont to do whenever a word wouldn't come to her. "Wingman! He radioed his wingman and then out he went." Mother swished the remains of her tea around the bottom of her glass and stared at the melting ice. "This next bit is…well, it's not very nice. But I think maybe you need to hear it because…well, because I see the way you look at your father sometimes, and I know, um…well, I know he can—and has been—hard on you and Ron…which is probably why Ron hasn't come home this summer. So maybe—just maybe—if you know something about what he's been through, you might think differently of him."

Mother tossed the remainder of her tea down her throat in an unladylike way that reminded me *of me*. And then she resumed her story. "When he landed in the water, he got rid of his parachute and then tried to inflate his Mae West. But it had holes in it from the Japanese gunfire." I was watching my mother intently as she related this unknown history of my father. Her eyes were darting back and forth as she pictured what he must have gone through. "Your father's clothes, his pistol, and the useless Mae West were starting to weigh him down, and he was afraid he might drown. So, he threw away his Mae

West, holster, and gun and then managed to take off his shoes. Because of his wounds, just trying to get rid of those things and stay afloat exhausted your father, you understand?" Mother looked at me for assent. I quickly nodded my head and she drew a deep breath, sipped the water from the melting ice in her glass and then bit her lower lip before continuing. "Jon, where your father parachuted from his plane…well, it seems he had landed amidst the…the…" she seemed to be grasping for words, "the *wreckage* of the ships they had hit that day and some days before. Because he was getting weaker and weaker from his wounds and loss of blood, he had to do *something*, you understand? He had no choice…other than to drown."

"What do you mean, 'he had to do something'? I don't follow."

Mother's eyes were beginning to fill with tears and she reached into the side pocket of her summer dress and removed a tissue. As she dabbed her eyes, Mother asked me, "Well, what would *you* do, if you were in danger of drowning?"

"Find something to hang onto, I guess."

"Exactly," mother nodded. "That's exactly what Phil—your father—did…but it's just that what your father found was…um…the bodies of dead Japanese sailors or soldiers. I…I don't remember." Mother looked down nervously.

"*Je-sus…*"

"Now, Jon!"

"Sorry, Mom…but *Christ*!" I was still young and inexperienced enough in the ways of the world to be horrified at the picture her words conjured in my head. "Dad used *dead Japs* as a *life-raft*? Is that what you're telling me?"

Mother just gave me one of her looks. "Jon, you wouldn't be here now if he hadn't done what he did. You also have to take into account that the Solomon Islands were surrounded by shark-infested waters, and your father was more than likely scared, and he was *bleeding*. Surely, you've watched enough *Sea Hunt* to know what danger that would put him in. Happily, your father was rescued after an hour or so by an Australian coast watcher who had seen his plane go down. He came out in a little boat and picked him up." Mother dabbed her eyes and stood.

She turned to look at me and said, with her voice breaking, "I just hope you might think a little more charitably of your father now," she sniffed back a sob, "and remember that, like you, he was young once and had to go off to war when he was not much older than your brother, Ron. And he has had to live with such awful memories." Mother sobbed loudly, and I didn't know what to do. I was in the no man's land between youth and manhood, and I didn't know how to be my mother's comforter. In fact, seeing her crying was bringing me to tears. Mother herself broke the impasse by saying, "Would you just look at the time?! And look at the state of me!" Mother leaned over and kissed me on the forehead. "Let's get our weary bodies to bed."

By the time I went to bed, I was wrung out with vicarious emotion at what my mother had related to me. Perhaps my brain had been more receptive to her account of my father's gruesome experience with the Japanese corpse due to the book I had been devouring—I don't know; but something in my young world had not so much changed but *shifted*. As I drifted toward unconsciousness, in my mind's eye, I saw the photo of Dad which depicted a confident twenty-three-year-old, standing on the wing of his fighter, smiling. Had he only been feigning the nonchalance? Just when I thought I had begun to have the pieces of the jigsaw puzzle that was my father put into place, the picture lost all recognition. I wasn't to know this would not be a singular occurrence.

~ * ~

My dreams that night were a fitful combination of my father's nightmarish incident in the Solomon Islands and Kesey's *Cuckoo's Nest*. I was relieved to be awakened by the bright summer sunshine flooding my room, but at the same time, I was exhausted. I pulled on a T-shirt and cutoff jeans and shuffled my way downstairs for some breakfast. A note lay on the breakfast table, telling me that Mother had already gone to the grocery store. She had also written reminders of the neighbors' yards that needed cutting. After breakfast, I went to our back porch, pulled on my grass-stained tennis shoes, and made my way down the street.

When I arrived at my first job of the day, the Linvilles' lawn, Doreen Linville met me at the door. She studied me for a minute and the asked, "You all right, Jon? The grass needs cutting, but I don't want you out in this heat if you're not okay."

I told her that I hadn't slept well but assured her that I was fine, reinforcing it with a big smile that took an amazing amount of energy to summon up. However, when I sneaked a look at my reflection in the window glass of the darkened garage where the mower was kept, I saw the reason for her concern. My hair, which had grown increasingly longer over the past school year, was sticking up, and there were dark circles under my eyes. Once out of sight in the garage, I fished my comb out of my back pocket, spat on it, and ran it through my unruly hair. My efforts were in vain as, after barely twenty minutes had passed, I looked like I had just stepped out of a shower. I pulled out an old bandana, rolled it up, and tied it around my head to keep the stinging sweat out of my eyes. By the time I had finished the next two jobs, not only was the bandana wringing wet, but the only dry clothing on me was the lower half of my cut-offs.

When I arrived back home, Mom was at the table drinking a cup of coffee and nibbling a sandwich while looking at the newspaper. "Jon, honey? As you got up after breakfast and have just about missed lunch, please make sure you're home for supper at five-thirty, okay? Your father will be back and I'd like for us to eat together." Mother took a good look at me as I was about to mount the stairs. "And Jonathan Braddock, don't you dare go upstairs with those grass-covered sweaty clothes on! You march right out and leave them in the utility room!"

Sighing heavily, I swung around and did as I was told. But at seventeen, I didn't like the idea of stripping naked and then walking past my mother. "Okay with you if I leave on my underwear?" I called out grumpily. I awaited her usual reply of "it's nothing I haven't seen before," but this time she just mumbled "That's fine," and left me to it.

After a long, cooling shower and wolfing down a couple of sandwiches, along with half a pitcher of iced tea, I grabbed my bike and wheeled off to Kyle's. He was washing his mother's car when I rode up, and, true to form, fired the hose at me. "Bastard!" I growled at him—but with a smile.

"Takes one to know one," came his reply.

I laid my bike on the grass and sat in the shade to watch him finish. "Hey, Kyle, that book I found? Man, you've gotta read it! I've nearly finished it and...well, it's like nothing they've ever had us read in high school."

"You mean it's not Dickens with his Pip Pirrups and Martin Chuzzlewits?" chuckled Kyle.

"Far from it, man. It's...it's really mind-bending stuff. It doesn't just tell a story; it makes you *think*."

"Well, shoot it my way when you're done," replied Kyle, as he "accidentally" let the hose drift my way while rinsing the last suds off the car. He was halfway to their back door before I tackled him.

Eleven

Pleasure's a sin, and sometimes sin's a pleasure.

—Byron

I did shoot *Cuckoo's Nest* to Kyle when I finished it; others would follow. But Kesey's imaginative romp inside an insane asylum set off a chain reaction in me as regards counter-cultural literature which has continued to this day. I have never been satisfied with viewing society from only one set of lenses. And it all started from simply picking up a book which had slipped from the top of a car onto the road in front of me.

My foray into the world of counter-cultural America took another twist the next morning when I was making my grass-cutting rounds. My second job of the day was the Taylors' yard. They lived about a half mile from us. My skin was gleaming with sweat as I cycled up to their front door. The Taylors were a retired couple whose age I could only guess, so I was taken aback when the main door opened and, through the screen door, I was greeted by a man in his late twenties or early thirties with shoulder length hair. He had on a tie-dyed T-shirt and beads around his neck. In the background, I could hear The Doors blasting out of a stereo, but I didn't recognize the album. The man looked at me for a moment and then, with a sly grin, asked, "Are you the local dealer?"

Flummoxed, I stuttered, "W-what…who? Me? Uh, no!"

"Pity," he replied laconically, "my parents said there would be a guy coming around about the grass. I thought maybe you were their dealer." I just stared at him. "*Grass*? Marijuana? Get it?" He looked at me and shook his head. "Never mind." He noticed me looking past him toward the source of the music. "You like The Doors?"

"Yeah, I have their first album. Their long version of 'Light my Fire' is a lot better than the cut-down single you hear on the radio."

"No shit," came the reply. And then he casually dropped, "I met 'em in San Francisco, just after they released that single."

Now it was my turn to say, "No *shit*?" The distance between East and West coast America collapsed in an instant, as did the gulf between rural North Carolina and that hip, capital of flower-power in California.

The mysterious son of Bill and Meredith Taylor just grinned. He knew he had impressed this country kid. Suddenly his grin became laughter. He extended his hand and said, "I'm Martin, the Taylors' reprobate son. Wanna come in for a minute?"

"Sure…um, yeah. I can come in for a few minutes."

Martin flopped on the sofa and indicated an armchair for me. The air-conditioning inside the Taylors' house was refreshing.

This epiphany of hippiedom from San Francisco had piqued my curiosity. "Um…What do you mean: 'reprobate son'?"

"Let's see…by 'reprobate' I mean I had the temerity to disappoint my parents by running a sound studio on the West coast where I record and produce rock and roll bands—that's how I met The Doors. Mom and Dad feel they wasted their money on sending me to Indiana University to study classical music. Actually, I use my education *all of the time*, but my mother and father refuse to believe it. Bu-u-t…they're still my parents, so I come back to see them from time to time." He grinned.

"Yeah, parents," I chimed in.

"So what's your name?" asked Martin.

"Jon Braddock."

"Braddock?" Martin seemed to roll my surname over his tongue like wine. "Braddock? You from around here, Jon Braddock?"

"Not really. My mother's family comes from here, though. Her family name is Lawrence."

"Ah—" was his sole and knowing response.

"But I grew up in New Bern. My dad was in the Marines over at Cherry Point."

"Marines, eh? Scary stuff." Martin feigned a shudder. "So, what about the hair then? Kinda long for a Marine's kid, ain't it?

"Yeah, I suppose. He's not in the Marines now though. He flies for Pilot Aviation."

"Hmmm," mused Martin, "but I'll bet your old man would want you to join up and do your patriotic duty in Vietnam. Right?"

I shrugged. "I don't know. To tell the truth, we don't talk about it that much." I paused for a moment, deliberating about whether I should speak my thoughts. "But I kinda think Dad wishes he were over there. His old squadron is there now."

Martin shook his head at my comments. "Man! I mean, why does anyone in his right mind *want* to go to war? Especially when our country isn't even in danger!"

"My sentiments exactly," I replied. "Vietnam's a big mistake." A light flickered in Martin's eyes at my last statement. The album ended, so he got up to flip it over.

"I haven't heard this album before," I mused aloud.

"No," smiled Martin as he returned, "Not many people have. It's a demo. Should be out in a few weeks or so."

Doubly impressed, I uttered the universal vocative of the sixties, "Wow!" Before I could ask to see the cover, Martin dropped it on my lap as "Spanish Caravan" flowed from the speakers. As I studied the cover notes for *Waiting for the Sun*, I could see—out of the corner of my eye—that Martin was studying me. Finally, I couldn't help but look up at him. It was clear he had something on his mind, but he wasn't in any rush to speak.

Trying to show I wasn't just another 'country cracker' I tried out my newfound literary taste. "You ever read Ken Kesey…*One Flew over the Cuckoo's Nest*?"

Martin's eyes really lit up. "*Read* him? I've *met* him!" Could I have been more impressed? I doubt it. "Kesey hangs out with some of the bands I record—when he's not dodging the cops. He and his Pranksters have put on some pretty far out concerts—if you want to call them that!" Martin laughed gustily and then, with a face full of mirth, said, "Acid tests. Man!" He seemed lost in happy memories.

"Acid tests?" I queried.

"Acid—LSD? Surely you've heard of LSD?"

"Yeah, I've…*heard* of it…"

"But I'd be safe in saying you're never tried it."

I shrugged and nodded, "Pretty much."

"Well, I'm here to enlighten you," said Martin. "*Cuckoo's Nest* is an acid trip, man! Kesey was paid to be a part of some sort of government experiment using hallucinogens on human subjects, mainly LSD. And it all took place in a mental hospital, you see? Just like in the book. Then the FBI goes and busts him for using LSD a few years later! Ha! Anyway, the book is a…a…" Martin's hands were floating around like drunken fish, as he tried to describe what his words couldn't capture, "a…metaphor—yeah, that's it," the hands clasped together, "for his experiences on acid in that hospital."

It was beginning to feel like the teacher and the taught as Martin filled me in on things Beat, hippy and generally counter-cultural. I realized there was a sort of parallel society happening within America, but not one I was likely to learn about in school.

"Hey—I know I'm taking a risk here—but do you ever get high?"

"Um...do you mean like *drunk*?"

"Not really. I'm guessing you've never smoked dope then?"

"You guessed right."

"Yeah. Figures." Martin drummed his fingers on the arm of the sofa for minute. "So you listen to 'head' music, but you've never smoked dope?"

Feeling like a babe in the woods, I merely nodded. Assuming I no longer posed any interest to this urbane hippie, I got to my feet. "Guess I'd better get the grass cut."

But before I could open the door, Martin leapt up and started rubbing his hands together. "Yeah, there's no point risking a bust here in redneck land—so let's get drunk then. Whaddaya say?"

Not wanting to appear what I actually was—a complete innocent—I replied, "Yeah, sure! Uh, when?"

"Why not tonight?" proposed Martin. "I know a great place for rhythm and booze. Have you got a car? I flew into Winston-Salem, and my mother met me at the airport so I haven't got any wheels."

I had to think for a moment. My father would be home tonight. Lately he had taken up what I could only imagine to be a perverse pleasure of insisting that, if his car were at the house, I should take it if I wanted to go out with my friends. Since my first driving lesson with Dad, that car had become my nemesis. It seemed to mock me whenever I was asked to wash it: "Whassa matter, Kid? Can't handle my clutch and gear box?" Not only that, but the years and weather had not been kind to this '54 Bel Air. Far from being a chick magnet, my youthful heightened self-consciousness convinced me that driving such a wretched machine would have made me a laughingstock.

Martin waved his hand in front of my eyes. "Yo, Jon? You still there?"

"Uh—yeah, yeah, I'm still here. I was just thinking…my…uh…my parents will be using the car tonight. My dad's flying in this afternoon, but…but I have a friend named Kyle and…uh, well, he'll probably be able to help us out."

"Kyle, huh?" Again Martin mused over a name, just as he had done with mine, as though by some sort of magic, he could discover the person who held the name. "Your friend Kyle, is he cool?"

"Yeah, sure. Don't worry about Kyle. What time should we come for you?"

Martin turned toward the clock on his parents' mantelpiece. As he turned back toward me, he had a slight smile on his lips. "Let's say eight o'clock. The place I know ought to be coming to life about then."

"Great! I'll see you then." I headed out to the garage to get the mower. From inside the house, I could hear Grace Slick's voice belting out: "If the truth is found…to be lies…"

~ * ~

At supper, my thoughts were preoccupied with what the evening might hold in store, and thus, I was suitably evasive when either of my parents questioned me about my plans. I never could lie—well, not convincingly—so I resorted to the adolescent language of ughs, shrugs, and grunts. Thus, I waited until my parents were in full-flow of conversation before I gulped down the last of my milk, jumped up from my chair and darted for the stairs. A short time later, I saw Kyle pulling up in front of our house. With the same speed with which I had mounted the stairs, I flew down them and out the front door, while shouting to my parents, "See you later!"

I jumped into the front seat of the Westons' Bonneville and flopped back with exaggerated relief.

"So, where're we headed, Jon?" asked Kyle as he released the handbrake and reversed the family car out of the driveway.

"First we pick up Martin. After that…well…I'm not really sure." I shrugged and added: "But it oughta be pretty cool, knowing this guy, Martin."

Kyle shrugged, grinned, and drove us the short distance to the Taylors' house. "Just give the horn a toot," I advised, "I don't want to go to the door and have to make small talk with Mr. and Mrs. Taylor." Kyle had no sooner touched the horn when the front door was flung open and Martin was making his way to the car.

When he had closed the rear door, I introduced Martin to Kyle. "What's happenin'?" he asked, grabbing Kyle's hand in a 'black power' style of handshake soon to be adopted by most counter-cultural types.

"Ask me when we get there," came Kyle's reply.

Martin laughed heartily. "Ha! I like this guy already! Let's slide!"

"Where to, boss?" came Kyle's cheeky reply.

"Just aim this rocket toward Main Street, and I'll guide us from there."

~ * ~

As we drove through the town, Martin chatted to Kyle and me as though we were all old friends. Before long, it was clear we were going to an area referred to locally as 'Milltown,' a predominantly black area where most of the housing was two-storey, pre-war duplexes. Although neither Kyle nor I could have been classified as *practicing* racists, we had both imbibed deeply from the springs of Jim Crow—quite literally, in fact, as segregated water fountains were one of the most visible of Crow's insidious social traditions. And we had used segregated toilets, eaten at segregated cafés, ridden in the *front* of buses, etc. We had done these things unconsciously because, as we might have answered if asked, 'that's just the way things were.' Thus Kyle and I found ourselves far outside our comfort zone. However, Martin was clearly at ease. "You're gonna love this joint! It's just along here on the right." He was drumming on the back of my seat and singing some bluesy number under his breath. "Hey—pull in here!"

"Where?" asked Kyle.

"The church parking lot. Lights are off, so God's probably not in! Ha! The place we're going is just half-a-block away."

Kyle dutifully drove into the parking lot of the Ebenezer AME Zion Church. "Are you sure we'll be okay here?"

"*Sure* we'll be okay? No. *Probably* okay? *Sure*! Ha!" Martin laughed at his tortured pun.

Martin was out of the car in a flash. Kyle and I gave each other searching looks as we slowly exited. Having got us into this situation, I felt I had better do the talking. "So…um…Martin? Exactly where are we going?"

Walking ahead of us, Martin looked over his shoulder and said, "Oh? Didn't I say in the car? Yeah, well, it's a kind of 'juke joint'— they often have some live blues or jazz. It all depends on who's doing the circuits. And they sell cheap bootleg booze. Whoooh! It'll cure what ails you, boys! Don't worry, you'll love it! It'll be an experience."

We turned down an alley beside a Mom and Pop kind of store, which also advertised "Soul Food to Go." A dim light beside a blacked-out door provided the only light. Martin strode up purposefully and knocked at the door. We could hear music pulsing inside. A curtain or shutter was pulled open inside and a person's face then filled the small window. The face was as dark as the night and only the eyes were visible to us. The eyes moved from Martin, to me, and then Kyle. They seemed to take in the measure of both Kyle and me before they returned their gaze to Martin—where they began to flicker with recognition. A chain was removed and a bolt slid back as the door opened a few inches. A sliver of light shone on Martin, accentuating his whiteness in the inky darkness of the alleyway. Martin threw back his arms as though to say: "Ta-da!" After a moment, a woman's voice said: "*Martin*? That *you*?"

"In the flesh!" smiled Martin.

The door then opened wider, the light from within catching us like escaping prisoners in a spotlight. A woman with intricately corn-rowed hair and radiant ebony skin stood before us. She placed her right hand on her hip and leaned in the doorway on her left as she turned to Martin. "Mah-*tin* Tay-*lor*! Look who done turned into a hip-*py*! Come give Marletta a big hug!" While they were embracing, Marletta looked over Martin's shoulder at Kyle and me. "Mmh-mmh!" she half-whispered into Martin's ear. "Where you be findin' young white meat like that?" Kyle and I were most definitely out of our comfort zone— way out! She laughed lustily and suddenly let go of Martin, who nearly fell through the door. Marletta then beckoned to me and Kyle with her hand, as though summoning children. "Y'all comin' into Marletta's or not? Tell y'all one thing. Y'all don't want to be hangin' round outside in *this* neighborhood after dark! Not with your shiny white faces. No sir-ree!"

Hooking her right arm around Martin, Marletta took me by her left hand and led me inside. Kyle quickly followed. Half of the people in Marletta's place turned to look at the only white faces in the house. The rest kept their focus on a group of musicians on a makeshift stage at the rear. In between, the air was blue from smoke. A rudimentary bar built out of planks and packing cases was set up on the left side of the place. It looked to me as though this juke joint could be set up or broken down in a matter of minutes. After she closed the door, Marletta studied Kyle and me up and down. She smiled and said, "Just look at them boys blush!" My ears felt like they were on fire. "How old're you?"

Suddenly finding my mouth dry, I left it to Kyle to reply, "Eighteen."

"Eighteen, my ass!" Marletta shook her head with laughter. "Dream on, white boy!" Kyle smiled nervously; I was so self-conscious and embarrassed I thought my face would spontaneously combust. Having let us squirm for a moment, Marletta let out another laugh and blurted, "Hell, I don't care how old y'all are!" Marletta waved her hand in a carefree manner. "*Everything* in here's illegal anyway." Then, with a wink, she added, "But if you got the *money*, you get the *honey*."

Beads of perspiration sprang from my forehead. Kyle's face was frozen in a shit-eating grin. Having only ever had the occasional sip of my father's beer or wine at holidays, I began to grasp, for the first time, what people meant when they said, "I could use a drink," even though I was blithely unaware of its effects.

"The way it works," advised Martin, "is that you buy a jug of their moonshine. What you don't drink here, you take home."

George, the bartender, smiled and nodded in accord with Martin's words, saying, more to himself than to us, "Thass right, thass right." George was a middle-aged man, with close-cropped salt-and-pepper hair. When he smiled, something I found he did a lot, a golden front incisor caught any ambient light and gleamed.

Kyle and I fished out the required money, which was then added to Martin's and handed over to George. George winked at us and disappeared through a small doorway. He came back with a glass gallon jug and plunked it heavily upon the bar. "No-o-ow," he said with a flourish and producing a lighter, which he set on the bar, "le'ss us light up a little of this juice and see what she do."

With two flicks of his wrist, George screwed off the metal cap and held it between his thumb and forefinger. With his other hand, he gently tipped the jug and poured a little of the clear liquid into the cap. George then set the cap on the bar—away from the jug—and flicked the lighter. He looked at each of us individually and said, "If it burn *blue*, then that'll *do*." The tooth gleamed. As soon as the flame came close to the innocuous-looking fluid, a tongue of blue flame shot upwards. George, obviously pleased with himself, stepped back and admired his work—as though he were a waiter in a fine restaurant who had presented us with a Baked Alaska. As George set three glasses on the bar, he asked, "Y'all drinkin' spo-dee-o-dee or do y'all be wantin' somethin' to mix that with?"

"What's 'spo-dee-o-dee'," I queried, "apart from a Jerry Lee Lewis song?"

Martin chipped in, "It's like a liquid sandwich! A sip of wine, a sip of whisky, a sip of wine."

George beamed. "Yassuh! Dis stuff can *burn* goin' down, 'specially if y'all ain't used to it, y'know."

Kyle and I balked, so Martin advised that we should go for mixers. Each of us handed over fifty cents for small bottles of cola, which George duly opened for us. As we turned to look for a table, we saw Marletta motioning us toward one that had just been vacated. The previous occupants, a man and a woman, were walking across the small dance floor, she leading him by the hand. They exited the barroom by a door to the left of the stage. Marletta winked, made a rocking motion with her hips and then laughed. We crowded around the small table while Marletta went to welcome some new arrivals. Guests at other tables nodded at us, a few smiled and one or two gave a black power salute. Martin leaned over the table, drawing in Kyle and myself. "I don't know why white folk ever had the nerve to refer to black people as 'spooks'! I mean—*look at us*—we're the ghostly white spooks! Ha!" Kyle and I were prone to agree and happy to laugh. We needed to relax.

On stage, a saxophonist was being accompanied by a piano and string bass. I nudged Martin. "How long have you known about this place? Marletta and George both seem to know you."

"I first came here when I was about your age, maybe a little older. Marletta's mother ran the place then. Now she mainly does the cooking. I'm told she does a mean chittlin marinara."

"A *what*?" asked Kyle.

"Chittlins in barbecue sauce!" laughed Martin. "Gotta admit to not liking soul food myself, but Marletta and her mama can make some mighty fine fried chicken! Now *that* I like!"

While we had been talking, Martin had poured about two fingers of booze into our glasses. He placed the jug on an empty chair next to our table and left us to mix our drinks to taste. Not knowing what I was doing, I followed Martin's lead. He had mixed his half and half, so I did the same. The first gulp took my breath away. It was not long down my throat when it felt like my head was beginning to expand and rise. I took a deep breath and said, "Wow!" Watching me with trepidation, Kyle added more cola to his glass and took it in slow sips.

Martin, with eyes closed, was swaying to the notes wafting from the tenor sax. Each of us let the mood of the music carry us as we nursed our drinks. From time to time, Martin would reach for the jug and splash more of the fiery liquid into our glasses. After half-an-hour or so, I caught Kyle's eye and he gave me his winning grin, but with slightly glazed eyes. He looked down at his glass and then back at me and raised his eyebrows as if to say, 'Can you believe we're doing this?' I just returned the grin as we raised our glasses in a toast. About then, the couple who had vacated our table came back through the door where they had exited. The man was mopping his neck and brow with a handkerchief in his left hand, while his right arm held the woman snugly around the waist. I watched in fascination as the woman looked up coyly while her partner said something that she obviously liked hearing. The man leaned forward for a kiss and the object of his affection placed both hands on his chest, as if saying, 'It stops here.' Clearly, the man wanted his lips to linger on hers, but she slowly and deftly pushed him away. He gave her a little wave and headed toward the exit, a satisfied smile on his face, while she drifted over to the bar, adjusting her hair.

I saw that Kyle had also been following the movements of the couple, so I leaned over and asked, a little too loudly, "Are you thinking what I'm thinking about this place?" I cocked my head toward the woman at the bar. My voice brought Martin out of his reverie. He quickly looked from me to Kyle and then followed our gaze to the bar. His head nodded as he cottoned on to our naïveté. He motioned for Kyle and me to lean toward him over the table.

"Zhentlemen—for that is what I a-shume you are—zhentlemen. You have heard, have you not, what the pro-p-prietor-ess said as we entered this fine eshtablishment? F-f'you got the money, you get th'honey! He-he-he!" Kyle and I joined in the moonshine-soaked laughter. Neither of us had noticed—until now—how much booze Martin had downed. Martin raised his hands solemnly to silence us. "Zhentlemen, please. That fine brown frame you see at the bar…well— *urp*—" belched Martin, "she is some of the honey on offer here. Right-'ere!" Martin used his left index finger to thump the table in making his point, while his right hand sloshed his drink. "Oops! He-he! Man, I had forgotten jush how pow'ful this stuff is. Been smokin' too much weed in California…" Martin frowned briefly and asked, "What was I saying?"

"You were saying the young lady over there is some of Marletta's 'honey'," chimed in Kyle.

"Thish is shrue," nodded Martin, "very shrue indeed. In fact, many a young man—black or white—for Marletta is not a rashist—has come through that door—" With his outstretched hand, Martin dramatically drew our attention to the door we had soberly entered not an hour before, "Many a young man has entered that door, only to leave behind shomething very important—very important indeed." Again Martin nodded at the veracity of his words.

Feeling my first ever stages of inebriation, I made the mistake of asking, "*What?*"

Looking aghast, and enjoying his ham performance, Martin placed both forearms on the table and gravely stared at me. "Sir—d'you mean to affront me? *What* indeed?!" Then, in silent film style action, Martin quickly looked left and right, before dropping low until his chin nearly rested on the table. "Your virzhinity, idiots! Are you fine shtrappin' shouthern boys tellin' me you walked in here with your virzhinity intact?"

Being too high to prevaricate or lie, I answered, "Well…uh—yeah. We didn't come here to get laid, just to get drunk." As with Martin's questioning regarding marijuana and acid earlier in the day, I thought I was in for a belittling from our worldly, older companion. But once more, Martin just laughed.

"Ha! Sho be it! Get drunk then!" Martin reached to the adjoining seat and brought up the jug of moonshine, gingerly pushing it to the middle of the table. "Here. Look after this. Now I am going to look for *mine…*"

"Your what?" asked Kyle.

"Virzhinity, my good man, my virzhinity. I left it here when I was about your age. It musht be around here somewhere. 'Scuse me."

Kyle and I looked at each other and just shook our heads with laughter. "This guy's a madman!" said Kyle.

"But he knows how to have fun!" I replied. We both turned to watch Martin, who was over at the bar talking with George and 'Honey.' From behind the bar, Marletta appeared with a plate of chittlins and fried chicken. She placed it on a table two along from ours and then turned and sashayed her way to Kyle and me. I felt my palms begin to sweat and my mouth suddenly went dry.

"Y'all enjoyin' Marletta's place?" We both just mutely nodded. Our huntress pursed her lips and made a slight frown. "Y'all just gonna sit there and *drink*? Ain't you gonna dance or eat or *some*thin'?" I meekly raised my hands and gave a quick shrug. Then she extended her hand to me and said, as much a command as an invitation, "C'mon, sugar. You gonna dance with Marletta." Glancing over her shoulder, she called to a young woman at the far end of the room, "Charlene, come dance with his friend!" My head was slightly spinning as I was led to the dance floor. Kyle and partner were right behind us. The musicians seemed to wait for Marletta's instructions, which weren't long in coming. "Somethin' sweet—and *slow*."

Before I could think, Marletta was leading me slowly around the floor. For the second time that evening, I started to sweat and could feel my face start to flush and my ears burn. Sensing my frustration and embarrassment, Marletta called out for someone to dim the lights on the dance floor. As the lights went down, I gulped heavily and breathed a sigh of relief. "What's your name, sugar?"

"J-Jon, it's…uh…Jon."

"So, J-Jon, what's got yo' white ass so uptight? And yo' face is so red you look like you're on fire! First time you ever been in a juke joint?"

I quickly nodded and stared over her head into the middle distance. But her interrogation wasn't finished, so Marletta took my chin between her right index finger and thumb and deliberately turned my face to look at her. "First time you ever been close to a *black wo-man, sug-gah*?" The deep brown irises of Marletta's eyes almost seemed to widen to the point that it felt as though I might be drawn in. I felt I had to look away, but Marletta was having none of it. Somewhere in my throat an inarticulate 'uh' was trying to form, but that same throat had turned into a labyrinth where thought could not unite with speech.

As I think back on that night, I know I responded to Marletta's question only a few seconds after she asked it, but in that same short space of time, my thoughts and emotions ran the gamut of excitement, fear, embarrassment, enticement, shame, and arousal. For a white, middle-class, God-fearing boy, dancing with Marletta that night was like dancing with a hybrid X-ray and lie-detector machine. For her part, living the life of a black, illicit-business woman in the American South—*in those days*—had made Marletta more self- and other-aware than most college-educated psychologists or social workers I would meet in later life—or at least until they had practiced for a dozen years or more. In short, Marletta was nothing short of a startling life-revelation for 17-year-old me.

"The answer to all of your questions is yes," I blurted—amazed both at the honesty and succinctness I had been able to muster.

"*I know*," came Marletta's surprisingly soft reply. "You too damn scared to be one of those white men comes here to 'dabble in the dark' and then go back and tell all his white friends" and here she put on a nasally white accent, "'the blacker the berry, the sweeter the juice' and all *that shit*." She shook her head at the very thought.

Involuntarily, I jerked my head around to look for Martin and Kyle. Martin was nowhere in sight, but Kyle was back at our table with Charlene. She was laughing and playing with his hair.

When we arrived back at our table, Marletta chirped at Kyle and Charlene. "Y'all make room for Jon here. I plumb tuckered him out."

I settled heavily into my chair and looked over at Kyle who was chuckling at me, while Charlene continued playing with his hair, with which she seemed truly fascinated. All I could do was raise my eyebrows, give him a wink and go, "Whew!"

As she started to leave, Marletta turned to me and said coyly, "Thanks for the dance, Jon. You're learning to *move*, baby." And then, more business-like, "Charlene, go over to the bar, honey, and fetch these young *men* some more colas." As she slinked out of her chair, Charlene gave Kyle's hair a twist, leaving him with a comical spike reminiscent of Alfalfa's in *The Little Rascals*. I started to laugh and pointed toward the top of his head. Kyle gingerly felt around until he found the object of my mirth. As he rarely combed it neatly, Kyle just tousled it to its normal, almost unkempt state.

I sloshed down the remaining drink in my glass, and shuddered as the white lightnin' hit and burned my gullet. "Man, Kyle," I gasped, "I can't believe this place!" Kyle and I continued to dig the music and chat with some of the regulars. As Kyle knew he had to get us all home, he drank more cola than booze, but in my blissful ignorance, I kept mixing my drinks half-and-half. Just when we began to wonder when or if we would see Martin again, he appeared through the same door as the earlier couple. Strands of Martin's long hair were matted to his forehead and he wore a dreamy smile. Jacqueline, his 'honey,' wore a lemon-chiffon, sun-back dress and looked like she belonged in the Supremes. She escorted Martin to our table, her skin looking darker than midnight in the bright yellow dress. And Martin—well, he was as drained of color as white can be. He fell into his chair much as I had done a short while before. Jacqueline kissed her fingertip and placed it on Martin's lips. Without a word she gave us all a little wave and walked away. Martin was more sober and less manic than when he had left us. "Man!" he beamed at us, "I have been transported! I feel like I'm floating." Comically, he checked to make sure gravity was still in control and he was still connected with the floor.

With Martin back at our table, the jug of moonshine kept getting passed around so that the three of us could refill our glasses—or so I thought. I later learned that only Martin and I did any drinking. Kyle told me he had more fun watching Martin and me make fools of ourselves. I do vaguely recall feeling terribly ill as we drove home. The nausea hit me when we were in the middle of a new subdivision of Lawrenceville, with lovely manicured lawns. Kyle had wanted to drive farther, so as to reduce the liability of my being caught heaving on someone's lawn or flowers. But my body's violent reaction to the alcohol wouldn't wait for a more convenient area, so I stumbled out of the car and proceeded to vomit on everything in sight. When it seemed there was nothing more to evacuate, I was later told I began howling at the moon, while running and crashing through people's small hedges and flower beds. As the most sober of the three of us, it was left to Kyle to chase me down and tackle me. We were fortunate in that, if anyone did hear or see us, no one called the police.

Once back to the car, Kyle and Martin placed my semi-conscious body on the back seat. Martin was dropped off first. Kyle knew he would not only have to help me to my house, but upstairs to my room as well. In any case, he knew he could also crash there and not worry about driving home. Kyle told me he tried to coast the Bonneville into our driveway so as not to disturb my parents, but he knew we were in for it when he saw not only the front porch light illuminated, but the living room light as well. I do have a grey image of Kyle bending over me, patting my face, calling my name and telling me to get up and try to walk. But I was totally blasted. Kyle recognized that he couldn't exactly leave me by the front walk and drive away quickly, so he did the only thing a pal could do. He hefted me out of the car's back seat and bore half of my weight as I schlepped toward the glow of our porch light.

How he managed my rubbery, near dead-weight is hard to imagine, but we were both young and fit then. Once we had made it to the front door, Kyle struggled to open the storm door without losing his grip on me at the same time. This involved a bit of bumping and banging. That done, Kyle said he hesitated as he reached for the doorknob. To his dismay, the door opened in front of him and there stood 'Blackie,' in his undershirt and boxer shorts. Dad and Kyle simply looked at one another. Before Kyle could open his mouth to excuse or explain our predicament, Dad wordlessly jerked his head to the left, indicating that Kyle should bring me in the house. After entering the threshold, Kyle said Dad slipped both of his arms under mine, removing my burdensome body from him. In recounting this momentous night, Kyle said that the shift from his to my father's arms, brought me around—ever so slightly—and that as my glassy eyes came into focus, I smiled sheepishly, and said: "Oh—hel-lo-o…Da-ad." Kyle swore that just for a brief moment he saw a smile crease my father's lips.

In any case, Kyle backed toward the door to make his exit. Before he could turn and leave, he said Dad, easily holding me up with one arm, reached out, took him by the shoulder and asked, with genuine concern, "You okay to drive?" Once more Kyle hesitated, so Dad again jerked his head—this time toward the kitchen.

I was placed in a chair placed sideways next to a wall. With the wall to one side of me and Kyle on the other, there was little chance I could fall and do myself any further harm than I had already done with the illegal whisky. Dad went to the coffee percolator and loaded it with rich-smelling ground caffeine. When the boiling water met the coffee grounds, the aroma, that heretofore in life had heralded mother's cooked breakfast, greeted me with the adverse effect of making me ill. I threw my hand over my mouth and Kyle helped me to the small toilet which was located just inside our back door.

And so, I made my first inebriate's call on the great white porcelain telephone. From what little I can recall, I was surprised to find anything left in my gut. My temples were throbbing and I found myself silently praying, as millions of sinners caught in their own webs had prayed before me, that I might be delivered from the suffering of my own devising. But that was not to be, for my father had other plans…a veritable purgatory in the form of hot black coffee. Leaning once more on Kyle, I shakily made my way back to the kitchen table where the first of many mugs of coffee awaited me. Whether from pity or amusement I will never know, but my father barely spoke to me that evening. Instead, he simply gazed at me as he handed me mug after mug of purgative.

My memory of events starts to return at about this point, no doubt burned into my brain cells by caffeine. On occasion, as I drank the bitter liquid, I was brave enough to lift my eyes toward my father, expecting a telling off or at least an 'evils of alcohol' lecture. But there was none of it. I remember being sick one more time, after which I wordlessly waved away any more coffee, which I have never liked since that day. I begged Dad just to let me go upstairs and die in peace, and he simply nodded. With Kyle on one side of me and Dad on the other, I was assisted to my bed where I fell, fully dressed, face down. Kyle took the other single bed in my room and was soon snoring. I envied him because my bed soon became a roller-coaster ride, fueled by the one-hundred octane mixture of alcohol and caffeine. When the room wasn't spinning, my head was, and so it went until complete and utter exhaustion overtook me. It might not have been sleep, as in the Bard's 'balm of hurt minds.' but at least I was unconscious.

Twelve

It is the nature of desire not to be satisfied, and most men live only for the gratification of it.

—Aristotle

The day after my first tangle with alcohol found me both subdued and repentant. After a late sleep-in, Kyle and I lay in our beds and chatted—in low tones—about my appearing drunk at the front door—in front of my father, no less. Having known nothing of alcohol's power, I knew nothing of moderation. Thus, I could only judge from my experience of excess. Just talking about it made me feel sick. Kyle's take on things, however, was slightly more phlegmatic, as he hadn't barfed his guts out. "You know, your old man was pretty cool. I don't know if my dad would have reacted the same way," he reflected.

"Yeah, I know. He surprised me as well. I wonder if he said anything to Mom?"

As though on cue, Mother called upstairs. "Boys? Are y'all awake? Kyle's mother needs her car to go shopping."

I called down and said we'd be ready in ten minutes. As I stood up, I felt a throb in both temples. I wobbled a bit as I tried to stand erect. Next, I shuffled to the bathroom where I turned on the shower to let the water warm up while I emptied my bladder. As soon as the water was ready, I stood, leaning against the wall with both hands, as I let the water gush over my head and face. I even found myself wondering whether this was the way people felt when they were fully immersed and were washed of their sins. I decided I had better not mention this thought to Wendy.

To avoid my mother's curiosity, I said I would ride with Kyle back to his house to return the car and that we would eat breakfast there. Along the way, we both re-played the previous night's events, laughing at our initiation into the world of whisky and wild women.

~ * ~

I ran into Martin again when I cut his parents' lawn the following week. As was his mother's custom, I usually received a glass of ice-cold lemonade or tea half-way through the job. On this occasion, however, it was Martin who brought it to me—Mrs. Taylor's refreshing, home-made lemonade.

"Hey, man! How's it going?" he said as I switched off the mower. He proffered the glass and added slyly, "Sorry, but there's no booze in it."

I accepted the glass and replied, "No problem! I don't think I'll drink so much the next time. It took me two days to get over that moonshine." I rubbed the chilled glass over my sweaty brow, enjoying the sensation on that hot, Carolina day.

"Yeah, that booze at Marletta's—whew!" He whistled softly, "It's the real deal."

"Yeah," I mused, "so was Marletta."

"No way! Did you get it off with Marletta?!"

"Well…I…um..." Despite my tanned and sun-flushed face in the heat of the day, I could still feel myself blush.

"Ha! You horny dog! Marletta's hot, isn't she? And she won't give it to just anyone." Martin slapped me on the shoulder.

Realizing that Martin thought I had got laid and, enjoying the approbation of my older comrade in debauchery, I decided not to disabuse him of his false assumption. It was nice to be able to look this world-wise hippy in the eye. As I finished the lemonade, Martin pulled a thoughtful look, rubbed his chin with his right hand, and asked, "Say, Braddock—have you read any Kerouac?"

"Who?"

"Kerouac. Jack Kerouac, one of the Big Beats. *On the Road*? *The Dharma Bums*?"

I shook my head.

"Well, man, we gotta fix that! I think you'll find a true companion in Kerouac." Martin took the empty glass from me. "Pop in the house when you're finished, okay? I'll fix you up with a book or two of his."

Twenty minutes later, I was sitting on the screened porch at the rear of the Taylors' house being given a primer in the Beat writers. Martin felt I should read *On the Road* and *The Dharma Bums*, as these two were his favorites. I hadn't a clue what 'dharma' was and decided not to show my further ignorance, which Martin was so keen to remedy. "But," he said with an air of defeat, "after ransacking my room, I could only find one of them. Still, it is *the* classic: *On the Road.*" He passed the book to me with reverence. "And dig this, one of the main characters—he's called Dean Moriarty in the book—well, he's actually a guy named Neal Cassady. Well, that is, *he was*. Sadly he died a little while ago. I met him a couple of times around 'Frisco. He hung out with Kesey and his crowd, and he was one way-out dude." Martin smiled with his eyes and shook his head at some mental image. "Oh—I also found this battered copy of *Lonesome Traveler*. It's interesting, but nothing to compare with *On the Road* or *Dharma Bums.*"

I accepted both paperbacks with genuine gratitude and interest; after all, the lucky find of *Cuckoo's Nest* had certainly been a mind-opener. "Thanks, Martin. I'll get these back to you as soon as I've finished them."

Martin pushed both open palms toward me. "No, man, they're a gift. I'm heading back to 'Frisco tomorrow, so we'll talk more about

Kerouac next time I see you. I'll want to know what you thought of him."

"It's a deal," I said, as I made my way out of the door.

"And—hey!" Martin looked over his shoulder to see whether his parents were in earshot. "Don't forget you're welcome at Marletta's anytime. You don't need me to get in there!"

"Thanks for letting me know." As I placed the two paperbacks in the small bag which hung from my bike's handlebars, I smiled to myself as I once more recalled that night at Marletta's. I had noticed that, as the effects of my first hangover receded into memory, so the pleasures of that evening emerged into high relief and beckoned to me.

Seeing what he thought was a self-satisfied smile, Martin once again gave me a slap on the shoulder and said, "You horny dog! Well, say 'hcy' to Marletta for me the next time you see her. Take care, Braddock."

"Will do. You, too." I mounted the bike and headed off to my next job.

~ * ~

That evening, I carried my two new "friends" upstairs with an anticipation I would later experience when escorting my college girlfriend into my dorm room—the new, the untested and untasted and untried. Following Martin's suggestion, I started with *On the Road*. It wasn't long before I was mesmerized by the free-wheeling lifestyle described by Kerouac. He actually made adulthood look *fun*. That was nothing short of a revelation. I took a look at the publication date: 1955. Then I turned to the back page where there a few brief words about the author. "Christ!" I mumbled to myself, "He's the same age as my father!"

I laid the book on my lap to cast this thought around in my mind. I tried to picture my father smoking dope and hanging out with poets and beatniks or stealing a car when he fancied going somewhere. It didn't take long for that picture to dissolve. But then it hit me: except for an accident of birth, my father could well have been a Sal Paradise or Dean Moriarty. But once I started tracking on my theoretical family tree and realized that my mother would not have married one of

Kerouac's characters, I gave up my musing and went back to enjoying the story.

And so, an inner alchemy began its work, its catalyst being no more than printed words on the pages of cheap paperbacks—but what words! Having grown up in a Christian family, which took its faith as a simple given, I had never had the opportunity to experience the power of conversion. But words, mundanely used by most of my teachers and the authors of school books, in the hands of people like Kesey and Kerouac had the power of *metanoia*, a fundamental change of mindset. What I discovered was, in effect, a parallel world, inhabited by people not so very different from me or those I knew. But the way they spoke and behaved was outrageously refreshing and honest.

~ * ~

How do you tell your white, Southern Baptist girlfriend that you got drunk in a juke joint in the black part of town and danced with a sensuous woman? Answer: you don't. But your hormones do look for ways to explore further that taste of carnal pleasure. And so began the "battle of the bra" in earnest. Whenever Wendy and I had the good fortune to be alone, we would fall into one another's embrace. Clearly Wendy was as swept away by our passion as I was, but she had two braking mechanisms that I did not possess: first, she was the only one of us who could get pregnant, and second, her superego was inhabited by a hell and damnation harridan in the form of her mother. As for the former, I was not sexually precocious, but was subject both to my innate shyness and the constraints of my moral upbringing. As for the latter, Mrs. Sullivan was herself the perfect form of prophylaxis, as who in his right mind would have wanted to risk having her as a mother-in-law? She was a living, breathing passion-killer, if ever there was one.

I had heard the term manic-depressive mentioned once in relation to Mrs. Sullivan by a friend of their family. I hadn't a clue what it meant, although I did have an inkling about the depressive part. So I dived into the encyclopedias Mom had bought for Ron and me. Clinical depression certainly fitted Mrs. Sullivan's personality, but what I failed to observe in her was any sign of manic. Whenever I was at their house, Mrs. Sullivan hardly ever left the kitchen, although I had long noticed that it was Wendy's father who usually cooked their evening meals, after he got home from work. In my effervescent teen outlook, I tended to view her simply as a mean-spirited and bigoted fundamentalist. But maybe there was something more. I knew nothing of psychiatry—and sometimes, I knew little of myself.

This had been unwittingly underscored by my father, who, after Wendy and I had been dating for a couple of months, took it upon himself to dole out some worldly wisdom to his shy and bookish son, a rare occurrence in my early years. He took me aside one evening, after I had been on the phone with Wendy. "Son, do you really like this girl?" I nodded sheepishly. "Well, just remember one thing: before you ever decide to marry a girl, make sure you meet and get a good look at her mother because that will be a good indicator of what she'll look like in twenty or thirty years."

Dubiously thankful, I replied, "Okay, Dad. Thanks."

As this was the first time I had heard such advice, I wrongly assumed it was a gem discovered by my father along life's way. I had no way of knowing just how trite a truism it was. After all, no one ever said to look at a girl's father to see what she might become, and his DNA was just as much a part of her. But my father's advice did have the effect of arousing in me the awareness that traits found in one generation might well appear in the next. Although not physically ugly, Mrs. Sullivan had, to my opinion, an ugly personality, that of a foul-tempered, joy-killing crone. Thus, I secretly harbored worries about Wendy's becoming like her mother. After all, something had once attracted Earl Sullivan to the woman who became his wife and mother of his children. Could the same metamorphosis happen to his daughter Wendy? It didn't bear thinking about. Thus, marriage had the appearance of a life-sentence without possibility of parole. I, of course, never ventured to voice any of this to Wendy because I always hoped our sexual explorations would somehow go further, my ineptitude and naiveté notwithstanding.

Occasionally, when I could get my mother's car, Wendy and I would drive up to the Blue Ridge Parkway. Like many others our age, we'd find a quiet overlook and park. We'd usually get to the stage where Wendy's bra was unfastened and I had a growing bulge in my jeans onto which I would try to push Wendy's hand, at which point Wendy would call a halt to our proceedings. As I was a young gentleman—albeit horny and frustrated—I would retreat to my side of the front seat. Wendy would protest her desire to go further, but then add the proviso that this would have to wait until we were married; we both had to be patient. And for Wendy, who had it all figured out, our marriage would take place after our sophomore year in college. It never occurred to me to ask *why then*? Why not when I had graduated from high school or from college? In retrospect, I suppose Wendy thought that midway through my college education was just close enough in time so as not to seem as good as never. Thus, sex became something of a Holy Grail for which I must earnestly search and endeavor. But the catch was always the same: marriage.

Thirteen

Death is a fearful thing...to die, and go we know not where.
—Shakespeare

A few weeks before the start of our senior year in high school, a small group of us rising seniors at Lawrenceville High decided to have a pre-school party. It was going to be a fairly tame affair: five or six dating couples gathering in someone's basement to play records, dance, make out, eat snacks, and drink sodas, which promised to be spiked with pilfered parental booze (although I kept this latter information from Wendy). The party was meant to start about 7:30, so I thought I would "splash out" with my meager earnings from mowing lawns and take Wendy to a new pizza parlor down in Winston-Salem beforehand. We planned to pick up Kyle and Jean on our way back to the party.

When I got to Wendy's house late that afternoon, her father's car was not in the driveway, so it was Mrs. Sullivan who met me at the door. Normally, she would take one look at me and then walk away from the door, usually to the kitchen, which had become her lair. But on this particular day, she simply stood in the doorway for a moment or two, while seemingly looking through me or past me. As I pulled upon the outer storm door, she started and said, "Oh!" as though she had been unexpectedly caught doing something of which she was ashamed. Mrs. Sullivan stepped back from the door and muttered, "I expect you'd better come in." At that she turned and made her way to the kitchen.

I sat in the front room and waited, hoping Wendy knew I was there. It wasn't long before she popped her head around the doorway, still brushing her thick brown hair, and said, "Hey, Jon! I won't keep you a minute."

No sooner had Wendy disappeared than her younger brother, Tommy, entered the room, dressed in his Little League uniform. Without any ado, he asked, "Where're y'all going tonight?"

"Down to Winston for a pizza. Why?"

"I was just wondering if y'all could drop me by the ball park on your way out. Mama says Daddy's working out of town today and won't be back till a little later on." Then his voice dropped. "I…I don't think Mama's going to feel like driving me today. Hopefully Daddy'll be back in time to come get me."

"Yeah, sure. Wendy and I can do that. Just make sure your mother knows, okay?"

Tommy smiled and nodded, then quickly disappeared around the corner to tell his mother and Wendy the plan. When both Wendy and Tommy were ready, I turned toward the front door. I had long ago given up trying to exchange pleasantries with Mrs. Sullivan. Wendy stood in the hallway and called to her mother, "Mama, we're going now. Okay?"

"All right," came the hollow reply. Wendy looked at me, rolled her eyes, and we set off. After leaving Tommy at the ball park, we turned up the car radio, rolled down all of the windows, and let the warm air rush over us as we drove the twenty-plus miles to Winston-Salem. The intense summer heat had brought out the smell of pine trees and ripening tobacco from the surrounding countryside.

Going out to eat was still novel for us and, having only lived in small, southern towns, pizza was about as exotic as it got in those days.

In my family, "eating out" usually meant going to the homes of their friends, colleagues or relatives. On road trips, we normally stopped at family roadside cafés where we sat in booths or the occasional drive-in where we ate in the car. So taking Wendy to a pizza parlor where we actually sat at tables and had waiters was "high cotton." In any case, it was soon time to drive back to Lawrenceville to meet Kyle and Jean.

However, as we drove into Lawrenceville, along the road near Wendy's neighborhood, we saw a dejected Tommy walking toward home. At Wendy's urging, I pulled up next to him. Wendy leaned out the window and asked her brother why he was walking.

"'Cause nobody came for me, *that's why*," came his petulant reply.

"Daddy didn't come for you?" asked Wendy, though the answer was obvious.

"Does it look like it?" Tommy was near to tears.

"Well, get in the car. We'll take you home." Wendy turned toward me, gave a quizzical look and a shrug. I answered with similar non-verbal signals and waited for Tommy to get settled in the car before driving off.

"So tell me what happened," solicited Wendy. And in that instant, she sounded more like Tommy's mother than his older sister.

"Well, after my game was over, I just waited for Dad—or Mom— to come get me. Coach Jarrett had practice scheduled for some older guys, so he had to get on with things. But after a while, Mr. Jarrett saw me still standing there and waiting, so he came over and asked me if I wanted some money to use in the telephone booth and call home. So I took the money and called—"

Starting to show concern, Wendy cut in, "Did Mama answer? What did she say?"

"No. That's just the point: *nobody answered*. And because there were the older kids waiting to continue their practice, I just had to walk home." Tommy stifled a sob. "Mr. Jarrett said he was awfully sorry, but there was nothing he could do. He thought Mama or Daddy would probably be on their way to get me and would meet me before I walked too far. Ha!" In the rearview mirror, I could see Tommy's lower lip tremble as he stared out the window.

"Tommy, I'm sorry," responded Wendy. "It's a good thing Jon and I were coming along here when we did." And then, more to me than to her brother, "I hope nothing's wrong."

"Well, we're not far now," I offered, "so we'll soon see." Within another two minutes, we were in front of the Sullivans' house. The little car that Mrs. Sullivan rarely drove was in the driveway. Before I had fully engaged the handbrake, Wendy had hopped from the car and was quickly walking to her front door. I followed behind with Tommy.

When Wendy attempted to open the storm door, it was locked. "That's weird. We never lock the storm door." Before I could respond, Wendy ran past the garage around to the back door. It, too, was locked. "Tommy—have you got a key?"

Tommy gave Wendy an impatient look and asked, "Since when do I ever need a key? Mama's always here, you know that."

"Maybe she had to go out and left a note. You look back here and I'll go to the front." I was already on my way before I finished speaking.

"But why is Mama's car here if she had to go out?" came Tommy's plaintive reply, as I rounded the front of the house. There was no note. I ran back to Wendy and Tommy. We all scanned each other's faces, trying to make meaning of the situation.

I began to have a sinking feeling, although I wasn't sure why, so I concocted a plan to get Tommy away from the house for a few minutes. "Tommy—uh, look—why don't you go check with your neighbors on either side, see if your mother's next door or told them anything. Okay?"

Tommy simply nodded and set off. Keeping my voice low, I moved close to Wendy. "Both doors locked from the inside?" She bit her lower lip and just nodded. "Okay. Then we've got to find some way to get in."

We began to check all of the windows, but they were latched, all except one window in her parents' bedroom, which had an air-conditioning unit. It was held in place from above by the lower sash window, and it was supported from below by a two-by-four. Our only hope was to push the unit inside the house and for me to climb in through the window. But to push a fifty- or sixty-pound air-conditioner in through the window was bound to do some damage when it fell, both to the floor and to the unit. I checked once more with Wendy before proceeding.

She looked toward the house next door where Tommy had gone, and then looked back at me with determination. "Something's wrong, Jon."

"Okay. Here we go." I placed my left shoulder under the air-conditioner, which released the weight off the two-by-four. With my right arm, I shoved the lower sash window open. Wendy took the freed plank of wood and pushed with me against the heavy unit. It dropped through the window with a heavy thud. I hefted myself up on my arms, ducked under the upper window, lay across the sill, placed my hands on the toppled air-conditioner and managed to do a head-first roll over it onto the bedroom floor. Just for a moment, I thought about how stupid I would look if either of Wendy's parents were actually in the house. "Oh—hello, Mrs. Sullivan…I just thought I'd uh…." Yeah. Right.

I got up, called to Wendy to meet me at the back door, and cautiously made my way through the house. What if Mrs. Sullivan had flipped and was waiting with a gun? All sorts of scenarios were running through my head. Just to be safe, I called her name a few times. When I got to the small utility room by the back door, the key was in the lock. I turned the key and opened the door and then unlatched the storm door. Wendy was inside in a flash. She stood for a moment looking left and right.

"Your mother's not in her bedroom or the hallway." I indicated behind me. Wendy darted toward the kitchen. I followed, half-expecting to hear a cry before I got there. But nothing came. I began to feel some measure of relief. Wendy then opened the door which led from the kitchen into the garage. It was dark and sweltering from the trapped heat of the day. We both paused in the doorway for a moment, peering into the inky blackness, but seeing nothing. I felt along the wall for the light switch and flicked it. Again, no Mrs. Sullivan. Needing to say something in the midst of our clueless search, I blurted out, "It doesn't look like she's here."

Wendy, arms folded tightly across her chest, just muttered, "Hmm," and headed for the hallway. Next, we checked the living room, bathroom, and Tommy's room. Lastly, we arrived at Wendy's bedroom door, which was standing ajar. Wendy looked at me; her eyes invited me to go in first. I took one cautious step forward. What did I expect? I had no idea. My eyes navigated the room: the bed, desk, and dresser. Nothing seemed disturbed or out of place. I entered the room fully and checked the far side of the bed. Once more, nothing.

As I turned to speak to Wendy, who remained just outside the room, my eyes caught something unusual by the closet door: a shoe, on its heel and with the toe pointing upwards. For reasons I couldn't have explained, all of a sudden, my breathing seemed labored and my heart was pounding. "Hang on," I said to Wendy, who had already taken note of my alertness and grasped the door-frame. "Let me just check something."

I walked around the bed to the closet, keeping my eyes on the shoe. As I opened the closet door, an arm slipped to the floor. "Oh my God!" burst from my mouth as I jumped back and followed the arm to its owner. I was greeted by a bluish-white, marbled face, peering through plastic clothing bags. It belonged to Wendy's mother. She was slumped back against the clothes in Wendy's closet. The cyanotic lips formed a near-perfect O and the eyes, which had never really looked at or seen me, stared blankly at nothing. The face was made more grotesque by the plastic bags twisted around and knotted at the neck.

"What is it?!" cried Wendy, as she came up behind me. I started to turn toward Wendy—to what? Shield her? Protect her? Whatever I intended, it was too late. I was rooted to the spot in shock. Wendy then uttered a sound that I cannot express in words, but the sound of which I can never get out of my head. She then began to retch.

Not knowing what else to do, I helped Wendy sit down on her bed. Her retching soon became hyperventilation. At last, there was something I could do. A boy in our Scout troop had been prone to hyperventilation, so we had all been instructed in how to help him. No brown paper bags being at hand, I grabbed a floppy, felt hat Wendy wore on our country walks or picnics. As I urged her to breathe slowly and deeply into the hat, it struck me that we didn't even know whether Mrs. Sullivan was alive or dead. I took Wendy by the shoulders and said, "I need to check your mother. Okay?" With panicked eyes, she quickly nodded assent.

I spun from my crouching position in front of Wendy to my hands and knees as I moved the short distance to the closet door. Relying on my rudimentary first aid from Scouts and a lifetime of watching television, my fingers sought to find a pulse on the extended wrist. There was none that I could detect. Knowing that a faint pulse would be easier to find on the neck, I forced myself to look toward Mrs. Sullivan's face. Whatever she had hoped to escape in this life, her countenance now bore the mute terror of the face in Munch's *The Scream*. The seal, formed by the filmy plastic bags, around the mouth and nostrils told me my efforts were in vain. I had tried to keep as much of the door between Mrs. Sullivan's lifeless body and Wendy. As I sat back on my heels, I looked around the door at Wendy and shook my head. Tears began to pour from her eyes as Wendy wailed, "Oh—Mama!"

At the same instant, I heard Tommy shouting from the back door. "Wendy? Jon? Where are y'all? What's going on?"

Galvanized by Tommy's voice—I had nearly forgotten about him—I scrambled to my feet. I whispered to Wendy, "We can't let Tommy back here. He mustn't see this!" I shouted, perhaps too loudly, "Stay there!"

Until that moment, death had always been the stuff of funeral parlors, my relatives looking like benign, waxy replicas of themselves. But this—this was death in the raw, unadulterated by the machinations of human fear and interventions. Tommy didn't need this etched into his brain as the last image of his mother. I sprinted to the back door, where Tommy was hovering, halted by the emotion in my voice. As I approached him, Tommy's eyes seemed to study every aspect of my face. I knew I had to keep cool.

"Jon? What is it? Is Mama…?"

"Tommy, something's wrong with your mother." Tommy looked past me toward the hallway. I gently took his upper arms in my hands.

"Wendy is with your mother, okay? Tommy?" I gave him a soft shake and his eyes returned to mine. "Here's what I need you to do. Please go next door to whichever neighbor you know the best, and ask them to ring for an ambulance." Tommy gasped. "Listen: ask them to ring for an ambulance, okay? And then ask them if you can stay there with them until it arrives. Got that?" Tommy mutely nodded. "It's important that you wait with your neighbors, okay?" Terror had marked a path across the thirteen-year-old's face, but he complied and let me usher him to the door. Once he was out, I decided to latch it; I couldn't risk his returning.

I made my way back to Wendy's bedroom and found her sitting, statue-like, on the bed, her hands clamped beneath her knees and tear tracks down her face. Bubbles of saliva had formed on her lips as she burbled, "M-mama…w-w-why did y-you…do th-this?"

I sat down on the bed beside Wendy and put my arm around her. I leaned my head against hers and took one of her hands in mine. Wendy turned and crushed her face into my chest, her fists absent-mindedly beating my chest. "Oh, Jon! How could she do this?!"

"I don't know…I-I just don't know," was all I could respond.

What else could I have said? We were both seventeen and, to this point in time, had been happy. Not depressed like Mrs. Sullivan had been. Life seemed to stretch out interminably ahead of us as something to be grasped, savored, enjoyed, not to be squandered in some desperate and secretive way. My nose and mouth were pressed against the top of Wendy's head as I held her. Her hair smelled of summer and of life— so incongruous in this macabre setting.

"Let's get out of here. There's nothing to be done, and it's no good looking at your mother like…like this."

Wendy mumbled, "Okay," and we slowly walked toward the living room, arms wrapped around one another.

~ * ~

There are times in life when having grown up with a Marine has come in very handy, and more often than not, those times have been a surprise to me. Such a time was in the moments following the arrival of the ambulance. The siren ensured that nearly every house on Wendy's street had at least one spectator on the front porch. Some neighbors had started to gather in the front yard. The fact that they lived within proximity to whatever tragedy had occurred seemed to have endowed them with the inalienable right to interfere. I stepped out onto the front steps and firmly asked them to back off and allow the paramedics a way through. They seemed reluctant at first, as I was a complete stranger to most of them, so I bellowed, "Please move!" They did.

Once the paramedics were inside, the door was locked behind them. And then, not long after their arrival, Tommy returned home and called to us from the back door. When Wendy and I met him, the next-door neighbors were there as well. This was becoming quite a community affair. I opened the door only partially and let Tommy in—after all, it was his house and his family disaster. But when the couple from next door started to follow, I said, "Sorry, but there's nothing you can do here, not right now," and went to close the door.

The husband took umbrage at being excluded and placed his hand against the door, "Hell, son, *we live next door.*"

To his amazement—and mine—I shouldered the door closed, and, as I turned the lock, said, "Then that's a good place to wait, sir." He started to mouth something at me, but I had already walked away from the door. Wendy had led her brother into the living room in order to break the news. As I went to join them, one of the paramedics came out from Wendy's bedroom and took me aside.

"Y'all find her like this?" I nodded.

"Okay…well…and I hope you'll understand, but we're gonna need to ring the police as well." Seeing the puzzlement on my face, he laid his arm on my shoulder and said, "Don't worry; it's nothing to do with you. It's just something the law requires when a…fatality occurs, for whatever reasons."

"Okay…uh…yeah. The phone's over there."

The next thing I heard was the front door opening—it was Wendy's father. Although people had followed him to the front door steps, Mr. Sullivan had had the good sense to ask them to wait outside. Once in the doorway, he looked at his two children sitting on the sofa, with tear-stained faces, and then at me, standing in the archway into the hall. "Wendy?

Tommy? What's going on? Where's your mother?" Both Wendy and Tommy started to cry. Earl Sullivan looked at me. "Jon?"

"Mr. Sullivan?" I began, "There's been…uh…well, there's been…" I gave up on words and simply motioned down the hallway. At the same moment, the paramedic who had rung the police saw Mr. Sullivan and motioned for him to come into the hallway. I took that as my cue to rejoin Wendy.

We three sat on the sofa with our arms around each other. Out in the hallway, I heard mumbled voices and then, "Oh, my Lord! Oh, oh, my Lord!" from Mr. Sullivan.

As if all of this weren't enough, the telephone started ringing and, as I was the only one not in tears, I told Wendy I would answer it. My head was starting to spin. What I wasn't prepared for was my mother's voice at the other end.

"Jon? Are you all right?"

"Mom…what...how did you know?"

"Know what, dear? Is everything all right? Kyle's been ringing and wondering when you were going to pick him up. He and Jean are waiting at his house. What's going on? Jon?"

The spinning in my head intensified. In the midst of such morbid chaos, I couldn't think of anything to say to my mother other than, "I'll ring Kyle," and I put the phone down. Numbly, I sat back down and held Wendy's hands.

Sometime between ten and eleven p.m., an exhausted Earl Sullivan came to tell me and Wendy that he and his children were going to spend the next few nights at his brother's place over near Pilot Mountain. He asked Wendy to grab whatever she needed; they would be leaving in ten minutes.

I took this as my cue to ring Kyle and ask if I could stay the night at his house. I told him in as few words as possible what had transpired that evening. I also asked Kyle to do me the favor of calling my parents to tell them where I would be and anything else he wanted to share so they wouldn't worry about me. Kyle came up trumps. "Sure. Yeah. Anything you need. I'll wait up for you and let Mom and Dad know. The back door will be open."

~ * ~

My dream-life has always been vivid; thus, I can sometimes awaken more tired than when I went to bed. Such was the night—or what was left of it—of Mrs. Sullivan's suicide.

At one point, I woke up shouting, "Give me some air! I can't breathe!" A pillow hit me and I woke up.

From his bed, Kyle dozily said, "Hey, buddy. You were having a bad dream. You okay now?"

"Yeah, I guess. I dreamt I was suffocating…or drowning…or something. I—uh…couldn't breathe."

Barely half-awake, Kyle asked, "You wanna talk...or go downstairs and get some food or something?"

"Nah—I'll be okay…I think. I'll just try to get back to sleep."

"Okay." Kyle was sound asleep again within seconds. I listened to his easy breathing. It was good to know he was there and that I had a best friend. The slow, regular pattern of Kyle's breath soon brought me under its power and I had a sleep—of sorts.

Late the following morning, Wendy called me from her uncle's place. Mrs. Weston let me take the call in the den so I could have some privacy. It wasn't so much a conversation as a word-spill, venting all of the mixed emotions Wendy was feeling, ranging from intense grief that her mother was dead, to intense anger that her mother should have used her elder child's bedroom to kill herself. And there was so much in between. I tried to assure Wendy that the choice of her bedroom was more a dig at me and Wendy's choice of me as her boyfriend as it was anything to do with her. I didn't say it just to make Wendy feel better; I actually believed it. Mrs. Sullivan had never cared for me, and somehow, even at that young age, I was fully cognizant of the fact that not just I, but no boyfriend would ever have been found suitable, because happiness had no place in Mrs. Sullivan's life, not even for her offspring. Wendy told me that they would be returning from her uncle's the next day. In a voice as full of angst as I was ever likely to hear, Wendy ended by saying, "Jon—I love you." Yet the words sounded more like the shout of a drowning person calling for a life-preserver. And with that, something changed.

"I love you, too, Wendy," I replied, but the words seemed to cleave to the roof of my mouth. I had somewhere crossed over the invisible boundary between the world of innocence and the world of experience. The love between girl- and boyfriend, a love that had seemed so simple barely twenty-four hours previously, was now an unknown territory I would somehow have to navigate.

As I came off the phone, the grandfather clock in the Weston's den told me that Wendy and I had been on the phone for nearly an hour. My right ear felt as though it had been ironed. My ear, hand, and the receiver were all coated with perspiration. I wiped them as best I could on my T-shirt and made my way into the hallway from where I could hear Kyle and his mother talking in the kitchen. Having slept through breakfast, Mrs. Weston kindly called to me to ask whether I would like to join her and Kyle in a bite of lunch. As my last meal had been nearly eighteen hours before, I suddenly realized I was famished. Even simple bodily functions like eating took on a profound significance for me, as so much had changed since the simple sharing of a pizza with Wendy the night before—and since pushing myself through the window into her house. I might as well have fallen down a rabbit hole into my own bizarre Wonderland.

Foundering under the weight of my thoughts and feelings, I didn't sit so much as drop heavily onto the kitchen chair, surprising even myself. Mrs. Weston just gave me a warm and placid look as she pushed a plate of cold-cuts toward me and gently said, "Time you had something to eat." Happily, Ellen Weston was "cool" by teenage standards. She didn't flatter herself that she was still young enough to relate to teens like Kyle and me, on their level, neither did she foist her maturity onto us. She took us as we were and didn't begrudge us our damn-fool teenaged years. Although she occasionally smiled to herself at Kyle's and my antics and our ways of speaking, the smile was not one of condescension. Her smile never said, "You'll learn," or anything of the knowing adult. Like many of those who had lived through the privations of the Great Depression and the war years, she knew how quickly youth's innocence could be swept away. In fact, it was not until I became a father that I understood the nature of Ellen Weston's smile.

After lunch, Kyle and I went back upstairs to his room, but I was too restless to sit down. I paced the room, pounding my right fist into my left hand. "Let's go…somewhere!"

"Where?"

"I don't know—let's just go." I continued my pacing and then blurted out, "Maybe the Smokies? We could hike the Appalachian Trail for a few days and…just get away…" I waved my hands around me as though trying to clear smoke from the room, "…from all of this! Whaddaya say?" I reached out and shook Kyle gently by the shoulder.

"Sure. I'm game. But how're we going to get there? Will your mother lend you her car? Or will someone have to drive us?"

I shook my head. "Mom won't lend us her car, and there's no one to drive us." But for me, the urge to go was too strong to be deterred by things like lack of transportation or even parental permission. "We could hitch-hike! Pick up the Trail off I-40, at Davenport Gap. The Trail crosses I-40!" I announced triumphantly. I stopped my pacing and looked at Kyle. "I've gotta do this. Will you go with me?"

I am certain that part of this desire to go was fueled by the Kerouac I had recently ingested at Martin's behest. Perhaps I thought a road trip would transform me or somehow cleanse me; perhaps it would help me forget what was now fixed in my mind's eye—I didn't know and couldn't have said, but I was anxious to move, to get on the road—*my road*.

"Um…yeah—why not?! When do we leave?"

"Wendy's coming back tomorrow…and then I guess there's the funeral…maybe a couple of days? Okay?"

"Fine. Anyway, we need time to buy food and pack our gear. But, Jon, what if our parents won't let us hitch-hike? What then?"

"Well, when we speak to my parents, we could…um…make it sound like one of your parents is driving us and vice versa! By the time they find out, we'll be gone."

Kyle gave it a moment's thought and then said, "Okay. Fine. Why not?!"

With that settled, I headed home for what seemed the first time in a very long time. But as I drove past our church, I decided to stop and see whether Rev. McLaurin had a few minutes to talk. As I pulled into the parking lot, he was walking out of the building. He saw me and gave a little wave. I parked the car and went over to where he was waiting for me beneath a huge oak, shaded from the baking sun. "Jon! I'm glad to see you. Your mother called to tell me what happened last night. Terrible! It's absolutely terrible! How are you? And perhaps more to the point, how is Wendy?"

"She's okay. Well, she's as okay as anyone could be in that situation, I guess. Wendy went with her dad and brother over to Pilot Mountain to stay with her uncle. I spoke with her on the phone today. She—uh—she's coming back tomorrow. I'll see her then."

"Jon, as you can see, I'm just on my way out—to see a church member who's in the hospital. But listen…" he placed both of his hands on my shoulders and squeezed, leaning his head forward and drawing my attention to his eyes. "What Mrs. Sullivan did…" he let out a deep sigh and shook his head in disbelief, "Jon, that's just the damnedest thing for a parent to do to a child. I just don't have the words to express how despicable it was to do a thing like that. It's the biggest guilt trip anyone could dump on another human being."

"Yeah, I know. I still can't believe it. Wendy's really messed up over it."

"And that's to be expected. Well, do what you can to support her, and keep letting her know it wasn't her fault. That lies solely with her mother, okay?"

"Okay. I'll try. Thanks."

Rev. McLaurin dropped his hands and started to move toward his car. "Okay, son, I have to go now, but come see me tomorrow or whenever you can, all right?"

"Yeah…okay…except…well, I might be going away. I mean, I probably *am* going away. Kyle's going with me. We're going to spend some time on the Appalachian Trail. I just need to get away from things. But I'll try to stop by before I leave."

McLaurin paused for a moment and seemed to consider my words. He pursed his lips, nodded to himself and said, "You'll know best what you need to do. If not before you leave, then come see me when you're back, okay?"

"I will. Bye." We both got into our cars and drove our separate ways.

~ * ~

Mother was sitting in a rocking chair inside the screened porch when I got home, obviously on the lookout for my return. She had an open book on her lap, but it was missing the decorative bookmark she normally used, so it was obvious, even to me at that time, that she had only absent-mindedly flipped through the pages. Within moments of stepping across the threshold, I was informed that Mrs. Weston had called and given Mom what little information she had about the previous night's events, thus her call to Rev. McLaurin. Clearly Mom was concerned for me and my state of mind because I had taken no more than three steps inside the screen door than she started asking too many questions. In the briefest of pauses, she called to my father, who was out back working on his old Chevy, to tell him I was home.

Dad downed his tools and made his way to the porch. At first, I feared that my father might give me some sort of interrogation about Mrs. Sullivan's suicide, but to my amazement, he was very much in the same vein as the night I came home drunk. In fact, compared to Mother, he was downright placid, so much so that, when Mother began her line of anxious questioning again, Dad spoke up: "Rachel— honey—that's enough. Can't you see this isn't going to help Jon one little bit? Why don't you go fix Jon and me a nice cool drink?"

Wringing her hands, Mother looked from me to Dad and said, "Well…if you're sure."

"Jon and I are fine." Dad gently patted her shoulder as a way of ushering her into the house. My father settled himself on the glider and gently rocked back and forth. It could have been a day like any other— except it wasn't. On any other day, my father and I wouldn't have been sitting there together and I wouldn't be trying to wipe my memory clear of Mrs. Sullivan's death mask. I could hear my mother rattling around in the kitchen.

"That must have been one helluva shock, son, what you walked into last night." Dad's voice was even and unusually soothing. His eyes almost seemed to be studying me as though for the first time.

"Yes, sir, it was. A real nightmare…except…it was no dream."

Dad nodded thoughtfully and said, very tentatively, "The first time you see death—I mean, *really see death*—it feels as though it is looking at you, like it could reach out and claim you for its own." My father's words reached somewhere inside me, at my life's core, where the recognition of our own mortality quietly resides until awakened by one of life's signal events.

Without meaning to at that moment, I blurted out, "Dad, I gotta go away for a while. Kyle and I are thinking maybe we'll head up to the Appalachian Trail for a few days, you know, just get away from it all. I'll cut all the neighbors' grass before we leave, I promise." I was looking at my father in earnest. And although I was trying to coax him to give his permission, my entreaties were nevertheless in earnest.

Dad was always a man of few words, and never more so than at moments of deep or raw emotion. I felt his right hand grip my left shoulder, firmly and tenderly at the same time. It was as close as he could come to saying "I love you" at that point in our lives. His eyes still fixed on mine, Dad simply gave me a little shake and said, "Just clear it with your mother as well, okay? I'll be up and off before five tomorrow morning. I'll be gone two days."

"I will…*and Dad?*" Perhaps from all of the emotion of the last twenty-four hours, my voice started to break and my eyes to mist over.

"Yes, son?" He had already let go of my shoulder and turned to go.

"Thanks," I said huskily before I dashed inside and up the stairs. I closed the door after I entered my bedroom and then paced the floor for a few minutes. "Out," my brain kept saying to me. "You've got to get *out of here.*" I went into the hallway and opened the closet where I stored my sport and outdoor gear. I set about assembling everything I would need for Kyle's and my trip. The activity served as an antidote to the awful event which kept circulating in my mind, and kept me out of my mother's reach and having to explain my desire to get away.

Supper that evening was a subdued affair. My thoughts were like tennis balls, bouncing between the racquets of Mrs. Sullivan's suicide and my need to escape. For the most part, we ate in silence, but it was clear that Mother was caught in the uncomfortable position of not knowing what to ask. Dad ate slowly, methodically, sipping a whisky and water with his meal. It was I who finally broke the silence. "Either of you ever know anybody who committed suicide...and did it...in such an awful way?"

Although discomfited by the silence at her dinner table, Mom was even more discomfited by my questions. "Jon—honey—that's not something we really want to discuss at supper."

"Well, *I do*." My reply came with more vehemence than I intended. Mother looked pleadingly at Dad, who quietly took us both in. He swallowed the food in his mouth, and then his tongue sought out bits around his teeth and gums. It was clear this was all in preparation of his saying something. We didn't have to wait long.

"Jon's right, Rachel. Things like what he's been through...well, they can eat a man up inside if he can't get it out." Dad then focused his attention on me, while Mother excessively patted her lips with her napkin. "To answer your question, son, no, I haven't known of anyone who committed suicide in such a fashion. I've seen a lot of death—and suicidal death—but that was in war, and it was all pretty ugly." Dad paused. "But then...well...I'm sure what you saw last night was fairly ugly as well." He paused again. "And all the uglier for what it did to Wendy."

"I-I knew a girl at school whose father killed himself." Mother had decided to join in. "The bank had taken his business—this was during the Depression—and...and I suppose he despaired at not being able to feed his family...so he...um...took a shotgun to the garage...and shot himself." Mother frowned and looked at her hands which were twisting her napkin around her fingers. "I-It must have been a terrible thing to discover..." Her voice drifted away and she stared out the kitchen window.

Dad finished his drink and pushed his plate away. "Rachel—hon? I've told Jon that he's free to go away for a few days, camping up on the Appalachian Trail with Kyle. I think it will be good for him."

Vacantly, mother responded, "Oh...okay."

Dad left the table to go out and finish the work he was doing on his Chevy, and mother started clearing the table. I was still hanging around in the kitchen, waiting for what I considered to be inevitable: that one of my parents would ask me just how Kyle and I were intending to get to the Smoky Mountains. It then occurred to me that it was daft to hang about and have my plans crushed. So I quietly slipped out of the kitchen to get on the phone with Kyle.

~ * ~

Kyle and I planned to hit the road the day after Mrs. Sullivan's funeral. It remained for me to explain to Wendy why I wanted to go away at such a time. But then, I couldn't quite verbalize that urge for myself. First I had to help Wendy get through the funeral, and then I would tell her about my going away for a while.

I wasn't—and couldn't have been—prepared for the Wendy who returned from her uncle's place. She was nervous and fidgety, unable to sit still for long, alternately wanting to be held by me and then beating herself up for her mother's suicide, saying it was her fault. She expressed the guilt and regret often felt by close family members in the wake of a suicide. But with my youthful inexperience, I was uncertain what to say or do. Whenever I tried to reassure Wendy, she would throw her arms around me and beg me never to leave her. This left me with conflicted feelings. Although I loved Wendy as much as a seventeen-year-old could, even at the time, I was fully aware that I had no plans beyond the immediate future. I knew I would be leaving home within a year, going away to college, and that would include parting company with Wendy, who was going to a college hundreds of miles from me. Thus, Wendy's imploring me never to leave her ironically had the reverse effect of creating an emotional gulf between me and her. I didn't fully understand it at the time and couldn't have put it into words, but I certainly *felt* it. And I couldn't pretend otherwise. Intuitively, I knew it was not the right time to tell Wendy of my feelings. But this had the adverse effect of leaving me feeling guilty. And so, I muddled my way through. Whenever Wendy fell into a spirit of despair and insecurity, pleading for my eternal love, I simply mouthed what seemed to be the right words at the time: "It's okay, I'm here," "You'll be all right—but it'll take time," etc.

What did take me aback was Wendy's more amorous approach to me when we were alone the night before the funeral. We had gone for a short drive to a nearby state park. As we started to make out, Wendy unfastened her bra for me and let me slip my hand underneath it for the first time. Not only that, but she rubbed her hand over the lump in my jeans until I ejaculated. She looked with some curiosity at the damp stain growing on my jeans. "It's a bit messy, huh?" Then she smiled sheepishly over her accomplishment and asked me how it felt.

"Good," I replied, and then asked whether she'd like for me to try the same on her.

That did it. "No," came her curt reply. "We'd better not. We…I…have to be back soon. You know…tomorrow and all."

Feeling relieved and frustrated at the same time, I slipped out of the car, made sure no one was in sight, and then used some tissue from the glove compartment to mop up some of the mess in my underwear. All the while, Wendy mused aloud what it would be like when we finally got married. Marriage again. It would be a blissful future, she opined, if I would just stay the course. I was totally confused. What I had thought I wanted with Wendy only a few short days previously had suddenly lost its appeal. Our relationship seemed to be a foreign country with a language I couldn't understand. I knew then that I couldn't stay.

~ * ~

To this day, what memories I have of Mrs. Sullivan's funeral seem like a black and white film viewed from the bottom of a well. I know it was attended by Kyle and many other high school friends. I remember I sat with Wendy, who gripped my hand and wept uncontrollably. I have a mental picture of being spoken to at the family's reception following the service, but here the mental film flickers and appears badly spliced together. There is a vague recollection of people, young and old, telling me to look after Wendy. I do recall having this thought: considering that Mrs. Sullivan had never liked me, it seemed supremely ironic that her suicide had had the unintended consequence of bequeathing her daughter to me. And although I perfectly understood it was the Sullivan family who had suffered the loss, it nevertheless occurred to me that, as the guy who found the body, there were no words of comfort or sympathy.

Fourteen

To travel hopefully is a better thing than to arrive.

—R.L. Stevenson

The night of the funeral Kyle stayed at my house. We fussed over our backpacks, checking and re-checking our equipment. We sat up on our beds and mused aloud about how many lifts it would take to get us into the Smokies. Neither Kyle nor I had ever hitch-hiked, so it was a time of nervous excitement for both of us. When we weren't talking about our impending adventure, our conversation drifted back to the funeral. Kyle and I puzzled about the message Mrs. Sullivan had sent by both the chosen method and location of her suicide.

"Jesus," Kyle shook his head in disbelief. "I mean, can you imagine finding *your mother* like that?"

I shook my head no and then added, "But my mother—and yours, for that matter—are nothing like Mrs. Sullivan. She was…well…*weird*. I never saw her happy. She just seemed to be…well…*less* down-in-the-dumps at some times than she was at most other times. She sure as hell

162

didn't like me…but then, Wendy says her mother didn't like any boy that was interested in her."

"Maybe she was jealous," offered Kyle.

"What do you mean?"

"Well, you know. She might have been jealous of Wendy's looks and personality."

"Yeah," I gave it some thought, "maybe you're right. But then, she did attract Wendy's father. Maybe she was different then. They managed to have two children."

"Sure," replied Kyle, "but that only means she had sex twice!"

I contemplated Kyle's words and mused about life's fundamentals. Sex. Death. *Sex and death.* If my relationship with Wendy had ignited my interest in the flesh, then staring into the lifeless face of her mother had shown me the end of that same flesh. And yet, at this point in my life, both seemed laden with guilt. It was all too much for my seventeen-year-old mind. My brain gave in to the solace of sleep.

When morning dawned, Kyle and I got up with the sun, donned our T-shirts and cut-off jeans, gulped down a couple of bowls of cereal, and slipped out the door with our backpacks before mother could wake up and question us.

Kyle had made us a few signs out of cardboard from boxes, each with a different destination written in marker pens on each side. His idea was that we should use intermediate destinations, as he thought people would be more likely to stop if they knew we were headed to 'local' places. It certainly worked, because Kyle had no sooner handed me the Winston-Salem sign while he adjusted his backpack, than a pick-up pulled over. We threw our packs into the back of the truck and climbed in the cab. The driver was a shift-worker in the big cigarette factory in Winston and was curious as to why two young men with backpacks were headed for the state's twin cities. When we told him where we were headed, he actually seemed envious, which only served to inflate my notions of our great road trip.

The pick-up's driver dropped us off at the busy junction of Highway 52 and Interstate 40. Traffic sped past us, the drivers barely giving us a glance. We wondered if we were in for a long wait. Kyle held up the sign for Hickory, but I suggested we should just go for broke and use the Asheville side instead. Kyle shrugged, flipped it over and, not unlike our first ride of the day, we heard a car hit the brakes. We turned to see a Cadillac grind to a halt about forty yards past us. Kyle and I looked at each other dumbfounded and laughed. Once again, we had barely been there two minutes. The Caddy driver hit the horn and waved us to the car, so we grabbed our gear and ran. Over his shoulder, Kyle shouted to me, "Looks like we're really on our way!"

The driver was standing by the trunk when we got to the car. He was a thin man, with black, Brylcreemed hair, combed back. He looked to be in early middle-age, and had a careworn face. In a taciturn voice he said, "Y'all can throw your things in here. I'm going to Knoxville." As part of my unspoken agreement with Kyle, I jumped into the front seat this time. I couldn't believe our luck—a Cadillac! And it was air-conditioned. When I turned to express our great fortune with Kyle, I noticed two sets of tiny eyes looking at me. They were so small that neither Kyle nor I had seen the children—a boy and a girl—in the back seat of the car as we approached it. The older of the two, a boy about eight, simply said, "Hey."

"Hey yourself," I replied. "I'm Jon and this is Kyle." I looked at Kyle and mouthed, "A Cadillac!"—rolling my eyes for effect.

"Those are my children, Darren and Hannah. Mine name's Delmar. Kids, y'all be good and don't bother these fellas none, okay?"

"Yes, Daddy," came their subdued voices.

Delmar checked his mirrors, saw a gap in the traffic, and floored the Caddy, which spewed gravel as it re-gained the road surface. Johnny Cash was belting out of the eight-track tape player. He was singing about how he had stripes around his shoulders and chains around his feet. I was feeling anything but chained—Kyle and I were on our way.

Unlike our previous lift, this time our driver showed no interest in us or where we were going. Only when the children showed signs of becoming fractious or started asking Kyle questions did Delmar take his eyes off the road and look into the rear-view mirror. Sometimes he asked them to keep still; other times he just returned his gaze to the front. As I studied our driver out of the corner of my eye, I wouldn't have said he was focused on the road or traffic ahead of us; rather, he was simply looking forward—but toward or at what?

After about half-an-hour, I realized I had heard the same Johnny Cash songs several times. In fact, I noticed that the tape seemed to consist of only three–and-a-*half* songs. Delmar didn't seem to notice or care. In order to make some conversation, I made mention of the unusually short tape.

Delmar cast me a quick glance and then said, "Oh…yeah. Tape player's broken—it only plays one track." And then, as though anticipating my next question, he added, "That's the only tape I brought…and it's stuck in there…" Delmar's voice trailed away. Wherever he was, he certainly wasn't with us in the car.

I was beginning to wonder why he had bothered to pick us up. And the quick repetition of three-and-one-half Johnny Cash songs was beginning to wear thin. I started to ask Delmar if we might listen to the radio instead, but the words died in my throat before I could birth them through my mouth. So instead, I turned and looked at Kyle. When he met my gaze, I raised my eyebrows in a 'this is a fine how-do-you do' fashion. But Kyle just shrugged. I couldn't really talk with Kyle as he was directly behind me and the music and the air-conditioning conspired to drown out any real possibility of conversation.

It was the kids who finally broke the oppressive atmosphere within the car. "Daddy? I gotta go to the bathroom!" came the urgent appeal from Darren.

"Me, too!" chimed in his younger sister.

"O-kay," replied their father laconically. "I'll keep my eyes open for a rest area or a filling station. Meanwhile, y'all hold on, okay?"

"I'll try," said Darren.

I cast my eyes over into the back of the car and saw little Hannah squirming on the seat. It didn't look good. I debated whether I should say anything to Delmar. If I intervened on behalf of his child, would he stop the car and put Kyle and me out? Happily, my quandary was resolved by Kyle.

"Uh, hey—Delmar? It doesn't look like Hannah's gonna last much longer back here…"

Delmar briefly came back from wherever his head was and looked at Kyle in the rear-view mirror. He bit his lower lip and then said, "Ah-right, ah-right. I saw a sign for a gas station a while back—it oughta be comin' up soon." He put his foot down on the accelerator and the car seemed to rise. "Y'all kids hang on—ya hear? Just one minute."

Not before time, we saw the sign for a filling station a mile ahead. I took what I hoped was a casual glance at the speedometer and it was hovering around one-hundred-and-ten MPH. To help take their minds off their bladders, Kyle said to the children, "Hey! Can either of you do this?" Kyle could make the sound of water dropping into a pool, by tapping the side of his jaw while expelling air from his rounded lips. Hannah and Darren laughed at the comical noise and faces Kyle pulled at them and then tried making the noise themselves. Seconds later we were coasting along the exit ramp with the service station in sight.

As soon as the car rolled to a stop, Delmar was out and hustling both of his youngsters to the toilet. Kyle and I got out and stretched. Heat was shimmering off the tarmac in front of the station. It was shaping up into a typical August morning during the dog days, "ninety degrees before noon." Once Delmar was out of earshot, I asked Kyle, "Do you want to keep riding with this guy?" Then I started mimicking Johnny Cash. "I got stripes, stripes around my shoulders…" while Kyle grinned and immediately joined in: "I got chains, chains around my feet!"

"Yeah, I know. It does get a bit repetitive, doesn't it?"

"But Delmar—isn't he just a bit…well…odd? I mean, he picks us up and then acts like we're not even in the car. What's that all about? Not to mention listening to the same few songs over and over and…"

"Yeah, I know," replied Kyle, "but it could be worse."

"How's that?"

"We could still be standing back in Winston under this sweltering sun! At least we're in a Caddy with air-conditioning. And this cat is taking us nearly all the way." Kyle looked around and then said, "Look, Jon, we'd better take a leak before Delmar gets back to the car. Seems like he just wants to keep rolling."

As Kyle and I approached the restrooms, Delmar came out with his children. He was running his comb through his shiny, black hair. He looked at Kyle and me for a moment, ran his tongue around his teeth, through which he sucked in some air, and then spoke. "Boys, it's up to you, but my kids..." Delmar looked down at Darren and Hannah, "...well, they ain't had much to eat today. Y'see I got 'em up early this morning so's we could get from Siler City back to Knoxville." Delmar paused, so Kyle and I waited to see where this veritable word-spill from our reticent driver was going.

"Darren, walk your sister to that café over yonder." Delmar nodded to a roadside grill on the far side of the filling station. "Just wait in the shade a minute...and watch out for cars as you go."

"All right, Daddy," replied Darren. He looked up at Kyle and me and with sad eyes, said, "Bye." Hannah gave us a last look and a little wave.

Both Kyle and I said "Bye" and waved back at Hannah.

"Boys...I, uh...I buried the children's mama—my wife—yesterday over in Siler City, where her folks live." Then in answer to our unasked question, he added, "She had cancer." Delmar stood for a moment, once more looking somewhere beyond the place and time. "And I...well..." he waved his hand in front of him. "I just need to feed my kids and stuff...maybe get myself some coffee. Point is, I need a break. Now if y'all want to wait...well, you're welcome to ride on with us...but I just wanted to give you the option of getting on the road. It's up to you." Delmar squinted from the bright sunshine.

I didn't know about Kyle, but I was stunned, saddened, and relieved at the same time. I reached out and squeezed Delmar's shoulder. "Gosh, that's terrible—for you and the kids. Look, Kyle and I will just get our backpacks and head on down to the road." Delmar just bit his lower lip and nodded. I turned to Kyle and said, "You're okay with that, aren't you?"

What else could Kyle say but, "Sure." Then he, in turn, said to Delmar, "Sorry about your wife."

Delmar unlocked the trunk of the car so Kyle and I could grab our gear. As we shouldered our bags, Delmar offered, "If y'all don't catch a lift, I'll stop for you again." He cut a sad figure as he walked toward his children.

"Man!" I whispered to Kyle, "Can you believe that?! Death again! I mean, I'm sorry for the poor guy—I really am. But first Wendy's mother commits suicide, and then we hitch a ride with a guy whose wife dies young. I-I can't seem to escape it." I shook my head at the irony of it all and headed toward the interstate.

"Yeah, it is weird," said Kyle, "but don't forget abo't one important thing…"

"What's that?"

"You and I are still alive." Kyle grinned and handed me some trail mix.

I took a handful and munched it as we walked down to where the entrance ramp met the highway. Kyle dusted off his hands and fished out our Asheville sign. It was beginning to be a long wait, and I started looking back up the ramp, half-expecting and half-dreading to see Delmar's Cadillac coming toward us. As cars flew past, some passengers gave us a peace sign while others gave us the finger. It amazed Kyle and me that a simple act like hitch-hiking could generate such opposite reactions in people. Sweat was stinging my eyes as we stood in the unrelenting sunlight. I took out a bandana, rolled it up and tied it around my head. I started to wonder whether Kyle and I should head back up to the greasy spoon by the filling station and grab a bite to eat, but then I recalled that we really hadn't brought much money. Our food was in our backpacks, and we needed that for the Trail.

As we discussed what we should do, neither of us took notice of an old school bus that lumbered past us. It was only when we heard its horn that we looked behind us and saw it had stopped. The door was open and waiting for us. Before I mounted the stairs, I glanced at the window over the driver's compartment. Where one would normally see the bus's destination or number, it read "Doo-Wah-Diddy." I looked up at the driver. He had shoulder-length hair and a long scraggly beard. He was wearing a top hat and tails. Which is to say, *that was all* he was wearing; everything beneath the hat and tails was bare. The driver doffed his hat, bowed and said, "Intergalactic Travel Service at your disposal, young sirs. Do hop aboard." I noted his accent was slightly English.

Kyle and I looked at one another for a brief moment—to check, I suppose, whether we were prepared for whatever might be in store for us. We both shrugged at the same time and climbed the stairs. Hippy beads were hanging from the rear-view mirror and sticks of incense were burning on the dashboard, although another smell—and it wasn't tobacco—was coming from somewhere inside. I looked along the length of the bus and saw a motley collection of counter-cultural types. "Where're y'all headed?" I enquired of the driver.

The driver looked at me curiously and replied, "Why, in that general direction." He pointed along the west-bound lanes of I-40. "You are going in the same direction, are you not?"

"Well, yeah…sure."

"Then this is where you want to be." He smiled knowingly and added, "There's plenty of room for your luggage in the rear." Our enigmatic driver closed the door behind us and put the bus in gear. It shuddered before the clutch engaged, such that Kyle and I nearly lost our balance from the weight on our backpacks.

"Far o't!" said Kyle. He had been taking in the bus and our fellow passengers while I was speaking to the driver. To my recollection, that was the first time I ever heard him use the expression. It would not be the last. And then, turning to the driver once more, "I thought we were going to fry o't there in the sun."

The driver nodded thoughtfully and replied, "I can excavate the place from which you originate."

"Uh—come again?" asked Kyle.

"I can dig where you are coming from," said the driver cheekily, and then changed gears as the bus picked up speed along the shoulder of I-40.

As we made our way through the bus, I noticed it had been fitted with bedding, a kitchenette and storage cupboards. There were eight or nine young men and women sitting on seats or sprawled on the floor. Kyle and I were greeted with friendly smiles. "Hey." "How's it goin'?" "What's happenin'?" After we stashed our backpacks, Kyle and I looked for places to sit. My eyes were drawn to four people in a circle on the floor, sitting or reclining on Indian rugs and cushions. They were passing what, to my inexperienced mind, looked like a tiny peace pipe. It hit me that this must have been the source of the strange smell that had greeted my nostrils.

A guy who introduced himself as Steve—and had very dreamlike eyes—invited us to join the circle. Kyle and I gave our names as we joined the group. A young woman, perhaps nineteen or twenty years of age, wearing a loose-fitting, tie-dyed cotton dress, smiled up at me and bade me sit on the cushion next to her. She was so attractive that I needed no further encouragement. Her hair was sandy-blonde, perfectly straight and nearly the length of her back. A leather band with beads adorned her head. She introduced herself as Carol. I sat cross-legged, rested my back against the wood-paneled side of the bus, and let out a contented sigh. "That's good," offered my new travelling companion, "just relax and listen to the music." A built-in reel-to-reel tape player was broadcasting what was, as I later discovered, *Electric Music for the Mind and Body*.

"You dudes goin' far?" asked Steve.

"Not really," responded Kyle. "We're just headed up into the Smokies to spend a few days on the Appalachian Trail."

"We're just *headed*," smiled Steve. He passed the pipe to Kyle.

"Uh…no, thanks…I don't smoke."

"Neither do I," blurted out Steve with a peal of laughter. He fell back onto a pillow and held his belly, which was convulsing as he laughed.

Steve sat back up and wiped the tears of mirth from his eyes. "Man, this isn't *tobacco*—it's *hash.*"

"Hash?" repeated Kyle.

"Yeah, you know—*hashish*." Steve laughed again as he pointed at the glowing ember in the pipe. "The surgeon general guarantees that this stuff will *not* give you lung cancer!" Steve started to wheeze with laughter again at his own humor. "But it will give you a hangover-free high!"

Those last words caught my attention. A way to get high without all of the vomiting and room-spinning? A young woman next to Steve took the pipe from him and said to Kyle, "Watch. Just draw it in slowly and let the smoke fill your lungs." She gave Kyle a demonstration, and then, in a whispery voice which was still sucking in air said, "Be sure—to hold the smoke—in your—lungs—for a while." As she finally exhaled, she let out a slow, "O-oh wo-ow," and grinned at Kyle.

Tentatively, Kyle took the pipe, put it to his lips and began to inhale the smoke. All of a sudden, his eyes widened and he started sputtering and coughing. Everyone apart from me laughed—not *at* him, so much as *with* him—as they had all been through the same rite of initiation. Steve gave Kyle a few hearty slaps on the back. Even Kyle started laughing as he shook his head and said, "Whoa! That burns!"

"Take it easy, Kyle," came the soothing instructions from his new teacher. "Just take small puffs and hold them." Kyle did so, and though there were a few stifled coughs, he managed to hold the smoke to the approval of our hosts. But that meant the pipe was headed my way.

To cover what was sure to be my coming embarrassment, I spoke up and said that, like Kyle, I had never smoked before. Steve crumbled up another piece of hash and packed it into the bowl of the pipe, as he said with his stoned smile, "There's a first time for everything." As the pipe headed my way, I noted the expectant smiles on everyone's face. Carol took a small toke on the pipe before she handed it to me.

I shrugged, raised my eyebrows in comical fashion and said, "Here goes." My reaction to the acrid smoke was the same as Kyle's. My eyes were watering so much I could barely see. At this point, Carol intervened.

"There's another way that can help you get used to it." She lifted the pipe from my hand and prepared to draw in some smoke. "When I blow the smoke to you, just breathe it in slowly, okay?"

I wiped my stinging eyes and gasped, "Okay," as I prepared for the next assault on my virgin lungs.

Carol looked at me over the pipe and there was both kindness and mischief in her eyes. With some nervousness, I watched as she filled her lungs with the mind-altering smoke. Carol nodded to me and then puckered her lips as though for a kiss. I opened my mouth woodenly, as though for a dental appointment, so Carol took her free hand and gently turned my head and drew it closer to hers. She looked in my eyes as she exhaled the smoke into my waiting mouth and lungs. Coming from her lungs, instead of the pipe's brass bowl, the smoke was more tolerable this time. When I had inhaled my limit, Carol blew the remaining smoke into the air and then placed a finger over my lips. "Hold it for a few seconds."

When I finally released the smoke, Carol smiled at me and asked, "Better?" I returned the smile, nodded, and leaned back against the wall of the bus, watching the pipe as it made it rounds.

Those who had smoked their fill of hash before Kyle and I had joined the party waved it off. Soon it just passed between Kyle and me until, like all of the others, we were too stoned to smoke any more. The pipe returned to its owner—Steve—who just looked at us all and said, "Ye-a-h."

I looked over at Kyle, whose grin had widened to the size of the Cheshire cat's. At that, I burst out into uncontrollable laughter. The rest of the group looked at me with bemused wonder, but no one seemed particularly surprised. Carol just looked at me with a smile that could have been painted by Renoir.

Having never been stoned, my inhibitions went on holiday; thus, I lost myself in staring at this beauteous creature barely an arm's length away. The object of my attention took it in her stride. Like a starving man stumbling into a banquet, my eyes devoured every aspect of her face: the sensuous curve of her lips, the down that grew just below her right ear, her hazel eyes and fine lashes, the hint of a dimple in her chin. After an indefinite period of time, Carol winked at me, then she reached out and gently tweaked the end of my nose. "You're staring," she said softly.

Somewhere from deep inside me an inhibition broke loose. "Oh, gosh…I'm sorry. I didn't…uh, I mean…I was…" I could feel the blood rush to my cheeks and ears.

Once more Carol's finger found its way to my lips, but this time its intention was to silence me. "Shhh—it's okay. You're stoned." She smiled kindly, and gracefully placed her left arm under her head and turned toward me on the cushions. "It's kinda nice being looked at that way."

"Um…in what way?"

"The way you were looking at me just now. You were staring, but it felt nice. Most of the time, if someone is looking at you and you look back into his eyes, then that person turns away." Carol took on a pensive look as her free hand lifted a loose strand of hair away from her face, "But you didn't do that, not until I said something. Now I wish I hadn't."

Stoned or not, I felt I was already on a level of honest communication with Carol that I had never experienced with any female in my peer group. She had piqued my curiosity, and I wanted to hear more from her. "Why?"

Carol paused before she spoke. She was obviously weighing her words. "Your eyes are soft and gentle…and…well…although you were looking at me intently, your eyes also seemed to be speaking to me—not in words—but still they were speaking to me."

My head was floating from the dope, but my soul was exhilarated at the immediate closeness I felt with this inviting young woman. Without noticing when, and oblivious to everyone and everything around us, we had each slid down on the cushions until our faces were within inches of the other's. Carol was cradling my face in her hands and looking at me with the same intensity I had shown her. My face, sill hot from both the scorching sun and my recent embarrassment, cooled under the touch of Carol's fingers, which I also found immensely comforting. She pulled the sweat-soaked bandana from my head and let it drop beside me. As her fingers traced their way around my eyes and then continued around the rest of my face, I could almost picture my countenance as a book written in Braille, which yielded its contents to fingers which held it in reverence. I had no need to ask further questions, because I knew implicitly that Carol would tell me what she had perceived.

"I see a real gentleness in you—and playfulness," a smile shot across her face and her eyes sparkled, "but…" and the tone of her voice darkened slightly, "but your eyes are also somehow full of sorrow…or pain."

Perhaps my eyes flickered with recognition, revealing the grotesque tragedy that they had only recently beheld. Perhaps they sought to explain why Mrs. Sullivan's face remained an undigested visual image, visible only to someone insightful enough to perceive it. I don't know. Carol neither wanted nor needed any explanation; she simply saw what was and accepted it. Since that time, I have sometimes wondered whether Carol greeted every chance encounter with a total stranger with such intensity, but I have never dwelt upon it. It didn't matter then and it certainly doesn't matter now. Whatever happened between us on that bus ride was special.

Our psychedelic bus bumped and clanked as it continued on its journey, and Carol and I continued our silent journey of self-revelation. Words would have only got in the way. Neither were there guidebooks for this journey, apart from what each other's presence disclosed. My hand had long since left my side and lightly stroked and touched the skin and hair my eyes had so hungrily devoured minutes earlier. I let my fingertips run along her face from her headband to the bottom of her chin. Then I turned my hand over and let the backs of my fingers experience the same topography. I took a long strand of her hair and let it play across my face and lips, inhaling its unique aroma, blended with sun, hashish, and incense smoke. But the most sensuous experience of my life to that point in time was the simple act of letting my index finger drift across her lips, which parted ever so slightly in the process. Could heaven have been any sweeter?

It was only when the bus jolted, jostling us about, that Carol and I became vaguely aware we were no longer on a main road. From the way the bus jerked and bumped, it was clear we were on an unpaved, washboard road. Our creaking transport came to a standstill, and then, as the driver ground the gears into reverse, our foreheads knocked together, causing both of us to wince and laugh at the same time. The entire vehicle shuddered as our hippy chauffeur backed our travelling wonderland under the shade of some oak trees. I pulled Carol's head gently toward me and kissed the spot where our heads had collided. She smiled, laid her head on my right shoulder, and stroked my hair and face with her right hand. Carol's soft breathing caressed the skin around my Adam's apple. "Where are we?" I asked languidly.

I felt Carol's lips part against my neck as she whispered, "We're *here*."

Fifteen

The innocent and the beautiful
Have no enemy but time.
>   —W.B. Yeats, "In Memory of Major Robert Gregory"

"Here" was a good place to be. It still is. And whenever it joins its natural partner, "now," then things come as close to perfection as this life allows. Suffice it to say that Kyle and I never made it to the Appalachian Trail. During that late summer of 1968, "here" turned out to be a makeshift hippy commune on the outskirts of a small town called Old Fort, nestled on the edge of the Pisgah National Forest. Without haste, the bus's occupants, including Kyle, got up, collected their things and made their way off the bus. Carol and I stayed where we were, firmly ensconced in both here and now. Our eyes were still locked in an embrace neither of us wanted to be the first to break.

In the end, it was urgent bodily needs that broke our ocular entanglement—both of us realized we needed to pee and, once one of us started to giggle, we both started in laughing—laughing so hard I nearly wet myself. As we stood, I moved to pick up my backpack, but Carol stopped my hand. "You don't need it; we can stay here." She motioned toward the back of the bus. Her words, spoken so matter-of-factly, echoed around the chamber of my brain. "We—WE—can stay here." Then, as we clambered down the bus's steep steps, Carol clutched her lower belly and groaned comically: "Gotta pee! Gotta pee! Gotta pee!" Without a hint of self-consciousness and in good counter-cultural fashion, we both headed for the nearest trees. In one swift motion, Carol hitched up her long, flowing dress and squatted beside a gnarled oak, holding herself steady with one hand on its wrinkled trunk. Modesty declared that I should turn slightly away and aim myself behind another tree. Although the effects of the hash were beginning to wear off, we were both giddy from relief, continuing to laugh and chat as we emptied our bladders.

"Oh man! I needed that!" I laughed as I zipped my cut-offs. "I'm starving! What about you?"

"Let's go see what's cooking up at the house." Carol took my hand in hers and our fingers intertwined. As we walked toward an old weather-board farmhouse, which had been extended two or three times over the years, I noticed a collection of vans and tents scattered around and about it. We occasionally looked at one another and smiled broadly. My brain was still somewhere back on I-40. *How had this happened?*

When we got to the front porch, I noticed our bus driver sitting on an old wooden swing suspended from the ceiling by creaking chains. He was eating what looked like lentil soup from a stoneware bowl. When he noticed us, he placed the spoon in the bowl and tipped his top hat. "Good evening. You will find supper being served in the kitchen."

Once inside the rickety screen door, I quietly asked Carol, "What's the story on the bus-driver?"

Carol laughed. "Oh, Reggie? Word is he used to be some titled person's chauffeur back in England. It seems he had got turned on to acid and thought he ought to introduce his employer to the joys of the same. As the story goes, Reggie put acid in the afternoon tea and then drove his boss to London to see the lights. The trouble was, Reggie was tripping as well. The police became suspicious when the Rolls or Bentley was reported going around the same roundabout a few dozen times. Reggie was fired and…well, here he is!"

"That's wild!" I remarked, shaking my head in amusement.

Inside the front room, I saw Kyle and a few others from the bus eating, drinking beer, and talking. He saw Carol's and my hands clasped together and grinned broadly at me. "Hey, buddy!" He lifted his bowl of soup and, nodding toward the kitchen, said, "Soup's on! And it's good, too." As Carol led me through the door leading to the kitchen, I saw Kyle wink at me.

"So…do you live here?"

"Well, just for now. I was hitching with a college friend of mine—Katy—and we…well…just kinda ended up here."

Carol led me into the kitchen where another young woman, about Carol's age, was standing over an old, wood-burning stove and stirring an institutional-sized pot full of lentil soup. She had wavy, dark brown hair that was pulled into an unruly knot at the back, and she was wearing a chef's apron. On an already hot day, the kitchen was itself an oven. "This is Katy," offered Carol. As Katy turned toward us and smiled, Carol lifted the hand she still tightly clutched and said, "Look what I found!" beaming from me to Katy. "This is Jon. Isn't he a beauty?"

Before moving to greet me, Katy ran the back of her wrist across her perspiring forehead, swiftly wiping it in her apron. She looked me up and down appreciatively and then proffered her hand. "Hey, Jon!" And then to Carol, "Did you find one for me?"

"As a matter of fact, he's got a friend. You've already fed him. He's sitting in the living room with Robert and the other 'Nam vet, whose name I forget."

"Hmmm," considered Katy. "Maybe I've spent too long over this stove. I'll serve you guys and then I'm done!"

Carol and I gratefully received two bowls full of steaming lentil soup. There were slices of fresh granary bread on the counter top.

Carol handed me her bowl with bread gingerly balanced on the side and said, "You take these out onto the porch. I'll get some cold beer."

I made my way back to the front porch and found the swing vacant. I carefully backed my bottom onto its wooden slats and then halted its movement with my feet as I awaited Carol. She wasn't long in coming, with a sweating bottle of Heineken in each hand. We transferred soup and beer to each other and tucked in.

"Mmhh! This is delicious!" I pointed toward the soup for emphasis.

Carol replied, "Jon, you must still be stoned! Katy's soup is good, but it's not *that good*!"

"Well, I haven't really eaten since this morning. It was midday when y'all picked up Kyle and me—and I was hungry then. Then you got us stoned…and well…" Our eyes again met and smiles broke out once more. I leaned back in the swing and took a swig of the beer. "Whoa! Nectar!"

Carol playfully punched me in the ribs. "There you go again!" She dipped her bread into the soup and then bit off a big chunk. With her mouth full, and eyes opened wide, she began mimicking me, "Whoa, Yon! Iss is 'e bess food I ewer ate!"

I nearly spewed beer out of my nose. Maybe I was still stoned— who could tell? It was fast becoming the most eventful day of my life: hitch-hiking, being picked up by the magic bus, getting stoned, and then meeting Carol…and the day wasn't even over. Her words on the bus came back to me: "We can stay here." I played that short sentence over and over again in my mind: "We…WE…we can STAY here. We CAN stay HERE." Every word seemed pregnant with promise.

We ate in silence for a few minutes. The sun had gone behind the mountains, but it would still be light for another couple of hours. Clearly Carol had as good an appetite as I—it was fun watching her eat. When I had emptied my bowl, I picked up my beer from the floor. The bottle was still glistening with condensation, so I rubbed the cool glass across my forehead. "That feels go-o-od." I turned to Carol. "Think I could have a shower? I'd love to wash the salt from my skin."

A mischievous look formed on Carol's face, and she raised her eyebrows Groucho-style. "I have a better idea. Let's finish these," she lifted her beer, "and then go for a swim. There's a *gre-a-at* pond down behind the barn." Carol pointed the beer bottle over her shoulder.

"Sounds good!" I turned up my beer and drained it. "Let's go!"

Keeping her eyes fixed on mine, Carol downed the remainder of her beer, stood, offered me her hand and said, "Follow me!"

We made our way from the front yard past a disused smoke-house, then picked up a path alongside a fast-running stream which led us to the pond. A willow tree grew next to the pond, its long branches overhanging the grassy bank and trailing into the water. Carol parted the branches and stepped through. With a motion of her hand indicating the semi-secluded grassy spot beside the pond, she said, "Here's the locker room." With that, she kicked off her sandals, then reached down and in one easy movement, whisked her dress over her head. Carol wore no bra, and so her largish breasts swayed in front of me. My eyes must have widened as large as her cinnamon-colored areolas—which stared boldly back. I felt a familiar stirring in my groin. She then threw her long hair back, removed the headband and used it to tie her flowing locks into a pony-tail.

Up to this point, naïve young man that I was, it hadn't even occurred to me that we would be skinny-dipping. In fact, ever since the doors of the bus had opened to me and Kyle, I had stopped thinking and simply gone with the flow. Now the flow had ebbed, leaving me upon the bank of a pond, gazing upon Carol's nearly-nude form. As she finished tying back her hair, Carol saw me standing frozen to the spot. She looked up at me and I tried to shift my eyes away from her breasts. "Come on, slow-poke!" And then she mischievously added, "Never seen a girl naked before?" Before I could muster a response, she bent down, removed her panties and threw them at me, at which point she turned and jumped into the water. My pulse had quickened and blood was pumping in two opposite directions at once: to my head and my penis. This realization led me to strip quickly and submerge myself in the pond before my state of arousal could embarrass me.

The stream-fed water was a shock to the system but refreshing nonetheless. As I surfaced, I shook the water from my eyes and looked for Carol. She was a few short yards away, swimming on her back and spewing water from her mouth. Her breasts kept motion with the movement of her arms, her nipples as firmly erect above water as I was below. Cool water is normally thought to have the opposite effect on the penis, but such was not the case. Cool as the water felt in the lingering heat of that summer's day, I had never been treated to such an erotic vision, other than in my fantasies.

When I swam closer to Carol, she quickly disappeared beneath the surface and just as quickly re-appeared in front of me. I wanted to search her eyes again to see where this nude frolic might be leading. What I got was a face full of pond-water as Carol spewed a mouthful straight at me. She laughed as she swam away from me. I entered the spirit of the chase and soon caught hold of her foot. Carol playfully kicked and struggled, and after a few moments, we were both panting and treading water. The colors of the evening sky were dancing upon the water's surface, adding to the Impressionist-like quality I had seen in Carol's smile earlier in the day. As my foot felt for the bottom of the pond, I reached out and took Carol's hand, pulling her to where the water reached my chest and her chin. I leaned down to kiss her, but my lips paused the moment they touched hers. I brushed them gently over Carol's lips and let myself become slowly intoxicated on her breath. "Your lips…" I did not know how to finish what I had begun to say.

"What about my lips?" Carol enquired quietly.

"When I touched them today on the bus, I don't think anything has ever felt so... felt so…my God—you're so beautiful!"

There's a Zen saying which goes, "What can't be said, can't be said—and it can't be whistled either." So where words fail, senses rule supreme. In this instance, touch and taste took charge. As I pressed my lips against Carol's, she pressed her body against mine—taking my erection for granted. After a few minutes we released our lips and drew our breath. Carol's arms were wrapped firmly around my neck and mine were around her waist. My erection was happily squeezed between her belly and mine.

Carol took her lower lip between her teeth and slowly released it as a thought formed in her head. "Think you can support both of us?"

"I can try." I spread my feet a bit in the silt on the pond's bottom, not sure what to expect.

Carol smiled and hoisted her legs around my waist. I wobbled about as I slipped in the soft muck underfoot, all the while trying to keep our heads above the water. Carol reached down between her legs and found my erection. "I think he's feeling kinda lonely, don't you?" I could feel my heart pounding as Carol slowly rubbed the head of my penis against her labia. "We'll have to take it a bit slowly. This water isn't as slippery as my juice." She winked. I was in her hands—literally. Carol rocked her hips gently, re-positioning herself a few times, using first her right and then her left hand, until I was fully inside her. Nothing could have prepared me for the contrast between the cool water surrounding our bodies and the delicious inner warmth of her body. "Mmmmhhh!" she uttered, throwing her head back. "Jon, you feel so good!"

"So…do…you!" My voice was barely a hoarse whisper so overcome was I from both desire and pure joyful surprise.

Carol lifted her head and forcefully pressed her lips against mine. She took my hands and placed them on her breasts, causing even more blood to flow to my nether region, and then began a rhythmic grinding against my pubic bone. Releasing my lips, she kissed and bit the skin of my chest and neck, while increasing the tempo of her movement. Looking up at me, and with a voice tense with passion, Carol asked, "Can you come this way, Jon?"

"I-I…um…I think I can." This stumbling, lame response had the effect of bringing an intrusive—and decidedly un-erotic—thought to mind: the childhood story of *The Little Engine that Could*: "I think I can, *I know I can*!" But having never made love to a woman, much less in a pond, I was indeed determined to try. Carol was using her body's buoyancy to arch her lower back and bring her pubis against mine, rubbing her clitoris along the length of my penis in ever-quickening movements. All of a sudden, she started to make little gasping sounds and the walls of her vagina started pulsating against my erection. She dropped her chin to her chest and groaned deeply, "O-oh G-o-d," squeezing me tightly in the process. That did it for me, and I joined her in the bliss of our mutual orgasm. I had never witnessed a female orgasm and had certainly never shared in one. Carol seemed almost to convulse, alternately pulling herself tightly against me and then pushing back. Meanwhile it felt as though my entire insides were pouring into her. I was transported to a realm of exquisite delight.

We were both panting from the effort and exhilaration. Carol's arms and legs remained locked firmly around me. "Please don't pull out of me yet," she whispered breathlessly.

"No—of course not! How could I? It...it's *too lovely*." As far as I was concerned, I could have remained inside Carol forever.

Carol "mmhed" her approval. Our breathing fell into the same tempo, our lungs expanding and exhaling together in time. At that moment, I couldn't have told you where my body ended and hers began. I felt more truly one with Carol than I had ever felt with anyone in my life, Wendy included.

After a few minutes of silence, Carol cleared her throat and said, "Somehow we managed to stay afloat! It's a wonder we didn't drown in the process." She began giggling. With Carol clinging to me, I swirled us about in the water, joining in the laughter. The thought of losing my life at the same time as losing my virginity did seem rather comical.

As that thought went through my mind, Carol spoke again. "Have you ever done that before, Jon?"

I didn't know how to respond. Had Carol realized that I was a virgin? Was it that obvious?

My silence earned me a splash of water on the side of my face. "Well...have you?"

"Um...well, gosh...to be honest...*no*..."

"Neither have I. So it's the first time for both of us—in the water." I simply smiled and nodded. Carol laughed softly to herself and, in the fading light, she interlaced her fingers behind my neck and leaned back to look at me. She seemed somehow shy and said, "I wasn't sure we could manage it. You handled...um...all of my gyrating *really well*." Carol dropped her gaze, released her right hand and ran a finger over my chest. "I'm...um...sometimes really embarrassed by how my...orgasms can really take over. But it felt so comfortable and natural with you." Looking back up at me she said, "That's special."

"*You're* special, Carol," I spoke without inhibition. "For the first time in my life...I...I can't think of another person I'd rather be with or another place I'd rather be than with you right here and right now."

"Me, too," Carol said as she leaned forward to kiss me once more. All of a sudden, she shivered. "Brrr! After all of that hot passion, I'm getting chilled! Let's get out, okay?"

"Sure," I agreed. My penis had greatly diminished in size, so I slipped out more easily than I had entered her. We then turned and, supporting one another in the slippery mud, made our way up the bank, where our clothes lay beneath the guardian willow. I pulled on my cut-offs, stuffed my underwear in the pocket, and slipped on my tennis shoes. There was no sense in donning my sweaty T-shirt. Carol pulled her tie-dyed dress over her head and then held onto me as she worked her wet feet into her sandals.

"What about these?" I reached down and picked up her panties.

"Got another pocket?" She grinned.

We slowly made our way back toward the bus, Carol holding my right arm with both hands and leaning on my shoulder. Everything had happened so fast, it hadn't really occurred to me that I hadn't taken any precautions before we made love. In truth, I had never even purchased a condom. A slight panic gripped me and I felt a moral imperative to say something, however much too late after the fact.

"Um...Carol?"

"Yes?" Carol gave me a quizzical look. "What is it?"

"Well...um...we didn't really...um...use anything before we...ah...made love...did we?"

With a look of complete shock, Carol turned toward me. "You mean you weren't wearing a rubber?"

Nonplussed, I blushed and stammered, "No...I...I mean...how could I?"

Happily, Carol's visage returned to one of mirth. She poked me in the ribs and said, "It's okay, Jon—I'm on the Pill."

A huge surge of relief flooded through me. Virginity—and its loss—had brought such ethical dilemmas to this young Presbyterian.

"I think I'll sleep well tonight." Carol yawned.

"You can say that again." Then I added, "I wonder how Kyle's doing?"

"I'm sure he'll be fine. Everybody's cool about sharing here. Who knows, maybe Katy's nabbed him?" Carol playfully grabbed my belly. "You can ask him in the morning, but right now I need you for my man-blanket."

We climbed aboard Doo-Wah-Diddy and made our way just past the spot where Carol and I had met not so many hours before—but how my life had changed in that short time-span. Carol pulled a towel out of a cupboard and we both used it to dry ourselves. The kitchen counter-tops were constructed in such a way that they folded out over the passageway to make a smallish double-bed. "This is where I have been sleeping," said Carol, as I helped her make the bed. "And now it's our nest for as long as you want to stay here." Carol paused. "Jon, I know you and Kyle were planning a hike on the Appalachian Trail…so…so I don't want you to feel you have to stay now. Okay?" Carol smiled wistfully, but honestly, at me.

I took both of Carol's hands gently, but firmly, in my hands. "Look…what I said a few minutes ago still stands. There isn't anywhere else I'd rather be than with you, right here, right now. Believe me—the Trail can wait." Carol smiled warmly and kissed me.

We undressed and climbed into bed. Carol snuggled up to me with her head on my chest. "I want to listen to your heart beat."

So Carol listened to the drumbeat of my mortality and I indulged myself once more in the scent of her hair and skin. But as I waited for sleep to overtake me, my mind wandered along different tracks, engaging in dialogue with itself. It went something like this: Over the past week, two days had started in their own innocuous fashion, and yet both had ended in such unpredictable ways. One brought abject tragedy, and the other found me lying in complete contentment, entwined with a gorgeous young woman I had only just met. Is this how my life would be, an erratic and incredible series of ups and downs? Were these events determined, the way that some of my Presbyterian fellow-travelers believed, or were they random? What would my parents think of this escapade? (*Why would I ever tell them?*) Could I ever see myself sharing this with Rev. McLaurin? If I did, would I be embarrassed or ashamed? On the other hand, how can something that *feels so good* not be *right*? Is this why sex was such a hush-hush secret subject in my family? "Free love" wasn't so free when one was brought up Presbyterian!

But what about Wendy? (Well, what about her?) I had barely thought of her today, only her mother's ghastly end. Now all I could think of was Carol. I wasn't engaged to Wendy or anything. Maybe my moral upbringing had been a con just to get me married off like generations before me? If so, why keep the wonders of sexual union a secret? Was I in love with Carol? I certainly felt something for her, more than the obvious desire. And at some point, a combination of fatigue and contentment overwhelmed my inner dialogue and I fell into a deep, peaceful sleep.

Sixteen

The whole world is watching

> —Antiwar protest chant,
> the Chicago Democratic Convention, 1968

The morning after the night before dawned brightly. The sun shone through a light mist as its rays evaporated the rain from the night's thundershower. Through the bus's open windows I could smell the fresh, damp earth. A rooster crowed nearby, but Carol remained fast asleep. I rose up from the pillow, rested my head on my hand and looked on her in wonder. My chest seemed to be full of helium—from the sheer joy of being *here*. Carol and I had known each other less than twenty-four hours and yet we had become more intimate with one another—in more ways than simple physicality—than I had ever been with Wendy, even after many months of dating. It would not only be trite but also dead wrong to say that having sex with Carol had made a man out of me, for I was still far from fulfilling that part of my destiny. Neither had it simply been a case of losing my virginity, but rather a case of *gaining* the fundamental insight that no one *has* a body in the sense that we can step in or out of it like a car or a suit of clothes, but that we *are* bodies: flesh, blood, bone, mind and spirit—all fused into one being. And with that realization, I was changed, and my life would never be the same.

Having reversed the conventional order of relationship formation and become emotionally and physically intimate with one another from the beginning, Carol and I took the morning to share the mere facts of our existence. We did this while we, along with Katy, prepared breakfast for those in this hippy haven who had not already arisen and eaten, which was the majority. Carol and Katy were students at Oberlin College. They had decided to spend the summer after their sophomore year hitchhiking around the US, which they jokingly referred to as their "state of the nation" survey. The two of them had been picked up by Doo-Wah-Diddy and its cosmic driver, Reggie, somewhere in the Midwest a couple of weeks back. When they scooped up Kyle and me, a bunch of them had been returning from the Democratic National Convention in Chicago.

"Democratic national *fiasco* would be more like it," came a male voice. I turned to look for its owner. "It was a goddamn police riot!" I recognized the face as one of the guys Kyle had been talking to over dinner the previous evening. He was wearing faded military fatigues.

"Robert—this is Jon, Kyle's friend."

"Hey. How ya doin'?" Robert offered me his hand. "Kyle says you're a pacifist." He seemed to be sizing me up. I nodded, but before I could say anything, Robert shook his black curly hair and laughed sardonically. "You wouldn't have liked Chicago! Not one little bit." His slate-blue eyes seemed to twinkle a dare to challenge his words. I didn't.

"Amen to that," chimed in Carol.

"Why's that? What happened?" I asked, looking from Carol to Robert. What with Mrs. Sullivan's suicide and all of its aftermath, I had been only vaguely aware of the goings-on at the Democratic convention in Chicago. My own little life had been enough to cope with.

"Man, haven't you seen the news?"

"Well…um…" I cleared my throat, "not really. Life has been kinda crazy lately."

"Oh yeah, Kyle mentioned something about you stumbling upon a suicide. Bad scene." I noticed a concerned look from Carol.

"Yeah, you could say that." Wanting to change the subject, I pressed Robert for information. "What did you mean about a police riot? What actually happened there?"

Robert looked at me impassively for a minute and then ran his hand through his mass of tight curls. I noticed the hand was shaking, as though he suffered from some sort of palsy. He was also missing a piece of his right ear. "It's like this," he began. "Me and Doug Slater—who's around here somewhere—well…we've done our patriotic duty by going to America's fucked-up little war in Southeast Asia. We *know* what's going on out there. So we thought we'd join other Vietnam vets, who are also against the war, in a peaceful protest outside the convention. We knew the world's news cameras would be there." Robert then looked at Carol and a few others who had joined us in the kitchen and smiled mischievously. "Doug and I thought we'd also take some of our peace-loving hippy friends with us." There were a few sniggers. "As soon as we rolled into Chicago, we knew something was wrong—man, cops were *everywhere*. There were so many uniforms and guns, I thought I was back in 'Nam. And when they saw our bus, they told us *to turn back or we'd be arrested*." Robert looked from face to face. "And this is the 'land of the free' that my buddies and I fought for!" Robert shook his head incredulously. "So we left the bus in the 'burbs and I rang some Marine buddies who were already in the city. They told us to take the train in and meet up in Grant Park—which is what we did. But when we got there it didn't look too good. There were thousands of us—but even more police."

While he paused to catch his breath, Katy handed Robert a mug of steaming coffee, which he accepted gratefully. He sat for a moment, cradling the mug in his hands and inhaling the aroma. Ripples across the surface of the coffee alerted me to the continuing shake in Robert's left hand. Before he resumed his story, a voice came through the doorway. "You telling 'em about how you and I single-handedly took on the entire Chicago police force—or is this about how we stopped the NVA cold at Hue?" A wiry, red-headed young man stepped into the kitchen, followed by Kyle, who winked at me and smiled.

"You wanna tell the story, Doug?" growled Robert—but his eyes belied his tone of voice.

"No way, man! Semper Fi! It sounded good to me."

Robert knocked back half the mug of still-steaming coffee. I thought he must have had an asbestos throat. As I looked at the faces gathered in the kitchen, it was clear that Robert commanded the respect of his audience.

"So anyway, sometime in the middle of the afternoon, a kid lowers the American flag, and that was all the cops needed. Man, it was like they were just waiting for any excuse, no matter how flimsy. The cops set about busting the kid's head and then taking swipes at anybody who tried to help him. Skulls were being cracked and noses broken. If Vietnam taught me anything, it was when to get out of a fight you can't win. The cops had the weapons and body armor, and they also outnumbered us. So it was time to split. Probably took us two hours to make our way back to the train station." Robert paused and drank the rest of his coffee. His eyes rested somewhere in the middle distance and he shook his head at his inner thoughts and memories.

"It wasn't quite that simple," added Carol. "Robert and Doug were helping us to escape the melee when a couple of cops tried to herd us back into the fray. Doug and Robert ripped up a park bench and used it as a battering ram to drop the cops and help us get away. It was awful! I thought we were going to be clubbed." Carol thought for a moment and with measured words added, "You know, I never thought I'd see the day when two US Marines would have to defend *me* against *American police*…how did our country ever get to this place?"

"No shit," responded Doug. "I mean, Rob and I just about get our asses blown off in 'Nam, only to come Stateside and nearly get our heads caved in by the police. This sho' ain't the country I took an oath to defend."

"And you know," Carol added, "you could almost understand the cops going after *us*…but as we were running through the fray, I actually saw a cop push an older woman, who was obviously not one of the protesters, through a shop window. It was surreal."

Silence pervaded the room as each person examined his or her own thoughts. As for my thoughts, I was trying to reconcile how here I was in the same country and state as the day before, and barely a hundred miles from my home, and yet it felt like I had crossed an invisible border and entered another country, populated with people whose life experiences were so different from mine—and was now looking back on the land I had left. I was amazed what could happen when one simply stuck up a thumb to hitch a ride. Slowly, in ones and twos, people started getting on with their days and entering into conversations. At that point Kyle caught my eye form across the farmhouse kitchen. Katy and Carol were talking with each other, so as I crossed the room, I gently brushed her shoulder and said, "See you in a while." She reached out, gave my hand a little squeeze, and I joined up with Kyle.

As I approached Kyle, he smiled knowingly, glancing from me to Carol. We walked out to the front porch and sat in old, ladder-back rockers. "Some twenty-four hours, eh buddy?" Kyle grinned at me. "You look like the cat that caught the canary."

I grinned back. "Yeah, what a difference a day makes, as they say. This time yesterday we were on the road, headed to the Smokies."

"And now we're not!" retorted Kyle.

I looked at Kyle, trying to judge how his words were intended. "Are you…um…okay…I mean—with where we've ended up?"

Kyle just looked at me for moment, poker faced—not like him. "Well, I know *you are*." The grin returned. "I guess this little journey will spice up your conversations with Rev. McLaurin."

I blushed. "Umm…yeah, I guess so."

"You and Carol seem…*really tight*…and it's all happened just like that." Kyle snapped his fingers for emphasis.

"I know—really, I do. I mean, nothing like this has ever happened to me. And it all seems so *easy*…and natural…and right. I'm still having trouble believing it's all real."

"Oh, it's real enough—or we're both dreaming the same dream! But I...um..." Kyle hesitated, looked at me sheepishly, and continued, "I hope I haven't spoiled things for you and Carol." I looked at him quizzically. "'Cause I kinda let it slip that we're upcoming seniors in high school when I was talking with Katy, and she was a bit surprised that Carol had...well... you know...with you." He looked at me searchingly. I shook my head with incomprehension. "Well, Katy and I were talking, you see, and she and Carol thought we were probably about their age, you know. I guess being o't on the road and unshaven helped give us that...um...'manly look.'" Kyle puffed out his chest, rubbed his stubbled chin and gave me a shit-eating grin.

"Oh..." I muttered, as the meaning dawned on me. "Oh! Yeah, I see what you mean."

"Yeah," said Kyle. "Sorry, buddy. I really hope I haven't screwed things up for you."

"Well...who knows? I mean, Carol and I hadn't ever got around to talking about age and stuff...things just sorta took off for her and me. But...I suppose I'll find out soon enough. But—hey, what're we gonna do now? That is, if things are still cool with Carol and me, shall we just hang tight here and then head back home?"

"I think I know *your* answer," replied Kyle. "And yeah—let's stay. This place is really cool."

Satisfied that I hadn't pissed off my best friend, I asked him, "By the way, where did you sleep last night?"

"I was carrying the tent for us, remember? I pitched it out back near some of the others." Kyle indicated with a jerk of his thumb over his shoulder. "But, hey, did you know that the two guys who originally bought this place make hammer dulcimers for a living? You gotta check o't their workshop and instruments. Who would've thought there'd be a place like this tucked away in the hills of North Carolina?"

"No—I didn't know...but then, I was a bit...occupied." The blush returned.

"By the way, I spent a couple of hours with Robert and Doug. Man, they've been through some shit in Vietnam. They say the news we get doesn't tell us half of what is actually going on over there. And if it did, nobody in his right mind would volunteer or allow himself to be drafted. You might want to talk with them if you get the chance…or if you can keep your paws off Carol!"

"Yeah, well you might have taken care for that for me, ol' buddy of mine!" I gave Kyle a gentle poke in the ribs.

He feigned injury and cried, "Ouch! Hey, I thought you were supposed to be a pacifist!"

"Oh, I almost forgot. Thanks for reminding me! Now, do you mind if I go look for Carol?"

"Nah," came Kyle's laconic reply; but as soon as I had walked five paces, he blurted out, "Pussy whipped!'"

I gave Kyle the finger and headed back to the farmhouse. Kyle just laughed and shook his head as I departed. Once back at the house, I went to look for Carol. She was still in the kitchen where a discussion was taking place among the commune's members about a cabin that was being built about fifty yards behind the farmhouse, on the edge of the woods. "Hey," I whispered as I moved in close to her, wondering whether Kyle's revelations might have changed things between us.

"Hey, yourself," Carol, slipped her hand around my waist. I put my arm around her shoulders and pulled her close.

"What's up?" When I looked down at Carol, I picked up a slightly studious look in her eye, but it quickly disappeared. Had it been a result of Kyle's revelation that we were still high school students? I decided not to pursue it.

"Cabin-raising!" she beamed, "And you and Kyle are volunteered!"

"W-what?" I stammered.

"If we're going to eat the commune's food, we have to share in their work! And as you are a very healthy young man—and to that I can attest," Carol looked me up and down and then ran her hand over my chest and gave me a wink, "you and Kyle are volunteered to help. There's a crane arriving in about half-an-hour." Shielding her eyes against the strong morning sun, Carol pointed toward a huge pile of chestnut logs. "The cabin's being built over there." I followed her over to a stone foundation. Indicating the stack of wizened, sinewy logs, she ran her hand along one and said, "These came from an old mill about two miles away. Aren't they beautiful?"

As my eyes took in the size of the logs, I whistled through my teeth. "I can see why you need a crane." I then noticed two young men, both in their late twenties, standing inside the foundations and looking over some plans.

"Let me introduce you to Nick and Danny," chirped Carol. "They're the guys who bought this place."

Nick had the looks of the classic beatnik: he was lean and lanky, with dark, unkempt hair and thin goatee. Danny, on the other hand, had an athletic build, slight freckling, and a mass of thick hair that resembled freshly stacked wheat-straw. We exchanged greetings and shook hands. Nick, the slightly more serious of the two, asked, "Got any experience in construction?"

"A bit." I nodded.

"Any fear of heights?"

"Not really. My Dad's a pilot."

A sly grin spread across Nick's face. "You'll do. What about your friend? He okay with heights?"

"As far as I know. He goes flying with Dad and me."

"Great. Y'all will ride the logs and help steady them into place."

Seeing the incomprehension on my face, Nick gave a wave of his hand and said, "Don't worry, it's pretty straightforward; I'll show you when the crane arrives."

As though on cue, we heard the blast of a horn and then the grinding of an engine. A battleship grey truck with a huge, fifty-five-foot crane on the rear flatbed came lumbering up the gravel road toward the farm, belching black diesel smoke as it approached. Two hippies in the cab bounced on their seats each time the wheels found a pothole. When the truck pulled up to the building site, Danny jumped onto the running board and grabbed the hand of the passenger. As he greeted his friend through the cab's window, I noticed the following sign painted in a flowing script over the cab:

Jack N. Lawson

Reed & Walker Erection Company
Specialists in Getting it Up

As I erupted with laughter, Carol rejoined me and gave me a quizzical look in quest of what had brought me to near hysterics. I simply pointed to the hand-painted sign over the cab. Carol joined in the laughter and then whispered, "After that performance in the pond, maybe *you* could work for them?" Although I blushed, I was pleased with the compliment.

Within a few minutes of the crane's arrival, most of the farm's inhabitants were gathered by the cabin's foundations. Danny mounted the pile of chestnut logs and took charge. "Okay. Here's the deal. My ol' pal Jeff Walker and his buddy Ty Reed have agreed to let us use their crane while they're in between welding and steel erection jobs. So we've got two or three days to raise the walls and beams of this cabin. Apart from being hot as hell, the weather looks okay, so let's get started."

Except for the modern equipment, it felt like being part of a Colonial barn-raising we had read about in history books. There was a lot of friendly banter, occasional cussing, plenty of cuts, nicks, bruises, and scratches along with copious sweating. From time to time, fellow-workers would take a break to dive into the pond and return, five minutes later, refreshed.

Just as Nick had said, Kyle and I rode the log beams into place. It started with our helping to lever them up from the pile, hook chains around either end, and then, holding onto the chain and standing on top of the wooden beam, all the while shifting our body weight as needed in order to balance the logs, we were hoisted up to the top of the wall. Doug and Robert used chain saws to notch the ends of the logs, while Danny and Nick used a 32-inch drill bit to bore holes through two to three courses of logs, into which they dropped steel dowels, thus giving the walls more stability. Those two helped Kyle and me release the chains which secured the logs to the hoist, then Kyle and I mounted the ball just above the massive steel hook and rode the crane back to the ever-diminishing pile of aged chestnut. Level-by-level, the walls began to take shape.

It was a revelation to me that manual work could be so satisfying, especially with no overbearing adult or parent telling us all what to do. It was easy to take directions from Nick and Danny or Jeff Walker from the crane's cab. During the hottest part of the day, we took an hour's break for lunch and rest. Carol, Katy and a few others served up piles of corn-on-the-cob, freshly baked bread, and apples from the farm's orchard. After lunch, Carol and I retreated to the pond, this time with many others. There was a mixture of skinny-dipping and those who kept on their cut-offs and/or T-shirts. Carol fell into this group, as did I. I was afraid to remove my cut-offs, both to preserve what modesty I had and for fear of what proximity to Carol might do to me. Carol and I floated around in each other's arms, just holding one another. She smiled indulgently when she felt a protrusion from my crotch, kissed me gently, and said, "Tonight." The promise of delights to come helped to ease my worries over what her knowledge of my age might have done to our budding relationship.

The end of the day saw the walls of the cabin ninety-percent completed. From our position on top of the last course of logs, Jeff bade Kyle and me jump aboard the crane's ball for a lift to the ground. As we clung to the chain, I heard Jeff's partner, Ty, shout: "Show 'em the penthouse, Jeff!"

"Oh yeah!" called back Jeff, "I nearly forgot! Y'all hang on, boys!"

With that, Jeff cranked the crane's chain nearly up to the end of the lifting arm, leaving us just enough headroom, and then extended the arm to its full fifty-five feet. The fact that the building site was located on the lower slope of a mountain only served to accentuate our height. Neither Kyle nor I shouted out the fear we felt inside; rather, we hung onto the chain for dear life and exchanged looks of "holy shit!" with each other. As there was barely foot-room for one person on the ball, the fact that there were two of us precariously perched upon it meant that we were treading on each other's feet, only adding to the discomfort. Sweat started running from my head into my eyes, but I was loath to release my grip in order to wipe my brow and eyes.

"How's the view from up there?" Ty called up to us.

Apart from looking at my white knuckles and insecure footing, I had barely cast my eyes elsewhere. But at Ty's question, I instinctively looked around—and, in fact, the view was stupendous. "You can see for miles!" I shouted back.

"Well," Ty drawled, "Y'all want to stay up there for supper or do you reckon y'all'd like to come down?"

"Down is good!" shouted Kyle. "My arms are abo't to give o't!"

Ty gave Jeff a wave and, with that, we felt the crane's gears engage as our descent began, which, thankfully, was at a slower pace than our ascent. Within a few feet of the ground, Kyle and I both jumped off before Jeff could change his mind. But Jeff's mind was on quitting work, so all we got from him was a big grin and a wave. Kyle and I both stretched and shook our muscles loose. It had been a strenuous-enough day, but the last few minutes of airborne adventure had served to tighten all the muscles in my shoulders and arms. At that moment, I saw Carol walking toward us. Her hair was tied in a pony-tail, but she was also wearing a bandana to catch the sweat. Like everyone else on the farm, she had been working all this scorching August day around the emerging cabin.

"He-ey, y'a-all." Carol twisted her Midwestern mouth around our Southern vowels in gentle mockery. "That looked a bit scary." Carol nodded her head toward the crane as she slipped her arms easily around my waist.

"Hey yourself." I leaned down to kiss her. "And yeah, it was a bit scary."

As Carol returned my kiss, she pulled her arms away from my sweat-soaked T-shirt. "Yuck! You need a splash in the pond! You coming, too, Kyle?"

"Sure. Why not?"

We ambled along together, discussing the day's work and the progress that had been made. When we arrived at the pond, a feast of flesh greeted our eyes. Those who were not already skinny-dipping jumped into the pond to rinse off their dirt-and-sweat-stained clothes, then peeled them off and threw them onto the bank. Happily, the sight of so many nude bodies—male and female—had the effect of stemming the erection I feared would arise when I saw Carol in the buff. Thus came another discovery during those few days in hippy paradise: when everyone is naked, eroticism diminishes. And so, like children, we splashed, laughed, hooted and hollered. Kyle looked at me, shaking his head with mild disbelief and simply said with a huge grin, "This is wild!"

I returned his grin and replied, "It's great, ain't it?"

Once everyone had both cooled down and cleaned off, people started heading back to the farmhouse in various states of undress. Kyle walked along with Carol and me, carrying his rolled-up clothes. As Carol and I turned toward the bus, Kyle headed toward wherever he had left his backpack and unrolled his sleeping bag. "See you at supper," he called over his shoulder.

Carol and I didn't make supper.

~ * ~

When Carol and I sheepishly entered the farmhouse to see what remained of the evening meal, the first person we met was Katy. She took one look at us, made a mock frown and said, "You two are like rabbits!"

"Jealous?" retorted Carol, wiggling her nose bunny-style.

"As a matter of fact, *I am*! Seeing you get laid like this is making me horny! Damn it, you two!" Katy turned her glance toward me, placing one hand petulantly on her hip. "So where's Kyle?"

"Beats me. He'll be around here somewhere."

Katy just nodded, but as we walked toward the kitchen, she remarked with determination, "I'll find him tonight." Carol and I looked at one another and smiled.

When we entered the kitchen, the farm's owners, Nick and Danny, along with Robert, were hunkered over the kitchen table, which was covered with an old-fashioned oil-cloth, busily scooping a brown, powdery substance into tiny gelatin capsules.

"Is that supper?" joked Carol.

Without looking up, Nick grunted, "Unh-unh. But it's the best mescaline you're ever likely to try. Just Danny's and my way of saying thanks to everybody for all of the hard work y'all did today. Ty and Jeff brought it for us. But if y'all are hungry, there's probably a little barbecued chicken and stuff out back on the picnic table." He indicated the direction with a tilt of his head.

We opened the rear screened door and saw a few people, Kyle included, sipping beers and picking at the leftovers. "Leave us anything?" I asked.

"Not much!" Kyle grinned. A couple of forlorn chicken thighs lay on a plate smeared with barbecue sauce; cold, fried okra was on the plate next to that; and the remains of what had been a huge salad, replete with homegrown, beefsteak tomatoes, was in a wooden bowl. Without ado, Carol and I hungrily tucked in.

Talking with her mouth full and with bits flying, Carol said, "'Ooks 'ike Nick and Nanny hab' an in'resting night planned."

I pretended to flick pieces of food off my T-shirt, which earned me a gentle elbow jab in the ribs. Laughing, I asked her, "What do you mean?"

Wiping her mouth on the back of her hand, Carol nodded toward the kitchen. "The mescaline."

"What's mescaline?" queried Kyle.

"We-e-ell..." Carol mused aloud. "It's probably the best drug experience I've ever had." Carol took note of our blank expressions. "It comes from the peyote cactus out in the Southwest. It seems Indians have used this stuff for years—I mean *centuries*. Anyway, I think it's much easier on the body than LSD." Carol licked some barbecue sauce from her fingers.

Kyle and I looked at each other, and Carol noticed our hesitancy. "Neither of you has tripped, right?" We both nodded. "Well, look, you two enjoyed getting stoned on the bus, right!" More nods from Kyle and me. "So, hey, this is even better! You're gonna love it!" Carol again gave her eyebrows a "Groucho" arch and grabbed me by the arm, pulling me in close. Looking up into my eyes, she said, with a kiss between each word: "I'll—look—after—you. Okay?" Turning quickly to Kyle, she winked and said, "Katy is looking after you tonight."

Kyle gave me a quick sideways glance as though to ask, "Does this mean what I think it means?" But I could only shrug.

Seventeen

And those who were seen dancing, were thought to be crazy, by those who could not hear the music

—Nietzsche

As night fell, the old farmhouse was illuminated from within by candlelight. There were also candles on the front and back porches, as well as by benches and chairs around the yard and even by the pond. Shadows rose and fell as the soft evening breeze tickled the flames. Our hosts, Nick and Danny, invited each of us to take a mescaline capsule from the kitchen table. They were already high from having loaded the capsules with mescaline and licked their fingers clean. Their smiles were contented and dreamlike, but they were also the knowing smiles of initiates watching novices like Kyle and me. A jug of fresh-squeezed lemonade sat at the end of the table with a stack of Dixie cups. Carol placed one of the capsules first on my tongue and then on hers; we washed them down with a shared cup of lemonade. True to her earlier words, Katy was waiting for Kyle. I gave him a little wave goodbye as Carol led me, I knew not where.

In addition to the warm glow of the candles, the house was filled with the sweet smell of incense. Several stereo sets were arranged throughout the house, each playing different music, ranging from Country Joe to Beethoven. Here and there were placed bowls full of succulent fruits, chocolate brownies, and other delights. Once we had made our first foray through the sensually arrayed house, Carol led me out to the front porch. We occupied the swing we had sat in the previous night, although that seemed a long time ago. I put my arm around Carol, and she snuggled against me.

"When will I start to feel anything?" I asked.

"Why? Can't you feel me?" Carol smiled mischievously at me.

"You know what I mean!" I gave her a tickle along her ribs.

Carol laughed easily and then said, "It won't be long now. We haven't had much to eat, so the mesc' will start to work soon."

I gently rocked us on the porch swing and the squeaking chains joined the cicadas, frogs and other night creatures in their nocturnal cantata. I placed my nose in Carol's hair, inhaling once more her intoxicating aroma, and rocked the swing by pushing off with the toes of my tennis shoes. Time evaporated, such that I had fallen into a continuous rhythm and hadn't felt Carol sit up beside me. I only noticed her again when I heard her giggling and felt her body shaking beside me. As I turned to look at her, I felt a sort of effervescence running up my spine and a broad smile spread across my face. Carol's eyes glistened at me and sparks seemed to emanate from them. "How do you feel *no-o-ow*?" she asked.

"Wow. Ooohh, wo-o-ow," I drawled.

Then she giggled again. "You've been watching your feet for what seems like ages!"

I looked down and it seemed almost like I was watching someone else's feet, still rhythmically pushing the swing back and forth. Carol dropped her feet to the floor and stopped the swing. She stood and offered me her hands. When I took them, she pulled me up from the swing and said in a hushed tone, "Let's explore!" Under the influence of the mescaline, whatever fatigue I had felt from the day's labors faded away. We began to wander the rooms, taking in the sights, sounds, smells and tastes. At one point, Carol placed her hand across my eyes and said: "Open your mouth." I obeyed and was rewarded with a slice of fresh orange.

"Whooaa!" was all I could articulate in response to the rush of sensation.

As we moved through the house, people appeared, first as shadows, as they approached the candlelight, then became their full, three-dimensional selves, only to return to shadow; all the while their forms taking Munch-like wavy lines due to the wavering candlelight and, of course, the mescaline. Sometimes Carol and I would stop and examine each other's faces, tracing the contours with our fingers. I remember at one point becoming lost in playing with her long, flowing hair. At another time, Carol had me sit with her and watch the flame of a candle. It felt as though I could feel the light reaching to the back of my retinas. All of my senses were awakened in ways I had never experienced. Carol and I continued to taste the fruits, brownies, and other goodies that had been placed here and there for our delectation. With each bite, our taste buds were stimulated anew. The passage of time disappeared, and I was fully immersed in the present moment. Everything we did commanded my complete attention. At some point, Carol suggested we go outside. As we started to make our way to the pond, I turned to look back at the house. With the warm glow from inside and the soft murmuring of music and voices, the house seemed to be alive. In fact, it occurred to me that the house looked like a friendly jack-o'-lantern, the rear, upstairs windows being its eyes and nose, and the back porch being its crooked grin. I was just about to say something to Carol, when a naked figure sprinted past me, shouting: "This is where it's at! This is where it's at!"

I laughed out loud and thought to myself: "That's funny! Kyle would love that!" And then, from somewhere deep inside myself I recognized that the figure *was* Kyle, which made me laugh even harder. I turned to look at Carol and found that she, too, was howling with laughter. Within seconds of Kyle's disappearance, the nude form of a woman swooshed by me, calling after Kyle. It must have been Katy. With that, both Carol and I fell to the ground and laughed as I had hardly ever done. I thought about what we had just witnessed and blurted out, "Kyle's being chased by a naked lady!"

"Yeah," replied Carol. "It's great, isn't it?" Followed by, "I hope she catches him!"

We lay there on the grass, looking at the night sky, which possessed an organic quality. The stars were vibrant and alive, their light pulsing and whirling its way toward me. Years later, when I stood in front of Van Gogh's "Starry Night," I was humbled and amazed that he had captured the essence of what I saw and felt that summer night on my first mescaline trip. After a while, it began to look as though the stars were below us and that, if we weren't very careful, we could detach from the earth and fall into infinite space…but it wasn't a scary feeling. It all looked so friendly and welcoming. As though under its own direction, my right hand rose skyward. I gently waved my fingers across the stars. Then I rolled my head toward Carol and asked, "Is all of this," I waved my hand, indicating the totality of creation, "in that little capsule?"

Carol kissed me on the cheek and said, "No, silly. It's in you…and out there. It's you…and me…and more. It's all here…and it's all now."

"Ahhhh…okay then."

"C'mon—let's go play!"

Carol took my hand once more and led me back to the pond. We weren't alone this time and could hear voices and just discern movement somewhere on the opposite side from us, but nothing seemed to matter. We sat by the pond and looked at its still, inky-black surface. After a moment or two, that same surface was alive with dancing stars. It was as though there were a hole through the earth and we were looking right through it to the stars on the other side. All of a sudden, that portion of the universe dissolved and re-assembled itself into Carol's face. It took me a second to realize that she had slipped into the water without my noticing. Still bemused, I looked to where she had been sitting only a moment before. I laid my hand upon her still-warm clothes. At the same moment, I was electrified by the splash of water on my skin. Carol splashed me again, and I howled with delight. Water had never felt so electrifying—so alive. In a flash, I had stripped off and jumped into the pond with her. I seemed to be able to feel every pore in my skin as well as every hair and follicle. "God!" I shouted, "This is amazing!" The ambient light from the night sky and the still-flickering candles along the banks of the pond made each drop of water look like diamonds. Overwhelmed with what I beheld, I called out to Carol again. "We're swimming in diamonds!" Carol just laughed and splashed me again.

How long did we spend in the pond swimming and frolicking like dolphins? I have no idea. I do recall, however, that where we got *out* of the pond was not where we got *in*; thus, we lost our clothes and spent the rest of our "trip" wandering around nude, not unlike Kyle and Katy. Had it only been two days since Kyle and I had boarded the psychedelic bus with a little trepidation because the driver was nude?

~ * ~

At some time during the wee hours, the mescaline had run its course and exhaustion took over. Carol and I dragged ourselves back to the bus and fell into a very deep sleep, punctuated by colorful dreams. When we awoke, the sun was high in the sky. As we lazily stretched and greeted one another, we noticed that our feet were dirty and that there were bits of pond algae and blades of grass stuck to our skin. We laughed at our mutual condition and, like our primate cousins, began grooming each other. While Carol looked for some clothes, I rummaged through my backpack for another T-shirt and pair of cut-offs. As I had only hiking boots, I decided footwear would have to wait until we could hunt around the pond for the things we had shed the previous night.

We were each lost in thought as we made our way, arms slung around each other, to the farmhouse in search of breakfast. Someone I didn't recognize was curled up on the porch swing, fast asleep. One or two people were moving around in the house, in various states of consciousness. Oblivious to our arrival, someone was still sacked out on the old sofa in the living room with his face turned to the back cushion. Detritus from the night before was strewn about the house: bits of food, fruit peelings, etc. Tables were sculpted with candle wax which had overrun makeshift candle-holders. We were soon met with the clacking sound of dishes and tableware coming from the kitchen. We followed the noise and soon heard low voices, along with the sound of a percolator. As we entered the kitchen, we saw Danny, Jeff, Robert, and Katy hunkered over their mugs of the black brew. They smiled as they saw us enter the kitchen.

"Coffee-coffee-coffee!" came Carol's staccato response to the fresh aroma. As for me, I fished around in the fridge for some orange juice. Having found a clean mug, Carol filled it to the brim and held it under her nose, letting the steam caress her face and nostrils, smiling at the sensation. I let my glass of Florida sunshine tickle my taste buds.

"Anyone fancy some scrambled eggs?" came an unexpectedly perky query from Carol. Several "mmphs" and grunts of reply signifying "yes" came in response to her offer. She took a deep draught of her coffee and then winked at me. "C'mon, manblanket! You can help." There were several chuckles at her moniker for me, resulting in my blushing.

"That embarrass you?" asked Carol with a quizzical look.

"We-e-ll…sorta," I replied.

"Ahhh," she said as she threw her arms around my neck and gave me soft, tongue-filled kiss. And then, just as quickly, she said, "Let's get to work! There are hungry mouths to feed!"

As the communal farm had its own chickens, there were loads of eggs in the fridge. I found a mixing bowl, cracked a dozen or so eggs, and gave them a swift stir. Soon they were sizzling in the iron skillet. We found a fresh-baked loaf of bread and began slicing it for toast. It was not long before all of us were diving into the eggs and toast, on which I put lashings of the farm's sourwood honey. When everyone had finished eating, Carol volunteered the two of us for washing up duty. As we collected the dirty dishes, more people began to drift into the kitchen, Kyle among them, perhaps enticed by the smell of our breakfast.

"Our shift is finished, but the skillet is still warm!" chirped a fully-awake Carol. "You're welcome to take over where Jon and I left off."

Like automata, the mescaline-dazed crowd started moving wordlessly toward the stove, the fridge, and the percolator. Before vacating the kitchen for this new round of diners, I stopped alongside Kyle.

"What sort of night did you have?" A smile broke across my face.

Not usually one to be embarrassed, Kyle turned crimson and dropped his head, although I could see his trademark grin. "Later, buddy. I'll tell you later."

As Carol and I made our way outside, I slipped my fingers inside hers, pulled her close to me and said, "I think Katy caught him!"

"I know!" She released my hand to give a little clap. "Katy gave me a little whisper when we were serving breakfast. I'm so happy for both of them. Katy gets a little grizzly when she hasn't had a man for a while." Carol smiled at her inner thoughts, and exclaimed, "That's why she was sitting there so dreamily at breakfast! Ha—the minx!"

We drifted aimlessly around the farm grounds, enjoying the morning sunshine. After a few moments, I nodded toward the new cabin and asked, "So no work today?"

"Of course not, manblanket—it's Sunday! Even hippies need a day of rest."

"After yesterday's work, not to mention last night's adventures, it's no wonder!" I stifled a yawn. And then my mind began to work. "Sunday—damn!"

"Why—what's wrong?"

"Nothing really…but…well, yeah, there is." We stopped walking and Carol looked at me intently, waiting for me to continue. "It's just that I—well, Kyle and I really—well, we really need to get back home…tomorrow." At that moment, I couldn't bear to look at Carol, so I studied my toes. "I-I think you know why."

"I kinda figured this was coming," Carol said softly. "I heard Kyle say something about you guys being seniors in high school." Being a half-foot shorter than I, she tucked her face under mine and looked up at me. "Hey—it's okay. Really."

"Really?"

I was torn between the teenager whose body, mind, and emotions I dwelt within and the young man I was fast becoming. Feeling somewhat gawky, my shoulders involuntarily shrugged and I asked,

"But what about the…um…fact that you're in college and I'm, well…" I put on a gormless, self-deprecating voice, "still in high school?"

"I'll admit it threw me at first—*but only at first*! You have to believe that—and you ought to know it!" Carol grinned and gave her eyebrows a wiggle. "I think it was meant to be."

"Do you mean it?"

"Yes. I mean it." Carol placed her hands on my upper arms and gave me a shake. "It's really wonderful what's happened between us."

I pulled Carol against my chest. "God, I'd love to stay. I mean, as crazy as this sounds—I love you. And I love being here with you."

"I know," came Carol's gentle reply, "because I love you, too."

Caught completely unawares, I felt my eyes well up with tears, while my heart swelled to twice its normal size. I thought its pounding would knock Carol over. Was it really this easy to fall in love? Still standing, she took my face in her hands and began kissing the tears from my eyes. My world was feeling ripped apart. Here I was with a beautiful, vivacious young woman, staying with a bunch of hippies who had simply accepted us for who and what we were. I felt free—really free—for the first time in my life. I didn't feel that I was my parents' son or that I was my brother's younger sibling. I felt *me*. Only a few days before, I had left a guilt-stained, high school relationship which had been marred by suicide…and now: *this*! It was as though by stepping out onto I-40 to hitchhike, I had indeed stepped into Alice's rabbit-hole and had either ended up in Wonderland or some other world in the space-time continuum. But, as Carol had said to me in the midst of my mescaline rapture, "It's in you…and out there. It's you…and me…and more. It's all here…and it's all now."

I was gripped by confusing and conflicting emotions. "So what happens now…between us?" I asked tentatively.

Carol clasped her arms around me and laid her head against my chest. "I don't know, Jon. I hadn't intended to fall in love—not with you, not with anybody. When Katy and I finished the spring term, I had just broken up with a guy I had been with for over a year. I've met some guys and had sex, of course, like we all do, as Katy and I have travelled about. But I never really felt so *close* to anyone, not even with

Craig, the guy I was seeing at college. I think you're special, and, as I've said, I think it was it was meant to be. But, whether this is the *right time* for *us* is another question." Carol's extra few years of maturation were evident. I had no idea what should happen next. We stood in silence holding each other.

"Will we…stay in touch…or…well…do we just walk away from this?" I had to force the words out of me.

"I'll give you my address at Oberlin…but, Jon, we'll both be going back to very different worlds. But I really do want to stay in touch. If you want to." I could only nod.

"Hey, come on now! We've still got a whole day! And there's something we need to do."

"What's that?"

"Find our clothes from last night!"

I even managed to laugh.

Eighteen

Verweile doch! Du bist so schön!

—Goethe, *Faust*

At some point in life, most of us discover that, in those instances when we might wish for time to slow down so that we might savor every moment, it is at these self-same times that the hours slip away like quicksilver. And to say, "Time flies when you're having fun," only trivializes the realization. No, at some point we each must discover that life is not a game in which time-outs can be called and during which the clock stops. In life, the game is always on. This basic lesson was brought home to me over the space of my last night with Carol, when I willed with my entire being that the hours we had left to us would last a lifetime.

At supper that evening, Kyle and I had agreed we would start hitching back to Lawrenceville after breakfast. As Monday was a holiday, we didn't know what the traffic would be like or how long it might take us to get home. Robert, one of the 'Nam vets, agreed to drive us bright and early in the morning down to the interstate. Kyle and I had to start school on Tuesday, so we thought an early departure would make sense. And it did make sense on the rational level; but on the emotional level, it was hell and made no sense at all. This was the first time I had given myself wholly to another person, and I was leaving her behind.

After supper, Kyle had gone to take down the tent and pack it and some of his things for tomorrow. He'd said he would sleep somewhere else. Whether this was with Katy or just somewhere else, he never said. Carol and I ambled back to the bus, which, over the space of a few short days, had begun to feel like home. Carol sat on the bed and watched as I grabbed T-shirts and other odds and ends and placed them in my backpack. Neither Carol nor I spoke much. When I had packed away all but the few toiletries I'd need for the morning, Carol suggested we take a walk.

As often happened during summer's Dog Days, the late afternoon's heat had slowly built up to a short and sharp thundershower. The clouds cleared just before sunset and a mist started to rise as the sun's steely rays made one last attempt at asserting themselves. As dusk settled over those lovely foothills, the air was rich with smells of waning summer: drenched earth, rhododendron thickets which bordered the farm, dying grasses, as well as wildflowers releasing their perfumes. Birds chirped, frogs croaked, bees hummed, and crickets strummed their individual tunes, as though attempting to drown out the Morse code-like clicking of other insects.

Carol led me by the hand as we strolled slowly in no particular direction except away from other people. Occasionally she would turn and look up at me; her hazel eyes seemed to be searching mine. It brought to mind our ocular conversation on the bus, only a few days before. We said little but kept moving, occasionally bumping arms and hips, sometimes accidentally, sometimes playfully. Finally, we came to an ancient chestnut tree stump where we sat down. It was on a rise overlooking the farmhouse below. We could hear odd snatches of laughter and conversation from people out on the porch. I sat with my arm around Carol, and she nestled her face into my chest. My nostrils once more drank in the aroma of her body. Unusually, Carol's hair was down, so I took both hands and gathered it like a bouquet, burying my face into it.

She laughed quietly and said, "Jon, I don't think anyone has ever adored me quite like you!"

With my mouth still muffled in her hair, I said, "I don't know why I'm leaving tomorrow, why I'm leaving you at all. It's crazy."

"I know, I know," Carol responded, "but you *know* at some level why you're leaving. And I'll be leaving here, too, just a couple of weeks later. But talking about it won't change things, and it probably won't help either of us now so let's just *be*. Let's just enjoy *here* and *now* because it's all we have."

Here and now again. But never had "here and now" formed such a combination that I wanted them to expand into one eternal now. I wasn't yet old enough to be able to move on easily from such an experience, but I was still young enough to want to kick and scream, hold my breath, and try to force my will onto time and being. I let go of Carol's hair, lifted her face to mine and kissed her, letting the taste and texture of her mouth imprint itself on my senses. I wanted an indelible memory. We sat on the stump for an hour or more, certainly until our bottoms were numb. When we finally stood, stiff of limb, I stretched my arms over my head and was stunned, as I always am, by the Milky Way and the immensity of our universe. Yet here, in our one, little corner of the universe was love.

Without a word, Carol and I headed back toward the bus. That old bus might as well have been a time machine or some sort of tele-transporter from science fiction movies, for it had certainly transported me to a very different reality. Carol lit some candles, along with some incense sticks, and switched on the tape player. I watched her undress for the last time, the candlelight dancing across her sun-tanned skin. Carol smiled and said, "Come to bed, Jon." I dropped my cut-offs, threw my T-shirt onto my backpack, and slipped onto the mattress beside her.

Carol and I made love slowly, deliberately, and passionately; we fell asleep with me still inside her.

~ * ~

The dawning of that Monday, Labor Day, brought with it an ache such as I had never experienced. Carol and I said little to one another. For me, there were just too many thoughts and feelings—and conflicting feelings at that—to put into words in the time left to us. Thus, in the same way as our relationship had started, a mere four days before, we looked at one another deeply, letting our eyes do the talking for us. When Robert brought his VW Beetle around to the front of the farmhouse to load Kyle, me, and our backpacks, Carol said that she wouldn't be going down to the highway with us. I just nodded. Katy came out of the house to say goodbye to Kyle and me, but also it seemed she was there as emotional support for her friend. In her hands was a large, brown, paper bag. "Vittles for the road," she smiled. She handed the bag to Kyle. We both thanked her and then she and Kyle had a quick hug and kiss.

Carol threw her arms around me, her face against my chest. "I don't remember where I heard this, Jon," she said, "but it's all I can—and want—to say to you right now." Carol laid her hand over my heart, looked me in the eye and pronounced, almost as a benediction, "Nothing lasts forever, all is meant to die, but may I say 'I love you,' before I say 'goodbye'?" Carol then turned to Katy, who placed her arm around her waist. Kyle and I got into the VW, waved, and drove away. The lump in my throat felt like a goose egg.

~ * ~

I'm convinced that special people carve out a space inside us, a space that only they will ever be able to fill. And if they never re-appear in our lives, that space remains, their presence having enlarged us. It was true of Carol and certainly true for Kyle. But it's a painful process. Thus, another of life's ironies: It's not the lack of love that hurts so much; rather, it's loving and being loved, so very deeply and intensely, that hurts. It's especially so when a loved one is lost to us, for whatever reasons. This is just one of the many lessons we must learn as we negotiate our way from the innocence of youth's Paradise to the often-painful realities of life east of Eden.

And Kyle and I were heading east, back to all that was familiar, and yet now, suddenly strange. With no ado, Robert dropped us onto the entrance ramp of I-40. "Y'all take care, ya hear? And don't let the Man get ya!" He winked, revved the VW, and drove away.

Kyle sensed that I was leaving a large portion of my heart back in Old Fort. He asked some questions, but not many. Kyle was good that way. We both had a few laughs as we remembered the night of the mescaline trip. I teased Kyle about his running naked and shouting, "This is where it's at!" He blushed ten shades of purple and insisted the episode should remain strictly between us. I assured him it would, but I knew I would always be able to get a laugh whenever I brought it up.

To keep me from thinking about Carol, I asked Kyle about Katy. Although there was clearly no emotional attachment between the two of them, Kyle only grinned self-consciously and mumbled, "Well...*you know*." And I did. What I also knew was that for two guys who had just lost their virginity, we side-stepped the subject like two Victorian vicars. I suppose our mothers would have been proud of our reticence about such a topic, even if they were aghast at our recent behavior.

Kyle's and my return trip was subdued. Going somewhere is nearly always more fun than returning. At least the getting in and out of cars kept my mind from dwelling upon Carol and all I had left behind. Kyle and I had numerous five- and ten-mile lifts, but the people were friendly and curious about where we were going or where we had been. Overall, the trip was uneventful, unlike the previous few days.

Nineteen

With all my will, but much against my heart
We two now part.
My Very Dear,
Our solace is, the sad road lies so clear.

—Coventry Patmore

After the experiences of the recently past summer, my senior year in high school seemed totally irrelevant. It was something simply to be endured. Though outwardly, nothing in my life had changed, everything was different. My relationship with Wendy was no exception. After the vibrancy of the few days in Old Fort with Carol, my life seemed to have gone from Technicolor to grainy black-and-white. It seemed incredibly odd that two so very different realities, though united in my life, could be connected simply, yet irreconcilably, by a ribbon of highway. I had to fight the urge simply to hit the road and return to Old Fort and to Carol before she left. The commune was still there; but here I was in a life that seemed passé, yet still had to be lived. And everyone noticed the change in me.

I had suddenly become more pensive and introspective. I weighed the value or lack thereof of just about everything I had to do. In an attempt to divine what was going on, my parents asked me searching questions, to which I gave non-committal, pat answers which invited no further enquiry. They had found out, of course, that Kyle and I had hitch-hiked on our trip "to the Smokies." Kyle's father was pissed off, but my parents cut me some slack, as first, Kyle and I were fine, and second, they were still concerned about what Mrs. Sullivan's suicide had done to me. And so, I indulged their worries, just to give myself more personal space.

I did what was required of me. I continued to make good grades, I played sports, and even continued to see Wendy. But I realized that my heart was in none of these things. Kyle and I even still went flying with my dad from time to time, but it was Kyle who was keen to take the controls when offered. I just went along for the ride and to be with my best friend. In so many ways, I was going through the motions and paying lip service to the life that was expected of me at that time and in that place.

I read a lot: Kesey, Kerouac, and other Beat writers. I daydreamed about Carol, mused about tripping again, and schemed about where to find some mescaline. But for me, life had moved somewhere over the horizon, and in each facet of my life I seemed to be playing a part in someone else's script. Only my private, internal world seemed to have any authenticity, and Kyle was the only person who had a clue as to why that should be the case.

My parents' concern for their increasingly Cistercian-like son became the occasion for another of life's ironic twists. A couple of weeks after school began, my mother, full to the brim with anxieties about her younger son, asked, "Jon, darling...your father and I are...well...we're concerned about you. Something's changed...that is, well, *you've changed* and you don't seem the same as...well...*before*...you know, all that business with Wendy's mother. You used to have regular chats with Rev. McLaurin..." Mother fidgeted nervously. "Well…that is…ah…have you thought about speaking to him again?"

I studied my mother for a moment. "Aw, Mom—you haven't said anything to him, have you?"

"No—well…yes. Yes, I have. Sweetheart, I'm worried about you—and so is your father. If you won't talk to us, then maybe you'll talk with the minister."

"What did Rev. McLaurin say?"

"Ah…well…I believe he said you'd speak to him again when you were ready."

"Smart man," I quipped. Seeing the hurt on my mother's face, I added, "Aw, look, Mom—I'm okay *really*. I just have things on my mind, that's all."

"Well, Jon, that's what worries me."

Seeing there was going to be no convincing her, I told her, "Okay. Look, I'll go see McLaurin, all right?" And pre-empting her next question, I added, "I'll see him this week. In fact, I'll call him this evening and arrange a meeting, okay?"

Mother's relief was palpable as I went to the hallway phone. I spoke to McLaurin and we agreed to meet after school the next day. It occurred to me that I had less than twenty-four hours to plan what I would and would not say to my minister. I really liked and respected Rev. McLaurin, so I was determined I would not lie to him; I just wouldn't tell *all* the truth. After all, he was an *ordained minister*. How, I wondered in my naïveté, could he understand what I had recently been through or the things I had done?

~ * ~

When I knocked at the pastor's study door the next afternoon, I was greeted in his usual warm and friendly manner. But after Rev. McLaurin had closed the door and I was seated, he came to where I was seated, laid his hand on my shoulder and said, "Jon, I hope you are here because this is what *you* want and not what your parents have pushed you into. I don't believe in forced confessions or inquisitions!" He chuckled in his easy manner.

"Yeah, well, it is a combination of both, I suppose. But it is good to see you again."

The minister took his seat and smiled amiably. "I'll put my cards on the table. Both of your parents have had a word with me."

"Both?" I asked. "Even my dad?"

"Yep, even the Flyin' Leatherneck," he laughed. "Seems you've got him worried as well."

I raised my eyebrows and mumbled, "Wow."

"So here's the dope. I understand you and your friend, Kyle, went hitchhiking to the Smoky Mountains so you could spend some time on the Appalachian Trail following that awful situation with your girlfriend's mother. I'll be honest. Your mom accepts that story—*I think*—but your dad doesn't buy it. He reckons something else went on. That's all I know except that both of your parents seem very concerned about you."

"Hmmm, yeah." I bit my lower lip in thought as I weighed McLaurin's words.

"Jon, unless you really want to say anything, I'm happy to leave it there. We can both tell your parents in all honesty that we talked. The ball's in your court. But anything you choose to say will stay in this room, just between you and me. Okay? I can take care of your parents."

I nodded as I scratched my chin and then ran my hand through my hair, which now reached over my collar. "Wow," I began, "so much has happened since you and I last talked." And then, without meaning to do so, I told him virtually everything that happened on Kyle's and my road trip. I even speculated that what had happened between Carol and me was the death knell for my relationship with Wendy. All the while, I kept my eye on every non-verbal cue I might pick up from the pastor, looking for any sign of disapprobation or condemnation. There was the odd raised eyebrow, smile, and even chuckle, but none of the moral judgment I feared.

When I had finished speaking, Rev. McLaurin cleared his throat and said, "Jon, I believe it is only fair that when a man shares as much as you have, I should reciprocate in some measure. However, with your permission, I won't offer quite as much detail." McLaurin smiled. "But let it suffice to say that when I got married, I was not a virgin. When I was a young man, away from home and at war, I did as most of my compatriots did: took solace in too much alcohol and sought female companionship when it could be found. None of us knew when our number would be up, so we wanted to live life to the full. There were scant few of us who did not want to taste life's pleasures before we were either killed or shot down and taken prisoner. You understand?"

"Yeah, sure." This incipient understanding was accompanied by the sweet irony that, apart from my parents, the person to whom I had least expected to relate my "road" experiences had met my revelations with understanding and acceptance. It was also the first time that a person of my parents' generation had ever fully treated me as an equal.

"So, Jon, I cannot sit in the judgment seat. I admit that we have both sailed close to the wind as regards our society's moral conventions, but those conventions aren't necessarily found in the Bible. Now I'd be the first to say that the Bible doesn't support sexual prurience or profligacy, but neither does it actually provide us with a manual for sexual behavior and relationships, at least not as we understand them in our post-Victorian world. Just have a read of the book of Ruth—and I suggest you do." I agreed I would.

"Jon, you don't have to answer this, but may I enquire whether you and Wendy have had sex?"

"No, sir—I mean, yes sir—you may ask, *but no*, we haven't had sex." McLaurin simply nodded and thought to himself.

"It sounds to me that you and Carol have honored one another in the love you shared, and sometimes that's enough. God knows, I have seen too many relationships which enjoyed married, legal status but in which one or both parties failed miserably to love one another," he paused. "Or, in fact, they outright abused each other. Being married doesn't necessarily mean a relationship is honorable or loving." We sat in silence for several moments. "Jon, I do feel you need to clarify your relationship with Wendy. And I don't mean that you should tell her what you've shared with me. That wouldn't help her one little bit at this point in her life, understand?" McLaurin looked me straight in the eye. "It sounds like you and Carol, however intensely you have felt for one another, are going in different directions right now. Am I right?" I nodded in the affirmative. "But nevertheless, you owe it to yourself and to Wendy to decide how best to end your relationship, if that is what you intend."

"Yes, sir, I understand."

As we got up to shake hands, McLaurin smiled and shook his head at some inner thought. He gave a little apologetic wave of his hand and said, "Forgive me, Jon. But it has hit me just how much your life has changed in these last few weeks and since we last spoke." He clapped me on the shoulder as he opened the study door.

"You're certainly right about that!"

As I stepped out into the corridor, McLaurin added, "It all kinda reminds me of a line from one of Browning's poems that I learned back in college." I turned and waited expectantly. "'How soon a smile of God can change the world.'" McLaurin gave a little wave as he closed the door.

Part Two

Twenty

No nation in the world has had greater fortune than mine in sharing a continent with the people and the nation of Canada.
—President Lyndon B. Johnson

The clientele at Jorgie & Beth's had all changed over the past three hours—except for us, of course. Beth came over with a pitcher of steaming coffee in her right hand and a baby clutched against her hip with the left. "Y'all staying for supper?" she joked as she poured for Ellen and Marie.

"Well, now that you mention it…" I chimed in. Beth turned back toward the service counter. "Hey, Beth—hang on a minute. You remember my friend, Kyle, who used to come in here with me from time to time? Well, this is his mother and his sister."

"It's good to meet you, but I'm so sorry for your loss. It must be terrible." Both mother and daughter nodded.

"Ellen and Marie are staying at my manse tonight, so you'll probably see them here again."

"I'll keep the coffee ready. Y'all ready for some dessert? I have my home-made pecan pie."

"I suppose we should," I offered, "It will help us not feel guilty about the café's 'bottomless cup of coffee'."

"That's right, Preacher Man," winked Beth. "Three servings of pie?" she queried. We agreed and she virtually pirouetted back to the counter, with baby and coffee pitcher as counter-balances.

After having discussed the details of Kyle's death and the immediate legal requirements, etc., our conversation had drifted over our common past history and events, all of which was peppered with remembrances of Kyle.

As we waited for dessert to appear, Marie looked at me and asked, "'Nother Brother? You've been divorced now for, what, twenty years or more?" Before I could assent, Marie continued, "Will you ever re-marry?" Her question caught me completely off guard.

"Wow—how to answer that one?" I expelled a chest full of air.

"'Yes' or 'no' will do," grinned Marie, and I could see Kyle in her face.

"Probably 'no,'" I replied. "And for more reasons than I have energy to discuss at this time."

Slightly changing the subject, Ellen said, "When y'all were young, I always thought you'd probably marry that girl—oh dear! What was her name?"

"Wendy Sullivan," I replied. Marie and I exchanged glances, wondering whether Ellen would remember the suicide connected with "that girl."

"We split up during my senior year in high school." I hoped to draw a line under the subject, but it was clear that Ellen Weston's mind was thumbing its way through past memories until she found whatever it was she was looking for—her eyes inwardly searching in the temporal distance. Ellen smiled at the success of her memory hunt. "Yes, you and Kyle used to double-date. He used to talk about you two a lot. And then something happened...what was it?" The smile on

Ellen's face faded away. "Oh. Oh my—yes, now I remember. How terrible!" She looked me in the eye and her hand reached out to mine. "Poor Jon! You've had more than your share of suicides, haven't you?"

"Enough for one life, eh?" I forced a weak smile.

"Whatever happened to Wendy?" asked Marie, as the subject was now squarely on the table.

"Well, I broke up with her a couple of months into my senior year. She was obsessed about marrying me, as though somehow that would fix the gaping hole in her life. I wasn't in a place even to consider marriage, not at the time. Wendy had a hard time accepting that it was over between us. Well, in fact, she didn't accept it at all. She used to go places where she knew I'd be, come find me in the school. It became quite difficult. It would be called 'stalking' these days. So, in the end, I had to be quite cruel and tell her just to leave me alone. In any case, she came to accept our break was final."

We sat in silence for a while, during which time Beth brought our desserts. Ellen was the first to break the silence. "I hope you'll forgive me for dredging that up that bit of your past, Jon."

I reached out and took Ellen's hand. "It's not a problem." I let loose an unintentional heavy sigh.

Ellen interjected, "Jon, please don't feel you have to talk, hon."

"It's all right—really. I'm just searching for the words. I only wanted to say that you could be forgiven for bringing up Mrs. Sullivan's suicide because it has certainly been on my mind. I have asked the good Lord more than once why I have had the spurious honor of stumbling onto two suicides during my lifetime—my girlfriend's mother and now my best friend. I'm hoping God will pick someone else next time…well…that is, if there has to be a next time."

"Maybe it's because God knew you could handle it." Ellen was patting my hand. "Not many people could, you know."

"Well, maybe…or maybe not. I don't know. But thanks for the vote of confidence."

Ellen wasn't finished. "I don't think Kyle would have wanted to be found by that Peebles fellow and those others, not if you weren't there.

Jon, he trusted you *to the end*—his end. And as odd as it seems, it shows he loved and trusted you."

I just bit my lip and stared at the empty dessert plate.

When Beth came to clear our table, Marie suggested we make a move to Kyle's house. Although I had started the process of packing and sorting Kyle's possessions, which were not numerous, there was still work for the three of us to do. Marie's suggestion came as a welcome distraction for all of us. As much as we had needed to talk, remember, question and cry together, we also needed a break from it. In many ways, our time at Jorgie and Beth's could have been likened to trying to assemble a jigsaw puzzle when the box lid with the actual picture was missing. No doubt, a fresh approach was needed, but even then, I wondered whether the picture we eventually created would always be many pieces short.

~ * ~

"Jon, you met your wife in Canada, didn't you?" Ellen was going through Kyle's chest-of-drawers and placing clothes bound for charities and clothing banks in plastic bags on the bed. I was going through the closet and doing the same thing. Marie was going through Kyle's study, sorting out the paperwork I hadn't yet gone through.

"That I did. I met her when I was studying at the Presbyterian College for my Master of Divinity in 1975. She was a junior at McGill University where I had finished my degree—you know…after…um…I left St. Edmund's because of the draft back in '71, just before the end of the spring semester." I had lost my 2-S—the student deferment from the draft—probably due to my activities with various anti-war groups.

"Yes, those were terrible times for so many families. I do recall speaking to your mother once or twice after you had left. It must have been difficult for you, going to Canada. How did you manage—I mean financially and whatnot—after just picking up and leaving like that?"

"Well, in some ways it wasn't as difficult as you might think. I had already experienced a number of problems with the draft board, so I had started to make some plans…*just in case*. Mother was my main support—morally and financially—and I'm sure she never told Dad about what she did for me. Vietnam had certainly divided our household back then. Mom was a Democrat and involved with Another Mother for Peace, and Dad was a staunch Republican. Anyway, Mom had inherited some money from her father; she had been saving it in an account for Ron and me for whenever we settled down, started a family or whatever. In any case, she helped keep me afloat. One of my professors from St. Edmund's, Richard Stein, also helped me out, both financially and with academic contacts at McGill. By the way, you know my degree is actually from St. Edmund's, don't you, even though I did half of my course work at McGill? And then there was one other person who supported me. As it was so long ago, I don't suppose he'd mind my telling you now: Rev. McLaurin. You remember him, don't you? The minister at my family's church in those days? With his wife's agreement, they kinda adopted me as a sort of 'wayward son' and helped me pay for books and the like. McLaurin also had contacts at The Presbyterian College in Montreal where I went for my divinity degree after I finished at McGill. It would have been a hell of a lot harder for me without the support of my mother, Stein, and McLaurin, that's for certain."

Marie had taken a break to make some tea for all of us and brought a tray to the bedroom where Ellen and I were working. "Don't let me interrupt!" she quickly interjected, "I'd like to hear more abo't those years you were missing from our lives."

I received a steaming mug with thanks and continued. "To begin with, I lived in a hostel run by two expatriate Americans—also war resisters—just over the border in Quebec. They were a couple of wild Jewish guys, Zvi Cohen and Dan Feinstein." I shook my head and chuckled at my memories. "You know, up until that time, I had only really thought of Jews as people in Bible stories. I mean, I never remember even meeting a Jewish person, not in white-bread, Protestant Lawrenceville or New Bern. Ha!" A funny memory leapt into the front of my mind. "When I told Zvi about where I had come from, he began singing a send-up of the song 'Toyland'—'Goyland, Goyland, uncircumsized girl-and-boy-land! Once you pass its borders, you can never return again!'" I laughed again at this zany memory. "Anyway, whenever a new 'refugee' arrived, he was welcomed with a steak dinner and then some of Zvi's home-grown weed…um—you know, marijuana." Marie just laughed and Ellen 'tut-tutted' her mock disapprobation. "In fact, Zvi, in his gruff New York manner, simply tossed the bag of dope to me and said, 'Roll your own. I don't go for this passing the joint around malarkey.' So I did—and we did, the ten or eleven people staying there at the time. Dan said the local cops didn't worry as long as the weed was grown for their own use! Man, you'd think I had entered the Promised Land, as just a few miles to the south I was a fugitive from justice. I don't think I'll ever forget those days."

"How long did you live in the hostel?" asked Marie.

"Oh, a month or two. It wasn't meant to be a long-term residence for anyone except Zvi and Dan, who ran the place. They had a steady trickle of war resisters coming to them, so Zvi, Dan, and another guy, who lived nearby but whose name I forget, tried to help everyone find a place to live and, if possible, a job. They also worked with the Montreal Committee to Aid War Objectors, which must have helped hundreds, if not thousands, of young men like me. As for me, thanks to Richard Stein back at St. Edmund's, I had already been accepted into the religion department at McGill. I soon hooked up with a few other students who needed a housemate and joined them."

Ellen looked up from her tea and asked, "Now tell me, Jon—my memory's a bit weak these days—was this after Kyle had left for the Army and then went to Vietnam?"

I stopped and thought for a moment. "Yeah, it was. Kyle dropped out of college to join the Army during the fall semester of our sophomore year in college. That was 1970. I-I couldn't believe it—and certainly didn't expect it. I mean, Kyle did what, for so many of us, was the *unthinkable*: he not only dropped out of college, which meant the end of his student deferment, the hallowed 2-S, but he had also joined up!" I shook my head at the decision made all those years ago as my own memories pulled me in.

Twenty-one

This war has already stretched the generation gap so wide that it threatens to pull the country apart."

—Senator Frank Church,
speaking on the Senate floor on May 13, 1970.

"Are you crazy?" I grabbed Kyle by his shoulder and shook him gently. "How could you do it, especially at a time like this? Do you *want* to go to Vietnam?" Kyle just smiled that winning, lazy smile of his and pulled free of my grasp.

I had driven over to Kyle's house my first evening home at the beginning of the Thanksgiving break. Only that morning, I had received a short letter from Kyle, telling me of his decision to drop out of NC State, where he had been studying engineering. As soon as I had dumped my bags, I headed straight for the Westons' house. Kyle had written that he was tired of academics and wanted to fly helicopters. His letter had left me completely baffled.

"Shit, Kyle! I'm the one with the Marine for a father. Remember 'Blackie,' the flyin' Leatherneck? Why're you enlisting at a time like this? I mean, Vietnam is serious business."

Kyle just shrugged and grinned once more. "Even Vietnam can't go on forever. Besides, not everybody gets sent over there—there's Germany, Korea—plenty of other places. You know I like flying and always have, ever since those days we used to go up with your old man."

"Yeah, but you've joined the *Army*, Kyle, and Vietnam is where most guys like you get sent," I countered, "and it's already gone on longer than the US's involvement in World War Two. Think about that. Even my dad no longer thinks the US is fighting to win over there. Tricky Dick and Kissinger say they're going to wind down American involvement, but it certainly doesn't look that way...not yet anyway." But my pleas and appeals to conscience had no effect. Kyle left for boot camp the week after Thanksgiving.

~ * ~

I didn't hear much from Kyle during his time in boot camp, but that changed once he made it to preflight training, where he frequently reported his progress to me in letters. As he had always been a fast learner and had an aptitude for things mechanical, preflight went smoothly. The worst of it was that the sergeants enjoyed tormenting him and his fellow preflighters as though they were back in boot camp. Still, with the goal that lay ahead of him—silver wings—Kyle said he could ignore all the shit that was thrown at him. He wanted to fly, and fly he would. All the loudmouth stuff from sergeants, instructors, and senior classmen was just meant to weed out the wimps. It was a game, so he could simply let it slide. Kyle wanted to get on the flight line and into helicopters.

That day arrived soon enough. I clearly recall how excitedly Kyle wrote about his first flight with his IP— instructor pilot. I could feel the excitement as his handwriting was nearly illegible. "The guy's a natural—his hands hardly look as though they are moving on the cyclic stick or collective control. He seems to *think* the chopper where he wants it to go. Man, I'm half scared and half chomping at the bit to have my first shot at flying."

"Cyclic stick?" "Collective control?" I had only the vaguest idea of what Kyle was writing about; but what clearly came through was the fact that flight training was contagious, and Kyle had the bug. I had lived with Blackie long enough to know the effects of "aeroholism."

If I'm honest, Kyle's letters left me with mixed feelings. It was kind of cool to hear about his hands-on learning, as opposed to the academic education I was receiving. Having grown up with a Marine father, it had seemed natural to me that I would serve my country in some branch of the military. But Vietnam had changed all of that. For the life of me, I couldn't see what real difference it made to America who was elected to run Vietnam. After all, it was *their* country. I tried to picture hordes of Viet Minh running rampant down American streets, making off with our burgers and cheerleaders, but nary a flag-waving tingle called me to arms. The Vietnamese had their minds on other things closer to home. What the hell did America have to fear from Ho Chi Minh or his successors? If they wanted to fight a civil war, wasn't it their business—just like the War Between the States? But, as regarded my best friend, I couldn't separate Kyle's training from its intended purpose, not the way Kyle could. Kyle wasn't a militarist. After all, we had both opposed the steady escalation of the war in Vietnam. But there it was. Kyle received his wings as a Warrant Officer.

~ * ~

Meanwhile my life took its own oblique turns. One day, in the late spring of 1971, I went to my campus mailbox, where I found an ominous letter waiting for me. It was from the Selective Service System and managed to darken the luster of that otherwise bright morning. It was full of officialese regarding the Selective Service Act of 1967 and, as I was no longer to be considered 2-S, I was now 1-A and should report to my local draft board on such-and-such a date. Happily, classes had started to wind down as we were approaching the final exam period. I had already completed the few term papers that had been assigned, so no worries there, but I needed to enact the plan I had concocted with Richard Stein and start my journey to Canada without delay—exams notwithstanding.

In addition to being a professor of philosophy at St. Edmund's, Richard Stein—or Dick, as he preferred—was also a Methodist minister and peace activist who had counseled many a young man with regard to the Vietnam War and the draft. Born of German-American parentage in Wisconsin, with more than a little Mennonite influence, pacifism was second-nature to Richard. He had like-minded colleagues in both Church and university right up the east coast and into Canada; thus, together they operated their own version of an Underground Railroad for war resisters. Stein also shunned formalities of any kind and was always on a first- or last-name basis with his students. Thus, it was always "Dick" or "Stein," but never "Professor!"

Against the possibility of a day like this one, Dick had written a letter of introduction for me to present to a professor friend of his at McGill University in Montreal. He had it in a file cabinet in his office for safe-keeping. I managed to catch Dick just before he left to teach a class. Having run all the way to his office, I breathlessly told him the state of play. Dick stopped a passing student who was on the way to his philosophy class and asked him to tell everyone he'd be a few minutes late. Meanwhile, he unlocked his file cabinet, retrieved the letter of introduction for me, which was in an addressed, sealed envelope. "Keep this safe," he said. "You can use it at the Canadian border if need be." I carefully slipped it in my day pack with my books. Stein then returned to the file cabinet and, after fishing around underneath the files for a moment or two, pulled out a thick brown envelope which he thrust into my hand.

"What's this?" I enquired.

"About four hundred dollars," he replied. "You'll need it to get started in Canada, and you might need to prove to the border guards that you aren't indigent."

I looked at the envelope and started to speak, "Dick, I-I can't—"

Stein put his fingers to my lips to shush me; then he smiled, somewhat wistfully, at me. "You may be a degenerate hippy, Braddock, but at least you won't be indigent! You can repay me by doing the same for someone else one day, okay?"

"You got it! And—hey—thanks, Dick."

His mind racing ahead, Dick asked, "What time can you be ready for me to drive you to Greensboro for the evening Amtrak to New York?"

"I'll need about three hours to get back to the house and pack my bags and then I'm all yours."

Speaking more to himself than me, Stein mused aloud, "Okay. Okay. Hmm…my last class ends at 4:00. Right! I can be at your house around 4:30. Leave whatever you don't absolutely need, got that? I'll take care of it, okay? We'll grab some dinner en route to Greensboro. I've got to go now, but you can use my office phone to book your train ticket."

From that point on, the sequence of events happened so quickly that only some memories remain clear while the rest are like the blur of a film on fast-forward. I remember filling my backpack with clothes, toiletries, and some nibbles and throwing whatever else I thought I might need into an Army surplus duffel bag—my life in two bags! Stein drove me the eighty or so miles to Greensboro and, although my departure was a late one, he wouldn't let me wait alone. As we sat together in the station, Dick assured me that he would contact my mother and let her know what was going on. He would also send a letter to his colleague at McGill, as well as try to catch him on the telephone in case I got there before the letter arrived.

By the time the train rumbled into the station, I was feeling both the strain of the day and the high emotional excitement of the journey ahead. Dick helped carry my bags onto the train, gave me hug, and waited on the platform to wave me off. I gave him the peace sign and then rolled my eyes heavenward as though saying, "What in God's name have I got myself into?" The train jerked forward, Dick disappeared, and before long, the train was rolling through midnight darkness of the Carolina countryside.

My anticipation notwithstanding, I was soon lulled into a heavy sleep. I was awakened a few hours later when someone slipped into the seat beside me—was that in Richmond or Washington? But I didn't fully awaken until Philadelphia. The seat next to me was as empty as my stomach, so I made my way to the dining car. When I returned, there was a young—and not unattractive—woman sitting in the seat that had been vacated by my former fellow traveler. Her name was Melanie, and it turned out she was on her way back to New York University, having just spent some time with friends in Philly. We chatted for a while and compared notes on New York student life versus that of rural North Carolina. Melanie seemed surprised at the drug-taking and counter-cultural activities that went on down South. My journey northward naturally piqued her curiosity, and for a while, I avoided saying anything about the real purpose or destination of my trip. However, not long before we reached New York City, I felt I could probably trust this young woman. Thus, I told her about my situation and where I was headed. Melanie thought it was both a brave and scary thing I was doing, but respected my decisions for leaving the US. She even agreed to direct me to the right bus station once we had arrived in Manhattan.

I had only ever seen New York City once, and that was from the air when flying with my father, so I savored the skyline as the train approached Manhattan. Melanie pointed out the various bridges and buildings for my enlightenment. As we neared the terminus, Melanie asked whether I'd like to stay over a day or so with her and her friends. She assured me it would not be very likely that the Feds would find me in a city like New York. It was a tempting offer, but disappointing as it was to me—and seemingly to my newfound friend—plans had been made and I had a timetable to keep. So we quickly exchanged details before the train stopped in the station. Melanie then directed me to a good delicatessen to buy food for the bus journey ahead and then hailed a taxi to get me to the bus station and her back to her university digs. It was a short journey to the bus station, but a relief not to have to carry two heavy bags. As the cabby went around the car to get my bags from the trunk, I reached for my wallet, only to have my hand stayed by Melanie's. "This is my treat. I'm sure you'll need every penny you've got." With that she gave me a hug and kissed my cheek. "Take care, Jon."

"I'll do my best," I replied. The cabby jumped behind the wheel, and with that the taxi—and Melanie—roared away. For the first time since my sojourn had begun, I felt alone and lonely. I wanted to kick myself for turning down Melanie's offer of a night or two in New York. Chances were that no one would have begun looking for me for weeks yet. And there had been the slight hint of the amorous about Melanie's invitation. As I stood there recriminating myself in front of the station entrance, I slowly became aware that my bags and I were being considered something of a nuisance by the nasally New Yorkers trying to get past me into the ticket hall. So I slung my backpack over one shoulder, hefted the duffel with the opposite arm and made my way to the ticket counter. Basically, I was to make my way up the west bank of the Hudson River to Plattsburgh about twenty miles south of the border with Canada. I had been given the name of a motel run by a couple, James and Alison, whose son had also taken refuge in Canada. They knew Zvi and Dan, and were very supportive of the work they were doing.

When I got to Plattsburgh, I was road-weary from almost a thousand miles of train and bus travel, but I was equally heartened that I was near my destination. After checking into the motel, I had a hot meal in their café. Meanwhile, James rang Zvi to let him know I had arrived safely. Zvi then arranged for a Canadian friend to drive over the border the next day and return with me to the hostel. Before turning in for the night, Alison approached me somewhat abashedly and quietly suggested that she might give my long hair a trim. "You know, just to tidy it a bit. It might attract less attention on the US side of the border." I took her point and agreed to go under the scissors. In fact, she was a dab hand at hair-cutting, and thus, after a shower and a good night's sleep *in a bed*, I looked much less the part of a fugitive from justice.

My driver, Bob Stillman, turned out to be a middle-aged Canadian, who taught school on a part-time basis. The rest of his time, he volunteered for the Montreal Committee to Aid War Objectors. Bob arrived in time for lunch and gave me the protocol for our short journey. I was informed that, for the purposes of the border crossing, Bob was my uncle and I was paying his family a visit following my spring semester in college. As a fallback, I also had the letter from the professor at McGill to say I was considering transferring there. Bob chose the busy time of the day, when people who worked either side of the border were travelling home, to make our crossing. It worked like a charm.

However, at the same time, it was hard to take on board that by simply crossing an arbitrary geographical point, a state-imposed border line, a line that could not be discerned on the earth's surface from any spacecraft, that I was now a "free" man. How far was it between the US and Canadian border posts, a handful of yards? But what couldn't be measured—nor could I have even anticipated—was the gulf of separation that border would create in me over coming years, the separation between me and my family, between me and my friends, and the country and culture which had nurtured me. It was more than homesickness and the culture-shock of having to learn French in order to get on with a normal life in Montreal; it was the cost of following conscience and the moral imperative of non-violence. That cost involved giving up all that was comfortable and familiar about "home," for the life of self-imposed exile.

The dismissive term used by right-wing conservatives—"draft-dodger"—carried the connotation of shirking duty or hardship for a life of ease or even indolence. But such are the ways we minimize the lives of those with whom we disagree. There was no way I could have known, when I entered Canada in that late spring of 1971, that I would miss my grandfather's funeral and that I would not be there when my father suffered his first major illness and hospitalization, or that I wouldn't be there when my best friend returned home from Vietnam a very changed man.

~ * ~

After my first few months in Canada, it became clear from Kyle's correspondence that he would eventually be sent to Vietnam. There was a gap in our communication when he moved bases for further, intensive training. Whenever our addresses changed, we kept in touch by sending our letters to his mother. Ellen kindly acted the part of postmistress and re-routed them to each of us at the correct address.

With the start of the autumn semester at McGill, my life as a student resumed its familiar routines: studying, working at part-time jobs, attending occasional rock concerts, getting stoned, and, when fortune smiled, getting laid. I kept Kyle informed about how my life in Canada was unfolding, but I noticed, at the same time, that Kyle's letters became terser and he showed less interest in my Canadian adventures. I took no offense—and why should I? Kyle was preparing to go to war. As a pilot, he would have the lives of others literally in his hands. I did wonder sometimes whether my trials and triumphs as an ex-pat war resister in Montreal must have seemed rather mundane to Kyle, if not downright trivial. In any case, he never said so. Although we had chosen very different paths, neither of us ever passed judgment on the other. Our friendship was solid, and we both accepted and respected the vastly different lives we had chosen.

~ * ~

Kyle was sent to Vietnam in the autumn of 1971, as a part of an air assault battalion of the 1st Cavalry Division (Airmobile) during the waning days in that God-forsaken war. These were the heady days of "the Vietnamization of the Vietnam war." Oxymoronic at best, "Vietnamization" was a term coined by the then US Secretary of Defense, Melvin Laird. It was the new and preferred flip-side to his previous term: "de-Americanizing" the war. In stark human terms, it meant that more South Vietnamese were meant to die in the war than their American counterparts. But the sad fact was that the number of American dead hadn't even reached its peak.

Yet what I am telling you is the story of my friend and our friendship and not a war, so I will keep it to the personal facts and events during that time which were to irrevocably shape Kyle's post-Vietnam life, which is to say, the rest of his life.

Kyle was assigned to fly "slicks"—so called because, unlike the helicopter gunships, they were relatively unarmed, the exception being the M-60 machine guns mounted in the cargo doors and manned by the chopper's crew chief and gunner. In his last letter to me before being shipped overseas, Kyle had justified his part in the war by writing, "Hell, Jon, as a pilot, I can't even shoot anybody, but they can sure have a crack at me! I'll just be flying in and out of LZs, carrying grunts, ammunition, and stuff like that. Don't worry, buddy; ol' Kyle ain't a warrior."

Kyle's cool head and sure hands on the controls meant he would be the pilot of his slick. It was only in the remaining days before shipping out that he met the men who would form his crew. Dave McChesney, a Californian, was the crew chief for Kyle's ship and soon to become his "main man" while in Vietnam.

The gunner was Frederick Douglass Armstrong, a black kid from Maryland. His parents had given him his first and middle names in honor of the 19th century social reformer, orator, and statesman. It had been their hope that bearing such a name would inspire their son to the same heights. Frederick, as he insisted on being called, carried both his name and his parents' hopes proudly. But there was never a proverbial snowball's chance in hell that his fellow soldiers were going to call him "Frederick." Instead, because his initials were FDA, the same as the acronym for the Food and Drug Administration, he was christened "Food'n'drug" by one of the regimental wits, and it stuck. In any case, his fate was not to be determined by his noble name, but rather, like that of so many other 18-year-olds, by an anonymous white bureaucrat pulling numbers for the draft lottery. "Food'n'drug" was drafted before he could begin his first semester at Howard University.

To complete the crew of Kyle's chopper was the co-pilot, a Cajun from Louisiana named François Duquesne. He wasn't even out of basic training before he was re-christened with the somewhat predictable "Duke." All things considered, Kyle and his crew were a near perfect cross-section of young American manhood. Some were to have their names inscribed upon a wall made of black gabbro years after their deaths—but they weren't to know that in 1971.

~ * ~

Kyle's letters from Vietnam were few and far between and usually late in arriving. He mostly told me about the funny stuff that happened and the crazy characters he met. He rarely wrote about the war itself unless someone he particularly cared about was killed or wounded. I kept up with the Vietnam situation through the TV news and newspapers. It was interesting to be so close to the US but to get such a very different take on the war by Canadian pundits and political analysts. I even stuck a map of Vietnam on the wall of my bedroom so I could follow Kyle's whereabouts whenever he mentioned them. As for my side of the correspondence, I tried to write Kyle about once every two weeks, with the hope that news from his old friend might help him in some way. I could only judge this by how much letters from home helped me not to feel so far removed from loved ones.

Meanwhile, in the US, Nixon's re-election campaign was well under way. Hardly anyone in Canada could understand why the electorate south of the border would vote again for such a dodgy character. The only good things to come out of his great lead over his democratic rivals were the political cartoons of a Pinocchio-nosed Nixon and ironic slogans such as, "Don't change Dicks in the middle of a screw, vote for Nixon in '72!"

In the early summer of 1972, Kyle's by then infrequent letters stopped. Before I could read anything dire into this lack of communication, I received a letter from Kyle's mother. She wanted to let me know, in case I hadn't heard anything, that Kyle had been wounded but was "basically all right" and was being shipped home "any day now." I tossed around in my mind just what "basically all right" might mean. "Basically all right"—but with one leg missing? "Basically all right"—but blind? I tried not to let my imagination run wild, so I wrote Mrs. Weston, asking for any further details.

A few weeks later, I received a reply from Ellen Weston that Kyle had survived a chopper crash and had then been wounded in the left shoulder and hand while trying to escape the wreckage. His left hand needed re-constructive surgery, but his left shoulder was less serious. Ellen had managed to speak to Kyle once on the telephone and thought he sounded "remarkably well." That was something. She ended her letter saying that, as Kyle might be moved several times in the near future, I ought to send my letters to her and she would see that Kyle received them.

I wrote about a half-dozen letters to Kyle over the next two to three months without one reply. When autumn arrived, I decided to write once more to Ellen Weston, to try to discover Kyle's state of mind. Ellen wrote back to tell me that she had gone to see Kyle when he arrived at an Army hospital in California. She said he "seemed to be very glad to be back in the States, but was reluctant to speak about what happened over there." Kyle was spending a lot of time in physiotherapy for his shoulder, but would need another operation on his left hand. He would then be moved to a VA hospital in North Carolina as he was being discharged from the Army. Ellen said she tried to make Kyle promise to write me before long.

Showing that there's nothing like a mother's influence, I indeed received a letter from Kyle about three weeks later—well, a brief note actually. It read:

Hey Jon,
Mom says you want to hear from your one-handed, shot-to-shit, former flyboy friend. So here I am. Sorry if I don't have much to say, except, I'm alive.
Love,
Kyle

P.S. You, Jon ol' Buddy, made the RIGHT decision. Never doubt it.

That was the last missive I received from Kyle until we met again, face-to-face.

~ * ~

In the late summer of 1972, my brother Ron got married to a woman in Louisville, where he had moved for work after graduation from college. It was just such significant family events that intensified the sense of separation with my former life. Ron and I had never been close, but his marriage and settling far from our family home only served to make permanent the distance between us.

When Tricky Dick was re-elected in November 1972, I began to despair of ever going home again. But as '72 rolled into '73, news began breaking about a White House scandal which involved men in Nixon's employ burgling the Democratic National Committee's headquarters at the Watergate Complex in Washington, D.C. As evidence mounted, the US Senate voted to establish a select committee to convene hearings which began at the end of my last term at McGill. It was chaired by none other than one of North Carolina's senators, Sam Ervin. Nixon's predicament and Ervin's appointment seemed like a dual sign from heaven as far as I was concerned, and so I thought it was time I made a trip across the border to my home state. I hoped that, with most of North America glued to its television sets watching the Watergate hearings and the government in turmoil, a small fish like me wouldn't be worth catching.

My desire to go home was driven by two factors. Not only did I want to track down Kyle, from whom I had heard nothing for nearly a year, but I also wanted to see my parents and particularly my father, whose cigars and scotch had seemingly caught up with him. Mother had rung me just after Easter to say that Dad had been taken into hospital. He was released after a few days but had been grounded for the immediate future while he recovered and went through various fitness tests to make certain he was still able to fly. The icing on the cake would be that, if not arrested when I crossed the border, I could just make graduation at St. Edmund's where all of my academic credits from McGill had been transferred.

When I called my mother to discuss my plans, she broke into joyful sobs and told me that under no circumstances was I to chance the border crossing; if I were going to get myself arrested it would be closer to home! Thus, she would buy me an air ticket to fly from Montreal to Greensboro. Mom also said she would buy a ticket for my brother, Ron, if he would fly home for even a day or two, to make it a real family reunion. I next rang Dick Stein, who was delighted and offered any assistance I might need. Two years after having left under difficult circumstances, it was love for my family and best friend that drew me back, dangers and all.

~ * ~

During the flight from Montreal to Greensboro, I was able to watch the retreat of winter and the advance of spring on the landscape below as we hurtled southward. And with the miles, I felt my spirits lift as I saw the season of new life being painted on the earth's canvas: brown yielding to the pale green of budding leaves and, as we entered North Carolina's air space, the deeper green of fully-fledged trees. It was when I stepped off the plane that I knew I was over-dressed for a Southern spring. The warmth embraced me, and I knew I was home.

My homecoming was, thankfully, a legally uneventful affair as neither the FBI nor the police were there to greet me, but it was emotionally laden. For the first time, my father, who had always looked "mature" to me, had now begun to look old. His recent illness had left him wan, and his hair was much greyer than when I last saw him. I wondered how he would react to his pacifist, émigré son, but such things didn't seem to be on his mind. What surprised me most was that, when I reached out to shake his hand, our normal way of greeting or parting, Dad opened his arms to me and hugged me close to his chest. Overcome with emotion, my eyes welled with tears and a lump rose in my throat, leaving me speechless for a few moments. Over his shoulder, I could see my mother beaming with joy.

It was Dad who spoke first. "I'm very glad to see you, son. It's been too long."

"I know, Dad. I know." I started to say, "I'm sorry," but Dad shushed me.

"Vietnam is the wrong goddamn war; it's all been a mistake." And that was all we said about the war that had separated us for years; and yet, it was all that needed to be said.

~ * ~

On the drive from Greensboro back to Lawrenceville, Mother explained that Ron, due to work pressures and newly married life, hadn't been able to fly in for the reunion. It was clear that she was disappointed, as our family foursome hadn't been together for several years. Now it would be unlikely for the foreseeable future. Mom seemed to take it as a failure on her part that she hadn't been able to coax Ron away from Louisville, if only for twenty-four hours. I felt my mother's disappointment more keenly than my own and tried to help lighten her mood by saying that Ron and his wife were probably busy trying to make a grandchild for her. Mom blushed, but giggled at the

238

thought. Although I would have liked to have seen my brother, I had instinctively known, since our early days, that Ron and I walked very different paths; thus, this gathering, however important for our mother, wouldn't come as a priority for him. Nevertheless, if only for the three of us, there was much catching up to do, and so we filled the evening with our stories.

The following morning, I borrowed my mother's car and made my first port of call the home of Rev. McLaurin. I wanted to thank him in person for the moral and financial support he and his wife had provided over the past two years. And while I wanted to discuss with him my upcoming theological training, I also wanted to pick his brains regarding Kyle, as McLaurin, too, was a war veteran. I needed any advice he could give me as to why Kyle had become so incommunicative.

My next stop in Lawrenceville gave me a sense of what the Prodigal Son must have felt when he returned home. I hadn't told Kyle's family I would be visiting, so when Marie opened the door and saw me on the front porch, both her eyes and her mouth widened in shock, and she seemed to stop breathing. Then she threw her arms around me and squealed, "'Nother Brother! It's really you!"

Kyle's mother, Ellen, came out of the kitchen, wiping her hands on her apron and asking, "Honey? What's wrong?!" When she saw me, half in and half out of the doorway, Ellen beamed. "Jon Braddock— well I never!" And then she burst into tears. Ellen threw one arm around me while the other brought her apron to her eyes to dab away the tears. "You certainly know how to give a body a shock! Marie! For heaven's sake, let poor Jon into the ho'se!"

The three of us virtually stumbled through the doorway. Then, in good Southern fashion, Ellen rushed into the kitchen and returned with tall glasses of iced tea. All three of us squeezed onto the sofa, where Marie kept hugging me and Ellen kept patting my knee and telling me how good it was that I had returned.

When I told them that my return was only temporary—eight days, in fact—Ellen drew her breath and said, "Oh, your poor mother!"

I explained that legally I was still a "fugitive from justice," however unjust the Vietnam War might be, and therefore had to return to Canada after graduating from St. Edmund's and, more importantly, after catching up with Kyle. I noticed a shadow cross Ellen's face when I mentioned Kyle. She told me Kyle was living in an apartment "not very nice" close to the veterans' hospital in Fayetteville.

"Jon?" Ellen reached out and touched my arm. "You may find that Kyle is…well, *changed*. His father and I had hoped he might want to come back home to live, at least until he had recovered from his wounds and operations. But Kyle decided to stay near Fort Bragg and near the VA hospital where he was being treated. But some of his 'friends' we met when we've gone down to visit him…*well*." Ellen shook her head and looked out the front window. "Kyle drinks a lot, too—more than he ought to." She turned back to me and patted my arm once more. "Your mother ought to be glad you didn't go to that horrid war. I know she must miss you terribly, with you in Canada and all, but at least you're…*whole*."

At this point, Marie broke in. "Mama, I'm sure Jon can handle Kyle when he goes down to see him. But surely you want to hear abo't what's been going on with Jon in Canada!?"

I welcomed the change of topic. Truthfully, I had worried enough about Kyle over the last couple of years. I had often thought back to our hitchhiking trip to Old Fort, where we had met the two Marines, Robert and Doug. Their experiences had seemingly chastened Kyle *at the time*. As for myself, I hadn't really needed any encouragement to stay away from war, and Robert and Doug's admonition to stay the hell away from 'Nam had only strengthened my resolve. But then Kyle had surprised me by joining up and going to Vietnam. I had already noticed changes in Kyle from the few letters he had sent. There was a cynical and acerbic quality in the way he wrote that I'd never seen in my friend before then. In any case, I didn't actually want to hear any more from Ellen; rather, I wanted to see Kyle for myself.

After Ellen, Marie and I had caught up on the high points in our lives, and as I got up to leave, Ellen offered to ring Kyle. It took him quite a while to answer the phone. In fact, his mother had nearly replaced the handset on its cradle when he picked up at his end. I noticed a strained look on Ellen's face as she tried to make conversation with her son, saying that I was back in town and was planning to pay him a visit after my graduation at St. Edmund's in three days' time. When she offered to pass the phone to me, Kyle must have demurred, for a pained expression spread across Ellen's face, and all she said was, "Well, if you're sure. All right then, I'll tell him." For a brief instant, I worried that Kyle had refused to see me. Ellen set the phone down overly carefully as though it were made out of fine porcelain. Forcing a smile as she turned toward me, Ellen said, "I'm sorry, Jon. Kyle's not himself today. But he said you're welcome to stop by after your graduation." A heavy silence settled over the three of us, so it seemed best that I take my leave. I told Marie and Ellen that if I could stop by before flying back to Montreal, I would do so. We hugged and kissed once more and I drove back to my parents' house.

That evening, I sat out on the screened porch drinking my mother's iced tea. I mused that, had I still been in Canada, I would not have been sitting outside in my shirtsleeves. I also noted how noisy and alive spring was in North Carolina compared to what I had left behind. Apart from the traffic and the occasional human voice, late April nights in Montreal were relatively silent. I felt welcomed by the unseen choir of insects and night creatures as they joined together in the "hullabaloo chorus." I rose to my feet and lifted my glass to signify my approval.

~ * ~

My mother and father drove me down to my graduation ceremony. I list them in that order because it was, in fact, my mother who drove, another change since I had left the country and one which bespoke my father's ill health, for it was almost unheard of for my father to ride as co-pilot. They had booked us two rooms at a motel in Southern Pines, as that was the nearest town of any size close to the college. I rang Dick Stein as soon as we were checked in. All he said was, "I'm on my way now—and dinner's on me! I've already booked a table at the Pine Crest Inn."

Thus, my week of reunions continued in fine fashion. Dick, knowing that my father and I had fallen out over the Vietnam War, was encouraged to see that some level of reconciliation had been obtained. Happily, we steered clear of the reason I had gone to Canada and focused upon the impending commencement ceremony and my plans to study for the ministry at The Presbyterian College in Montreal. Dad made good-humored jokes about the fact that, although neither of his sons had become a pilot, at least I was on my way to becoming the family "sky pilot"—military slang for a chaplain or minister. The evening remained relaxed; we enjoyed superb Southern cooking at its best and, Mother excepted, imbibed much wine "to gladden the heart of man."

It was agreed that, following graduation and the evening reception, my parents would stay that night in Southern Pines, whereas I would probably party all night on the college campus with classmates whom I had not seen for two years. We arranged to have lunch the day after graduation with Dick vowing he would get me there no matter what condition I was in. My mother and father would then return to Lawrenceville, leaving me to spend two nights with Dick, as Fayetteville, where Kyle was ensconced, was only a short distance away. Dick had kindly offered to lend me his car to drive over to Kyle's as he could walk or cycle over to the college.

It was all a bit hectic and also emotionally overwhelming to see so many people who were important to me—not to mention to graduate from college—all in the space of eight short days. In addition, there was a slight edge to it all, given the real possibility that, at any moment, I might be apprehended by Federal agents for draft evasion. However, I tried not to let my very active imagination get carried away with such images.

~ * ~

The day of my college graduation was a whirlwind of hellos and goodbyes. For the first time since my hasty departure in the spring of 1971, I was seeing friends with whom I had spent those heady, first two years of undergraduate education, most of whom I would never see again. Thus, like with so many of life's rites of passage, it was all tinged with poignancy. I also noticed a change in me, one for which I wasn't quite prepared, especially as the afternoon wore on and the formal reception for parents and families was supplanted by the student parties, with cocktails giving way to kegs of beer and riotous graduates. Whereas at one time I would have thrown myself wholeheartedly into the drinking and dancing, I felt at a certain remove from all of the boisterous festivity. Two years of émigré life and a price on my head in the US had effected this change. I was no longer care free; rather, I had very real cares, which were to have a profound bearing on my life, even to this day. Dick Stein, who was always a welcome addition at any student gathering, picked up on my mood not long after we met up that evening, and so he gently guided me from gathering to gathering with us sometimes chatting quietly and other times shouting over the music.

Dick and I filled in the gaps of our lives that we had not disclosed in the many letters we had written. We discussed my future plans, both short- and long-term, beginning with my theological training which would begin in September, and then looking toward any future I might have back in the US. Would the way ever be open for me to return legally? Neither of us could say. Of course, the Watergate hearings also formed a major part of our discussions. The thought that Nixon and his cronies might possibly be brought to book and ousted from power filled us with hopeful elation. We drained our beers in toast to a future without Tricky Dick and, in that same moment, realized that we both had had our fill of partying, so we made our way to the car.

At breakfast the next morning, I began to talk about Kyle and my fears regarding his long silence. I told Dick about the short and seemingly uncomfortable telephone conversation I had witnessed between Mrs. Weston and Kyle and worried aloud that perhaps Kyle really didn't want to see me. Dick listened thoughtfully as I expressed my anxieties regarding my friend. He then reached across his small breakfast table and laid his hand on my shoulder. "Jon, I can't tell you what to expect. However, Kyle could have told you not to come—*but he didn't*. All I can encourage you to do is just to be the same as you have always been with Kyle. Sometimes…well…that's all we can do, simply be there for the ones we love and accompany them on their journey." I took Dick's advice to heart and hoped for the best.

Twenty-two

We seem bent upon saving the Vietnamese from Ho Chi Minh, even if we have to kill them and demolish their country to do it.
                                        —George McGovern

I think history will record that this may have been one of America's finest hours, because we took a difficult task and we succeeded.

                                        —Richard Nixon

"Welcome to Fayette-nam!" Kyle greeted me at the door of his apartment located on the second floor of a building from the 1930s. In what was once a nice area of Fayetteville, the building and its surrounds were now shabby; but that somehow befitted Kyle's outward appearance. In fact, as he stood in the doorway, I was taken aback. I wasn't prepared for the apparition that stood before me. Kyle's face was drawn, his lips chapped and peeling, his hair longish and greasy. He motioned me inside and pointed to a chair. Kyle dropped into a well-worn easy-chair. A bottle of Jim Beam stood on the table next to Kyle, and he balanced a half-filled glass of the amber liquid on his thigh, secured there by the languid grip of his badly-scarred left hand. A grimy shoulder sling hung over the back of the chair. Kyle looked up at me with bloodshot eyes and managed a broken smile. "Hey, buddy. What'sa matter? Scared of your old pal?"

"No. No, I'm not scared. But neither was I expecting to see you in…*this condition.*"

"What? Not middle-class enough for you?" he jibed.

I hadn't envisioned things starting off in such a contentious fashion. So in an effort to smooth things over, I simply waved off Kyle's barbed remark with a smile and said, "Oh cut the shit, Kyle. I'm here, aren't I? You could at least catch me up on what has happened to you and how it is that you come to be living here in Fayetteville and not back at home in Lawrenceville."

To my relief—and surprise—the ploy worked. Kyle slowly took a drink of the Jim Beam, closed one eye, cocked his head, and studied me for a moment. He began with his return stateside—the operations on his shoulder and hand, followed by rehabilitation. Kyle told me that his original reason for staying in "Fayette-nam," as he and other 'Nam vets liked to call it, was because it was close to the VA hospital and their rehab services. Over the succeeding months, however, Kyle said he stayed because there were a lot of guys like him hanging around, vets with whom he didn't need to explain anything, unlike with his family and old friends in Lawrenceville.

The events which had led to Kyle's wounds and his need for subsequent medical attention were conspicuous by their absence in his narrative. As we sat in Kyle's dark and dingy apartment, I thought about my conversation with Rev. McLaurin a few days before. When I had asked him about how it had been for wounded GIs returning from World War II, he said that most veterans felt that people wouldn't be interested in what they had been through and, even if they did tell of their war experiences, who would have understood apart from other GIs? I turned this over in my mind as I looked at Kyle. Should I ask about his war? Had I the *right* to do so? Kyle said nothing, but seemed to be waiting.

As I looked at my friend, I saw something in his visage of an old dog my family had owned when I was very young. One day it had been hit by a car. Limping and howling, our dog had dragged itself under our old, wood-framed house, which had sat on brick piers where it stood near the banks of the Neuse River. It had retreated as far into the darkness as it was able. My father came out of the house with a flashlight and the old blanket on which the dog slept. I remember waiting at the entrance to the crawl-space and seeing the hollow yet reflective glow of the animal's eyes as my father took the flashlight and, inching along on his belly, made his way toward the dog. He gently wrapped the bewildered creature in its blanket and pulled our family pet to daylight and a quick drive to the local veterinarian. My brother and I sat on the back seat of the car with the dog between us, keeping it securely wrapped in the blanket. It stared at us with wounded and suspicious eyes. Such were the eyes fixed on me that day as Kyle and I met for the first time in more than two years.

"Kyle, if you can, why don't you tell me about it? I mean, Vietnam—what happened?"

Kyle looked into the middle distance; his eyes seemed to glaze over a bit. "Tell you *abo't* it…tell you abo't *it*," he repeated those words, varying the emphasis—more to himself than to me. Kyle seemed to be debating my request, but then he started talking. His words sounded as though they came from far away, and in a very real way, I suppose they did—12,000 miles or from somewhere so deep in himself that his voice took on a different tone.

"Things hadn't gone too badly for us, me and my crew. We had flown by then…what…" his eyes moved as though checking flight logs, "…maybe five hundred and sixty combat hours? Our ship had taken a few hits, couple of canopies shot out, but nobody wounded…*scared shitless* maybe—but nobody wounded." Kyle nodded to himself and smiled at me. His eyes seemed to search mine in order to determine whether his pacifist friend was ready and willing to fly this mission with him. I held his gaze.

Kyle moved forward in his chair and continued. "Well, there was this one day...we were taking a load of grunts to a hot LZ, near the Cambodian border. There were six Hueys in this assault. The aim was—" and at this point Kyle's voice took on that of a television reporter "—*to interdict the flow of supplies along the Ho Chi Minh Trail.*" Kyle took a sip of his whisky, shook his head at the vapidity of what he had just said, and continued. "Cambodian border, *my ass.* Politicians—and even some generals—seemed to think we could actually *see* borders marked out on the ground below—like on a globe or a map. For those of us involved in the whole ordeal, it was all very simple: We took the fuckin' grunts where the fuckin' enemy *was*—and if the NVA or Viet Cong wanted to take their asses over some invisible borderline with the hope that we'd leave them alone, we obliged the little bastards and went after them. Hey, fuck 'em if they can't take a joke." He laughed sardonically.

Kyle checked my eyes again for—for *what?* Shock? Disapproval? Or maybe just a tacit assent for him to continue, to take me where he had been, to a place that made him look the way he did at that moment. I just kept my focus on him, because I *knew* Kyle, and I knew he needed to tell me something. My distraught friend paused, flopped back in his chair, and breathed deeply. He ran his hand through his unwashed hair, then set his glass down and rubbed his temples with the first two fingers of each hand.

"So..." Kyle suddenly returned to his narrative, "...so the slicks take off first. We were supposed to have three gunships with us to provide cover while we flew in and out of the LZ. But before their crews could get aboard, our base came under attack from VC mortar fire. We received orders from battalion to proceed to the LZ ASAP, drop the grunts, and bring o't as many wounded as we could safely load—fat chance of that with no cover! And so we come in low and fast only to find o't that we can't get more than two ships in at one time! The LZ was a small grassy knoll, and whoever was on the radio calling for support somehow missed the fact that there were *six* of us coming in *formation*—get in, drop the grunts, and get the fuck o't—right!" Kyle snorted and shook his head again, disgust written on his face.

"We were in the number three position as the first two ships went in. Man! Charlie opened up with everything he had—small arms, rocket-propelled grenades, fifty-calibers, mortars—you name it. They knew our tactics as well as we did; they knew we were most vulnerable when we hovered and dropped the grunts or picked them up, so they let loose. Whenever possible, the first grunts, if they are experienced, are already standing on the landing skids, ready to jump and head for cover as soon as we skim the grass." Kyle looked at his glass of Jim Beam and gently shook it as though trying to divine the image he wanted to describe for me.

"Well, as only two ships could get into this piece o' shit LZ, I had to overfly and try to stay low enough not to present a target for very long to the NVA hidden in the trees and high grass. Still, I could hear the *ding* and *clack* as they caught a piece of us. The gunners on the lead and second ships were blazing away, over the heads of their disgorged grunts. I could hear the chatter of our door guns as Ches and Food'n'drug opened up. I could occasionally see tracers from Ches' M-60 o't my side window. Then I see the first two choppers gaining altitude, so I head toward the LZ with Cal Northrop's ship on my left. Captain Martin, who was in the lead ship, radioed that they were going to keep circling at about seventy-five feet and provide some badly needed covering fire from their door guns. Talk about a hot LZ! I couldn't see how we were gonna fly through all of the shit Charlie was throwing in there. In such a small area, we *had* to be hit. But, Jon—let me tell you—at times like this you don't *think*, you just *act. That's what training is for*," Kyle burst forth in a mock-training film voice. He laughed at himself and then resumed.

"We'd hardly received the message from Captain Martin when his ship bursts into flames—I saw somebody jump—crew chief or gunner, I don't know...but he was on fire—then it just nosed into the jungle. I saw all of that, but it hardly registered because, by then, I was coming in to drop my guys. You take stuff in when you're in combat, but it's almost like watching a movie, you know, like it's happening to someone else. It's only later—*after* the adrenaline rush—that you look back and think, 'Shit!' I used to get the shakes bad after some air assaults—that's when I started on this medication." Again, the bottle of Jim Beam was waggled at me, now nearly empty.

"So anyway, 'into the valley of death' flew the Air Cav." Kyle laughed grimly. "I suppose it's a good thing the engine and rotors make so damn much noise. That, plus the helmet and headphones, keeps pilots from hearing all the noise of battle...but you can still *see*." Kyle stopped for a minute, looked at me and asked, "Have you ever tried to *forget* something you've seen—something you'd rather not remember?" Before I could respond, he answered his own question. "You can't do it; it's impossible. Man, once something is burned into those brain cells, ain't no amo'nt of trying will erase it. Drugs and booze help a little." Kyle waggled his bottle at me again, "But apart from *really* burning o't your brain, mental images stick. Man, they're there for *good*. I mean, I reckon *sight* has to be the strongest of the human senses, don't you?"

Without having to reflect, an image shot straight into the forefront on my mind: the bluish, ghastly face of my high school girlfriend's mother, when we discovered her suicide. Kyle, of course, remembered the event, as I had related to him every last detail at the time; but at that moment with him, it was as though he could read my mind or even control my memory selection. I had been the first of us to witness death firsthand in the raw, not in some funeral parlor with a manikin-like relative lying neatly in a coffin. His eyes met mine and he nodded. He knew.

"You agree, don't you?" A tired smile creased his chapped lips.

I nodded and simply said, "Yeah."

"Where was I?" queried Kyle as he studied his empty glass and then took a slow draught from the whisky bottle.

"Getting ready to drop a load of soldiers in a hot landing zone."

Kyle nodded. "Yeah, so there was a lot of shit flying around— bullets, ricochets, shell fragments—the works. So in I go: me, my crew and eight grunts." Kyle took on an instructor's tone. "Here's the deal. If we can help it, we don't actually *land* in a hot LZ. And in one that's too damn small to begin with, you bring the ship to a creeping hover, get the grunts to jump, and then gun it, leaving room for the next ships while getting your ass the hell o't of the line of fire. That's what we did." Kyle paused, then said, "So far, so *bad*." He grinned.

Kyle then ran his hand through his oily hair and closed his eyes. Without opening them, he took another sip from his bottle. The next thing I knew—and I could never understand how Kyle was able to do this at such a time—he pulled his top lip back above his front teeth and made a sucking sound through his teeth—in imitation of our junior high school PE teacher, who always had a bottle of cola on the go. Kyle popped one eyelid open, knowing damn well that if I caught this reference to our childhood, not to mention the incongruity with the topic at hand, he would catch me smiling. And he did. Even in the midst of his obvious pain and discomfort, he could still make me—and himself—smile…even laugh. We remained silent for a moment or two, each present to the other but at the same time locked in his memories.

"That's when Food'n'drug got it."

"What?"

Kyle's voice brought me from my reverie. He was looking straight at me. "That is when Frederick Douglass Armstrong *got it*. Ches said an NVA round blew a big-ass hole right through Food'n'drug's middle just below his ribcage." Kyle patted his midriff. "Ches got splattered with bits of his intestines and other shit. I never saw it—and you'll understand why in a minute—because, at the time, I was trying to get all of our asses o't of there. According to Ches, poor Food'n'drug flopped on the deck of our Huey like a fish o't of water, eyes bulging and lips struggling to make some sound. Hell, maybe he was praying— Ches couldn't hear a word though, not over the gunfire, engine noise, and rotor wash. And there was nothing he could have done for poor FDA anyway, not in those conditions. He just told me over the intercom that Food'n'drug was hit bad. We were trying to get some altitude and speed, and we needed Ches's finger on the trigger of his M-60. Hell, even if he couldn't *hit* anything, it sure felt better knowing somebody was firing back there. Duke and I couldn't do anything except *fly*. And *that we did*...that we did." Kyle closed his eyes again, but I could see them quickly twitching beneath the thin veil of flesh. It reminded me of films I had seen in psychology class of people experiencing REM sleep. But in this case, it was no dream, but a waking nightmare.

"I had to clear the treetops," Kyle continued, "firstly, so I didn't crash and kill the rest of us," Kyle again looked at me but didn't smile this time, "and secondly, a low, fast-moving target gives less time for gunners to train their weapons on you, especially when they're concealed amid the trees. I demanded maximum power from my ship, gauges were running in the red, but I got us up and o't of that LZ, and at least three of us were still alive. I told Duke to keep a close eye on the gauges as our ship had taken so many hits. As we headed back to base, the Huey felt heavy and rotors were making an unusual sound. Duke and I kept looking at each other. Guess we felt that if the other wasn't dead or freaking out, we'd each be okay...I don't know."

Kyle emptied his bottle of its last contents. He shook it forlornly and pronounced a one-word benediction over it: "Shit." The deceased was tossed carelessly onto the sofa. Surveying the empty glass on the side-table, Kyle wryly grinned and asked, "I don't suppose you..." I shook my head. "Nah, I didn't think so." With elbows on his knees and hands hanging limp at the wrists, Kyle's head joined them momentarily. It was the wordless clue that he had drunk far too much. Slowly, almost painfully, Kyle lifted his head. The veteran's bravado had disappeared, and in its place a weak, boyish smile creased his lips as he croaked, "Be a pal and get me a glass of water, would you? This story ain't over yet, and I want to finish it 'cause I don't think I could bear telling it again."

"No problem," I replied. Yet, before I could turn to go to the kitchenette, and without meaning to, I stopped and laid my hand on his unwashed hair. I tousled it gently. Kyle's bloodshot eyes turned up to meet mine. As he held my gaze, his right hand rose from its inert position and rested upon mine. As Kyle's eyes slightly moistened, I felt a gentle pat from his hand, followed by an equally gentle command. "Get me that water, okay?"

I nodded and went to find a glass. Everything was filthy. Despite the fact that Kyle wouldn't care about the cleanliness of the glass, I felt the compulsion to give it at least a cursory wash. It was as though his mother and sister were looking over my shoulder and they'd want it to be clean—for Kyle.

I returned to Kyle and proffered the water. It was veritably snatched from my hand, sloshing it in the process, and Kyle gulped down the rest. His head dropped back on his shoulders in satisfaction. He smiled and pushed the tumbler toward me while nodding toward the sink. I returned his smile, gave a sloppy salute, and went to refill the glass. Kyle took it more gently the second time, drank half the refreshing liquid, and set the remainder on the table. Kyle rubbed his hands through his hair once more and then rubbed his face in long, slow movements as though trying to massage the image forming before his inner eye. He let out a long sigh and retrieved the thread of his story.

"We were well away from the LZ, and I guess that Food'n'drug had bled o't by then. Ches never said much abo't it. Anyway, at abo't the same moment, both Duke and Ches called o't to me on the intercom. Ches was saying maybe we'd better find a place to set the ship down and Duke was making a similar suggestion due to the gauges showing us running hot. We had just passed over a village, and as nobody had fired at us, we decided it might just be safe enough to set the Huey down on a dike alongside the rice paddies. Duke and I would give cover on the M-60s or our sidearms while Ches gave the engine a quick check over. There were a few people working in the paddies some hundreds of yards away, but the emergency LZ seemed clear. As soon as we were down, I jumped o't and ran to have a look at Food'n'drug. His lifeless eyes stared up at holes made in our equally inanimate ship, probably by the same ground-fire which hit him. It's crazy what goes on in you at a moment like that—and maybe's it's some sort of primal self-protective instinct—but Food'n'drug's eyes, against his jet-black skin...well, they looked like ivory. And crazy as this sounds, I couldn't help but think of an Egyptian statue I had seen in *National Geographic*—I think it had been found in Tutankhamen's tomb. It was of this Nubian guy or something, and it had ivory eyes, just looking forward at nothing and no-one. Anyway, Ches brought me o't of it when he sho'ted, 'Get o't and help me give the ship the once-over! Duke can keep an eye o't for trouble and handle one of the machine guns if necessary.'"

"But before I jumped o't, I closed Food'n'drug's eyes. Man, I hope never to have to do that again." Kyle gave an involuntary shudder. "So Ches and I quickly walked around the Huey. I whistled when I saw several chunks shot o't of our rotor blades—that accounted for some of the noise. But Ches was more concerned with a leak from the oil cooler. At about that time, another of our company's ships came over. When he saw we were down, he started to circle. I waved at him and pointed toward the pilot's station, gesturing that I would put on my radio earphones. Turns o't it was Greg Masters. He quickly told me that nearly everybody had got shot to shit and that two ships were down. Greg asked if he should pick us up, but I told him to keep circling; we were giving the ship a safety check and hoped we could limp back to base. I told him we'd sure appreciate his company 'cause, if the engine quit, I'd have to autorotate into the first clearing we could find, and they'd have to pick us up. As I put the earphones down, I caught sight of three children making their way toward us along the dike, abo't one hundred yards away. I alerted Ches and Duke. Ches was so involved with the oil cooler that he just sho'ted, 'Well, go check it o't!—*sir.*' Duke was on the '60, so he gave it a pat to say he'd got Ches and the ship covered." Kyle looked for his water glass, picked it up, and dashed the rest down his throat. I started to move to get him some more, but Kyle shook his head.

"I don't know why—'cause they were just kids—but I unholstered my .45 and started to make my way toward them." Kyle's eyes started to squint into focus as though he could see them now. "I had gone abo't thirty yards when I saw that the middle child was carrying something. He was holding it very gently, o't in front of him. He was maybe six. There was another boy and a girl with him—maybe his brother and sister, I don't know. The girl looked slightly older and the other boy was maybe four or five. The girl waved at me...she seemed to be smiling. The children were saying something in Vietnamese. As the distance closed between us, I finally saw what the middle boy was bringing to us—a grenade. I'd heard about this kind of thing before—

some kind Viet Cong would give a child a grenade, make him hold the spoon tight, then pull out the pin and say, 'Go give this to a nice American. Don't let go until the American takes if from you.' I mean, using *children* as fucking walking bombs!

"So anyway, I sho'ted back to Ches and Duke, and gave them the situation—while keeping an eye on the kids. I saw both of their heads peer around the Huey and then saw them waving their arms and heard Ches—and maybe Duke, too—hollering, 'Shoot 'em! Shoot 'em, goddamnit!' The kids were barely fifteen yards away and starting to pick up their pace. I-I guess the grenade was getting heavy for the little guy, and he wanted me to have my 'present.' So anyway, I ran back, maybe ten yards, cocked the pistol, but I couldn't fire. I mean—for Christ's sake—they were *kids*. I tried waving them back, showing them the pistol and all, *but they kept coming*." Tears were streaming down Kyle's face. "I-I knew...that...if they kept coming, they could take me o't—and maybe all of us. I don't know. Meanwhile Ches and Duke were screaming at me to shoot them. So I did. I flattened myself on the ground and fired twice at the boy carrying the grenade. His little body flew backwards at the impact...and the grenade...well," Kyle licked his parched lips, "just fell to the ground and went off. It exploded before I could duck my head. Evidently the bastard VC had shortened the fuse. I *saw* the other little boy and girl blown away like ragdolls."

"When I got to my feet, I was shaking like a leaf. I mean, I never even did that when flying into hot LZs. I mean, you know, I held it together—usually. But not *then*." There were beads of perspiration joining the tears streaming down Kyle's face.

"Before I knew what was happening, Ches was dragging me back to the ship and telling me to 'get into this goddamn thing and fire it up.' When I got into the pilot's seat, Duke was already strapped in with his helmet on. He slapped me on the knee and said, 'It's okay, buddy. It's okay. Want me to take her up?' I just said, 'You got it,' and slumped into my seat. He radioed up to Greg Masters what had just happened. Masters and his crew had seen something happening on the ground but, from five-hundred feet, couldn't be sure what. He told Masters our ship was flyable but not sure for how long. It was as we started to take off that I realized I still had my pistol in my hand. Duke had rightly decided to get moving before the VC among the villagers came o't to see what had happened. I holstered my weapon and pulled on my harness and helmet. Duke looked at me, winked, and nodded... then he slapped me upside the head—or, at least I thought he had." Kyle wiped his nose and face on his sleeve and then continued. "At the same instant—and, Jon, all of this happened in a second—the Huey starts to shudder, the canopy fucking disintegrates, and I see tracers fly past us. The ship then starts to bank sharply to the left, so I instinctively grab the control stick. Then I notice blood all over the gauges and that Duke is still holding onto me—or so it seemed, until I find that his right arm is lying *across* me!" Kyle's body shuddered so hard I thought he was having convulsions.

"Jon, it was like it was a snake or something. I just picked up Duke's arm and threw it into the cargo area. Can you believe that? I mean, I tried to get control of the ship and take a quick look at Duke at the same time: he was already dead or damn close to it. He had been hit by at least two or three rounds, one of which took off his arm. Shit. Meanwhile, Ches is screaming through the intercom to get us o't of there or down—or anywhere but where we were. Now my adrenalin was really pumping—I mean, man, I had already forgotten abo't blowing away those kids. All I knew was that two of my crew members were dead, and I didn't want Ches and me to be next. But it was too late—we lost power, heeled over, and went into the rice paddy." I offered Kyle my handkerchief and he mopped his face.

"Between my adrenalin and the water pouring into the cockpit, I had my harness unbuckled in a split second! The good news was that my door was on the *up* side of the chopper. I took one last look at Duke. His half of the cockpit was flooded. I tried not to step on him as I scrambled aro'nd to stand upright. Still strapped into his harness, what was left of Duke's broken body was face down in the murky water. For that I was half-glad. I-I didn't want to see his face."

"I could hear machine gun and small arms fire o'tside, so I waited before I threw back the door to get o't. Whoever had brought us down was a good shot, that much was certain, so I hoped he would think we were all dead. I could hear Masters' ship circling the area and his door gunners firing bursts at targets somewhere nearby. The closest so'nd was the hissing from the Huey's partially submerged engine. Then I remember hearing someone calling my name! It's funny. At that moment, I wondered if I was *dead* and that maybe an angel was calling me to get o't of the chopper and...and *what*? Catch my ride to heaven? Or maybe to hell, after what I had just done. It took a few seconds to recognize the voice as belonging to Ches. He was asking if I was all right. I sho'ted back to him that I was okay but that Duke was dead and that I was going to jump o't of the door if all was clear. Ches said, 'Fine, but keep your ass down. There's still a lot of shit flying around o't here.'"

"I distinctly remember not wanting to step on Duke in order to boost myself o't of the Huey—isn't that funny? I mean, he was *dead*. He couldn't feel anything." Kyle's arms were demonstrating his words. "So I supported myself by putting my right foot on the aluminum frame of Duke's backrest, pressed my head and shoulders against the pilot's door, and then flung it open, while at the same time pressing upward with both arms on the doorframe. The moment I threw myself o't that door, a VC gunner opened up. I couldn't believe the bastard was still targeting my ship! A whizzing, snapping noise replaced that of the engine rapidly cooling in the rice paddy. The water started dancing as well—remember how those heavy summer thunderstorms used to churn up the water on the pond at your ho'se?"

I nodded and said, "I do recall."

"Well, these were *lead* raindrops! Anyway, Ches was waving to me from abo't twenty yards away by the bank of a dike. He was pointing toward our ship and sho'ting to 'keep it behind you and make your way toward me!' So back I went. And the sound of swarming, demented mosquitoes flying past my ears was changed into the metallic thud, ping, and ricochets of bullets making contact with the Huey— now the coffin for two of my friends. I did my best to keep the Huey between me and the VC bastard trying to kill me. Meanwhile Ches was keeping low with his head just above the water. I tried to bend double as I sloshed through the rice plants and mud—and do you know what I was thinking?"

I shook my head. "I haven't a clue."

"I mean, I know I've been drinking and everything," Kyle nodded toward the bottle on the sofa, "but—and this is the God's honest truth!" Kyle held up his right hand as though taking an oath in court. "I was thinking: what if I get a ro'nd up my ass like that rat your dad shot all those years ago?!" Kyle laughed for the first time since starting his nightmare narrative. "No shit. I really thought that! I thought, what if that gunner puts one up my A-hole and it comes right o't my head just like the rat your old man put away? Wouldn't that be a helluva way to die?" Kyle looked around. "Man, I could use a drink!"

"Will water do?" I stood up and realized how shallowly I had been breathing and how rigid my muscles had become, listening to Kyle's story.

"Guess it will have to do." Kyle dropped his head and surrendered his glass to me—using both hands, one of which bore a pinkish, white scar reminiscent of the stigmata. He held it up in the same way I would later see him hold up the chalice at the communion—but that was still many years—and a lot of whisky—away. I received the glass and went to refill it. When I returned, he again lifted both hands to take it from me. Kyle saw me looking at his scarred left hand. Holding the glass in his right hand, he slowly and painfully flexed his fingers. "It ain't perfect, but it just abo't works." He turned the hand back and forth, studying it. "I suppose I should be thankful to 'Charlie' for giving me this."

"How do you mean?" I couldn't follow his line of reasoning.

"We-e-ll," he drawled, "it means I ain't of no use to Uncle Sam no mo'. The shoulder wound I got only fractured my shoulder blade; it didn't enter my body 'cause I was bending down, running toward Ches." Kyle leaned forward in his chair to show me the angle at which he was hit. "But the one that went through my left hand, that ended my flying days; which means I ain't gonna study war *no mo'*. Hallelujah!"

I sat back in my chair. As Kyle had recounted his Vietnam experience—*the* critical experience with regard to the "why" and the "how" he was as I had found him—I had listened with bated breath, feeling the tenseness of what he described. I noticed a slight cramp and ache in my neck. I rolled my head from side to side, trying to release the tension. But Kyle's story wasn't finished.

"Hey, I haven't told you abo't Ches yet, how he got o't. Well, when we started taking fire and then lost control of the ship, we were barely two hundred feet in altitude. When I threw Duke's arm back into the cargo area, Ches figured maybe both Duke and I were dead or wounded and that, either way, we were going in. So he had unbuckled his safety harness preparing to jump. Then, when the ship heeled over suddenly, Ches was thrown clear. Splash! Thank God for rice paddies, eh?" Kyle laughed and shook his head. "Lucky bastard! Ches said it took a few moments to gather his wits and catch his breath as he was winded by the force with which he hit the water. By the time he got the mud o't of his eyes, the Huey was already down. Ches saw a few bursts of tracers fly past the ship, so he knew that if he wasn't careful, he could be the next target. That's when he made his way over toward the dike where I saw him.

"By the time I got to him, our boots and clothes were so soaked with mud and water we couldn't move very fast. We tried to climb the dike, but kept slipping and sliding back into the water. Ches finally said, 'Enough of this shit!' turned around backwards, and dug his heels into the bank. Ha! He looked like a giant, muddy-green inchworm, bringing his heels up to his butt and then pushing himself up with his hands and heels! Once he was on top of the dike, he drew fire, but did he jump clear on the far side of the dike? Hell no. He just lies flat on his stomach, looks down at me and says, 'You comin' or not?' Can you believe that? 'You comin' or not?' Then he grins and shoves his beefy hand at me. I take hold and up I go. Well the dirt's kicking up where the bullets are hitting, so Ches sho'ts, 'Keep your ass *down*!' And just as I start to comply, one bullet smacks into my left hand and the other plows a furrow into my left shoulder blade. *That* got me down, all right!" Kyle laughed and shook his head as he looked at his disfigured left hand.

"According to Ches—'cause I really don't remember—I was cussin' and hollerin' as he dragged me over the dike and down to the safety of the other side. Ches looked me over and said, 'It ain't as bad as all that!' Although he did tell me later he thought I might've been hit worse than I was because I had Duke's blood all over me as well. Anyway, Ches got me calmed down, and it was then that we saw Greg Masters' Huey coming in low. One of his door gunners was motioning for us to get up. As they weren't taking any fire, we reckoned we were safe—finally. Turns o't that the gunships which were late in joining us on the run to the LZ had silenced—or sent running for safety—the VC gunners who had brought us down. But we had been too busy trying to save our own asses to notice, especially as I had got peppered. The upshot is that Masters gave me my first—and last—ride as a casualty in the back of a Huey. I was patched up back at camp and then sent to a hospital in Da Nang where a specialist could look at my hand. After examining me, the doc said I needed reconstructive surgery and, as I was clearly not in condition to fly anymore, I might as well be sent back to 'the world,' as we affectionately called these United States. So the doc cleaned, packed and stabilized the wounds, and I was homeward bo'nd."

Kyle tossed the remaining water down the back of his throat, replaced the glass, and then flopped back in his chair. He was silent for a minute or two and then rolled his head sideways to look at me. Suddenly, Kyle put on a child's voice: "What did you do in the war, Daddy?" Taking a mock paternal tone, he responded, "Well, let's see…Oh, that's right! I blew away children, just abo't your age!" Kyle lifted both hands in the air in a show of helplessness and let them flop onto his lap. "So here I am, the returning warrior and baby-killer. What do you think of your old friend now?"

"I don't think you're a 'baby-killer.'"

"No? Well, I guess you wouldn't. You're all 'peace and love,' aren't you?"

I felt myself bristle at Kyle's words. I had resented the fact that many of my fellow Americans had taken the stand that the only way one could prove one's patriotism was to go to war—an undeclared war and invasion of a foreign country at that. I resented the fact that there seemed to be some sort of upside-down moral logic, that only those who had killed their share of Vietnamese were deemed worthy enough to be called America's sons. Kyle studied me as I fought my internal battle rather than cross emotional/verbal swords with my dear, damaged friend. Still, I lamely opted for a pedantic response. "You didn't kill any babies, Kyle."

Still spoiling for, what, verbal jousting, an angry reaction from me?—Kyle replied, "Okay professor, I killed *children*. Happy now? That make it any better?"

"Kyle, goddamnit, you know better than I that you were *at war*. Those kids had a grenade, and you had barely escaped from that landing zone—and one of your crew was dead. And besides, you tried to scare them off. You didn't just open fire."

"Yeah, but I could've fired high to scare 'em off, couldn't I?"

"But you were scared, Kyle. Who wouldn't have been in your situation?"

"I just acted."

"No, damn it; you *re*-acted!" I countered. "You told me yourself that Duke and Ches were shouting at you to shoot them."

"Well...I shoulda fired *high*."

"Then they might have killed *you*—unintentionally, I grant it—but they might have killed you."

Kyle's head fell back on the chair. "They *did*."

~ * ~

I was awakened about 10 p.m. by a combination of mumbling and whimpering. It was Kyle. He was having a nightmare. Little wonder. He had fallen asleep in his chair not long after recounting the horrors of his Vietnam experience. I must have drifted off not long afterwards, no doubt from emotional exhaustion. I had lifted Kyle's feet onto the coffee table and thrown a blanket over him. I rang Dick to tell him that I would be staying overnight with Kyle and then had made myself as comfortable as possible on his worn-out sofa.

It was still early when I awoke, just after dawn. The time of day I liked. The time of day Kyle and I used to set off on our bicycles or for our adventures in the woods. I got up as quietly as I could and stretched. Man, my neck ached. I made my way to the bathroom and then to Kyle's filthy kitchen. There were some eggs in the refrigerator and a loaf of bread which would pass muster as toast once I had scraped off the mold. I found some instant coffee on the counter top, put some water to boil on the stove, and then peeked into the living room to see if Kyle were still sleeping. He was. However, in looking for a skillet in a cupboard where everything was a jumble, pans rattled about, and I heard Kyle stir. "You auditioning for a one-man band o't there?"

"Something like that. It's a little tune called 'breakfast in ten minutes.'"

"You should leave the dead in peace," came Kyle's retort.

"Well, you should be pretty well embalmed with all the booze you had yesterday evening. But I'm going to see if I can bring you back to life."

"Yeah, just call me Lazarus." Kyle got up, tossed the blanket aside and then looked at it. As he scratched himself, he asked, "You tuck me in last night, Jon?"

"You could call it that." I took a look at Kyle. He did look like death warmed over. I hoped I could convince him to shave and shower after breakfast. "How do you take your coffee?"

"Black. No sugar."

"Good , 'cause you don't have any milk. And probably no sugar."

"Uh-huh," Kyle mumbled as he shuffled into the bathroom.

We ate our meager but warm breakfast in near silence. Kyle ate slowly and thoughtfully, for it was certain that his mind was working. His eye movements made it clear that he was focusing and re-focusing on something only he could see in his mind's eye. Kyle snorted a laugh and looked up at me. "Know how the Cav' used to welcome 'cherries' like me and my crew to Vietnam?"

"No idea," I shrugged, glad to have Kyle back somewhere near the present moment.

"Well, once we were settled in the camp, they'd lay on a beer bash for the new guys or 'cherries,' and those with the old-style cavalry hats would be wearing 'em and they would sing a little song to us. You remember the 'Camptown Ladies' song?" I nodded. "Well, they used that tune, but different words. Kyle began to sing: "You're goin' home in a body bag, doo-dah, doo-dah, you're goin' home in a body bag, oh de doo-dah day; shot between the eyes, shot between the thighs; you're goin' home in a body bag, oh-de doo-dah day."

"Charming," I said.

"Yeah, ain't it?" mused Kyle, holding his mug of coffee to his lips, but not drinking it, just inhaling the aroma. "I guess it was supposed to toughen us up to the reality of war, a sort of gallows humor or bravado, however you want to look at it. It sure proved true for a lot of guys, including two of my crew." Kyle closed his bloodshot eyes and drank deeply. "I never liked coffee growing up...but *man*...after a mission in 'Nam...it seemed to taste like...*life*. Maybe it was just the warmth and the caffeine rush—I don't know—but it sure made a difference." Kyle smiled at me: "Of course, if there was a little whisky to go in it; that helped, too!"

"You're clean out—if that's a hint."

Kyle shook his head. "There's plenty of time for that later."

We slipped back into silence as we finished our breakfast. My mind traced the path of our conversation and Kyle's revelations from the previous evening. My friend had been forced to find a solution to one of the greatest moral dilemmas any of us ever has to face: *Do I take someone else's life?* Is it murder or self-defense? All of his Christian upbringing and moral instruction had to be distilled into one instant and filtered through his military training. And Kyle had had mere seconds in which to make a judgment call...to act...or react.

We used to have ethical discussions and debates during late nights at church camp or in our youth group. It was all so safe and theoretical then. You know the sort of thing: There are four people in a lifeboat, but only food and water enough for three. Or, you are in a burning building with your mother and your best friend, but you can save only one of them, etc. Funny, we had never discussed the ethics of blowing away a kid with a hand grenade.

As I mused on these things, my father sprang suddenly into mind. Having downed twelve Japanese planes in World War II; he *must* have killed people—at least the number represented by the flags on his airplane—and somehow come to terms with it. But then, as I thought of his deep silences and his drinking, I began to wonder whether, in fact, he had ever come to terms with killing. I studied my friend's face, the lines and weariness this one regrettable action had imprinted upon him. He had gone to war, and he had killed three children. That was his contribution to the American effort in Vietnam. He had also flown a lot of young men into combat zones who were later returned to their families in flag-draped coffins. But for Kyle, the one and only time he drew his weapon in Vietnam was to shoot a child who had unwittingly been turned into a walking bomb.

~ * ~

After the joyful return to my home, family, friends and graduation, my reunion with Kyle had been fraught with tense emotion and anxiety. My old friend was a changed man. Oh, I still recognized 'the Kyle within him,' but the easy-going friend I had known for so many years was buried beneath the weight of his wartime traumas. Before I drove back to Dick's house, I took Kyle out for a late lunch at a local diner. He drank three or four beers to my one, and they did seem to help him relax. Every now and then I saw the old sparkle in his eyes, but seeing it damn near brought tears to mine. I offered to drive Kyle back to his apartment before I left, but he declined, saying the walk would do him good. As I got behind the wheel of Dick's car, Kyle came and stood by the door. He smiled his old smile and said with a chuckle, "Would you just look at the two of us?! I mean, you're on the run from the Feds 'cause Uncle Sam's got a price on your head. And me? I've done my patriotic duty, and now I'm one of Uncle Sam's rejects—a gimp." Kyle gave me a mock salute. "Who'd a thunk it when we were in high school?"

"Not I." I shook my head at the life-changing events neither of us could have foreseen a few short years ago. And not knowing when we'd next see each other, it seemed that neither of us could say 'goodbye.'

~ * ~

My mind was racing as I drove back to Dick's house; I could feel my pulse throbbing in my temples. To help calm both down, I opened the car windows so I could enjoy the spring warmth, still some weeks away in Canada, and inhale the rich scent of the pine trees. I breathed slowly and deeply. It worked. I let my eyes take in the color of the dogwood trees and crepe myrtles. But still my mind kept returning to Kyle's appearance and state of mind, not to mention the loss of his friends and his killing of the three Vietnamese children. I had hated leaving Kyle behind in that condition; he seemed to be in a place so dark that even shadows couldn't exist. But neither would it have been safe for me to remain in the US—and there was a flight to catch the next day, back to my life in Canada. Over lunch, I had encouraged Kyle to answer my letters in the future, and he had said he "would work on it," but I wasn't sure he meant it. I even suggested he come to Montreal and stay with me for a while, just for a change of scenery, but all he said was, "They got Jim Beam up there?"

As I drove through the colorful Carolina spring foliage, I thought once more about my father. As a post-war baby, I had only known the man he had become *after* the war; I mused about what he had been like before he went to war. Had his parents or my mother been shocked by the changes war had wrought in him? Was he as different to them as Kyle had appeared to me? I was still pondering these things when I pulled into Dick's driveway.

Dick was sitting in his favorite rocker on the front porch of his little house. He looked up from the book he was reading and gave me a genial wave as I parked the car. Tired, both from the restless nights with Kyle and my mind's incessant churning, I yawned and stretched as I got out of the car.

"Need a nap?" asked Dick as he stood up to greet me.

"Not right now, but I might catch a few winks on the drive up to Lawrenceville."

Dick nodded. "Let me just do a few things and we'll hit the road."

A half-hour later, we were driving north through Carolina's peach groves and "pottery region" on our way to hit 220 North. I watched the heat waves shimmering off the tarmac ahead of us, turning the road into a watery mirage, a rare phenomenon in my adoptive northern homeland. The road signs announced the colorful names of the Sandhills area: Samarcand, Troy, Carthage, Biscoe, and Whynot. The names conjured up the image of a Tar Heel Marco Polo! I always wondered who had bestowed these small towns and villages with their names and why—or Whynot, as one of the towns proclaimed! When we saw the road sign for 'Erect,' we both laughed out loud and began to share names given to towns and hamlets by the Quakers, such as 'Intercourse,' Pennsylvania, and 'Climax,' North Carolina—names which, these days, were not exactly associated with spiritual confraternity.

Our conversation then moved to the last time we had taken such a car journey together, my flight to Canada two years before. Although many things had changed, much remained the same: American youth were still in Southeast Asia and I still lived the life of a fugitive.

As we relaxed into the journey, Dick enquired about my visit with Kyle; so I recounted what I had seen, heard, and felt over the last two days. As always, Dick listened thoughtfully and with few questions. He wasn't one of those people whose listening is actually waiting for a gap to say something. Rather, Dick was one of those rare individuals who seemed to sift or savor the words flowing his way. When my words had run their course, Dick mused aloud, "You know, I was a little boy when my father went off to the Second World War. I hadn't yet started school. I was in second grade when he returned. Prior to the war, I have no memory of my mother ever stopping me from running to jump on his lap when he came home from work—or perhaps I was just too young to remember. But I do remember that after he returned from Europe, my mother always insisted on her greeting my father *first* before she let me or my siblings go to greet Dad."

Dick remained silent for a few minutes as we drove, perhaps examining his memories or simply enjoying the countryside. The balmy spring air had nearly lulled me into a sleep when Dick spoke again. "As we had come from a German immigrant family, I believe my father had a hard time reconciling not only what he had had to do and see in an infantry regiment, but also the horrors of what the German people— 'our people'—had done across Europe. The pictures we have of him before he went into the army almost always show him smiling. Afterwards—and at least until I was in high school—he wore a somewhat pensive expression. Cracking a smile seemed almost to hurt his face. His smile did return, little-by-little; but even now, when I visit my parents, Dad will get up and leave the room when news of the Vietnam War is on television. And he'll remain silent for an hour or so afterwards." Dick paused, lifted one hand from the steering wheel, palm upwards, and briefly looked my way. "Jon, none of us has any way of knowing for certain what happens to another person in wartime. But if anyone ever needed our love, patience, and friendship, then it is people like my father and all of the young men returning home from that thankless conflict in Vietnam."

Twenty-three

And when he gets to heaven,
To St. Peter he will tell,
"Another Marine reporting, Sir,
I've served my time in Hell!"

—Marine grave inscription on Guadalcanal

Mother had supper ready when we arrived, so we were ushered straight into the dining room for fried chicken, mashed potatoes with gravy, and turnip greens. Even before food was served, Mom pressed Dick to stay the night rather than drive the hundred-plus miles back to the Southern Pines area. Despite my mother's best efforts to impose our Braddock hospitality on him, Dick declined. He said he felt that, as this was my last night at home before returning to Montreal, my parents ought to have me to themselves. Perhaps feeling that Dick might die of starvation on the journey home, mother did her best to tempt Dick to linger "just for a taste of home-made caramel cake and a cup of coffee. That won't hold you up too much, now will it?"

At this point my father chipped in. "Rachel, hon, don't kill the man with kindness. If Dick says he has to go, then he has to *go*." Mother harrumphed and smoothed her apron, which she wore even at the dinner table unless, of course, it was a formal meal.

Not many people have succeeded in thwarting my mother's culinary onslaught, but Dick achieved that distinction. He passed on both dessert and coffee but praised my mother's cooking as he heartily thanked her. My mother, father, and I stood up from the table and accompanied Dick as far as the front porch, where he bade us farewell. Before driving away, Dick wished me the best of luck and gave me a thumbs up.

My parents and I made our way back to the dining room, where I gladly ate my share of mother's cake as well as the piece meant for Dick. As we got up to clear the table, Mother shooed Dad and me out of the way. "Phil? Jon? Why don't y'all go out on the screened porch and enjoy this lovely spring evening?" It was, of course, an order and not a suggestion. This was quickly followed by, "And I've also got to prepare some material for the women's Bible-study group tomorrow." Dad threw up his hands in surrender and I followed him out onto the porch. As the screened door closed behind us, Mom added, "Oh—I'll bring some iced tea out in a few minutes." It was far from subtle that Mom wanted my father and me to spend this last evening together. We could hear her rattling around in the kitchen, from where she soon re-appeared with our tea. After finishing in the kitchen, Mom took herself upstairs.

Despite the warmth of our reunion several days before, I was still not fully at ease with my father. I had never talked unreservedly with Dad the way I had with others of his generation, such as Rev. McLaurin. I suppose not many young men do so when they are in their teens or early twenties. When Dad was sure that mother was out of earshot, he asked me to fetch two glasses from the kitchen. I saw him duck into the study from whence he emerged with a bottle of scotch. Dad winked at me as he said, "Your mother knows I hide a bottle somewhere and does not approve, so let's keep this between us, okay?" He poured us each two fingers of the amber liquid, placed the bottle out of sight behind a planter and raised his glass to me. As simple as it was, there was something of the sacramental about that moment. My father had let me into his life.

We both sipped our drinks in silence for a moment or two, and then I decided to take a risk. Over supper, I had told my parents about catching up with Kyle and an abridged version of how he had been since his return from Vietnam. Yet there I sat in my family home with another war veteran: my father. Apart from showing me his photo album from his days in the Second World War, Dad had never really talked about the war itself or how he experienced it. Dad and I were sitting in two of our ladder-back rocking chairs, slightly angled toward each other. As was often the case with my father, especially when he was drinking scotch, he seemed absorbed in his own thoughts, somewhere deep within himself.

"Dad?"

My father blinked a couple of times and then looked at me. "Yes, son?"

"Dad...um...during the war?" My father's eyes focused upon me more clearly, inviting the rest of the question. "Did you...I mean, well...you must have killed some people, right? Like when you shot down Japanese aircraft?"

"Yes, I did. I killed men when I shot them down, and I'm pretty sure I killed men on the ground. As a military pilot, that was my job. We had a war to fight—and win." Dad took another sip of scotch and looked at me evenly over the rim of his glass, waiting to see where I was going with my line of enquiry.

"Well...how...how did it make you *feel*? I mean, how did you *deal* with it at the time? Because...well...Kyle's really...um..." I struggled for words but then settled on, "fucked up." I saw a slight twinkle in Dad's eyes. He had never heard me use the F-word, and I had never heard it from him. I proceeded to relate to my father the basics of Kyle's story and the root of his *dis*ease. "He seems to spend most of his time drunk," I added.

Dad looked at the remaining scotch in his glass and wiggled it at me as he raised his eyebrows. "Self-medication," he said, as he finished the drink. "I believe that's how our medical officer used to refer to it. Like a lot of my fellow Marines at that time, I decided it was best *not to feel*—or even to think too much. How we felt about the war or about what we had to do—and see…well…it wouldn't change our circumstances; and, in fact, it could have a negative effect on us." Dad paused as he seemed to collect his thoughts. "Beer was a nickel a can when I was out in the Pacific. But it was only 3.2 percent alcohol, and it took a *lot* of drinking to wash away…the fear…*and the nightmares*. So we did some wheeling-dealing with enterprising Navy boys who brought cases of scotch, gin, and the like to sell—*at a price*—to desperate sorts, like Marine pilots. And so began a lifetime's…" Dad searched carefully for the next word, "*dependency*—if I'm honest—on booze." He looked at his now empty glass. "Speaking of which, I'm out. You game for more?"

This was the most my father had ever told me about his experience of war. As I was keen not to break the mood of the moment, I quickly nodded to his offer of another drink and knocked back the rest of my scotch. Dad retrieved the bottle from its hiding place, so I held out my glass and he poured us each another two fingers. "You seem to hold your liquor better than I remember." His eyes sparkled with mirth and we both chuckled at the memory of my first experience of inebriation. Dad stared at the liquid in his tumbler as he swirled it gently, without spilling a drop. Not looking at me, he said, "And, yes, I am breaking doctor's orders—and, what's worse, *your mother's*. But after thirty years or so, well…honestly, it's hard to stop." Dad looked at me again. "But I am cutting back. I am trying."

A silence settled over us for a few moments, but I could tell my father wanted to say more, and so I waited.

Looking into the middle distance, Dad mused aloud. "I never really saw the faces of the men I killed. Oh, I could see a figure in a cockpit or a gunner behind Plexiglas—but only briefly." My father's left hand rose from his lap and pointed toward some distant memory. "Things happened really fast in aerial combat. As for men on the ground…well, they were soldiers *and our enemy*. Maybe some of the bombs I dropped killed civilians—I don't know. But, unlike Kyle, I don't have to live with the certain knowledge that I did kill civilians—or children." Dad shook his head and then looked at me. "That's got to be tough. But, Jon, I'm glad he has a friend like you. Just be advised that between his pain and the drinking, Kyle might say, and perhaps *has said*, some things that…well, that test your friendship to the limit. I've seen it with some of my war buddies. You've just got to be patient. A lot of people who've never experienced combat tend to see behavior like Kyle's as simply self-pity or bitterness at what he's been through. They don't take the time like you've done to try to listen…to hear— *really hear*—what the person has been through…and done."

Dad pondered his glass for a moment and then lifted it to his lips, slowly tilted his head back, and drained its contents. He reached for the bottle and topped his glass. I waved him off when he proffered it my way. Dad just nodded and took a draught of his scotch. He then twisted his head around, as though trying to work out a kink in his neck. Dad jutted out his chin and then ran his tongue over his lips. All of a sudden, he seemed ill-at-ease. Before I could ask whether he was all right, Dad spoke again, quietly and in the same sort of faraway voice I had heard Kyle use. "I did see *some* Japs face-to-face…once…and maybe this will help you with Kyle…I-I don't know. My squadron had been on a mission to attack some Japanese ships that were bringing reinforcements to the Solomons. On the last pass, I got hit pretty badly. I had barely gained enough altitude to jump when my engine caught fire and then cut out, so I jumped…" As my father talked to me, I realized I was hearing finally and *firsthand* the account that my mother had shared with me years before. Although it was thirty years after the event, it was clear that relating his story to me was causing him real anguish. It was an anguish that had kept him at a remove from his own flesh and blood. As he talked, Dad screwed up his face, frowned, bit his lower lip, took deep breaths and exhaled heavily: "…and as I was having a difficult time staying afloat, I had to do…*something*."

Dad glanced at me quickly—not unlike Kyle had done when relating his experiences in Vietnam. It was a tentative, are-you-still-with-me look.

"The area where I came down had a number of dead, bloated Japs floating around, no doubt killed days before on our earlier raids. I still had my combat knife, so I used it to cut the cords from my 'chute and—" Dad took a gulp of air, "I used it to lash a few of the bodies together—for a sort of raft." Dad paused and raised his eyebrows in a sort of how-does-that-grab-you fashion as looked at me searchingly.

"Dad, I-I can't begin to imagine what that must have been like for you…but I can understand *why* you did it."

Dad nodded his head slowly and thoughtfully. "Yeah," he sighed and dropped his head. "The will to stay alive is a powerful thing. And unless you've been there…" He lifted his left hand and then it fall onto this thigh with a slap. Dad knew there was no need to finish the sentence. "I did tell your mother about it…*once*." He gave his hand a little wave. "Oh, years before you were born. Your mom was getting pretty annoyed at me for coming home a little too tanked-up from the officers' club. We had an argument and…well, it just all came out." Dad raised his eyes from under his brow and smiled at me. "She was shocked! I even think she was a little scared…*of me*…for a while. I guess she wondered who she was climbing into bed with every night, and I can't really blame her. Jon, war turns civilized men into brutes. But that's how you survive. You do things in war that you could never even dream of doing in peacetime." Dad looked at me and his eyes misted over. "So I know what your buddy, Kyle, is going through."

Then, before I knew what was happening, my father was out of his chair and on his knees with his arms around me, weeping, his face pressed into my chest. At first my arms floated upwards like frightened birds, not knowing whether or where it was safe to land. Then I slowly lowered them onto my father's back, and held him, as he must have done with me so many years before when, as a child, I had needed comforting. "Jon…" his words were choked, "You don't know how much I love you, son. Can…you…forgive me?"

To say I was overwhelmed is an understatement. *"Forgive you?* But Dad—*for what?"*

"The things I've done…the things I haven't done…the way I treated you and Ron."

Imagine a glacier, which has stood for millennia, suddenly melting. Such was the onrush of emotions that picked me up and carried me with them. The image of my father—an image I had carried throughout most of my youth—was being washed away in an instant. And I wondered: had I become my father's comforter?

"Dad, whatever you did in the war, you had to do. You had good reasons. And as for me and Ron…well, we're *here*, aren't we? And that's because of you." It suddenly seemed apposite to use his nickname of old. "Hey—no Blackie, no Jon or Ron. Right? Everything I am or have, it's thanks to you and Mom. Dad, there's nothing to forgive. I love you." My father simply nodded into my chest. Words, whose use and abuse over the years had helped create the gulf between us, were no longer necessary. I wept with my father.

Twenty-four

The web of our life is of a mingled yarn, good and ill together.
—Shakespeare

Marie, Ellen, and I were all in a fellowship of tears as we sat, with arms around one another, on Kyle's bed. I hadn't really intended to relate the account of my reconciliation with my father, but so much had come tumbling out. The remainder of the tea Ellen had brought us earlier had grown stone cold; so, in search of tissues and more tea, we all left Kyle's bedroom and went into the kitchen. I fished out fresh cups while Ellen put more water on to boil.

"So...how did you feel when you left your mom and dad to fly back to Montreal?" queried Marie.

"How did I feel?" I repeated her question. "God, there were so many feelings! And there was so much to think about on that flight! I don't know that I had ever had so much to ponder and digest, even including the suicide of Wendy's mother. There was Kyle, of course, and then my father. It's funny, but when I had left for Canada back in '71, it hadn't felt like

274

running away—from life, the draft, or anything. It simply felt like what I had to do. It was about my beliefs and principles." I paused to collect my thoughts and rubbed the stubble on my chin, as I hadn't shaved that morning. "But…when I left my parents that day—and just two days after seeing Kyle—well…that's another matter altogether. There seemed like so many reasons why I should remain in North Carolina—good reasons. But then, there was always the possibility of my being arrested, and I was starting seminary in a few months' time."

"Jon, honey," Ellen spoke to me over her shoulder as she poured water into the tea pot, "you did the right thing. There was really nothing you could have done for Kyle back then. He was so *messed up* that…well, he just had to figure things o't for himself." Marie nodded her agreement. Ellen brought the tea pot over to the kitchen table and we all sat. For a few minutes, no one spoke. We stirred our tea, gently blew over the steaming surface, and took small sips.

"'Nother Brother?" I looked up from my tea. Marie was studying a framed photo of Kyle dressed in full clown regalia. "Did you ever have any inkling that Kyle was going to train as a circus clo'n after he left Fayetteville? Did he ever talk with you abo't it? We all just got a postcard from Florida one day saying Kyle had moved there and was using his GI Bill money to train as a clo'n!"

I laughed as I remembered my reaction as well. "Kyle always did have good timing!" I chirped. "But, no; I really had no idea. He'd never even mentioned the possibility. Like you, I received a post card one day, with the picture of a clown sitting on an elephant's trunk! On the back Kyle had written, 'This'll be me soon!' Then he said he'd enrolled at the Ringling Brothers' Clown College and gave me his new address. I thought it was a joke at first; but then I found out he was dead serious." I winced at my bad choice of words.

Ellen chimed in, "I think it gave his life a focus again. Before he went to Vietnam, it had all been abo't flying helicopters. Becoming a clo'n gave him…I don't know…a new lease on life, I guess."

"No, it was more than that," I blurted out with more urgency than I had intended. "It actually *saved Kyle*." Both Ellen and Marie looked at me quizzically.

"What do you mean, 'Nother Brother?" asked Marie.

I shifted around in my seat as I retrieved an old letter from the back pocket of my jeans. "I wasn't sure when to share this…but, well…these last couple of days have been a time of revelations; and, as we've now got onto the subject of Kyle's clown days, I suppose one more revelation can't hurt." I opened the crumpled, yellowed paper and smoothed it on the table before reading.

"Anyway, I think I got this letter in either 1975 or '76. It wasn't all that long after he had taken to the road with the circus. If you don't mind, I'll just read the important part." My audience nodded assent. I cleared my throat and took a deep breath. "Kyle wrote: 'Every time I make children laugh—especially young children—it's like a layer of clear varnish has been spread over the faces of those Vietnamese kids I killed. Over the years, I've found that no single layer can blot them out, but with each successive layer, their image becomes just a little more obscure. And the laughter of the children I entertain does that.'" Ellen bit her lip as the tears welled up in her eyes once more—and not just in Ellen's. Tissues were passed around again among the three of us.

Marie pulled her chair next to Ellen's and put her arm around her. She looked at me and started to speak. "Kyle never told us…" but Ellen stopped her.

"Honey, he could only have told us *why* he did the clo'ning if he had told us abo't killing those poor children in Vietnam." Ellen dabbed her eyes. "But isn't it good he had Jon to tell?" She reached out and squeezed my hand.

"I know, I know. It's just all so…" Marie left her thought unfinished.

"And at least my boy was *living* again. I hated seeing him just 'existing' down there in Fayetteville…in that filthy apartment of his— oh!" Ellen shuddered involuntarily.

I nodded in agreement. "Yeah, I have to admit, from that point on, Kyle's communications became more upbeat. He really seemed to have turned a corner. There was less looking back and more looking ahead. And when the circus wasn't on the road, Kyle even managed to finish his college degree. That was really something! It took him eight years or so, but he did it."

"When he put his mind to something, there was no stopping him," mused Ellen.

We all retreated into our own thoughts and memories of Kyle as we sipped our tea. As I stared into my cup, I found myself chuckling again at some recollections of Kyle's clown days. When I finally looked up, I saw Marie and Ellen looking at me quizzically. "Sorry. I was remembering a particular incident Kyle wrote about. He used to send me long letters with wild stories about life in the circus. Did he ever tell you two about the Ku Klux Klowns?!" Both Marie's and Ellen's eyes widened in bemusement as they shook their heads.

"Well, then, I've gotta tell you! Kyle said the circus had a team of midget clowns who performed various routines of their own devising. One of the clowns, Grady, who stood about three-foot-nothing, had no tolerance for prejudice *at all*. Seems he'd suffered enough throughout his life for being small. So this one time, when they were in Alabama, he and the rest of the team got roaring drunk before they went on. Grady and the others had made themselves KKK capes and hoods, so first, out came Grady, wearing his Klan outfit and riding backwards on a donkey and dragging an effigy he and the team had made with a picture of George Wallace as the face! Next, out came the other Ku Klux Klowns with a makeshift scaffold onto which they lynched the Wallace effigy and then set it alight! It all happened so fast the ringmaster couldn't stop it. Kyle said the crowd went wild—with some laughing, and others shouting and cussing. When a few hard-core rednecks ran out into the ring and tried to catch the little guys, the audience started laughing even harder as they thought it was part of the act! Then the security men started chasing the rednecks and it all became pandemonium! With all of the confusion, the midget clowns slipped under the bleachers and disappeared." By the time I finished, both Ellen and Marie were again wiping tears from their eyes, but this time it was from hilarity.

"Oh, it does a body good to laugh. It's certain that this poor ol' heart of mine has had enough of sadness." Ellen smiled sweetly at me and, for just a brief instant, I could see Kyle's smile. "Thank you for sharing that story, Jon. It's so important at times like this to remember that Kyle had some happiness after Vietnam."

Marie sighed unconsciously as she looked out the window toward the driveway. She seemed lost in her own thoughts for a few minutes. "Penny for your thoughts, Kid," I offered.

"Oh!" Marie smiled and looked at her mother and me. "Sorry! I was just thinking abo't when Kyle bought that camper van of his." Marie nodded toward the van and I also turned to look at it.

"His pride and joy," I said. "It's more than thirty years old now, but you'd hardly know it." The classic VW camper van gleamed in the sun as if it knew we were talking about it.

We sat in silence for a few minutes, and then I pushed my chair back from the table. Stretching my arms toward the ceiling, I slowly intoned, "We-e-ell, I guess it's time to get back to sorting out Kyle's things." Both Marie and Ellen nodded.

But then Marie said, "Mama, why don't you just rest for a while? Jon and I can do this together."

"Well, if y'all don't mind. It would be nice to stretch o't on Kyle's sofa."

"Not at all," I said. "We'll finish Kyle's bedroom and then work on what's left in the study."

When we reached Kyle's room in the rear of the house and out of earshot of the living room, Marie turned to face me. She laid her hands on my shoulders and looked me in the eye. "'Nother Brother, there's just so much I want to ask you abo't Kyle, but…well, not in mother's hearing. She's stood up to everything pretty well so far but…" Marie released a heavy sigh, "…but I can see the weariness in her face. And I'm not sure she's up to hearing some of the things I'd like to know— that is, if you can tell me."

"Sure, Kid. I'll tell you whatever I can."

Marie hugged me and then turned toward a box she had been filling with Kyle's clothes. Over her shoulder, she asked, "Was Kyle ever…*in love*? I mean, he lived over *fifty years*, but I've never known if he ever truly loved a woman."

"Hey, why don't you ask me a tough question?" I joked, but then paused for reflection before answering. "The short answer is 'yes,'

Kyle had some loving relationships. But before you ask, they always faltered over one issue: children."

"I did wonder," replied Marie.

"Well, you know Kyle." It hit me that I was still using the present tense when referring to Kyle—but then, standing there in his bedroom, and among his things, his presence was all around us. "He was good-looking, witty, warm, and...*truly human*. So a number of women wanted to have his babies. A couple of women thought they could change Kyle's mind, so he broke off with them. Others left Kyle when they came to understand he couldn't or *wouldn't* help them fulfill their maternal instincts."

I taped shut the last box of Kyle's clothes and paused. Having sealed him in his grave and committed him to life eternal, we were now sealing the remnants of his life in cardboard for their own afterlife in the homeless shelter down in Winston-Salem. I looked over at Marie. "Shall we attack the study before dinner?" She nodded and so we made our way along the hallway. We could hear Ellen lightly snoring as we passed the living room. We each grabbed an empty box from the stack we had left there earlier.

"Speaking of women and *chi-ild-ren*..." Marie drawled out the last word, giving it special emphasis.

"Yay-yes?" I drawled in return, knowing full well what was coming.

"How often do you see or hear from your daughter?"

"Karen? Not as often as I would like, that's for sure. After years of single fatherhood, I kinda got used to having her around. But Karen's a teacher now, living up in Asheville and married to a teacher, a great guy. It's so hard to believe. She seemed to grow up so fast, especially after the divorce. Looking back, it seems like every time I turned around, she seemed to be missing a tooth or growing a new one, or she seemed taller by a foot...or dating..." I looked up from the box I was packing and stared at the blank, white ceiling, where Karen's face appeared to me, moving through various ages and stages of her life.

"If it's any consolation—and I'm sure it's not—children change fast even when you haven't been divorced. What was it John Lennon wrote? 'Life is what happens when you're busy making other plans'—or something like that? It's true, you know. None of us can envision just how quickly and radically life or people can change. I mean, look at us here now, going through Kyle's things."

"Yeah…I know."

"So, what actually brought you and Elaine together? And how long were you two together before…well…you split up? That period of your life is kinda sketchy for me."

I was looking at a copy of Bonhoeffer's *The Cost of Discipleship* that I had given to Kyle for his ordination, the title of the book strong in its irony. "What? Oh…gosh—so you really want 'Jon: The Lost Years,' do you?"

"Well…*yes*—but only if you don't mind." Marie smiled and shrugged, and then added quietly, "As I've said, 'Nother Brother, you're now the *only* brother I have left."

I looked at Marie and smiled. "Fair enough. Well, let's see…Elaine and I met when she was a fervent American peace activist working with the Montreal Committee to Aid War Objectors while doing her degree at McGill. She was there in some loose, volunteer capacity with the American Friends Service Committee. From time to time I needed help and advice from the Committee, and that's how we met. It also turned out that we both came from North Carolina, so I suppose it gave us something in common."

Marie was silent for a moment and pursed her lips as she studied a book title and looked for the appropriate box in which to place it, as we were organizing them by rough categories: systematic theology, pastoral theology, biblical commentaries, etc. I was beginning to think she hadn't heard me when she said, "So, Elaine was a Quaker? I don't think I knew that."

"Yeah, well, I don't think she did either!" I laughed. It had taken me years before I could laugh about that part of my past. "I suppose it seemed sincere enough for the first few years I knew her, but then, after I got to know her family and discovered they were all Methodists, I came to see her 'Quakerism' as some sort of puerile rebellion against her parents and siblings. It certainly added nothing to her moral character. But those discoveries only came *after* we had moved back to the States."

I stopped and looked up from the box I was packing. "It's funny, you don't really see the whole person before you meet their family and discover a bit of their background. Before that, they remain in a sort of two-dimensional reality. Anyway, Elaine and I got married when I graduated from seminary, and she from McGill, in '76. It was a small Quaker service at Elaine's Meeting House. My parents even managed to attend. Of course, as you will well remember, 1976 was the year Jimmy Carter was elected president. What you might not recall, however, is that one of his campaign promises was to offer full, unconditional pardons to all war resisters. The upshot is, on Carter's first full day in office in January '77, he fulfilled his promise and I—" I raised my arms in thanksgiving, "I was a *free man*! After six years, I could return home. If for nothing else, I will always be grateful to Carter for that. In any case, I applied for and got a college chaplaincy job and off we went. Elaine was less sanguine about the move. In retrospect, I think she over-identified with guys like me and enjoyed what for her was the 'romance' of expat life. And why not? Elaine could cross the US/Canadian border without a worry and visit her family and friends *any time she liked*. There was no possibility of her being arrested!" I mumbled a few vile epithets for Elaine.

"So…um…when did things start to go wrong?" asked Marie.

Annoyed at myself for feeling vestigial anger after so many years, I virtually barked, "When were they ever *right*?" Immediately, I saw the discomfort on Marie's faced and apologized. "Hey, forgive me, Kid. Elaine and I had some good times—*in Canada*. We seemed right for one another—*in Canada*. Problem was, by the time we moved back to North Carolina, Elaine was already pregnant. Well, I-I mean," I stammered, "it…it wasn't a problem *then* that Elaine was pregnant. The problems came *later* when she wanted both her 'freedom' *and* her family life."

"Did she come right out and tell you that?"

"No, not at first. I-I kinda knew something was up, but whenever I asked, she either avoided the topic or said nothing was wrong. And that's how we limped along for three or four years. You know, when Elaine had her 'Quaker head' on, she was always espousing '*peace* and *love*', '*peace* and *love.*' But then came one afternoon, when I caught her in the act of—if you'll excuse the pun—sharing a *piece* of her *love* with a co-worker."

"No!"

"'Fraid so," I continued. "I had taken Karen to a swimming lesson, which got cancelled, so we returned home early...and to Elaine's surprise, and our shock, discovered her 'in the act.' For some reason, however, she was bewildered to find that I was less than understanding, even though our five-year-old daughter was with me." I stood and looked off into the middle-distance. The image of that day was stained into my memory bank. I shook my head, trying to dispel the image. "What fun," I added sarcastically.

"I'm so sorry, Jon. I know it doesn't help to say it—especially now. But you didn't deserve that."

"No, I didn't. And neither did Karen. But she got over it—as kids so often can and do. Sometimes I think they are more resilient than their parents when it comes to divorce. I can't say how it is for other divorced parents, but I think Karen and I looked after each other, each in our own way. She was—*and is*—a good kid. But it took some years before she really wanted to go visit her mother during holidays or summer vacation. And truth to tell, even to this day they aren't very close."

"None of us gets to choose our parents, eh?"

"Nope. Anyway, being a divorced, single dad minister left the Presbyterian Church feeling awkward about me. I didn't fit the nice, middle-class profile: wife, two kids, and all that shit. Seems to me that Mr. Jesus never did fit that profile either. But then I have learned that one should never make the mistake of mixing up Jesus and the institutional church. I mean, look what it did for Kyle."

"But...I thought you liked the small churches you serve along the Blue Ridge."

"Well, I do—or at least I *did*—but not at first."

"Umm...you kinda lost me there, Jon. Care to explain?"

"Yeah—sorry. It's like this: after the divorce, I was a single father—and don't forget that this was long before such things became anything near acceptable. So, as I said, the strait-laced Presbyterians didn't know quite what to do with me. I guess I was something of an embarrassment for them. And, although I had done nothing wrong, I was nonetheless viewed with suspicion. Thus, the churches in larger towns and cities were deemed off-limits for me. So when I decided to leave the college chaplaincy and start my life anew with just Karen and me, my personal information form only found its way to churches in the rural backwater. They were desperate for ministers in those areas, and, well, I was desperate to find a church. After all, I needed to make a living to support my daughter and me. At first, I have to admit, it felt like a punishment—or at least a kind of *banishment*. But, over time, I came to like the smaller churches and their communities. The women really took Karen under their wings, so the church community became a sort of extended family." I laughed aloud. "Why they even got to the point that they would listen to my views on non-violence." Under my breath I added, "*That* took some time!"

"So what abo't now?" Marie queried gently.

"So…what…about…*now*?" I mused over the question. "Yeah, well…*now*…having accompanied Kyle on his journey to hell…*now* I can't see the institutional church in the same light ever again, not like I did when I started my ministry…or when Kyle started his. You see, I had joined the institutional church and become an ordained minister because of men like Rev. Gavin McLaurin and figures such as Martin Luther King, Jr., and Daniel Berrigan. It hadn't really occurred to me at the beginning of that process that those men were the *exception* when it came to living a truth-filled, godly life, rather than the *rule*. I had actually been naïve enough not to realize that. For so many ministers, it's simply a nice way to make a living—better paid than many and less challenging than most—but only, I hasten to add, if one doesn't take this Gospel living too seriously."

Suddenly I felt very weary and slumped down into the nearest chair. With my elbows on my knees, I cradled my face in the palms of my hands and slowly rubbed my brow. I was feeling full of self-recrimination: Hadn't the Vietnam War been enough for one life? Why did I help commit my best friend to another—and in some ways—more insidious conflict, a moral conflict that was hidden and papered over with pious platitudes and unctuous smiles and handshakes? I heard Marie walk over toward me and felt her cool, soft hand gently stroke my neck. Without looking up, I muttered, "You know, whatever happened to Kyle in Vietnam…in the end, it was the church that killed him…and yet…somehow I can't help but feel that I helped slip his head into their noose." I felt Marie's hand jerk involuntarily.

"Jon! How could you say that?! You did no such thing!"

"Yeah, well, he came to me when he started thinking seriously about training for the ministry, didn't he? And I encouraged him."

"That may be, but you helped Kyle because you were his friend. And don't forget he was a grown man; Kyle could make his own choices."

I nodded in response to Marie's words, my head still lodged between my hands and feeling like it weighed a ton. Not for the first time in my life, I was experiencing the hell of suicide's aftermath: all of the self-questioning and rehearsing of events—and all prefaced with "If only…"

~ * ~

The distinctive sound of a Volkswagen engine roused me from my sermon preparation. I had just been describing how the Moabitess, Ruth, was just about to go sashaying in her finery down to the threshing floor for an assignation with an intoxicated Boaz. I chuckled to myself how—under just the slightest scrutiny—the story of Ruth easily turned into a titillating tale and knew full well that some of my congregation would be squirming in their seats. I rolled my desk chair over to the window and saw Kyle's van in the driveway. Karen, who had been watching Saturday afternoon television, was at the door before me. Still pre-adolescent, I heard her squeal, "Uncle Kyle!"

When I reached the front door, I was greeted by a clown—with Kyle somewhere beneath the make-up and regalia. I shook my head in mock disbelief, but when I extended my hand, I received a face full of water from the fake flower in Kyle's lapel. Karen doubled over with laughter, slapping her knees. This was quickly followed by two honks from an air horn in the giant pocket of Kyle's checked suit. "Really funny, Kyle," I responded in feigned anger and wiped my face with Oliver Hardy-style, exaggerated slowness—partly for Karen's benefit, as I loved to hear her giggle with delight.

"Hey, what do you expect?! I'm a clo'n!" Two more honks on his horn. "That is to say, the clo'n is in to'n—so don't you fro'n!" Three honks, as Kyle tickled Karen under the chin.

Having wiped my face, I made a show of replacing my handkerchief and said, "I would shake your hand, but you've probably got a joy buzzer ready to shock me."

Kyle laughed in his easy manner as he stepped forward to embrace me and said, "Always keep the audience guessing!" Looking down at Karen, he added, "Right, Princess?" Karen nodded assent. Like her father, she, too, had come to love the man she called Uncle Kyle. Smiling, I opened my arms to hug him.

"Good to see you, ol' buddy."

"Yeah, you too. It's been too long," replied Kyle. "And…um…I'll try not to get my make-up on you—people might start talking!" We both laughed as we broke our embrace.

Turning back to Karen, Kyle knelt and looked furtively left and right. He cupped his hand to the side of his mouth and motioned for her to draw near. In a stage whisper he said, "Psst, Princess? Think your old man would let you have some chocolate straight from the circus?"

I then received one of those expectant looks to which fathers who have daughters can rarely say "no." "Yeah, go on. It's still a couple of hours before supper." Karen snatched her prize as though I might have a sudden change of mind and dashed back to the television.

"So, what brings the clown to town? Did you come here to do a one-man show?"

"Nah. I just finished the afternoon performance in Winston-Salem and thought I'd drive up to see my old pal. I've got another show at eight this evening, so I thought I'd stay in costume."

"We-ell," I drawled, as I looked Kyle over appreciatively, "them clothes sho'nuff suit yew."

"Ha! Little do you know!" grinned Kyle. "Little do you know! Hey, got anything cold to drink—iced tea or a soft drink?"

"Sure, come on in and sit." Kyle followed me into the kitchen and sat at the table while I grabbed a couple of glasses and the tea.

Before I could sit down, Kyle blurted out, "I'm thinking about training for the ministry."

"Say *what*?" I said, sloshing the tea on the table.

Kyle laughed and said, "Why so shocked? *You* did it."

"Yeah…well…I didn't mean it *that way*. It's just that you hit me with this news out of the blue…and you're dressed as a clown, for heaven's sake."

"Would you have preferred a pie in the face?" Two honks from the horn. "I wouldn't be the first clo'n for Christ, now would I?" Another honk—quickly followed by a squirt from his flower. I laughed. What else could I have done? This was Kyle.

"I think the Apostle Paul referred to himself as a 'fool for Christ,'" I said as I wiped my face with a handkerchief, "but point taken. Okay, so talk to me. Are you actually talking about becoming a 'Christian clown'?"

"Maybe. Who knows? I don't know—it's too early to say. But what I do know is this: Jon, I want to be a means of grace; I've already been a means of destruction." I started to interrupt, but Kyle raised his hand to silence me. "I know what you're going to say, and no, it's not just abo't 'Nam and what happened there. Being a clo'n all these years has helped lay that to rest—an uneasy rest at times, mind you, but it's no longer in the forefront of my mind. No, what I'm talking about is this overwhelming desire to do something that builds up and encourages people—and doesn't just make them laugh for a short time—although God knows most of us need that! But I have to do more, Jon," and at this point Kyle leveled his eyes on mine, "and I know I am *called* to do more. And, whatever God may want me to do in the future, I fully believe I am being called to work with other Vietnam vets now—or as soon as I can get ordained."

As I contemplated my friend's words, the incongruity of having such a conversation with someone dressed as a clown was dissipated as both the essence and earnestness of Kyle shone through. In a racing instant, the evolution of my sense of call to ministry, and all of the people and incidents that confirmed it, played out in my mind. Although they might bear some superficial similarities, each person's call to ministry is as unique as the individual. Thus, the more I considered Kyle's sense of call, the more I recognized the air of authenticity of God's hand at work. Unconsciously, I had begun nodding my assent. It was Kyle who brought me back to the moment by saying, "You know it's right, don't you?"

Still slowly nodding, I looked at my friend, the clown, and replied, "Yeah, Kyle, I do.

"You know, I've learned a few things over the years I've worked with the circus as regards personal healing and spirituality. If we truly regret the way we have been or something we have done and seek to rectify it in the way we live now, then that's a big part of the battle. No shame, no gain, you might say." Kyle grinned.

"Anyway, as you have no do'bt observed, I wasted too much time dwelling on the past and getting sucked into the trap of 'If I'd only done *this*, then *that* might not have happened.' But, of course, the past always comes o't *the same way*, because it's done, dusted and dead. I've even read some the works by your favorite philosopher/theologian, Kierkegaard. How did he put the problem? We can only understand life backwards, but we must live it forwards. The trouble is, life keeps moving forward and thus our supposed grasp on the past becomes more tenuous. So I guess that I, for years, was like a man with one foot on the platform and one foot on the train. There comes a point of decision: climb on board or stay behind."

"Or fall off the platform," I added. Kyle laughed and gave me two honks from his horn.

"Anyway, I had to wrestle with my past until it finally hit me that I could just get on the damn train—let go of the past and move on. And although you, ol' buddy, and a few others could see what I needed to do, it was no use until I could see it. But don't get me wrong. If you'll pardon the paradox, although I alone could do it, I couldn't do it alone. I have no do'bt the love and prayers offered by you, my sister, my mom, and her church all helped get me to the place where I could see for myself what I needed to do. But I needed that time on my own." Kyle wiped the moisture-clad glass of tea across his brow. Sitting up with a start, he gasped, "Oops! I might spoil my make-up!" We both laughed.

"You know, a few years back, a small group of us from the circus did a tour of Western Europe. One day, when we were somewhere in the so'th of Germany, I went to visit an old palace and gardens. I was on my own. It began to rain as I walked through those enormous grounds, so I took shelter in what must have been some sort of summer house or tea room. On the wall, I saw a plaque which read: *'Einsamkeit ist besser als böse Gesellschaft.'* Roughly translated, it means: 'Solitude is better than bad company.' It seemed like a message from God! The circus life has given me that solitude. I suppose a lot of us circus people are loners for that matter. When we're not rehearsing or performing, I have a lot of time alone. Hell, I live alone." Kyle jerked his thumb of his shoulder indicating his camper van. "In any case, I feel like my forty years in the wilderness are coming to an end."

"How can I help?"

"Good ol' Jon—always cutting to the chase. Well, the thing is, I need references. And…well, at least one of them needs to be from a holy man, like you. As I haven't had a fixed address for the last eight years or so, I don't exactly have a local pastor."

I said nothing for several moments and rubbed the beard stubble on my chin. When I spoke, I kept a poker face. "Well, I don't know. I really don't." I raised my hand plaintively. "I mean, put yourself in my shoes. Some clown shows up at my place on a Saturday afternoon—interrupting my sermon preparation, I might add—and then asks for a *reference*?" I leaned forward conspiratorially. "What's it worth to you?"

My efforts at winding Kyle up earned me a complete showering from his plastic flower. I threw my hands up in surrender. "Okay! Okay! I give up—you win!"

Kyle made a frown of disappointment. "Don't worry…" he said, as he looked down the 'barrel' of his flower, "I'm o't of ammo anyway." This was quickly followed by a huge grin and a double honk.

Kyle then began to fill me in on the enquiries he had made to various seminaries and the responses which had followed. His desire was to be ordained in the Presbyterian Church as he had felt most comfortable there during our younger years, and when on the road, or during the winter when the circus was encamped in Florida, Kyle most often worshipped in Presbyterian churches. Although it's not the sort of thing most men or women who feel the urgency of a call by God want to hear, I led Kyle through the various steps that would be required of someone who wanted to serve in the Presbyterian denomination—or at least our branch of it. It's also true for those same women and men that these steps appeared as more of a hindrance than a help toward their goal. Happily, as Kyle had served in the Army, he knew quite a bit about procedures, regulations, orders…and bullshit.

With those basics covered and understood, we turned our thoughts to matters more mundane: supper. I gave Karen a shout and asked if she would help her dad and "Uncle Clown" prepare a meal—so that the clown could get back to his circus performance. It was a repast abounding with joy and punctuated with laughter. How could dinner with a clown be otherwise?

Twenty-five

The nearer the Church the further from God.

—Bishop Lancelot Andrewes

"Think it's time we woke Mama?" asked Marie. "It's getting near suppertime."

Marie and I had nearly finished packing away the books and papers from Kyle's study. "Yef," I mumbled, as I tore a piece of packing tape with my teeth. I stood up straight and stretched my back muscles. "My back is telling me we should probably call it a day. I know I'm ready to eat. Any problem with going to Jorgie and Beth's again?"

"No. I kinda like the fact that you and Kyle used to meet there regularly. It somehow feels like he's with us when we eat there."

I rang Beth from Kyle's study and reserved a table. When Marie and I got to the living room, Ellen was already awake, so we switched off the lights, locked up and walked out to my car. As I opened the

290

doors for my passengers, Marie suddenly said, "I don't know why it's taken this long to dawn on me!"

"What's that?" asked both Ellen and I at the same time.

"Well, you know how I asked you abo't why you had never married again? It's just occurred to me that the answer's been staring me in the face all along!"

"And I'm guessing you're about to share it with us," I teased.

"You dedicated your life to the two Ks."

"I beg your pardon?" I hadn't followed Marie's train of thought.

"Karen and Kyle, silly. Being a father to Karen and a support to Kyle."

"I suppose you're right." I started the engine and we pulled away from Kyle's manse. "But I can't say it was a conscious decision...I just did what I felt I had to do at the time. I assure you it wasn't a deliberate case of 'forsaking all others' for Karen and Kyle; but between the pastoral demands of my congregations and then trying to be a good father and friend...well...there wasn't much time left over for romantic interests. As so often happens in life, one thing simply led to another."

"Well, I think you'd still make someone a wonderful husband," chimed in Ellen.

"That's kind of you to say...*but*...since Karen left home for college, I've been on my own. So after all these years of bachelorhood, I'm not sure how adaptable I'd be as a husband and housemate."

The road to Jorgie and Beth's wound its way through some deep hollows. Some were so shrouded by trees that, despite the bright afternoon sunshine, the blanket of leaves gave the illusion of night. As I followed those twisty, mountain roads, I was reminded of that "hell drive" I experienced with my mother and father so many years before, when Dad got the cruise control stuck. It hadn't happened very far from where we were currently driving, but it now seemed like another life, and someone else's at that. I suppose that, more than the simple passing of time, it is the deaths of those who had been integral to one's life that help to create the sense of separation from the events.

My father had passed away some ten years before Kyle's death; he had gotten out of bed one morning and, on his way to the kitchen for his morning coffee, dropped into his favorite arm chair and died. It was that fast, that simple, and—for those of us still living—that shocking. My mother never fully recovered from the shock. Although still living, my mother had developed senile dementia, which left the woman I had known and loved without personality or memory—as good as dead. Lost in such thoughts, I was surprised to see the sign for Jorgie and Beth's illuminated in the near distance. I eased the car into the gravel parking lot and apologized to my passengers for having gone so quiet during our journey.

"Oh, that's quite all right," said Ellen, as I opened the car door for her. "I think each of us needs some time to sort through our thoughts and feelings."

As we made our way into the café, Tammy Wynette was on the juke box plaintively telling everyone that "sometimes it's hard to be a woman."

Marie joined in the song, mimicking Wynette's nasally twang, as Ellen and I laughed. We were soon greeted by Jorge, who escorted us to our booth. As we sat, Marie touched my arm and said, "I can see why you and Kyle liked to meet here. It's got character, just like the two of you."

"Yeah, it was our own little oasis away from pastoral cares and concerns." I swiveled my head, as though surveying the café for the first time. "Just wish I could have steered Kyle away from parish ministry that evening we met here a year and a bit ago. He was better off counseling vets and working with PTSD sufferers. After all, our country never seems to run out of unnecessary, thankless wars to which it can send its young people. Ha! Kyle thought he'd focus his ministry on fellow Vietnam vets, but within a few years of finishing his seminary training, along came the Gulf War and then Afghanistan and then Iraq *again*." I shook my head in disbelief at the human waste. "But then, the church, in its wisdom, didn't want to keep paying for that sort of—how did they put it? 'Non-essential' ministry. For heavens' sake, I was a college chaplain to a bunch of middle-class students. What was 'essential' about that? Kyle's ministry was every bit as important, if not more so. Why couldn't his work have been considered something of a 'roving chaplaincy'? But…that's the institutional church for you. Even Mr. Jesus would seem suspect: itinerant preacher, no fixed address, no wife and kids, no degree. Who needs a guy like that?"

"Well…the *world* does," croaked Ellen—sounding both very old and very tired.

"I'm sorry," I interjected. "We're here to eat, not to listen to me rant and rave." I picked up the menu and began to look at it without actually reading it.

"I think…" offered Marie very quietly, "…that the way you just described Jesus fits pretty well with Kyle. Don't you? He lived alone in his camper van for years, both when he was a clo'n and when he worked at various VA hospitals. He, too, brought joy and healing to people."

"That he did…that he did. I…I just can't come to terms with how the church could snuff that out." The words which Rev. McLaurin had said to me some forty years before came to mind. *The real challenge for you in this life will be to retain your integrity in the tug-of-war between simply "selling out" to the powers of this world and being crushed beneath their wheel.* Had I done enough to warn Kyle of the church's darker side?

~ * ~

"Parish work? Are you shitting me?" Bits of food came shooting out of my over-full mouth. It was a noisy lunchtime at Jorgie & Beth's; the juke box was unusually loud, with Merle Haggard mournfully telling the world about how he was in prison for life—no chance of parole."

Kyle looked down at his food-spattered shirt both dolefully and comically—as only a trained clown can. He slowly lifted his eyes at me and then offered out his hands, palms upward, as though he were asking, "What…are…you…doing?"

"Sorry." I wiped a napkin across my lips with one hand while I picked the flecks of food off Kyle with the other. We both cracked up laughing.

In parental-sounding tones, Kyle looked earnestly at me and asked, "Jon? Have you finished spitting food? If so, then I would like to continue this conversation in a calm manner."

I pointed at my now closed mouth as I chewed my "Che's Burger" and "Fidel Fries." Kyle nodded his approval. He was having the "Las Tunas Salad."

"Yeah—parish work. I've even been looking at churches up in this neck of the woods. I figure you need someone to keep an eye on you." Kyle flashed his grin and winked.

"Well—hey—it'd be great to have you nearby, I have to admit. It's just that…and I don't mean to sound patronizing, but do you know what you're letting yourself in for?"

"Did you?"

"*Touché, mon ami.* But now that I have the experience, I just don't want you to be blindsided."

"Fair enough. So fill me in." Kyle sipped his cup of "Gitmo-Joe"—Jorge's own blend of coffee.

I whistled softly through my teeth. "Where to start? Being a minister in a church could be likened to being the screen in a movie theatre…except it's made out of toilet paper. People project onto you all of their hopes and fears about life and God. And when you don't live up to *their* expectations, they tear you up and flush you."

"Whoa. Flesh that out a bit for me."

"Okay, take something like Augustine's *Confessions.* The guy really examined his life in minute detail, right? His desires, passions, motives, etc. The average person in the pew has not only *never heard* of Augustine, but neither does he or she even begin to examine their Christian life in such a manner. Hell, for most of 'em, being a Christian is simply a matter of going to church on Sunday: sing a few hymns, say the Lord's Prayer, doze through the sermon, and that's it! All of the stuff that goes on inside each of us to make us uniquely who we are, for good or ill, *never gets examined.*" Kyle cocked his head and squinted at me.

"Look, say you have an elder in the church who comes to you one day and tells you he's banging his secretary at work. You listen politely and then try to get more information—you know: does he actually *love* his secretary? What's missing in his life or marriage? Is he planning to divorce his wife?, etc. But he clams up and says he has to go. You realize he just wanted to unburden his conscience but didn't want to have to think. A few weeks later, his wife turns up. After a few pleasantries, she confesses she's sleeping with a member of Calvary Baptist Church down the road. As with her husband, attempts at helping her to reflect about the ethical implications of this affair, as regards the Christian life, fail miserably. You never hear from either of them again, but you notice that, over time, they attend church less frequently and become brusque in their dealings with you. The subtext is: 'You know something damaging about me, Pastor, so I'm keeping my distance from you.' It's as if they think that, should they enter into casual conversation with you, you'll suddenly blurt out something like: 'Still getting it from your secretary?' Or: 'Is ol' Baptist Bob still parking his pork-wagon in your garage?!' Wink-wink."

Kyle shook his head as he chuckled. "Ah, Jon. You still have a way with words! Maybe I should jot some of these gems down so I can use 'em sometime?"

"You may well laugh, ol' buddy, but I'm telling you the real deal."

"I know, I know. I'm not dismissing what you've told me, but look at it this way: the Presbyterian Fund for Mission is cutting the grant funding for my work with war veterans, and I need a job. I either go back to clo'ning or I do what I feel called to do: be a minister for Mr. Jesus. What would you do?"

"I take your point, I do…it's just that…oh, I don't know…"

"Hey—look. I survived Vietnam, right? I'm sure I can deal with a bunch of un-self-aware parishioners. But what's eating you? There seems to be something else bothering you other than my being bushwhacked by a crazed congregation."

"Oh, I guess it's quite simple really. After three decades in ministry, I'm tiring of so-called Christians who don't want their lives disrupted by the gospel. You know, back when Reagan was president, if I ever criticized any of his policies, it was considered blasphemy! The old Ray-gun was untouchably holy! But if I had said to one of my congregations, 'You know, when you stop to think about it, the Holy Spirit knocked up that young Palestinian girl, Mary, and then dumped her on her fiancé, Joseph. So doesn't that make Jesus a bastard?' In that case they'd have said: 'Well, gol-lee—yew got sumpthin' thar, Pastor!'" Kyle smiled sympathetically as he listened to me.

"I came into ministry with the firm belief that—how does Paul put it?— we should 'not be conformed to this world, but that—'" and here Kyle joined in "'—we should be transformed by the renewal of our minds, so we can discern the will of God, and to know what is good, acceptable, and perfect.'"

Kyle raised both hands and said, "Let the congregation say 'Amen!'"

"Bastard."

"Hey, I'm not being sarcastic—I'm with you—and the Apostle Paul. Look at how I was after 'Nam. I was a mess and was just drifting wherever life might take me. You helped change that. And why have I spent the last nine or ten years working with stressed-o't and emotionally screwed-up vets? Because I believe our lives can be transformed. That's what Mr. Jesus is all abo't—and you helped me to see that."

"Yeah, well I guess the difference between your work with vets and the average congregation is that people who are hurting are more receptive to change. Sadly, the average congregation is simply happy to be confirmed in their prejudices, greed, materialism, lust, and more. Worship has begun to remind me of those old Jack-in-the-box toys we used to have as kids. People come in, the organ cranks up, out pops God-in-the-box; we all clap and push him back in until the next week. The church has spent too much time trying to tame God. We don't want the unexpected and sure as hell don't want to be challenged."

"Okay, I hear you. So let me join you in the good fight. What do you say?"

"I say: Welcome!" I extended my hand. Kyle took it and gave it a squeeze. We spent a few minutes in silence as we finished our meals.

"The good folk of Carson Memorial Presbyterian Church have invited me for an interview." Kyle drained the last of his coffee.

"Carson? Over near Mt. Airy?"

"That's the one."

I nodded thoughtfully. "Well, it's a moderate size church...and Mt. Airy continues to grow. It ought to keep you busy."

"They seem to have a heart for their community, as they run a fairly large pre-school that serves a lot of the families employed in the nearby textile mill. It runs from six a.m. until six p.m. to help the mill workers. Funnily enough, it's one of the mills where my father used to do some work—and one of the few still operating. There's a lot of blue-collar poverty in that area, so at least the church is helping in some small way. I'm given to understand that the pre-school operates damn near at a loss, so that the workers can afford it. I've also been assured by the pastor nominating committee that the pre-school has recently received a positive assessment by the state board. So that's one less worry."

I nodded again. "Kyle, it sounds like a place where you could do a lot of good."

"There's something else," added Kyle. "You've leveled with me regarding where you are with ministry these days, so let me do the same."

Wondering what might come next, I looked Kyle in the eye and said, "Shoot."

"While it's true that the Presbyterian Church is yanking the funding for my work with vets, and I wish that the ministry could continue—'cause God knows it's needed—at the same time, it's given me the nudge I've been wanting in order to move on."

"How do you mean?"

"As I've said, this country can't begin to do enough for the young men—and now women—it sends to war. And the church needs to be involved in this." Kyle was looking down at his empty coffee cup, twisting and turning it between his fingertips. "But in some ways, working with war survivors and PTSD cases day in and day out hasn't helped me to move on. In some ways, it's dragged me backwards..." Kyle paused and then looked up at me. "Sometimes I feel I'm just too close to it. Sure, it helps them to know I've been where they are...and I know I've done a good job; but for the last year or so I've felt their trauma becoming...I don't know...my own...and that's not good." Hesitantly, Kyle added, "In fact, the nightmares have started to recur. And *that* definitely ain't good. So you see, it's *time* to go. The Fund for

Mission has unwittingly done me a favor, although the vets I work with might not see it that way. But I've read the writing on the wall, and I know what the message says to me."

"Okay. 'Nuff said. I'll do whatever I can to help you make the move to parish life."

"As always, writing one of your A-1 reference letters will do just fine. And maybe meeting me here once a month to help keep me sane!"

"Keep us both sane, more likely! And you're on. I'll provide the reference and you can buy me lunch!"

~ * ~

"Going to Carson Memorial really did sound like a good move for Kyle," Marie murmured pensively, sipping her soft drink. "Especially the way you tell it now. I'll admit I was surprised when I heard he was planning on moving into parish ministry, but then he never told us as much as he told you. What abo't you, Mama?"

"Oh, I was pleased for Kyle. I thought that maybe he was finally settling do'n—and I suppose he was. It's just that…" Ellen's voice and thoughts trailed away. I suspected that from then on, whenever Kyle was mentioned, a lot would be left unsaid.

"'Nother Brother, when did you find o't that things were so wrong at Carson?" asked Marie. "Mama and I didn't really know there was trouble until the court case started."

"Sadly, it was only a couple of months after Kyle was installed as the pastor at Carson. I hadn't heard much, if anything, from Kyle after the installation. But I didn't see anything unusual about that. Getting started in any new parish is time consuming. But then, late one evening, I received a phone call from Kyle. He apologized for calling at that hour and said he really needed to see me soon, and could we meet for lunch the next day—here, at Jorgie & Beth's. I said fine and he hung up—short and sweet. I didn't give it too much thought."

"What happened first?" queried Marie.

"Well, when Kyle and I met that next day, he only had suspicions about the financial side of things at Carson—and not without reason. He had brought along the ledgers to show me his concerns."

Twenty-five

To what extremes will you not drive the hearts of men, accurst hunger for gold!

—Virgil, *Aeneid*

"Hey, buddy. Looks like you're getting ready for an IRS audit." Kyle had arrived at the café ahead of me and laid out several large ledgers on the table.

"Hey, Jon, thanks for coming. And, yeah, the IRS might be involved in this before it's all over…maybe even the police."

"Police? Sounds serious."

"I'm hoping there's a rational explanation…or just something I'm missing, as I'm no accountant." And then, sotto voce, "But I'm no fool either."

We ordered food, and then Kyle gave me a summary of his concerns. "Abo't a month after I started at the church, I decided it was time to get some idea of the finances. You see, I've learned something from you about churches as charities. So one day, when I saw Ted

Clayton hanging about the office of the pre-school manager, I thought I'd approach him about the accounts. Ted was the elder who was head of the pastoral nominating committee, remember? You met him."

"Yeah, I remember. Kind of a gruff character, right?"

"Yeah, he's the one. Well, I invited Ted into the study and said it was probably time I got a feel for the overall financial picture of the church and pre-school. Ted kinda straightened up and pointed toward the office of Bernice Byers, the pre-school manager, and told me to 'leave the pre-school alone. I'll handle that. Your job is the church.' I told Ted that as pastor, I was also Chairman of the Trustees, so I both wanted and needed to know abo't all the church's business and finances. Although it was a civil exchange, Ted was visibly disturbed by my request. But I didn't think too much abo't it at the time. I kinda reckoned he meant what he said in the best light and just wanted me to get on with the pastoral work. But then he added something sorta strange."

"How so?"

Kyle bit his lower lip and scratched his head as he re-ran the encounter in his mind's eye. "Well, he said to me, 'We might not be able to give you a pay raise, but we're gonna take care of you.' I tried to assure him that the salary they offered me was fine, but the guy kept swingin' after the bell, saying, 'we're going to take care of you.' It just got me to wondering why he kept making the point. I mean, was he going to offer me some kind of backhander or bribe?"

"Yeah, I see what you mean. So how'd you finally get the books?"

"Well, I let it ride for a few weeks. I got on with visiting the members, planning services, and the like. I started to notice that Bernice became a little edgy whenever I popped into her office in the morning just to say 'hello' and ask how things were going. Her reaction was like the guy in the Monty Python sketch—if you recall: 'No one expects a Spanish Inquisition!' Anyway, to cut a long story short, I waited until the second monthly meeting with the elders, and let it drop that I had yet to see the financial records. Except for Ted and one other elder, Shirley Huntley, the rest seemed to take in their stride and were even glad that I wanted to check over the books; so I suggested they be brought to me first thing the next Monday morning. And, well, *here they are.*"

Kyle opened two of the ledgers and turned them to face me. He had also prepared a brief summary of his findings which he handed me. "Now look at this. There are two sets of accounts—one for the church and another for the pre-school. I've found this puzzling, as the pre-school is church-owned and operated. But here's where it starts to get fuzzy. If you look here in the church ledger, it would seem that the church has actually been *underwriting* the operation of the pre-school." Kyle pointed toward one or two lines where transfers had been made to the pre-school. "And if you look at my summary sheet, you will see that the pre-school is only posting income of just over a hundred thousand dollars per annum. Are you with me?"

I nodded and asked Kyle to continue.

"Okay, so now we do our sums. Considering the pre-school has a maximum, licensed enrolment of forty-two children, and all are registered full-time at seventy-five dollars per week, the pre-school should have an income in excess of a hundred sixty thousand per annum. But, somehow, the pre-school is *losing* around sixty thousand a year, and the church seems to be making up the loss!" Kyle sat back in his chair and ran both hands through his hair. "Am I missing something, or am I sitting on a problem?"

Equally puzzled as my best friend, I looked more closely at the pre-school accounts. Something caught my eye. "Shit!" I whispered under my breath.

Kyle leaned forward onto the table and asked, "What is it?"

"Oh, Kyle. You've got another problem, buddy." I swiveled the ledger around for Kyle to see. "Look here." As Kyle studied the entry, I pulled out my cell phone to use its calculator. One quick calculation and my suspicion was confirmed. I pointed at the ledger entry. "See this amount of income for the first week of February? Well, forty-two children times seventy-five dollars equals three thousand one hundred and fifty, right? But if you notice, this entry shows three thousand eight hundred and twenty-five, which would mean…" I entered the figures into the calculator, "...that your pre-school had fifty-one children in attendance that week—well over the legal maximum."

"Wow...I missed that. I was too busy totaling up the overall income..." Kyle's brow was as furrowed as I had seen it since our first encounter after Vietnam. He was nervously rubbing his chin and biting his lower lip. At that moment our lunch arrived. Kyle was still distracted, so I smiled and thanked Beth as I moved the ledgers aside for our meals.

"Okay, it's clear there's a problem," I said as I shoved a chunky Fidel Fry into my mouth. "But...it *might* just be *bad bookkeeping*..."

"Yeah, *very bad*," Kyle added dejectedly.

"But just to be safe, I think you ought to go have a word with Milton Peebles. It might not hurt to have the General Presbyter aware of the situation, just in case there's deliberate wrongdoing." I sipped some water as I considered who else might need to be informed. "And why don't you request that the chairman of the Committee on Ministry be there? Neil Bullins. If you want, I'll go with you. Hell, I owe you that much. After all, I helped get you into Carson."

Kyle slowly chewed a mouthful of his burger and nodded at my suggestion. "Yeah, you're probably right. No use trying to sort this o't by myself. I don't yet know whom to trust at the church. I'll set something up as soon as I can and let you know."

"Great. Whatever date you can get, I'll make it a priority." We finished our meal with less chatter than would have been usual as both of us, no doubt, considered the various implications of the dodgy accounts.

~ * ~

Only two days after I had met with Kyle over lunch, I received a telephone call at my church office from an obviously harried Kyle. In clipped tones he asked, "Hey, Jon—you got a fax machine on your phone?"

"Uh, yeah. Why?"

"Just make sure you have paper in it. You'll see why. Ring me back when you've read it."

"Okay, sure—" but Kyle had hung up.

A minute later, the fax was coming through. Impatiently, I watched two pages print out. I glanced at the heading and the opening sentences and then slumped into my chair. "I don't believe it!" What I held in my hand was a joint letter from the North Carolina State Child Abuse/Neglect Consultant, the Licensing Officer, and the officer for Child Advocacy. The two sheets of paper seemed to weigh a ton. It seemed the pre-school at Carson Memorial had been under threat of closure or a heavy fine—or both—for at least a year. The further I read, the more my spirits sank. Fully half of the two single-spaced pages contained breaches in the state's standards for pre-schools. Most worrying was the fact that there were reports of child neglect and abuse—including sexual touching—and an ongoing lawsuit against the church from parents whose child had sustained a broken arm in the playground! Could this be the same pre-school which, as had been reported to Kyle, had only recently been given a positive assessment by the state board? My mind was in a whirl. I could barely take in the other charges, such as having under-aged children in their care, exceeding the licensed maximum number of children, the wrong staff-to-children ratios, etc. My only thought was how Kyle must be feeling. The bottom line was, as pastor of the Carson Memorial Church, Kyle was ultimately responsible for the goings-on there, and the three signatories to the letter wanted to meet with Kyle as soon as possible. I dropped the letter on my desk. How had all of this been covered up until Kyle was installed as the new minister there? How many people must have known about it? What the hell was going on?

I picked up the telephone receiver and dialled Kyle's number.

Kyle's voice was taut. "You've read it?"

Without intending to do so, I let loose a heavy sigh before speaking. "Yeah…yeah, I've read it."

"*Children*, Jon. This place has *abused children*."

"I know, buddy, I know. What're you going to do?"

"Well, for one, I've already called both the abuse and neglect consultant as well as the licensing officer. They've agreed to meet with me here, in just over a week's time on Tuesday morning. From what they told me on the phone, there's been all kinds of shit reported abo't this place for well over a year. Parents have yanked their kids o't and given damning reports. Seems the only reason it's been kept running is that it's the cheapest day care in the area and serves a lot of needy families. Thus, the state had given them some time to get their act together. Anyway, these two officers want the pre-school manager, Bernice Byers, and as many of the elders as possible, at the meeting. Oh—and you'll love this. They want to examine the pre-school's accounts as well. You know those discrepancies I showed you at lunch the other day? I've got a sinking feeling they're more than just bad bookkeeping."

I thought the same thing but chose not to voice it. Kyle had enough on his plate. "They know you've been at the church barely two months, don't they?" I asked. "You can't be held responsible for what happened *before* you arrived at Carson!"

"Yeah. Yeah, they know. I think it's one of the reasons they shared so much with me…that and the fact that I called them so quickly." Kyle's voice became a mumble, "So listen…um…think you could join me at the meeting? I could sure use some support."

"I'll be there. What time?"

"Ten o'clock." And then, as though he hadn't heard or believed me, "You'll be there—right?"

"Absolutely. I said I would, and I will. Don't worry. And, Kyle?"

"Yep?"

"It might be a good idea *not* to tell Bernice about the meeting. I know you'll have to contact your elders, but try to keep it low key for now, okay?"

"Yeah, will do. Anything else?" All the lustre was gone from Kyle's voice.

"Yeah, there is: call me any time, day or night. Got it?"

"Got it."

~ * ~

My phone was ringing before I had finished breakfast the next morning. Still swallowing a mouthful of toast, I picked up the receiver. "Yef?"

"How fast can you get to Carson?" It was Kyle.

"Forty minutes, maybe?"

"Do it. There's a shit storm going do'n." The pre-emptory click at Kyle's end underscored the urgency in his voice. I wolfed down the last of my toast and finished my mug of tea. Then I rang my part-time secretary to tell her that I would be unavoidably detained today. As I was already dressed, I made double-time to my car.

When I pulled up in front of Carson Memorial, Kyle was having a heated argument with Bernice Byers. Kyle held a water hose in his right hand and there was a smoldering pile of papers on the gravel parking area. Bernice, a corpulent woman, was purple in the face and spewing verbal invective while pointing a chubby finger at Kyle. In her other hand, she held what looked like files. As I got out of my car, she looked nervously at me, but never stopped her oral assault. "You don't have no right to stop me! These're my files and I can do what I want with 'em!" A few parents who were dropping off their children, seemed both bemused and confused at the standoff between the minister and the pre-school manager.

"Who called you and told you abo't the meeting with the state licensing board?" demanded Kyle. "I know good and well that's why you're destroying these files!"

"Warn't nobody called me!" huffed Bernice.

Kyle nodded at me as I approached the two of them and then turned back to the pre-school manager. "Bernice," Kyle's voice and face both revealed his exasperation, "why are you burning pre-school files in the parking lot?!" I could see Kyle was clenching his teeth and trying to keep his anger in check.

"I done tole you," began Bernice, at which point an enraged Kyle pointed the nozzle of the hose at Bernice's face and let loose a torrent of water. Like a beached baby whale, Bernice gasped and spluttered in total shock. There were peals of laughter from a few of the children in the playground. Their supervisors stood with mouths agape.

"Get o'tta my sight!" growled Kyle. "You're suspended until further notice. And don't you dare touch anything else in the pre-school office!" Pointing toward the files in Bernice's left hand, Kyle barked, "You can leave those on the doorstep."

Bernice opened her mouth as her befuddled brain searched for words, but one look at Kyle told her silence was her best recourse. She dutifully laid the files on the step and waddled through the door, with Kyle on her heels. Over his shoulder, Kyle called to me, "Jon, keep an eye on that pile of papers for me."

"Sure thing." In the meanwhile, I walked over to the smoldering pile of files, which appeared to be attendance records and ledgers, and stamped out the few glowing embers that remained. A moment later, a much-chastened Bernice puffed her way down the church steps and plopped herself into the seat of her souped-up Camaro. With much spinning of wheels and spewing of gravel, she sped away.

Kyle popped his head out of the church door and asked me to join him in the pre-school office. When I joined him, Kyle was standing in the middle of the room with his hands on his hips, surveying the mess. File drawers were flung open and papers had been dropped on the floor. Shaking his head, Kyle said more to himself than to me, "That woman was in one hell of a hurry."

"You think Clayton warned her about the impending meeting with the state officers?"

"Probably," Kyle muttered, "or Shirley Huntley." Kyle turned to look at me, and I was taken aback by his tired, drawn face. As though reading my mind, Kyle said, "I couldn't sleep last night. I kept thinking abo't all of this." His hand languidly gestured around the room. "Something told me that I'd better get here early today. I wanted to secure the pre-school records in my office. Man, am I glad I got here when I did! And only just in time, from the looks of it. I don't think Bernice was able to destroy very much."

"You're lucky she didn't pour gasoline on the records," I added. Kyle raised his eyes in a gesture of thanksgiving and breathed a dramatic sigh of relief.

Kyle clapped me on the shoulder and said, "Glad you're here, buddy! I can sure use some help moving all of this stuff into my office."

"Not your office, Kyle. It's all going to my house." Kyle looked at me questioningly. "Clayton has keys for the whole building, right?"

Kyle nodded. "Well, isn't it likely he told Bernice to get rid of the records? And if he finds out you stopped her—and I'll wager she'll be on the phone to him as soon as she gets home—what would stop him from raiding your office tonight? But he and Shirley would never think of the records being at my house."

Kyle chewed his lower lip as he listened and thought. "Yeah—it makes sense. I'll go o't to the van and grab the boxes I picked up at the grocery this morning. Why don't I start on the paperwork o'tside and leave you to load the files in the office?"

Before we could set to work, two curious pre-school staff wanted to know what was going on and what had happened outside with Bernice. Kyle briefly explained that Bernice was suspended and that he could not discuss the matter further. He asked them to carry on with their jobs, and he would speak to them later in the week. It was clear they wanted to know more, but they could see that Kyle was resolute, so they left.

An hour-and-a-half later, Kyle and I unloaded the pasteboard boxes full of pre-school records at my house. I chose Karen's old room for our "forensic lab," as it was unlikely to be needed anytime soon. Kyle thought we ought to make a cursory examination before deciding what to do and whom to involve. I made coffee for Kyle and tea for me, and we set to work. I had found the pre-school checkbook lying on Bernice's desk, so I began my investigation there. When I opened it, I immediately noticed that the latest check had been written that very morning.

"Hey, Kyle—get this: Bernice paid herself *three weeks in advance*! She obviously knew her days were numbered."

"The fat cow!" he growled. "And it gets worse. Here are some of the things Bernice tried to burn first—bank deposit slips." Kyle studied them for a few minutes and then handed me the singed, damp papers. "Notice anything odd abo't them?"

"Apart from the fact they're toasted?" I joked.

"Wise ass!" Kyle made an annoyed grunt and handed me another handful. "Apart from *that*, what do they have in common?"

"I don't know, buddy—they show the number and amount of the checks deposited each week."

"Exactly—the *checks* deposited. I know for a fact that abo't a third of the pre-school's parents pay in cash. Many of 'em haven't got bank accounts. These deposit records only show *checks*, not *cash*. That might explain where sixty grand a year has been going."

I whistled softly. "Man! If that's the case, this place has been hemorrhaging money!"

Kyle suddenly sat up and said, "Let's take a drive! We can get some lunch while we're o't."

I was caught off guard by the abrupt change of plans. "Um…okay…uh, sure. *Where exactly are we going?*"

"I want to drive by Bernice's place—and also Ted's and Shirley's. Let's take your car. They'd know my van."

Our fresh discoveries had left me feeling a little paranoid, so I closed the curtains in Karen's former room and checked that the back door was locked and bolted. As Kyle looked at me evenly, I shrugged and said, "Better to make sure. There are at least three people who don't want us to find out what's been going on at Carson." Kyle sucked his teeth and nodded, obviously lost in thought.

As we got into my car, Kyle simply said, "Just head toward Mt. Airy, and I'll tell you where to turn off." And so we retraced our earlier journey across Stokes County. Just north of Pilot Mountain, Kyle indicated a turn onto a gravel road. "Bernice lives up along here somewhere. We'll look for her Camaro." Dotted along the road were clear-cut areas where we saw trailers and the occasional double-wide. After about a quarter-mile, Kyle pointed to our right. "There!" He slipped down in the seat and said, "Just keep going slowly. Let's use the ol' revenuers' trick and see what Bernice and her hubby have parked around the place."

As I eased the car past Bernice's house, I heard Kyle blurt, "Ha! Check o't that double-o'tboard motor boat! And that Silverado pick-up!"

"With extended cab," I added, using my radio announcer's voice. I then pointed toward an aluminum out-building. "There are a couple of four-wheelers parked by that shed."

"Yeah, and at least two other cars sitting around the back." Kyle was smiling to himself. "That'll do for now, buddy. Let's turn aro'nd just up here," Kyle waved toward a driveway about fifty yards ahead, "and cruise by Mr. Clayton's place next."

As we drove the back roads of Surry County, Kyle started piecing evidence together out loud. "Bernice's husband works at the mill. He's a line operator, and I gather that neither of 'em has more than a high school education. I know what Bernice earns—and it sho' ain't no 'manager's' salary. So all of those high-priced toys that we just saw back there weren't paid for from their salaries. That's for sure."

"So just how did Bernice come to be 'manager' of the pre-school?" I asked.

"Yeah! I've wondered that, too. From my conversations with the state licensing and neglect officers, I've gathered Bernice's reports to them border on functional illiteracy. So somebody in the church must have put her in charge. We can be pretty sure the trail will lead to the fellow whose ho'se is just up the road a way."

As we approached Ted Clayton's place, Kyle slapped his knee and shouted, "The goddamn answer's been staring me in the face—in the church parking lot every day!"

"How so?"

"Just look what's parked outside Ted's house! He drives a Cadillac, and his wife drives that Lincoln Continental. Not bad for a guy who's been retired at least five years from a fitter's job at the mill. And his wife's never worked outside the family home! And then there's Shirley, with her Lexus LS! The missing money has been staring me in the face!" Kyle was shaking his head in exasperation and gently beating his forehand with the heels of his hands. "Of course! Of course! Of course!"

"And don't forget that Bernice's Camaro is a classic—" I began, when Kyle interrupted.

"Jon, forget going to Shirley's! Let's go to Jorgie & Beth's. I'm famished!"

"Yeah, you do seem to be running on nervous energy. When did you last eat?"

"Yesterday…sometime," Kyle mumbled into the hand his chin was resting on as he stared out the car window.

Wham! A sudden, sharp noise made me jerk the steering wheel such that I nearly swerved into the oncoming lane from the shock. Kyle had slammed his hand onto the dash board. "What the hell?!" I shouted. "You want to kill us both?!"

"Sorry, buddy! I didn't mean to scare you." Kyle flashed what he could muster of a smile. He then let out a deep breath and lifted his hand, palm open, toward whatever he could see in his mind's eye. "It's just that…well, God! If our suspicions turn o't to be true, these so-called Christians are driving aro'nd in their nice cars—purchased with embezzled money—and they don't seem to give a shit that this purloined money has come from the coffers of a pre-school that abuses the very children they're supposed to be looking after!" Kyle flopped back in his seat. "Man! I'd love to have a Huey gunship right now! I'd be Bernice, Ted and Shirley's worst nightmare! *Death from above!*" Kyle's smile was more of a grimace.

"Yes," I said in a patronizing voice, meant to de-fuse Kyle's anger, "that would be just the sort of Christian chastisement they would need: being blown away in gentleness and love!"

"Bastard!" Kyle laughed despite himself and then added, "Well, fuck 'em if they can't take a joke!" Kyle drummed his fingers on the dashboard. Turning to me, he asked, "You know I wouldn't actually do them any harm, don't you?"

"I think I know that, Kyle."

"Not that I wouldn't mind scaring the shit out of 'em!" I was glad to see Kyle's grin return in its full majesty.

~ * ~

Jorgie & Beth's was situated in southernmost Virginia, only a few miles from the North Carolina state line. However, the very fact that it was *across* the state line brought a certain sense of freedom from the fishbowl existence of ministry, pastoral concerns, and the headaches of institutional church life. The café was its own little counter-cultural oasis. And the old-fashioned, high-backed booths created a greater sense of confidential space. For beleaguered clergymen, it was a real sanctuary.

On this day of difficulties for my old friend, the sound of the Velvet Voice—Jim Reeves—came as a soothing welcome, even though he sang about the sorrows of love. A few people at the bar were doing their best to join in the song—happily, without managing to butcher it. Jorge gave me a wave from behind the bar and pointed to a booth at the back. I wondered whether our need for privacy was that painfully obvious. Once seated, Kyle ignored the menu and started to flip through the juke box selections. I noticed, as he pressed in his quarter, that he had settled for Hank Williams' "I'm So Lonesome I Could Cry." Inwardly, I hoped that it was not a reflection of Kyle's state of mind.

However, my concerns were soon put to rest. After we had ordered our meal, Kyle started talking about any- and everything except the storm brewing over the Carson pre-school. Following Kyle's lead, we chatted and laughed about incidents from our childhood, high school days, and more. Kyle shared funny events from his flight training and even Vietnam. At points, we laughed so hard tears streamed from our eyes. "Just look at us," quipped Kyle, "a couple of damn fool teenagers!"

"Ah yes, your father's favorite phrase." I shook my head, thinking back to the intensity Ed Weston put into those words. "Your father was a trip," I added.

Sipping and staring into his soft drink, Kyle nodded. "That he was…that he was."

"He died quite young, didn't he? I forget; when was it?"

Kyle set his drink down and began nibbling at the salad garnish on his plate. Without looking up, he responded, "Oh, not long after I came back from 'Nam, when you were up in Canada. He was diagnosed with lung cancer and died soon after. He had barely started chemotherapy." Kyle shook his head at some mental image. "You know, whenever I try to visualize him, he's always got a damn cigarette hanging o't of the corner of his mo'th. That clo'd of smoke he constantly had aro'nd him is an apt metaphor for his constant, smoldering anger. But anger *at what*? I could never figure that o't when he was alive, so now I'll never know." Suddenly Kyle sat bolt upright and looked up. "You know something else? I don't think I ever heard that man say he loved me. I wonder if he ever said it to Mom or Marie?" Kyle pointed his fork at me. "That reconciliation you had with your father, Jon, when you came down from Canada to see me?"

"Yeah?"

"That, my friend, is something to be treasured." Kyle stabbed a slice of cucumber to make his point.

"Don't I know it," I responded. "It gave us a relationship we'd never had before. Ironically, it made losing him a lot easier—no unresolved issues."

"Man, I envy that," said Kyle.

"You know, I haven't thought about this for some time, but the very first hospital call I made as a pastor was to see an eighty-nine-year-old woman who was dying. When I arrived at her room, she had already slipped into a coma, and there was this fifty-something woman, who turned out to be the dying woman's daughter, flopped across her mother's bed, crying uncontrollably. As best I could make out from the daughter—in between fits of wailing and sobbing—she had had a falling out with her mother many years before and had refused ever to speak with her mother again. She had made that fatal error of pride, assuming there would be plenty of time for her mother to come crawling back to her, begging her forgiveness. Of course, that time never came. Truth to tell, it was tragicomic, because the old woman looked like she was in the most peaceful sleep, without a care in the world. Her lips were flapping with each exhalation—" I imitated the sound, "while her daughter blubbered and wailed. What a contrast! Whether people in comas are actually able to hear and understand what's going on around them, I don't know. All I know is that this lady seemed totally oblivious to her daughter's pleadings for forgiveness. And the woman died that night." I shook my head at the mental images of that scene. "As for the funeral—whoa—it was emotional, to say the least."

"It is pathetic, isn't it? It reminds me of something I heard one of our Army chaplains say: 'Most people live as though their lives are determined and everyone else has free will.' The longer I live, the more I see that to be the case. It was certainly my father's problem. Nothing in life ever seemed good enough or right enough for him—including me. For my old man, everything in life seemed tinged with a sense of tragedy and failure."

"Didn't you say your father used to troubleshoot electrical systems for Farrington Mills?"

Kyle sipped his iced tea and nodded.

"Well, maybe he just got used to finding faults and problems as a way of making a living and it carried over into family life. What do you think?"

"I'm not sure. Was it nature or nurture? It just seemed to be in his blood. But then, it's also the case that he grew up having his paternal grandparents living in the family home. They had lived through Reconstruction and freely shared their memories of what a beaten-down place the South was. Dad shared some of their stories when I was young. And they also related their parents' experiences of the War Between the States. Maybe it's all that and more which gives us Southerners a tragic sense of life. In school, our history books taught us that America had never lost a war. Bullshit! Tell that to the eleven states who engaged in the Lost Cause..." Kyle's voice lowered in volume, "...and tell it to the Vietnam vets! I wonder how future historians will treat that fiasco?"

Kyle tapped the table with his knife, looking into the middle distance. "And then I think that maybe this Southern stuff is itself so much bullshit—at least as far as I am concerned—and that it's really just Vietnam that has made me see life as so full of tragedy. It seems to be wherever I look. I mean, what abo't the shit that's been going on at Carson! For the church to be engaged in that kind of wrongdoing—*isn't that tragic*? And then again...I think: Am I just being my father's son, smelling the shit and not the roses? I don't know." For reasons not readily apparent to me, Kyle's mood was dropping fast. I decided to try the direct approach.

"Yes, you are your father's son, but you are *not* your father. Listen, Kyle, I knew your dad well enough to know you two are very different people. Whatever issues Ed Weston had, they're not yours. For one thing, you are *not* an angry man. That just isn't in your blood.

And how you might or might not be like your father in sharing a tragic sense of life has nothing to do with the reality of the mess at Carson. That is a *real tragedy*—particularly for the children and their families—but it's also sinful and illegal and despicable! No matter how you might *perceive* or *feel about them*, those things at Carson are *real*. And, hell, they're *not about you*, Kyle. They are only your responsibility because they are happening on your watch. But that's as far as it goes. You didn't create those problems."

Having been reminiscing, laughing, and joking only a few minutes before, Kyle seemed to be struggling deep within himself. "You're probably right, Jon. But, you know, I sometimes feel, when I look at a crucifix, that Jesus is winking at me from the cross, as if to say: *'Didn't I tell you it'd be this way?'"*

"Yeah, I know. Jesus got attacked by the religious establishment *and* the political overlords. Seminary training seems to overlook the fact that, today, the church itself is often part of the very evil we are meant to combat—Carson Memorial being a case in point. The automatic assumption that the church is the 'good guys' gets in the way of preparing ministers for the real challenges of trying to live a faithful life." I was going to say more, but Kyle broke in—raising his hand to make a point.

"You know something, Jon? A lot of people worry about death; they fear death. But *dying* is *easy*—I've seen enough death to know. It's *living* that's hard, and this business of taking up our cross for Mr. Jesus…well, that's harder still." Kyle let out a deep breath and his hand fell limp on the table. "Jon, Jon," Kyle looked at me with devilment in his eyes, "how have you managed all these years in parish ministry? I'm surprised it hasn't driven you to drink or led you to an early grave, like my father."

Trying to inject some humor back into our conversation, I retorted, "It probably has something to do with the fact that I'm not a hypertensive smoker who is angry with the world. Oh—I suppose *not having cancer* helps. Where are you going with this? You do remember I'm on your side, don't you? Anyway, whatever made your father so angry in this life no longer matters now, does it? His trials and tribulations are over."

"Yeah, but doesn't that depend upon whether he's in heaven or hell?" I hadn't seen Kyle in this kind of argumentative state for many years. My friend looked me in the eye. "Rev. Jon, what do you think hell is?"

"You're shitting me, right?"

Still looking me in the eye, my friend shook his head. With Kyle in this mood, I didn't know whether to make a serious reply or not. It was hard to read his true emotional state. I opted for a middle line. "Kyle, we've both seen enough of hell on this earth to know what it is."

Kyle was quick with his rejoinder. "I reckon hell is the realization, the eternal *awareness* that we're fuck-ups, who refused every chance at redemption."

"Yeah, that works," I replied. "What about heaven?"

"Heaven? Hmmm, let me think abo't that." Kyle screwed up his brow and rubbed his chin in a mock-thinking pose. "I figure we all project onto heaven what we long for most on this earth, just like we project onto God either the best or the worst of our earthly parents."

I reached across the table and squeezed Kyle's shoulder. "Kyle, it's me you're talking to here—*Jon*. You don't have to do this shit."

I thought I saw a glint of moisture in the corners of Kyle's eyes before he spoke again. "Heaven, eh? Okay, I'll give it a shot." Kyle's voice gave the faintest suggestion of a quiver. "I so much want to think that, in heaven, all of the things that plague me most on this earth won't just be forgotten—*they won't even matter*. Think of that!" As his darkness and anger dissipated, Kyle warmed to his subject and his eyes began to shine. Gesticulating with his fork like an artist with a brush, he continued. "Streets paved with gold don't hold any appeal for me. Who needs gold when he's dead? But I do like to think that whatever is left of us might indeed be refined like gold...with all of the dross burned away. I'd like to think that what actually remains of us will be the love we had for other people and the love that others had for us—and that we could *bathe in that love for eternity*." Kyle sat back, closed his eyes, and smiled at the image he had just created. "That's what I would like: to dip myself in that love, just like getting into a nice, hot bath when your muscles ache after a good worko't. You know the feeling: when you're just getting into the water and it's almost too hot—not scalding—but *hot*—just hot enough to make you go 'Ahhh'…and you can feel the tension leaving your body. And you think to yourself, 'I could stay here forever.' That's what I want."

"I could sign up for that," I heard myself say. I looked deeply at my friend. I hadn't seen or heard Kyle in full flow like this for some time, and it was as meaningful as any Eucharist.

~ * ~

On our way home from Jorgie & Beth's, Kyle and I agreed we needed to have an emergency meeting with Milton Peebles and Neil Bullins as soon as possible. Kyle would need the backing of the church's hierarchy in the row that was sure to develop at Carson. We rang the Presbytery office when we got back to my manse. I listened as Kyle briefly laid out his concerns regarding the pre-school for the General Presbyter; he also explained I was helping him out a bit.

Afterwards, Kyle seemed reassured. He said Peebles made the right noises and seemed to be genuinely supportive. Peebles had told Kyle he'd arrange to have Bullins meet with the two of them when the office closed at five o'clock the next day.

"Shall I drive, so you can focus on the meeting and what you need to tell them?" I asked.

"You'll probably need to," replied Kyle, "as I'll more than likely spend most of the night sifting through the records in Karen's room."

"Well, you know where the coffee is—and I'm sure I can rustle up some grub for us. But I hope you don't mind if I get back to some of my pastoral work?"

"Nah—I'm just glad for what you've done so far. It's great to have your support." Kyle smiled and winked at me. "I'll owe you one."

"I'll try to remember to collect."

As Kyle walked down the hallway, he said over his shoulder, "Into the valley of debt rode the Air Cav!"

Twenty-six

The Church is like Noah's Ark; if it weren't for the storm outside, you couldn't stand the stench inside!

—Variously attributed

"This meetin's only with Kyle, Jon. Didn't he tell yew that? I'm sor-ree if he didn't." Milton Peebles smiled unctuously at Kyle and me while blocking the partially opened door to his office with his considerable paunch. I was dumbstruck at this turn of events. "Why don't yew come on in, Kyle?" Peebles opened the door enough for Kyle to squeeze by him sideways and motioned toward Neil Bullins, who was seated across the room. Neil nodded an acknowledgement at Kyle, but ignored me.

Kyle hesitated at the door, looking from me to Peebles. "But…uh…Jon has been helping me sort o't this problem," replied a befuddled Kyle. "I-I thought I mentioned this to you on the phone yester—" but Kyle was cut off by Peebles, who raised his hand magisterially for silence.

"Jon can wait for yew out he-uh, Kyle—cain't yew, Jon? After all, it's not his church's pre-school that has the problem, now is it? These thangs are sens'tive—and confidential." Meanwhile, Peebles extended his flabby arm, which enveloped Kyle's shoulders and pulled him into the office. It was like watching the corpulent tentacle of some vile creature pull my friend into its lair. Before the door closed tight, Milton's plump visage appeared once more in the doorway. "Oh, and Jon? Yew'll be more comf'table in the reception *a*-rea." He pointed his pudgy index finger down the corridor. "There's some bottles of pop in the little kitchenette. Make yo'sef comf'table, okay?"

Reluctantly, I turned to go. "Yeah, okay." I then stopped and turned. "But if you need me…"

"Ye-e-s, ye-e-s," Peebles intoned with his nasally diphthongs. "We'll know jest right where yew are, Jon." I always hated when people over-used my name—a habit Peebles made into an art. He gave me a little wave of his hand that looked more as if he were shooing away a fly.

"Shit," I mumbled under my breath as I walked back to the reception area of the Presbytery office. I spent the next hour thumbing through the denominational magazine and sipping cans of soft drinks.

When I finally heard Peebles' office door open, I stood, half in expectation that they were going to call me in. I heard some indistinct voices coming from the end of the corridor and then saw a pale apparition approaching me, for that is the only way I could describe Kyle.

"Let's go," was all he said.

Flummoxed, I stammered for words. "Well…okay…b-but…what happened?"

Kyle, walking woodenly, was already going out the door. "I'll tell you in the car."

I remained fixed to where I stood for a brief moment, baffled at what had occurred during the last hour, and then dashed out to open the car. Kyle was standing by the door, staring off into space. "Glad you could join me today," he said, poker-faced.

As we pulled out of the parking lot, I glanced over at Kyle, who looked catatonic. "You okay, buddy?"

"I'm under-dressed," replied Kyle, with a voice flat as a pancake.

"Come again?"

"Said I was under-dressed...*I should have worn a wire.*" Kyle looked out the side window and exclaimed: "Those sons-of-bitches!"

"Who? Bullins and Peebles?"

"Who else?"

"Well, I could name a few..."

"Either they didn't believe me or they're in it up to their friggin' eyeballs!" Kyle made a fist of his right hand and slammed it into his damaged left. I saw him wince.

"Okay, well...start filling me in."

"Well, they made some weak-assed apology abo't not letting you come in and then 'wham!' They started hitting me with one question after another—except it was bad-cop and *bad-cop. Whap!* What did I think I was doing starting my first parish job by investigating the church and pre-school accounts? *Whack!* Did somebody put me up to it? *Slam!* Didn't I know Ted Clayton and Shirley Huntley were fine, upstanding elders and great supporters of Carson Memorial Church *and* the Presbytery? And on it went. They wanted to know what evidence I had of embezzlement or wrong-doing. They told me I had acted hastily in suspending Bernice Byers—but get this: I *never told them* I had suspended Bernice. It felt like I was in some kind of Inquisition—*they* asked the questions and *I* gave the answers. And everything—and I do mean *everything*—I had to say abo't the situation was cast into do'bt." Mimicking Peebles, Kyle drawled, "Yew ain't no lawyuh, son. Yew ain't no detective or accountant. There might be a reas'nable ex-pla-nation for all thee-yus. An' we only have yore word for it."

"Sounds like they've spoken to Ted or Shirley—if not both," I offered.

"Yeah, but the question is: who called whom? Not that it matters now."

"Kyle, what did you mean when you said you should have worn a wire? What else happened?"

"Ah! Now we come to the clincher! Just before I left, Peebles takes me by the arm and asks, 'Yew haven't reported any of this to the sheriff's department, have yew?' When I told him I hadn't, Peebles looked visibly relieved and gave just the faintest nod to Bullins. Then he became all avuncular with me and said, 'Now don't yew worry about a thang, Kyle. We're gonna take care of everythang, y'unnerstand?' When I tried to get him to explain what he meant as regards 'taking care of everything,' he simply ushered me out of the office and repeated once more, 'Don't bring the law or other o'tsiders into this. Neil and I'll take care of it.'" Kyle shook his head in disbelief.

"But what about the allegations of abuse? And the lawsuit over the child who had his arm broken? Not to mention the concerns of the state licensing board and the abuse and neglect officer? None of those is simply a matter of your word. Weren't Peebles and Bullins interested in any of that?"

"Apparently not, although I did try to discuss those matters. It all seemed to be abo't the money, the money, and the money." Kyle let his head drop against the side window.

"I guess that's why they didn't want me in the meeting with you. If the shit hits the fan, they can deny ever having spoken with you about any of this." My fingers drummed along the steering wheel as my mind raced forward, trying to decide what to do next. "Look, Kyle—you're right to wish you had worn a recording device. I mean, why the hell did Peebles press you about not calling the law? Obviously, he knows something's wrong. And how are he and Bullins going to 'take care of it?' Maybe you don't need to ring the sheriff right away, but I think you do need to speak with a lawyer—and I know just the man: Derek McIver. He's a member of my church and honest as the day is long, so there's no worry about anything getting back to the folk at Carson."

With a voice sounding old beyond his years, Kyle said, "Yeah, that'd be good." Then he put his seat back, mumbling, "I need some shut-eye." Kyle folded his arms across his chest and released a slow sigh. But then one eye popped open as he said, "Hey, buddy, I'm sorry you've been dragged so deeply into all of this." A moment later he was breathing evenly and soundly. I reflected that nearly everyone I knew who had served in the armed forces had a knack for falling asleep when time afforded it.

~ * ~

"A *what* of felony?" I asked.

Derek McIver, a native of Lumberton and consummate Southern gentleman, had lived and practiced law in these parts for more than forty years. "A misprision of felony, Jon, is in effect the concealment of a felony or serious crime." Turning to Kyle, Derek said, "Let's say that the IRS runs an audit on your pre-school manager and that audit does show—for sake of argument—that she had purchased cars and other items that are far beyond her pay grade and that of her husband. And then let's say that she confesses to embezzlement but says that you, Kyle, as chairman of the trustees for Carson Memorial Church, had access to pre-school accounts and were most likely aware of it. Then under North Carolina law, you could be tried for the misprision of felony as you did not report it. It can carry a stiff prison sentence."

"Whoa!" groaned Kyle, raising his eyebrows as he looked my way. "Nothing like going to prison for something I didn't do."

"Exactly," nodded Derek, "which is why, if things are as bad as you think they are at Carson, you'd do well to report it." McIver rubbed his chin thoughtfully for a moment as Kyle and I absorbed his legal advice. Pursing his lips and tapping his chin with his index finger, McIver mused aloud, "You say that Rev. Peebles has told you he'll take care of this situation; is that right?"

"It's what he said. He just didn't say how." Kyle lifted his arms in a gesture of helplessness.

The wise old lawyer nodded and quietly hummed thoughtfully to himself. He cocked his head to one side as he looked Kyle in the eye. "You trust him?"

"Not one iota," replied Kyle.

Derek veritably exploded with laughter. "Ha! You're a good judge of character! I've long thought of our General Presbyter as a fox in the chicken coop. The man has about as much Christian 'character' as my gardening shoes—and a lot more manure on him!" Kyle and I laughed at McIver's unexpected revelation and honesty. "Peeble's main—and perhaps only—concern is to do things by the Presbyterian Book of Order. Funny thing is, he finds ways to do things that would make the pages of the Bible curdle! Kyle, if you're seeking my legal advice, then I say this: Find out exactly what Peebles means by 'taking care' of the mess you have at Carson, and if it's anything less than ethical, above board, and *legal,* then you'd do well to call the sheriff's department yourself. From what you've told me, you and Jon have dug up enough evidence to justify an investigation. And the fact that your pre-school manager has paid herself three weeks in advance…well," McIver chuckled, "you won't be seeing her again." Derek leafed through an address book and began writing on a note pad. He tore off the page and handed it to Kyle. "Here's the name of the deputy who deals with this sort of fraud and financial crime. He's a good man. Tell him I gave you his name."

Kyle took the note from Derek without saying anything. McIver and I sat in silence as we awaited Kyle's response—after all, any decision rested with him. Kyle was nervously drumming his fingers on the arm of the leather chair. I could hear his teeth grinding against each other. Finally, more than to himself than to us, he mumbled, "I gotta shut that place down."

"What *place?*" I asked. "The church or the pre-school?" I genuinely had no idea which.

"Both—I wish—but I mean the pre-school. The place is a rats' nest, and not only has the church ignored the filth, it's made money on the suffering of children! It's a goddamn travesty!" Kyle slammed his hand hard on the chair's arm for emphasis. His mind seemed to be racing. "I've still got that meeting arranged with the state's abuse and neglect consultant and the licensing officer—they're driving up from Raleigh on Tuesday…hmm…in four days' time." Kyle bit his lower lip as he considered his next moves. "I'll make doubly sure that I can get as many of the church's elders there as possible. We'll anno'nce the closure of the pre-school for the end of that week and we'll let the staff know at the same meeting." Kyle nodded in agreement with his own planning.

"What about Peebles?" I enquired.

"Porky?" Kyle flashed a grin at Derek and me. "Well, I thought we could mosey back over to your place, Jon, and I'll call him from there. Maybe you could listen in on another phone? I might need a witness this time."

"I have a better idea," offered McIver. He was fishing around in a deep desk drawer from which he produced a tape recorder. "It's an old lawyer's trick: record the call. If he gives you any bad advice, you'll have it on tape." McIver smiled at us.

I laid my hand on McIver's shoulder. "You've been a great help, Derek."

"Well, that's what I'm here for—and Kyle? If you need me, you know where to find me."

Kyle shook McIver's hand and thanked him. Armed with the tape recorder, we headed back to my house. As it was midday, I fixed us a couple of sandwiches while we discussed the next steps Kyle would take. Following lunch, we attached the tape recorder to the phone in my study and then Kyle rang Peebles from the phone in my kitchen. Happily, he was in his office. I listened to the conversation through the tape recorder.

"Hey, Milton, this is Kyle Weston. Got a minute?"

"Why hey, Kyle," came the decidedly wary response, "what can I do fer yew?"

"Well, it's about our conversation at the Presbytery office the other day—I just need to know exactly what you meant when you said you and Neil would take care of this business with the pre-school…"

Before Kyle could say another word, Peebles cut in. "Yew've kinda lost me there, Kyle. What meetin' was that?" Peebles was obviously playing dumb. I wondered whether he knew or suspected he was being recorded.

"The one I had with you and Neil Bullins—abo't the pre-school at Carson. You said I shouldn't involve the sheriff's department, because you and Neil would take care of the situation." As a result of Peebles' caginess, I could hear tension in Kyle's voice, but he held himself together pretty well under the circumstances.

There followed a brief silence on the line before Peebles spoke again. He chuckled before he spoke. "Oh, yew mean when yew stopped by the Presbytery office and caught me between meetin's a couple days back, right? To tell the truth, Kyle, I have so many meetin's it's hard to remember all that gits said. So, have yew called the sheriff about sumthin'?"

"No, I haven't called the sheriff. And if you remember, I didn't just drop by the office, *you arranged* the meeting with you and Neil Bullins—"

"Well, whatever..." interjected Peebles.

But Kyle was not to be put off. "Milton, for my peace of mind, I'd just like to know what you have in mind for dealing with the pre-school situation. I feel like I'm in a...well...a very delicate position here."

Once again, Peebles was silent for a few seconds and then said, "Look, Kyle, I'm leavin' town tomorrow for a few days, going to a conf'rence, y'unnnerstand? Kyle, just try to relax, Son—yew sound a bit overwrought—and let me git back to yew when I return, all right?" I knew Kyle would bridle when Peebles called him 'son'—for they were of similar age—but once more, Kyle kept cool. It was clear he could get no further with Peebles.

"Sure. Fine. I'll speak to you then." Both men hung up.

A moment later, Kyle appeared at my study door. His face spoke of both dejection and disgust. "Guess it's time to ring John Law."

"Guess so," I nodded.

A sly smile crept across Kyle's face. "It would be kinda cool, wouldn't it, if the deputy turned up at the meeting between the state licensing and abuse officers and the church elders on Tuesday? I could watch Ted and Shirley squirm!" Kyle positively beamed.

"Ha! They'll think Peebles has everything in hand," I added, "and that he has you under his thumb. Peebles has probably told them that you won't do anything before he returns."

"Peebles! What a slime-ball! How do guys like him get into such positions of authority in the Church?"

"Wish I knew," I shrugged. "But if my thirty-plus years as a minister have taught me anything, it's that the higher people like our

General Presbyter go up the institutional ladder, the farther they get from any kind of genuine spirituality or personal integrity."

"So you're saying that the secret of 'success' in Christian ministry is what," queried Kyle, "*downward* mobility?"

"Yeah, that about sums it up."

~ * ~

Marie stirred her iced tea with the straw, pushing the mint leaves around the glass, while her mother listened impassively. "So, Jon, you're basically saying Kyle's ministry at Carson was virtually over within a few months of starting there—and the next year or so was…well…*what*?"

"Dealing with the legal mess, closing the pre-school, and working with a forensic accountant to determine the full extent of the wrong-doing…not to mention the ensuing court case. As Bernice was no longer there to intercept the daily post, Kyle discovered she was having all of her personal bills—credit cards, cable TV, etc. —sent to the church. The pre-school bank account had become her personal piggy bank! And, despite all of this, Kyle continued to preach, visit the sick, conduct weddings and funerals, etc.; but his main energies were spent dealing with the fallout from the pre-school."

"God!" Marie shook her head in despair and disbelief. "Kyle told us so very little. Why didn't my brother ask the rest of us for help and support?"

"I don't know. But what I think is that Kyle saw what needed to be done and simply put all—and I mean *all*—of his energy and time into seeing it through to the end. And after that…well, I don't think there was a lot of Kyle left, if that makes sense."

Marie nodded slowly. Ellen listened wordlessly.

I continued my recollections. "I don't think either Kyle or I had any idea of the depth of corruption we would uncover, nor could we have guessed at the rapidity with which the situation at Carson would unravel. The meeting that was held with the state's abuse/neglect and licensing officers opened the flood gates. The two church elders, Ted Clayton and Shirley Huntley, had been duplicitous and clever enough to fool most of the church members at Carson, but they were not smart enough to fool the state licensing board for pre-schools. And then, when the sheriff's deputy arrived—Ha!—you should have seen their faces! They didn't know if they were shot, fucked, powder-burned, or snake bit!" Marie stifled a laugh at my quip, but I felt the need to apologize to Ellen for my language, although I noticed just the faintest smile crease her lips.

Gesticulating with her fork and using her other hand to grab a bit of salad stuck to her bottom lip, Marie exclaimed, "But how could this Ted and—what's-her-name?—Shirley even in their wildest imaginations, think they could get away with all of it? Did they think they could somehow just dump the problems on the new minister while they got off Scot free?" Marie raised both hands in exasperated wonderment.

"I don't know." I shook my head. "There might have been some of that, but it's pure speculation. Peebles and Bullins knew about Kyle's problems with PTSD after Vietnam and his former alcohol problem. All of that was in Kyle's file and had been discussed when Kyle first went forward for ministry training. I did wonder if those things made Kyle an easy mark for them." I looked up at the ceiling fan for a moment as I gathered my thoughts. "But then, all of the records clearly showed that the wrongdoing at Carson had been going on long before Kyle arrived." I shrugged as I looked at Ellen and Marie. "I wish I knew. You don't know how many hours and sleepless nights I have spent going over all of the possibilities. Maybe they panicked," I offered. "Or perhaps they never thought about the long-term implications of what they were doing—or that they'd ever get found out." I then laughed at my own words.

"What's so funny?" asked Marie.

"Oh, it's just that if people really did think about the long-term implications of their actions or the unintended consequences—like getting caught, going to jail, etc.—then there would probably be very little crime. Problem solved!"

"People are stinkers!" quipped Ellen. Marie and I burst out laughing. "No, I really mean it," added Ellen, feeling somewhat aggrieved that we might be laughing at her contribution.

"Oh, Mama, we're not laughing at you!" Marie leaned over and gave her mother a squeeze.

"It's just that you summed up the Christian doctrines of the Fall and Original Sin in three words!" I interjected. "And, you're absolutely right: people *are* stinkers."

"Jon, how could so-called Christian folk allow themselves to get involved in…in…" Ellen searched for the right word, "…in all that…*mess*?" Ellen pronounced 'mess' as though her mouth were full of sewage. But that one syllable said it all.

I took Ellen's hand. "I'll tell you what Kyle thought. As regards the financial side of things, Kyle said to me that Bernice, Ted, and Shirley probably didn't start out to deliberately do anything wrong. It was simply—and I liked Kyle's turn of phrase—the 'casual culture of corruption.'"

"Okay," Marie quickly interjected, "they were casual crooks. So what?"

"Kyle wasn't *excusing* them, Marie," I said. "But he was trying to *explain* their behavior. Kyle said once the moral boundary had been moved, it was much easier to move it the next time and the next and so on. According to the deputy sheriff who arrested and interviewed Bernice, it was Shirley Huntley who first noticed something wrong with the accounts. Shirley went to her fellow elder, Ted, as they had oversight of the church's pre-school. When they went to confront Bernice, she confessed everything to them. Bernice told them how, at first, she had taken some of the pre-school's cash payments when she and her husband had gotten behind on their mortgage. She said she had meant to pay it back except that no one had seemed to notice. A month or two later she wanted some new living room furniture—and voila! After a while Bernice had moved that moral boundary so many times, she forgot where she left it."

"So why didn't the embezzlement stop once Shirley and Ted confronted Bernice? How and why did they become involved?" asked Marie.

"I'm afraid the only answer I can give you is your mother's." Marie gave me a quizzical look. "People are stinkers!"

"Oh, Jon!" Marie mock-punched me on the arm. "You know what I mean."

"Yes, I do—but what can I tell you? Bernice wasn't privy to what Shirley and Ted discussed after their confrontation. All she said—and I heard this in court—was that Ted and Shirley came back to her the next day and threatened her with the law. Bernice said that she started to cry and begged them not to call the sheriff. She said that Shirley and Ted then changed their tone. They even congratulated Bernice with pulling the wool over their eyes for so long. Bernice said that when she had calmed down, Ted and Shirley questioned her about exactly how much she had embezzled over the months it had been going on. When Bernice told them—and I forget the exact amount—she said they actually seemed impressed. According to Bernice, it was at this point that Ted told her that he and Shirley had decided not to call the law, and that from this point on, Bernice should only ever discuss the pre-school with him or Shirley but no one else in the church. Bernice said that, when she started to thank Ted and Shirley, Ted stopped her and said that there was one more thing: Bernice could show her gratitude for their 'kindness' by cutting the financial pie *three ways*."

"Good Lord!" Marie shook her head in disgust.

"Yeah, well, it gets worse. As they became greedier, they started enrolling 'phantom' children in the pre-school."

"*Phantom* children?" Marie shook her head in bewilderment. "You're gonna have to explain that one, 'Nother Brother."

"What I mean is that Bernice got friends of hers who were receiving welfare payments to register their children with the pre-school—but the children *never actually attended* the pre-school. What Bernice did was to submit bogus receipts for these phantom children to Social Services, so that the pre-school would receive the co-payments from them. When the co-payments arrived, Bernice split the proceeds with the parents, Ted, Shirley and herself. This fraud scheme went on for several years! The three of them were netting upwards of twenty-thousand every year—tax free."

"They're as bad as TV evangelists!" spat Marie.

"Probably worse," I added, "because all the while they were bilking the pre-school of money, children were being mistreated and neglected—and their greed blinded them to all of that, not to mention the cost to one very good minister."

Marie banged her forehead with the palm of her hand and looked at her mother. "Mama, can you believe what we're hearing?" Ellen's face was pale and drawn. Her visage brought to mind the way Kyle looked the first time I saw him after Vietnam. Marie shook her head despairingly. "They as good as killed my brother."

"I can't disagree, but…um…there was…uh…something else that…well… helped push Kyle over the edge." I bit my lip nervously.

Both women simply looked at me, as though their weary eyes were asking, "Something *else*?"

"Do you ever remember Kyle mentioning a guy called 'Ches'—his name was Dave McChesney?"

There was a flicker of recognition in Ellen's eyes. "Yes, I believe Kyle wrote to us abo't him—didn't he fly with Kyle?"

"That's right. He was the crew chief on Kyle's helicopter—and…um…the only surviving member of the crew…well, apart from Kyle." I winced at my words. "And what's more, Ches was the only person other than me—until now—to know what had happened to Kyle all those years ago in Vietnam. Kyle and Ches didn't see much of each other after Vietnam, but they did exchange letters from time to time; and every now and then Kyle would say Ches had called. Kyle said that Ches had become something of a recluse after Vietnam. His marriage broke up, and he had trouble keeping a job. He lived in a trailer on a piece of land he bought in northern California." I continued biting my lower lip and felt myself fidgeting over what I was about to say. My eyes darted between Ellen and Marie. "Anyway, the week before the trial began…uh…Kyle received a letter from Ches's lawyer…" I filled my lungs and slowly exhaled, "saying that Ches had died a few weeks earlier—of natural causes—and that Kyle was the sole beneficiary." I stopped speaking and took a long, deep breath.

Marie plopped her elbows on the table and her head dropped into her hands. She lifted one hand in a "halt" position toward me. "Jon, please, *please* tell me there is nothing *else*. I know my brother's gone, but I don't think I want to hear any more of…of *this*…of what led him to…" Marie waved her hand, as though to dispel whatever image she had forming in her mind.

I took Marie's hand. "No, nothing else. I promise." Marie's fingers squeezed mine. "From where we sit, here and now, I would say that Ches's death somehow released Kyle's demons from Vietnam. And they joined forces with the shit storm he encountered at Carson. Once the investigations took place and the stories of child abuse emerged…well, I think all of that must have re-kindled both Kyle's memories of killing those children in Vietnam as well as his self-condemnation…and even—dare I say it?—his self-hatred. It had taken him so long to lay all of that to rest…and well…" I shrugged, "I guess the thought of trying to work through it all again was just too much."

As though from a great distance, her voice fragile and tremulous, Ellen's rasped, "My son. My poor son."

Marie put her arm around her mother and drew her close. She kissed her mother's pale forehead. "I know, Mama. I know."

Twenty-seven

No good deed goes unpunished.

—Various

I drove into the gravel, circular drive in front of Kyle's manse and stopped behind his camper-van. It was the day after the trial ended—five days of accusations and counter-accusations, pleadings of ignorance and innocence, and the inexorable turning of the wheels of justice—such as there was. My energy level was lower than the reading on my fuel gauge, which sat a fraction above empty. Although I had passed two filling stations, I couldn't be bothered to pull in and fill up. I knew I needed to be with Kyle, but was not at all clear about who really needed whom at this stage of things. As I got out and walked toward Kyle's house, I noticed he was standing just inside the screen door. He was unshaven and wearing a T-shirt and shorts; a large mug was in his hand, and I hoped it was only coffee.

"Hey," I nodded as Kyle pushed open the door for me.

"Hey, yourself." As though reading my thoughts, Kyle raised the mug and said, "Straight coffee—black. The bastards won't make me go back to the bottle. I won't give them that satisfaction." The screen door banged behind me as I followed Kyle toward the kitchen.

"How're you doing?"

"Fan-fuckin'-tastic! What will you have to drink, Rev. Braddock?" asked Kyle, "Scotch, gin—strychnine?"

"The latter sounds good—but with a dash of tea, please."

"Tea and strychnine, it is, coming right up." Kyle set about boiling water and gathering the necessary items. He shuffled as he moved about the kitchen, and I noticed he hardly glanced at me.

The morning paper lay on the table, and I saw that Kyle had been reading the account of the trial. The bold headline read, "One Convicted, Three Acquitted in Church Pre-School Scandal." Kyle saw me looking at the article and said, "Kinda funny, ain't it? The headline focuses on those who walked and not on the guilty. What's wrong with this world?!"

"I don't know, buddy. I just don't know. When I was a lot younger, I thought I'd have things pretty well figured out by this time of life. But it ain't so."

Kyle handed me my mug of tea but didn't take his seat. Instead he moved from place to place around the kitchen, drinking his coffee. Whenever he did stop, it was to stare out the window toward the woods behind his house. Kyle spat out the word "Justice" and shook his head. My friend turned toward me and I saw the dark circles beneath his bloodshot eyes. "You know that statue of justice with the upheld scales and blindfold?" Kyle raised his hand in imitation.

"Yeah."

"Well, I think she should be bent over with her head so far up her ass that she needs a glass navel to see what's going on."

"I couldn't agree more…"

"The whole trial focused on *the money*. The fact that children were abused under the care of the church barely featured!"

"I know…but at least a few choice sentences from the state abuse and neglect officer's report got into the article—and even more on last night's late TV news."

Kyle threw up his hands despairingly as he paced the floor. "But it was the money—the dollars and cents—that took center-stage. And even then, you can scarcely call it justice! Bernice—that dimwit—gets three years and a modest fine, that her hubby gets to pay after a liquidation sale of all their motor toys! Ted Clayton receives a *suspended sentence* and a fine—whoopee! And Shirley Huntley?—well!" Kyle started to gesticulate such that he sloshed coffee over himself. He swore softly to himself and continued, declaiming his thoughts as though on a public rostrum. "Shirley Huntley, upstanding citizen, long-standing member of the county board of elections, and elder in the Carson Memorial Presbyterian Church—Shirley Huntley is *totally exonerated*! And despite all of Bernice's testimony!" Kyle turned toward me. "Can you believe that shit, Jon? Can you really believe it?"

I shook my head and—when I tried to raise my arms in a Gallic shrug—they limply fell to my lap. "Let's face it, Bernice cried so much during her time in the dock that hardly anyone could understand a thing she was saying. But then, all of the financial, attendance, and enrolment records were in Bernice's handwriting...all the receipts, real or bogus—*everything*. Shirley played that right—by getting Bernice to do *all* of the record-keeping, nothing could point directly to her or Ted. Who were the members of the jury going to believe: a blubbering dumbass like Bernice or the upstanding citizen who had been falsely accused by a dishonest church employee? All of the hard evidence pointed to Bernice. Ted only got his slap on the wrist because he kept a "pastoral eye" on the pre-school on behalf of the church leadership. After all..." and here I put on Ted's gruff accent, "I ain't no account-tant or innything of the kind. An' the church lay-dership only gives extra money to the pre-school 'cause they was heppin' so many needy families. Leastways, that's what we thought." I lifted my hands in supplication as Ted had done in court. "I had no real ideer what was goin' on."

Kyle waved his hand at me. "Stop, Jon! I'm still trying to get over the real performance." He took his mug to the coffee maker and re-filled it. Over his shoulder, Kyle asked, "Want to know who should receive the Oscar for best performance in the trial?"

"I'm pretty sure I can guess."

Kyle then adopted the style and tone of a game-show host. "That's right, studio audience, our winner is that pork-faced Presbyterian and lying lump of lard: Milton Peebles!" Kyle quickly gulped some coffee and then changed his voice to that of cartoon character Porky Pig. "Th-th-th-thanks very m-much, everybody. Y-y-you duh-duh-don't kn-kn-know how hard I've w-w-worked for thi-th-th-uh-this award. I re-ra-re-ra-really appre-pre-preciate it so m-m-much—I re-ra-ruh-really do!" I started to applaud but then Kyle raised one finger and said: "But wait! Let's have a few clips from the performance that won the award for Porky Peebles: 'Chi-chi-child ab-ab-b-b-buse? At Ca-ca-carson Me-me-mo-rial   Ch-ch-church?   Wh-wh-why   that's   ri-ri-ri-…uh…ridiculous!" And let's not forget: "Ke-kuh-Kyle W-w-weston n-n-n-n-ever reported nu-nu-nuthin' to me!' *And finally*: 'W-w-why I'm as su-su-surprised as ev-ev-everyone e–e-e-else!'" Kyle took a fake bow, and then looked at me, rolling his eyes and shaking his head.

"I know, Kyle. He committed perjury in a court of law—and what's worse, he got away with it. And don't say it—I wish you had worn a wire that day at his office. I also wish I hadn't let them keep me out of the meeting with you. But, hell, neither of us knew then what we know now!" I was becoming more emotional than I had intended. "We didn't know Peebles, Clayton, and Huntley were corrupt; that they were liars and thieves; that they could care less about the children who had suffered at the hands of Bernice's inept, perverted, and slovenly staff!" My voice started to break into sobs as I tried to finish what I needed to say to Kyle. "But at least you got that shit-hole of a pre-school closed down, at least it's become public knowledge, at least no more children will be hurt there—and no more money pilfered! *At least you did that*!" Without knowing fully why, I broke into a flood of tears and sobbing. Kyle walked over and pulled my head into his chest. "I-I'm sorry, Kyle. I wish I'd never helped get you into all of this."

"Hey, buddy, it's okay. I'm sorry if I've been too focused on myself and the problems at Carson…to the point that maybe it seems like I've taken your support for granted—which I haven't. I really couldn't have gotten this far witho't your help. And I've been so absorbed in it all that…well…I admit I hadn't seen what it was doing to you. You've always been so resilient, Jon, and taken what life's thrown at you…"

Kyle's embrace was strong and tender, and for an instant I lamented the fact that no child would ever feel his fatherly touch. "Resilient? Ha! Just look at me now," I said, stifling back another sob. "And it's not like I've been through anything like you in Vietnam…"

"Let's not compare stories. Just take the compliment. And for the record, Jon, that war was overrated. But, yeah, we're a couple of real heroes."

"Damn fool teenagers, more likely," I offered and managed a chuckle.

"That's my Jon!" Kyle gave me a squeeze and looked me over. "You gonna be okay if I let go of you for a minute?"

"I think I can just about manage." I nodded toward the paper towels. "Hand me one of those, would you?" Kyle grinned for the first time that morning and tossed me the entire roll.

"Bastard," I intoned while blowing my nose into a towel.

"Probably," said Kyle as he walked over to his answering machine and pushed the button. "I think we can both use a dose of this."

The robotic sounding woman's voice said, "You have…thirty-six messages." All of them were in response to the results of the trial surrounding Carson's pre-school. Over the next thirty minutes or so, Kyle and I listened to the voices of members of Carson Church, parents of children who had attended the pre-school, and members of the public. They fell into two categories: messages of ill will or expressions of support for Kyle. Happily, the latter far outnumbered the former. Not surprisingly, the people who expressed sympathy for Kyle and gratitude at his closing down a toxic pre-school identified themselves. Those who excoriated Kyle for closing the pre-school or upsetting the congregational life of Carson Church hid behind cowardly anonymity.

There was one message that stood out among the others: it contained the voices of both parents of a child from the pre-school. They began by saying what an inconvenience it had been for them when the pre-school closed, as one of them had to quit work in order to look after their child. They admitted they had sent Kyle an anonymous letter at the time, because they had wanted, in their words, "to blow him out of the water." Kyle and I looked at each other as we waited for the latest barracking to begin, but then the parents said they had changed their minds after reading the morning's newspaper. Although it had not received much print, they realized that some children had suffered physical neglect, sexual touching, and bodily harm at the hands of the pre-school staff. After they had talked and prayed about it, they decide that Kyle's decision had removed their daughter from harm's way. Thus, they had decided to keep their daughter at home, and ended up by thanking Kyle for making them see what was truly important.

At that point I got up from my chair, walked over to the answering machine, and hit the stop button. As I did so, I said to Kyle, "I don't think we…no…*you* need to hear any more." I looked straight into my friend's eyes, pointed at the answering machine and, with a cracking voice, said, "You saved their child, Kyle. And if that's all the justice you get—*that's something.*"

~ * ~

"It wasn't enough for Kyle though, was it?" asked Marie, as we stood in front of Kyle's newly-installed headstone, illuminated by the evening sun. Ellen sat in a folding lawn-chair I had brought in my car, basking in the sunshine and her memories of Kyle. We had all wanted to spend some time together with Kyle before she and Marie drove home.

"No, sadly not." I slowly shook my head. "I did wonder at the time what went through Kyle's mind at that moment. I know I had made the conscious link between Kyle's having saved children from future abuse at Carson, with his having killed the children in Vietnam. But I was afraid to voice my thoughts; I…I think it was because it seemed unfair of me to suggest that one good and noble act could—or perhaps *should*—offset that one terrible act performed decades ago. Ultimately that resolution rested with Kyle's conscience and God's mercy. And who was I to say how Kyle *should feel* about it? Of course, I wondered whether Kyle had made the same link. Perhaps he had. But the sad fact is that none of us can ever undo the past. But I hoped and prayed that in some way, however small, by closing the Carson pre-school, and making public all the wrong that had been done there, Kyle had managed to atone for that one horrific incident in Vietnam." I rested my hand on the granite headstone that simply bore his name and dates, and watched as my silent tears rolled down its polished surface. Without looking at Ellen, I addressed...*whom?*—God or American society? "*Where* is the memorial for all of the young men whom the Vietnam War killed—like Ches and Kyle—*but years after the conflict ended*?" I patted the gravestone. "Because they, too, were casualties of that war, just as surely as those who died at the time."

Marie laid her arm across my shoulder. "I suppose this stone—and tho'sands others like it—will have to suffice."

"I guess so," I agreed. Turning to Marie, I said, "I've sent a letter of resignation to my two churches," and let out a deep sigh. "I had wanted to talk it over with Kyle." I patted his headstone again. "But I reckon he knows."

"Mama and I kinda thought that was coming. Well, I for one am glad." Marie gave my arm a squeeze. "You need to get away from..." Marie searched for words, "well...I mean, all of this—especially these corrupt Presbyterians."

I smiled at Marie. "You're right, Kid. And I appreciate the vote of confidence. Kyle had mentioned a similar move in one of his e-mails to me. I suppose I'd hoped he and I could ride into the sunset together— maybe go on a major road trip and put this chapter behind us." I looked down at the still fresh earth on Kyle's grave and said, "But...well...you had another journey didn't you, buddy?"

"Where will you go, 'Nother Brother?"

"Ah—" I laughed softly.

"What is it?" Marie gave me one of her gentle punches on the arm, her curiosity reminding me of her as a little girl—more years ago than I cared to remember.

"A monastery. I'm going to a Trappist monastery—not so very far from here...just over in Granville County. It's an off-beat sort of place, founded by monks who've all lived very human lives prior to joining the order. I started going there for retreats after Karen left home. I've been an oblate there for some time." I looked at Marie and smiled. "Perhaps now it's time to take the plunge?"

"Jon Braddock the monk. Why does that sound so unlikely and yet *so you* at the same time?"

"Guess I'm just a damn fool teenager." Now it was Marie's turn to laugh.

A shadow was suddenly thrown over us as the sun dipped behind the Blue Ridge. Although the air was still warm, Marie shivered.

"Are you okay?"

Marie nodded and then said, "Guess Mama and I need to get on the road soon. We have abo't four hours of driving ahead of us."

"Let me walk you to the car, then." I hooked my arm through Marie's and we went the few paces to where Ellen sat, eyes closed but wakeful.

Ellen looked up at both of us and smiled. "I suppose I'd better move these old bones of mine." I offered her my hand.

When Ellen was safely on her feet, I hugged mother and daughter close to my chest and kissed them each on the forehead. "I'll miss you both. Drive carefully."

"We'll miss you, too, son," said Ellen. Her calling me 'son' struck me to the core—had it been unconscious or deliberate? It mattered not; after all, I was ''Nother Brother.'

I walked the remainder of my best friend's family to their car and opened the door for Ellen. She hugged me again before letting me help her into her seat. Across the car, Marie asked me, "Jon? Does this monastery of yours allow visitors?"

"Of course, and I'll expect to see you both there. I can even speak to you—at certain times! In fact, if I behave myself, they might even allow me out from time to time! Who knows?"

"You're family now—for real; and you know where we are."

"I'll write. I promise."

I could see Marie was struggling to restrain her emotions. She simply nodded at me and got behind the wheel. Mother and daughter both gave little waves and the car pulled away.

I watched Marie and Ellen drive out toward the highway. When they were out of sight, I walked over to my car and opened the trunk. I carefully pulled out my sleeping bag and unrolled it. Inside was a bottle of Jim Beam—Kyle's tipple from the bad old days, but it seemed somehow appropriate as the last few days had been far from good ones for me. I threw the bag over my shoulder and closed the trunk. With my free hand, I picked up the lawn chair and carried it to Kyle's grave. It would be several hours before I needed the bag, so I draped it over the chair for comfort. Sitting down, I opened the bottle of Jim Beam, lifted it high and began my private wake with a toast: "To damn fool teenagers!" I started to take a swig, but changed my mind and poured a dram over Kyle's headstone. "Absent friends first!" I then put the bottle to my lips and took a large drink. I swished the warming libation around in my mouth and then felt its power as it slid down my throat and into my stomach. Unaccustomed as I was to hard liquor, it made me shiver. "Bllluuhh," I gasped. "How did you manage it all of those years, Kyle?" I took another draught and it felt like my skull was expanding. The feeling brought to mind the night Kyle and I first tasted liquor at Marletta's place. I laughed aloud as I remembered the rank naïveté and innocence of our youth.

And so I drank and talked to my best friend. "Kyle, ol' buddy. You're dead, and now I'm left with your story. So tell me, can we ever truly rise above what we are? I mean—" and I pulled at the skin on my arm and chest, "—this marvelous and chaotic coalescence of blood, bone, synapses, emotions, thoughts, mind, and soul?" I took another deep drink. "I'll grant you that, on occasion, we might forget ourselves—in moments of heroism, passion, or spiritual ecstasy. But can we ever be who we are, or are meant to be, without all of the corporeal history we carry with us and within us? I mean these corporeal boundaries which both delimit and define us?" I splayed out my arms and legs. "Or am I just drunk?" I laughed out loud. "S'matter, Kyle? You're as silent as the grave!"

My private wake continued in this vein. When I was three-quarters finished with the bottle, I climbed inside my sleeping bag and curled up next to my friend's stone marker. "Sorry if I can't stay up through the night, ol' buddy. Age and—" I hiccupped, "not being accustomed to the booze, I guess. But nothing you have to worry about anymore, eh?" I took one last drink and poured the rest into the broken earth. "Bottom's up. Bastard!" I belched, laughed out loud, and said, "Just kidding!" The gathering evening stars seemed to arrange themselves into Kyle's grin and I felt warmed inside.

"Oh, one more thing, buddy. If you run into Ches, Food'n'Drug an'...an' Duke, could you please ask 'em this for me? If those tens of thousands of American youth whose lives ended during or as a result of America's inglorious Vietnam conflict and who exist now only as beloved memories, if...if they could rejoin us once more in this life, would they merely resume their lives as before, with the same loves, hates, and prejudices?" I laid my hand on Kyle's headstone and felt the residual warmth from the day's sunshine. "Or, having now tasted death, would they instead become brigades of loving-kindness?" I spread my arms as though addressing an audience. "After all, war stories are only ever written by people whose bodies and souls have remained relatively intact. Only the dead really have the wisdom we so badly need on this war-ravaged planet. Christ! Now I'm preaching...s'a real liability for preachers, ain't it?

"Oh well, I'm doing what I suppose you did in your own way: leaving institutional church life behind—just not as dramatically as you did, ol' buddy. This preacher is leaving preaching behind so I can simply try to practice what I've preached all these years. But like St. Francis, without the words. People will just have to figure things out for themselves. In fact, if the monastery will have me for the long haul, then I intend to work, serve, live, pray, and die there."

Meet Jack N. Lawson

Jack Lawson grew up in North Carolina. As an ordained minister he worked as a prison chaplain in North Carolina and Ohio. He later served as a parish minister in the US and the United Kingdom. After earning a PhD in Hebrew Bible, he taught both ministerial candidates and lay people in the English counties of Kent and Norfolk. After leaving parish ministry in 1997, Jack worked for The Rural Community Council in Kent, focusing on rural economic regeneration and managing a European Social Fund grant between Kent and Nord-Pas-de-Calais. In the process he developed an intense love of France and the French people. Later, Jack spent more than 12 years as training and development officer for the Methodist Church in East Anglia.

His book, *The Concept of Fate in Ancient Mesopotamia*, is an exploration of early human attempts at working out how much free will we human beings actually have. It examines poems, myths, prayers, rituals, divination and more.

The author's first novel, *Doing Time*, reflects his years as a chaplain in a Southern US women's prison. It expresses how the harsh reality of domestic violence is the path that leads most women to prison.

Jack is married to Chris, a former mental health specialist who worked with children and families in the UK. They now reside in North Carolina.

Works from the Pen of
Jack N. Lawson

No Good Deed - A Vietnam veteran seeks to find peace within himself, first as a circus clown and later as an ordained minister. Events in his church conspire to reignite his PTSD.

Criminal Justice - A prison chaplain uncovers criminal victimization of inmates by the staff and must decide to risk his job/life for the sake of justice.

The Woods - Life in an enchanted retirement community opens the residents to their deeper selves—for mirth or madness, good or ill.

Dirty Business - An animal scientist uncovers the deliberate dumping of toxic waste, but the notoriety opens the door to further intrigue, danger and murder.